UP IN SMOKE

UP IN SMOKE

A Dr. Zol Szabo Medical Mystery

ROSS PENNIE

ECW Press

Published by ECW Press
2120 Queen Street East, Suite 200,
Toronto, Ontario, Canada M4E 1E2
416-694-3348 / info@ecwpress.com

LIBRARY AND ARCHIVES CANADA CATALOGUING IN PUBLICATION

Pennie, Ross, 1952–, author
Up in smoke / Ross Pennie.

"A Dr. Zol Szabo medical mystery".
ISBN 978-1-55022-967-7 (bound) / 978-1-77041-185-2 (pbk.)
ALSO ISSUED AS: 978-1-77090-465-1 (PDF)
978-1-77090-466-8 (ePub)

I. Title.

PS8631.E565U6 2013   C813'.6   C2013-902496-4

Cover and text design: Tania Craan
Cover image: Adam Hirons/Millennium Images UK
Author photo: John Pegram
Printing: Friesens   5   4   3   2   1

The publication of *Up in Smoke* has been generously supported by the Canada Council for the Arts which
last year invested $157 million to bring the arts to Canadians throughout the country, and by the Ontario Arts
Council (OAC), an agency of the Government of Ontario, which last year funded 1,681 individual artists and
1,125 organizations in 216 communities across Ontario for a total of $52.8 million. We also acknowledge the
financial support of the Government of Canada through the Canada Book Fund for our publishing activities,
and the contribution of the Government of Ontario through the Ontario Book Publishing Tax Credit and
the Ontario Media Development Corporation.

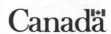

AUTHOR'S NOTE

As an infectious disease specialist in southern Ontario's Brant County, I've looked after countless smokers. After all, the lands north of Lake Erie have been the centre of Canada's tobacco industry for two thousand years.

Many of my patients — lungs shot and legs amputated after years of tar and nicotine — always had money for their smokes. Why? Because in this part of the world cigarettes are cheap. Dead cheap. Made on the local reserve (rez), free of most taxes and quality control.

Are tax-free, Native-brand cigarettes easy to find? Absolutely. At least 40% of the tobacco smoked in Ontario comes through clandestine channels. Is this harmful to anyone but the tax collector? Read *Up in Smoke*, a work of fiction (the plot and characters are purely from my imagination), and see how we all could get wrapped up in this menace.

My thanks go to the many people who made this book possible, especially my patients for speaking candidly about their addiction to Native cigarettes; Claire Pennie for her enthusiastic help with the research; Larry Kramer for his insights on tobacco farming; Edna Barker for pointing me in the right direction; Jack David and Crissy Calhoun for leading a dedicated and talented team at ECW Press; Cat London for breathing new life into the manuscript; Jen Knoch, whose eclectic knowledge made her an exacting proofreader; Jenna Illies, who skillfully pushed the word out; Tania Craan, who designs intrigue into my covers; my readers for encouraging me to keep writing; and my darling Lorna, who is always by my side, cheering me on.

Ross Pennie, June 2013

CHAPTER 1

He shivers inside his sleeping bag, rolls to the right, and groans. It's been a couple of years since he lost his Rolex to poker, but his body knows it's three hours past midnight. Bloor Street's sidewalk is playing hell with his shoulder. With no smokes left and the Canadian Club well out of his system, he should've taken a couple of Percs when he had the chance. And thrown on the flannel jacket that's at the bottom of the shopping bag. Under the good stuff.

At least he's out of the wind, thanks to that wild metallic thing looming above him, the giant zit stuck to the front of their museum. They call it the Crystal, and its weird angles would've sent him spinning if he was wasted. But tonight he's dead sober and not complaining. Not here, where their chi-chi extravagance overhangs the sidewalk, and the zany geometry makes a sheltered spot where a guy could catch a few z's. At least, until the busloads of school kids turned up in the morning.

He opens his eyes a crack at the sound of footsteps. Two kids in jeans and hoodies give him a wide berth and pretend not to stare. The taller one is carrying a gym bag that looks hefty enough to be loaded with a bottle of sherry and two twenty-sixers of rye. More likely, it's a set of tools they're packing — like a crowbar, glass cutters, and a couple of sledgehammers. Guys on their way to a job. And not shy about it.

He scratches that damn thing on his lip and it starts oozing again. He can taste the blood. Friggin' sore's been there for weeks and won't go away.

He shivers and shifts, sucks at his lip, and shifts again.

Minutes later, maybe more, the two kids slip out the museum's side exit, hoods raised. A third guy, a bit older, follows them out. He's got the gym bag, and it looks heavier than on the way in. Older Guy stops and scans for trouble. Sees only a wino on the sidewalk sleeping it off, waves the other two on. The light above the door catches the printing on his sweatshirt: ANISHINAABEG NATION. BIDING OUR TIME.

Really, eh? And then what?

The three of them head for the retaining wall. It's not a proper barrier, just a decoration between the museum and the music faculty next door. They don't run, but walk quick. Less likely to attract attention that way. Everyone in Toronto walks, bikes, drives like that — full of purpose.

But not everyone is a target.

He rolls onto his front and checks the street. No one else in sight.

He reaches into the sleeping bag and whips out the Glock.

They're down in three shots, before they even touch the wall.

He squirms out of the bedroll and grabs the gym bag from Older Guy's dead fist. He tosses out the crowbar and the hammers, throws in the Glock, and zips the bag closed. Then he heaves himself over the wall and drops into the black shadows of the campus behind the museum, telling himself it's okay he couldn't look at their faces.

Two blocks south on Hoskin Avenue, the Ford-150 flashes its lights. He jumps in and stows the gym bag at his feet. His twin brother hands him the throw-away cellphone.

He punches in the number, ten digits to show them who's boss.

He presses SEND, and they wait for it.

One, two.

The Crystal explodes with a satisfying roar. Smoke swirls way above the streetlights.

There must be shit all over the place. Too bad he can't see it, all that shattered glass and tangled steel. Wicked.

The Big Guy will be pleased. Might even buy him a new Rolex.

When the sooty cloud descends on the Royal Ontario Museum, it shrouds the ruins, the tools, the blood-spattered hoodies. And the neat holes in three skulls.

All that remains of the shopping bag is scattered ash.

CHAPTER 2

Zol Szabo measured six scoops of Kenyan Bungoma — shade grown and fair trade — into the grinder. Mornings were impossible without a large mug of coffee at breakfast and a booster around ten-thirty. And afternoons a sleepfest without a pick-me-up at three and often another at five. The public-health doc in him sometimes worried that his caffeine dependency might not be entirely innocent.

He pressed the switch and counted five Mississippis, reminding himself that he'd smoked fewer than one hundred cigarettes in his life, that his half-hearted experiments with marijuana were more than a decade behind him, and that one single-malt Scotch savoured every evening didn't constitute another addiction. Did it?

He dumped the coffee into a number-six cone and set it over his favourite mug. He poured in the six hundred millilitres of water he'd heated to a few degrees short of boiling, as recommended by the barista who'd sold him the beans yesterday at the Detour Café. That was the first time in almost a decade that he'd shopped on Norfolk Avenue in dear old Simcoe.

The sleepy town he'd been born in, an hour's drive to the southwest, was a few klicks from the farm that had raised him, and on which his parents still lived. But the town had little pull for him until two weeks ago. Now, Simcoe and adjacent Norfolk County were his top priority, professionally speaking. A massive stroke had felled the region's incumbent MOH, the medical officer of health in charge of the health unit. Zol had been swiftly promoted into the position. His Hamilton boss, Peter Trinnock, made certain Zol understood this secondment to Simcoe was temporary. And warned that Zol's performance would be under the meticulous scrutiny, from Toronto, of Dr. Elliott York, the province's public-health uber-boss. It was well known that York was grooming himself for an eventual cabinet post and would tolerate no embarrassing screw-ups by his underlings. Trinnock had warned Zol: Don't get any notions of selling that fancy house of yours over there on the West Mountain; plenty of good candidates in the running for the permanent position down in Simcoe. We'll keep your office here in the Hammer nice and warm for you. Trinnock was going to miss Zol toiling under his thumb; it would be just like him to engineer his early return.

Zol paused, revelling in the coffee's rising steam and cheery trickle, warm comforts on this grey October Saturday. Through the window, low cloud obscured the hawk's eye vista that on a clear day stretched to the glitzy towers of Toronto and jacked up the real estate prices in this part of the humble Hammer.

When he thought about it, the town of Simcoe had always been a quirky place. It sat alone, not quite on the north shore of Lake Erie. And owed its foundation to the tobacco farms that used to blanket every inch of the surrounding sandy loam. Now that the nicotine weed was no longer king, fair-trade coffees, pesticide-free veggies, and stone-ground grains were sidling up to Simcoe's fast food joints, tattoo parlours, and farm supply stores. How well the beer and white-bread town would embrace the organic scene was an open question, but his new posting was going to show him.

The Kenyan's aroma rose from the cone and tickled his nostrils. He braced himself.

A split second later, there she was.

On cue.

No audio gadget of any kind was playing in the house. No radio, no CD player, no iPod. Yet Céline Dion was belting the theme song from *Titanic* as clearly as if she was standing beside him. His neurologist had an explanation for the phenomenon: post-concussion synesthesia. A knock on his head a few months ago had crossed the wiring in his brain, creating a bizarre set of pathways between his sense of hearing and his sense of smell. Strong scents now conjured snippets of music inside his head so vivid they sounded like the real thing.

Almost every time he got a whiff of freshly brewed coffee, Céline showed up with ten or fifteen bars of "My Heart Will Go On." She was impossible to suppress and damned difficult to get used to. He'd prefer Amanda Marshall, Ray LaMontagne, or Royal Wood, but at coffee time he was stuck with Céline and *Titanic*.

He should have noticed that patch of black ice in April. Instead, he'd fallen prey to winter's last gasp. He was down in a second, his head whacking the sidewalk on Concession Street in front of the health unit. He was out cold, splayed in full view of his colleagues and the lunchtime traffic. Hours later, regaining consciousness in the intensive care unit of Caledonian University Medical Centre, he caught the scent of the hand sanitizer his nurse was rubbing between her palms. In a heartbeat, the Tragically Hip were at his bedside strumming the opening bars of "Wheat Kings." He'd thought either he was going crazy or had awoken in the afterlife, especially since the song opened with the ghostly cry of a loon.

Céline finished her kitchen breakfast concert, and, relieved at the silence, Zol lifted today's *Globe and Mail* from the counter.

The front-page photo grabbed his gaze and wouldn't let go. Yesterday, he'd heard a brief report on the radio, but he'd never imagined it was this bad.

The Royal Ontario Museum was in ruins, its ultra-modern entrance gaping like a great white shark with broken teeth. The Michael Lee-Chin Crystal — Toronto's latest engineering marvel, lauded and condemned for its cost, elegance, and flamboyance

— was now a rubble of twisted beams, shattered glass, and police tape.

He scanned the article. Halfway through, the story got worse, then worse again. "Colleen!" He turned and called again through the doorway, "Come look at this." His perennially unruly hands, now flapping like startled crows, knocked the coffee fixings across the counter and onto the floor.

He was staring at the sludge and shattered stoneware when she breezed in. His navy bathrobe — huge on her trim, five-foot frame — flapped at her ankles.

"Goodness, that was your favourite mug," she said, grabbing a wad of paper towels from the roll. "Never mind, you've got a cupboard full of others you never use. You'll just have to pick a new favourite. That Scott Barnim one from your mother is very nice."

Not sure he felt like picking a new favourite, he crouched beside her to help with the cleanup. His nose caught the scent of his bergamot shower gel wafting off her skin. Immediately, Marvin Gaye began singing "I Heard It Through the Grapevine." Oil of bergamot, in concert with her skin, always brought out Marvin.

As they cleaned up the last of the coffee grinds, she started to speak, but Marvin was still crooning at full volume. Zol touched his right earlobe.

Her hazel eyes glinted with understanding, and she adjusted the towel she'd wrapped around her waist-length ponytail. She threw him a smile that flared, then faded quickly. "Enough, already. You're as white as a sheet. And it's not just your broken mug. What's up?"

He pointed to the *Globe*'s front page. "That."

It took two headlines to tell the story: *Three Bodies Pulled from ROM Rubble* and *First Nations Artifacts Missing*.

She tutted in deference to the wreckage and the loss of life. "Extraordinary. Who are the victims? People you know?" Usually, her South African accent made everything — even the sordid details she occasionally divulged after an all-night stakeout — sound upbeat and musical. The story in the paper was making him too angry to appreciate that now.

"No idea."

"Surely the police must have some idea. And by the look on your face, I think you do too."

He shook his head. "It doesn't say . . ."

"You mean, it doesn't say whether the victims have been identified — or it doesn't say the names of the victims, even though the authorities know who they are?"

He glanced at the article and wished she'd read it for herself. He couldn't cope with being grilled before his first cup of coffee. "If anyone knows who they are, they're not saying."

"But surely, someone is speculating. Is it suggested that the victims are innocent bystanders, ROM employees, or the perps themselves?"

He handed her the paper's front section. "See for yourself. You're the private eye."

She flashed him a look that warned his cheap shot was *uncalled for* and only glanced at the headlines. "Do they at least say which artifacts were stolen?"

"A couple of wooden clubs, a ceremonial tomahawk, and . . ."

"And what? Why are you looking so sheepish all of a sudden?"

He didn't feel sheepish. Not in the least. But what he had to tell her would either stop her in her tracks or trigger another barrage of questions. "My . . ."

"Yours? What are you saying?"

"Yes, *mine. My* ancient stone-carved pipe."

She paused, eyes huge, mouth open so wide he could see her uvula. A few seconds later, she found her voice. It never left her for long. "You'd better start from the beginning."

He took a deep breath. "I gave the Royal Ontario Museum my priceless Hopewell Culture pipe, carved two thousand years ago in the shape of a gorgeous little loon. They were supposed to keep him safe. But now someone's stolen him from under their noses."

"This is extraordinary, Zol. But you've got to back up a bit further. In fact, a good deal more than a bit. What sort of pipe are we talking about? An ocarina? A piccolo?"

He turned to page four and showed her the photo of his missing treasure. "Tobacco. You know, tar and nicotine."

"And when did you donate said pipe to the ROM?"

He left her gawking at the photo and grabbed a can of Maxwell House from the cupboard. He'd fussed enough over the gourmet stuff for one morning. He put the kettle on to boil again and shook the coffee into a fresh cone.

She waved the newspaper and frowned. "The caption says this extraordinary loon effigy is possibly the most valuable piece in the ROM's First Peoples Gallery. Is that an exaggeration?"

"Probably not."

"You still haven't told me how you came to possess it and when you gave it up."

"I should never have listened to my dad. I damned well should have kept it."

"You're not serious."

"Why not? Finders keepers."

"But surely —"

"The ROM didn't do such a hot job of protecting it."

Through his anger at the theft, he could feel the excitement of his discovery raising his pulse as if it were yesterday, not fifteen years ago. There was something almost perfect about that little bird, nestled on an oblong block of stone the size of half a deck of playing cards. The entire object was carved from a single piece of charcoal-grey pipestone.

He cupped his right hand to mime its size and shape. "The first time I held that smooth little fellow, he felt . . . It's hard to explain, but he felt graceful and . . . alive. Yes, alive. I swore I could feel his heart beating, his garnet eyes boring through me."

Colleen looked surprised at his uncharacteristic burst of poetic enthusiasm. "Was it smoked every day, or just for show?"

"I haven't the faintest."

"Heavens, Zol. Surely some anthropologist has done a Ph.D. thesis on it. Have you never enquired?"

He shrugged, feeling like an overgrown, uncultured kid who

grew up on a tobacco farm on the outer margins of civilization. His father had taught him plenty about the history and cultivation of tobacco, but cultural anthropology had never been his thing.

"It's my guess," she continued, "that something so exquisite would not have been smoked every day. Used by shamans, maybe? Communicating with the spirit world?"

He poured the now boiling water over the Maxwell House. "All I know is the British Museum has almost a hundred pipes more or less like him. A menagerie of stone-carved effigies — sparrows, frogs, a cat, an otter. But no loons."

"Extraordinary! How did they acquire them?"

"Dug them up."

"Where?"

"Ohio."

"Shipped them from Ohio to London? From some punter's back garden in Cleveland all the way to Bloomsbury?" Ever the professional private investigator Colleen was intrigued by the outlandish. And had a natural sense of the absurd; you didn't survive childhood in apartheid South Africa — ride inside the cushy cab of your father's truck while your Black playmates rode behind in the unprotected flatbed — without a keen awareness of life's ironies.

"A long drive south of Cleveland," he told her. "Almost at the Ohio River. In two aboriginal burial mounds."

"And that's where you found yours? Outback Ohio? Then smuggled it over the border?"

He shook his head, then explained.

He'd found the loon pipe buried in a corner of his family's tobacco farm. He'd been about twenty years old at the time, playing around with his dad's metal detector. Dad used the homemade gadget to find old coins and such along the shores of Lake Erie. Zol had never taken much interest in the hobby, but one Saturday afternoon, when he was home from chef school for the weekend, he found himself with nothing to do. It was the end of the tobacco season and he'd exhausted the list of farm chores Dad always had waiting for him. Zol was goofing around with the detector when it screeched over a patch of dirt. He got a shovel from the barn and unearthed what turned out to be a rusty strong box. He forced it open and found the loon wrapped in a rag. He had no idea what it was, but his high school history teacher at Simcoe Composite understood its significance immediately and put Zol in touch with the Royal Ontario Museum in Toronto.

"The Brits have dozens of stone pipes, similar to that one?" Colleen said, pointing at the newspaper photo. "And they're all two thousand years old?"

He'd never figured out how the English had managed to scoop up a cache of priceless artifacts and speed them off to London without the Americans making an epic fuss.

"And carved from a type of rock called pipestone," he explained. The ancient workmanship was as fine as the best modern Inuit carvings he'd seen for sale in the classiest art shops. "The pipe fits in the palm of your hand. Nose to nose, eyes boring into yours when you take a toke through a hole in the base."

"Did you ever try it out?"

"A couple of times."

She studied the photo again, then said, "Amazing to think of the Indians smoking tobacco for the past two thousand years."

He flinched at the sound of that word, even voiced in her musical accent. He avoided it, *Indian*, especially now that he was a public official, representing the interests of a multi-ethnic society, and under constant public scrutiny. Only the federal government clung to the outdated term and used it in its legislation pertaining to Canada's indigenous people. The feds still called the land set aside for the country's original inhabitants *Indian Reserves*.

On the street, everyday Canadians were so caught up with the shameful plight of the country's Native people that no one knew what to call them. Political correctness inhibited constructive dialogue and strangled common sense. In the end, they were labelled Indigenous, Native, Aboriginal, First Peoples, First Nations, Status

Indians, Band Members, Metis, Inuit, Mohawk, Algonquin, Ojibwa, Anishinaabeg, Cree, Dene, Haida, or any of a host of other tribal designations. And did it really matter, as long as you were respectful?

"The original tobacco variety was *Nicotiana rustica*," he said, sticking safely to the biology of tobacco, as taught to him by his dad. Gaspar Szabo had made an excellent living as a grower because he used science to achieve high yields of top-grade product. "The original tobacco plant was harsher than the modern version and probably reserved for shamans and chieftains."

He explained that pre-contact, Native tobacco contained an almost poisonous concentration of nicotine and an untold number of hallucinogens. Smoking it would have been quite the trip: psychedelic visions accompanied by a rocketing heart rate, dilated pupils, and drenching sweats. Europeans found a tamer species when they landed on Bermuda, or maybe it was Bolivia — the story changed depending on what history book you read. Anyway, *Nicotiana tabacum* was less harsh on the heart and nervous system, and not hallucinogenic. But equally addictive. The Europeans quickly appropriated the ancient custom they'd stumbled on in the Americas and transformed it into a worldwide mega-industry. And governments everywhere taxed the hell out of it.

"No wonder Native shamans appeared to be possessed by spirits," Colleen said. "With all that mind-blowing dope and the addictive power of nicotine, they must have been running round half mad a lot of the time." She took her mug of Maxwell House and sipped it; her eyes lit with gratitude. She was no less addicted to caffeine than he was. After a moment of reflection she asked, "But how did your loon get from Ohio to Ontario?"

"Stolen and traded dozens of times, I guess. First between Natives, and then the Europeans got in on the act."

She threw him that smile of understanding he was coming to love so much.

After those rocky years with his ex, Francine, and the following seven years of hapless dating, it was wonderful to have a gorgeous, kind, smart, stable woman who understood him so well and expressed her appreciation both inside and outside of bed. True, he found it a strain when she pestered him with questions, but if that was her major imperfection . . .

Max, now ten, had asked a few weeks ago if he could call Colleen by a special nickname, since she was almost part of the family. Not Mum or Mummy, Max had said, because he already had a real mother who was waiting for just the right time to come for a visit. Zol had quickly changed the subject, worried they were living a dream that couldn't possibly last. Did he possess a flaw that drove women to nastiness once they got to know him? If he could ever remember how to pray, he'd plead on his knees for things to be different this time.

"Come to think of it," she continued, "that little loon did have a couple of millennia to make the trip. It seems to have been well cared for through the ages. Extraordinary. No chips in its beak, and its tail looks perfect."

"That's what my history teacher said. It had been handled with the same reverence as the British Crown Jewels."

"Did you trace the strong box to its owner?"

"Manufactured in Sheffield, England. Mid-1800s. That's all we could find out."

She cocked her head toward the newspaper. "What's this legend they're referring to? A second, almost identical pipe is out there somewhere waiting to make big things happen when the two of them are finally united?"

The front door opened and closed with a bang. Zol heard two clunks against the floor as someone kicked off a pair of shoes. The hardwood creaked beneath the approach of stockinged feet.

A few seconds later, Hamish Wakefield burst into the kitchen. He was soaked through and covered in bubbles.

CHAPTER 3

At Zol's first whiff of the bubbles, the Beatles struck up ten bars of "Hey Jude," and he watched as Hamish's jacket and slacks drained into puddles of industrial froth. There was no mistaking the smell of the cleanser from the Maxi-Wash, three blocks over on Garth Street.

Caledonian University's workaholic assistant professor — and one of Hamilton's ace diagnosticians — looked as if he'd been plucked from the brink of Niagara Falls.

"Good God, Hamish," Colleen said, pulling off his sodden jacket. "What in heaven's name have you been up to?" She fished two dish towels out of a drawer, threw one to Hamish and rolled his dripping jacket in the other. "Don't tell me you went through the Maxi-Wash with your windows down?"

Hamish shot her a look that said *Give me a break, I'm not that dumb.* "The track jammed," he said through blue lips and chattering teeth.

Zol clamped a hand over his mouth to stifle the laugh that was bursting to come out. He couldn't trust himself to say a word; Hamish was easily offended, and his limited sense of humour never included jokes on himself.

"So you got stuck in the Saab?" Colleen said. "With the water jets and rollers running?"

He rolled his eyes and backed away from Colleen, who was now attempting to relieve him of his soaking-wet shirt. "I honked and honked." He glared at his watch. "Sat there thirty minutes and no one came. Finally climbed out." He drew his hand across the back of his neck and made a face at the pink lather on his palm. "Ultra Wax." He swept anxiously at his flat-top. For once, his hair wasn't perfect. He patted his trouser pockets, and his face lit with alarm. "The keys. Hell's bells, still in the ignition."

"I'm sure the guys will take good care of your vehicle," Colleen reassured him. "Heavens, it's almost a member of their family."

Did Hamish get the irony of his predicament? Probably not — he was too cut and dried to appreciate satire — but he was the Maxi-Wash's best customer. Who else had their car preened at a carwash half a dozen times a week? Of course, Hamish's anxiety over his vehicle was understandable. The Saab had been stolen from outside a gay bar a few months ago, during his first experience drinking to excess. When the cops found the vehicle and returned it to him, he had the body repainted, the upholstery repaired, and the carpet fumigated.

Zol swallowed his laugh and clamped his jaw, then persuaded Hamish to come upstairs and change into dry clothes. Of course, Mr. Fastidious balked until Zol promised that the plaid shirt, Blue Jays sweatshirt, and slacks he was offering were freshly laundered. Zol conceded the pant legs were too long, but assured Hamish they'd roll up easily enough.

Back in the kitchen, Colleen handed Hamish a mug of hot coffee and excused herself to get dressed. Hamish sank onto a chair and drank in silence, the fiery blush on his cheeks broadcasting his mortification. More than anything, Hamish hated two things: being wrong and looking foolish. Socially, he was the Tin Man, largely unaware of the feelings of others and inept at idle chatter. Sometimes he came out with tactless zingers that really stung. He had no idea they were hurtful. Zol put it down to his lonely child-hood as a brainy kid — no siblings, few friends, and parents who bickered constantly.

Hamish drained his mug and thumped it on the table. He was scowling. "You should've returned my calls."

"Hang on," Zol countered. The sharpness of the guy's tone was a bit rich, dressed as he was in Zol's favourite sweatshirt and basking in the warmth of his kitchen. But he did have to admit, it was a relief to hear Hamish speaking in a normal voice again. The croaky whisper he'd been plagued with for a couple of years had disap-peared a few weeks ago as mysteriously as it had come. Colleen was probably right — the feeble voice had been some sort of psycho-somatic manifestation of Hamish's anxiety over hiding in the closet. Now that he was well and truly out, and he and Al Mesic were openly partnered, Hamish's voice had returned to full volume.

"All day yesterday," Hamish said, "and not a word back from you."

"I was in Simcoe. Didn't get home till late." Had Hamish for-gotten about his new job? He certainly hadn't called the Simcoe office. Zol's new secretary, obliging and efficient, wouldn't have forgotten to pass on a message.

Hamish scratched at the yellow stain on the sleeve of the sweat-shirt, then rolled back the cuff to hide the blemish. The Blue Jays logo looked out of place on his chest. He'd probably never been to a ballgame, never eaten a foot-long hot dog slathered in mustard.

"Next time," Zol told him, "message me on my BlackBerry. God knows, that thing can find me anywhere."

The BlackBerry had been the digital sergeant major Peter Trinnock used to keep Zol at his beck and call. Their three-year relationship was a Pandora's box of complicated, tacit understand-ings. Both were well aware that Trinnock couldn't cope without an underling thirty years his junior to take the heat. Trinnock pan-icked when the mayor, the press, or their politically ambitious boss Elliott York came calling. Zol could stay calm — at least outwardly — and blunder through. He chuckled at the thought of Trinnock forced to give up his three-martini lunches now that Zol was tied up in Simcoe. But would he?

Hamish stood up and began pacing between the stove and the kitchen table. "I've been dying to tell you about a couple of things. First, my fifteen-case cluster of atypical skin lesions." He was obviously feeling better. An intriguing medical dilemma always perked him up. "I'm hereby reporting it to you . . . you know, officially. A fascinating outbreak for your team to sink its teeth into."

Like most jurisdictions, the Province of Ontario required practitioners to report to their local health unit any sightings of certain contagious diseases on a specified list. Zol had a staff of inspectors and nurses who took calls from doctors and laboratories. Hamish insisted on reporting directly to Zol. Though he was flattered to have such loyalty, he wished Hamish would leave simple voice mails like everyone else.

"What've you got?" Zol asked.

"I'm calling it lip and finger eruption."

"You mean, like hand, foot, and mouth disease? Coxsackie virus?" Certain infections, such as syphilis, influenza, and meningitis warranted top priority because they were highly contagious and had devastating consequences if not managed promptly. This lip and finger thing didn't sound too serious, so why was Hamish so bothered? Especially on a Saturday morning.

"I don't mean that at all." Hamish was wagging that annoying index finger of his in full professorial mode. "Much bigger blisters that last far longer than Coxsackie. Weeks and weeks." He waved off Zol's suggestion, clearly disgusted at its feebleness. "The cultures are negative for Coxsackie. I made sure of that straight away."

"Could the blisters be herpetic?" Zol asked.

"Thought of that first. Negatory on herpes simplex."

"Shingles?"

"You're not serious. Lesions on the fingers and lips simultaneously? Impossible. Anyway, the cultures are negative for V-Z virus."

Hamish's demeanour had transformed itself over the past few minutes. Shop talk had replaced small talk, and the awkward Tin

Man was gone. Now, a short, blond version of Oscar Wilde was pacing the kitchen with extravagant confidence. Zol pictured Professor Hamish Wakefield strutting the streets of Victorian London, a cane in his hand a cape over his shoulders.

"You're right. Of course," Zol admitted. "What about an allergic reaction? Contact dermatitis. A plant? A herbal remedy?"

"Honestly, Zol. It's way too late in the season for poison oak or ivy."

"Easy now." Hamish needed reminding that he wasn't the only doctor in the room with a good brain. "Did you ask about firewood?"

Zol had once diagnosed poison ivy in seemingly the wrong season. It was mid-winter and the patient a farmer with a rash on his upper limbs: blisters that had persisted for weeks and perplexed three other doctors. Zol diagnosed poison ivy that had been contracted in the act of chopping firewood. The man's woodpile had been covered in poison ivy vines during the summer, and the plant had left its rash-causing resin behind when it died back in the autumn. He was still proud of that little diagnostic triumph.

"No," Hamish tsked, "I didn't ask about firewood. Many of the cases are skinny teenage girls. I doubt they've been going at woodpiles with an axe."

"How about giant hogweed? It's generated dozens of calls to our hotline."

Giant hogweed — a recent invader from China — looked like an enormous version of Queen Anne's lace, the delicate wildflower that no one could resist picking. If hogweed sap got smeared on the skin, it caused large, painful blisters when the affected area was exposed to sunlight. The health unit had been warning the public to stay away from the plant and had put an alert on its website, asking people to report hogweed sightings to their local city hall.

"I've seen your posters and bulletins," Hamish said. "But hogweed dermatitis erupts everywhere the plant touches the skin. Not only on the lips and fingertips. Besides, hogweed gets better with steroids. These lesions don't respond to anything."

Zol looked at his watch. It was almost time to pick up Max from his sleepover at Travis's house. No doubt the boys had been up until all hours playing a marathon of video games.

"Are you dealing with a closed population?" Zol asked. He hoped not. Health-unit staff were required to give immediate attention to group homes, retirement residences, and nursing homes. Regardless of personal weekend plans.

"Not closed, but several of their postal codes are clustered."

"Yeah?"

Hamish beamed. He loved hunting down a diagnosis, either in a single patient with symptoms that had stumped other doctors, or in a cluster of cases threatening to break into an epidemic. "A few cases come from Hamilton, and the rest live smack inside your new territory, Dr. Szabo. Town of Simcoe and a bunch of villages in Brant and Norfolk counties. Cool, eh?"

"Oh, great."

"I'll say. Now that you're the boss, you and I can call the shots on a full-scale investigation."

Zol shook his head. Outbreaks of contact dermatitis sat too low on his mandate to even think about. Hamish should know that.

"Why not?" Hamish said.

"For crying out loud, I'm a civil servant, not a magician. Your epidemic isn't on the list of reportable conditions, and there's nothing my staff can do about a non-infectious rash that's not a major risk to public safety. The Ministry frowns on us sticking our noses into every health problem we come across. We don't have the resources."

Hamish whipped off Zol's Blue Jays sweatshirt and tossed it over the back of a chair. And then, as if suspicious of the borrowed sport shirt underneath it, he straightened the collar and checked the buttons. When he looked up, he caught Zol's gaze. "Would it make a difference if two of the cases, both teenagers from Norfolk County, died yesterday morning?" His baby blues hardened as the pupils widened. "Jaundiced head to toe from galloping liver failure?"

CHAPTER 4

Colleen swished into the kitchen looking smashing in a white blouse, a funky multicoloured knitted vest, designer jeans, and her favourite silver elephant pendant dangling above her chest. Zol had never noticed the piercing intelligence in the animal's eyes before. Its trunk usually led him straight to her cleavage and its exquisite promise of warm softness and jasmine. But at this moment he wasn't feeling the heat of ardour, more the cold disquiet of unfocussed dread.

Never mind Hamish's fifteen cases of a more-or-less harmless skin disease. It was the second half of the story, told with Hamish's trademark flare, that had turned Zol's hands into blocks of ice. Five teens from four different villages in Norfolk County, Zol's new patch of the province, had been hit with galloping liver failure in the past few days. Two had died. Three others might be headed that way. Preliminary tests had ruled out the usual causes of infectious hepatitis, so it probably wasn't a virus or a parasite. It sounded like poisoning. But of what? Recreational drugs? The water supply? Had the teens been horsing around with agricultural chemicals? Pesticides?

"Has he gone?" Colleen asked.

"The Maxi-Wash called. Saab's fine. They picked him up, all super apologetic."

"Hope they're giving him a raft of free washes."

"Can't see him going back there. You know what he's like." Hamish had an impressive memory, and not only for the Latin names of a multitude of micro-organisms. The man never forgot a slight or injustice.

Colleen touched Zol's arm. "You okay? You look—"

"Hamish just handed me a couple of his diagnostic conundrums." That was the Hamish term for them. In public, Zol would have to call them "public-health challenges of a significant nature." Here in his kitchen, they felt like ordeals by fire. "And they both seem centred on Simcoe."

"Your first biggies down there."

He told her the little he knew from Hamish about the kids with devastated livers, their eyes and skin glowing with jaundice.

"Now what?" she said.

He wiped the sweat from the back of his neck. "It's hard to know where to begin. Natasha's out of town for the weekend."

Natasha Sharma, still under thirty, was the brightest light in the Hamilton-Lakeshore Health Unit. Zol had agreed to the secondment in Simcoe on the condition that Natasha would be assigned to help him whenever he needed her. With a Master's in epidemiology and a detective's nose for case-cracking details, she was a brilliant epidemic-buster. She had charm, dedication, and absolutely no ego. Furthermore, she was independent and very low maintenance. "Poor thing is somewhere in Toronto. At one of those big Hindu weddings her mother is dying to throw for her."

"Isn't she hot and heavy with a Greek guy? A surgical resident?"

At first, Natasha had passed off the handsome and dark-enough Dr. Kostos Stefanopoulos as a westernized Punjabi, an orphan with no Hindu family in Canada. It had worked for a while, but her mother had a meltdown when Kostos let it slip that he'd been an altar boy at a Greek Orthodox Church in East Toronto. "Yeah, but that doesn't stop her mother from praying that one day Natasha will come to her senses and settle down with a nice Punjabi engineer."

"I have a feeling," Colleen said, "her mother is going to be disappointed."

"I've got Hamish sniffing and digging on the liver thing until Natasha gets back on Monday." Hamish was as keen as Natasha at epidemic-busting, and because that wasn't part of his job at Caledonian University's medical centre, he was thrilled whenever Zol asked him to be a special consultant on a health-unit case. "He's going to update me in a couple of hours. Maybe by then he'll have something we can brainstorm with."

She poured them each a glass of orange juice and motioned for him to sit down. "Here," she said, "have a shot of this." She nodded toward the *Globe and Mail* still scattered across the counter. "You were about to tell me about your loon and the legend of a second one to match it."

"Was I?" If the ancient story had any truth in it, the repercussions would be too much to contemplate. It was better to leave it be. "It's nothing. Just silly hype."

"Come on."

He frowned and shook his head. Even though the legend had been told to him by the enthusiastic curator at the ROM to whom he'd relinquished his loon pipe fifteen years ago, it felt demeaning to attach superstition to such an exquisite artifact. Besides, it was ancient history compared to the urgency of the outbreak of liver failure among the Norfolk teenagers.

"Goodness, Zol. Anything that's two thousand years old is bound to carry folklore to spare. That's part of its allure." She crinkled her eyes over the rim of her juice glass. "Come on, it's not like you to hide things from me."

When she put it that way, perhaps the story did lend a harmless, mystical quality to the work of an ancient artisan. He downed his orange juice in three swallows, then told her about the two loon pipes that were said to have been carved as a pair.

"From the same block of pipestone?"

"That's the idea. A male and a female. One with garnet eyes, the other with black onyx. In life, male and female loons have identical plumage. Their eye colour changes with the seasons. According to the legend, the two carvings are indistinguishable, except for their eyes."

"Loons mate for life, do they not?"

He shook his head. "A popular misconception. More like serial monogamy." He'd done a project on loons in grade seven, his interest sparked by the pair that nested year after year on the small lake bordering his family's tobacco farm. As a kid, he'd seen two loons fighting to the death there on Smiths Mill Pond. One was defending his nesting site from an interloper who had designs on the site and the female who came with it. The winner had taken all. Zol never discovered whether the victor was the incumbent or the interloper. All the same, Mother Nature had taken on a new harshness in his thirteen-year-old eyes.

"And the legend?"

"The story goes that together the pipes bestow some sort of power that vanishes when they're separated."

Colleen smiled. A dreamy look flashed in her eyes and was quickly replaced by a frown of concentration. "Who had them last? And when?"

"Who knows?"

"And the power?"

Zol didn't answer.

"Come on, was it spiritual? Political? Sexual?"

He shrugged and said nothing, wishing he'd never mentioned the legend. He hated superstition. For centuries, the practice of medicine had been based not on logical deductions, but on myths and old wives' tales. His mentor and medical muse had been the most famous physician on the planet in the nineteenth century, Sir William Osler. Everywhere Dr. Osler went, he taught medical students to observe sick people systematically, to draw conclusions about their patients' illnesses using rational thought, not superstition. Sir William, known for his empathy and wit, grew up in Dundas, the crunchy-granola town Zol could see huddled in the valley below his sunroom. When preoccupied by a public-health ordeal, Zol often looked down from his affluent but lonely perch on the Escarpment's brow and pictured Dr. Osler at his desk, writing truisms for the ages by candlelight. With the cash from his first paycheque, Zol had purchased Dr. Osler's 1895 Parker fountain pen in a Montreal antique shop. Whenever he ran his fingers along the black ebonite shaft and sterling silver clip, the great man almost came to life. The instrument was stolen from Zol more than a year ago during a confrontation with a crazed butcher. The police had recovered it, but they'd been holding it in their evidence box for ages, always promising to return it to him soon. God, he missed that pen. And he could sure use some of Dr. Osler's wisdom now.

"For heaven's sake, Zol. By the look on your face, there's more to this than a couple of stone loons wielding some sort of nameless power."

He dug into his pocket for a loonie, the one-dollar coin he kept in his pocket for fingering when he felt anxious. The coin's reverse bore the image of its namesake swimming on a lake. He wove the coin through his icy fingers, passing it from one hand to the other and back again. The rhythm always soothed him.

He took a deep breath. "The legend says that whoever has possession of both loons will be empowered to take over all the lands he can reach by canoe in the months between the equinoxes."

Colleen thought for a moment. "You mean between March and September?"

"Two hundred years ago, the voyageurs could cover a lot of territory between spring breakup and winter freeze-up."

"The French fellows?"

"Europeans and Natives. The explorers and fur traders who opened up the country." He checked himself. Europeans opening up the country made it sound as though the continent were closed before they arrived. If closed meant unspoiled, he figured it was okay to think of it that way. As a public-health officer whose new territory included the largest First Nations reserve in the country, he was teaching himself to deviate from the old, Eurocentric path.

"But this is now," Colleen said. "No government is going to recognize the power of two ancient pipes."

"Of course not. But if a Native leader ever got hold of both pipes, he could use them in a propaganda campaign."

"How so?"

"Without believing in the legend himself, someone could appropriate the supposed power of the loons — incite a pseudo-legitimate call to arms. He could travel across the country from reserve to reserve, wave the loons, inspire cells of Native people to rise against five hundred years of oppression."

"Cells? Seriously?"

"Why not? Guerrilla warfare, Canadian-style. Might not take much to get them started." He could feel himself heating up, his voice rising. "They could demolish bridges. Block highways. Disable power plants. Blow up factories and government offices."

"Surely not."

"Our position on this land is a lot more tenuous than any politician or non-aboriginal citizen wants to admit."

Colleen clutched the elephant pendant in her fist. He could tell she was remembering why she and her late husband Liam, European descendants, had left post-apartheid South Africa. Was she picturing the nightmare of a similar scenario playing out here, in her adopted country?

"If Native gangs close the railways and highways, commuters won't get to work, goods won't get delivered. Large manufacturers like Toyota and General Motors will pull out. The U.S. will shut its borders. Banks, schools, offices will close. No car parts. No Corn Flakes. No artichokes or avocados."

"Okay, okay. I understand." She thought for a moment. "So where's the other pipe?"

"No one knows. Did it get smashed over the centuries, or is it out there somewhere, waiting to meet its partner?"

She pointed to the newspaper. "Is that what this bombing is about? Someone retrieving the loon pipe from the ROM because he's got the other one?"

"Or you're a Native guy who thinks he knows where it is."

"But why the destruction of the museum's Crystal entrance? It's not as hellish an example of contemporary architecture as the critics say. A fair bit of majesty in all that glass and aluminum."

Zol studied the photos of the damage. "The bombing doesn't make sense as a robbery. The First Peoples Gallery, from where they must have stolen the artifacts, is on the opposite side of the ROM from the Crystal." He knew that gallery well, had taken Max there to see the loon.

"You mean," Colleen said, "they stole the loon and a few other artifacts, then blew up the Crystal for spite?"

He mulled that for a moment. "Not quite," he told her. "As a manifesto: We've taken back the pipe, we have explosives, and we're going to use them."

He could feel his dread deepening. "They could be getting ready for the next stage. Trains and bridges." He gripped his coffee mug against the chill in his bones. "The railroad has always been a powerful symbol of European repression. It threw the continent wide open to epidemics of smallpox and measles. Millions of Natives died of infection without a shot being fired." He told her about the nineteenth-century prairie paintings in his grade-school history text, the images vivid with spilt blood. "The trains brought floods of settlers who slaughtered the plains bison to the brink of extinction. The prairie Natives starved by the thousands because their entire way of life depended on thriving herds of those buffalo."

Colleen shuddered and fastened the upper buttons of her vest. "Let's not get ahead of ourselves," she said, her tone cautious. "There's nothing you can do to retrieve the stolen loon. It's not as though you're responsible for it at this stage." She picked up her juice glass, seemed to consider its contents, then put it down. "What's happening with Max today? Shall I pick him up from Travis's? What time did they —"

The phone rang. Zol grabbed it on the third ring. "Hi, Dad, I was about to call you." Ever since his mother's diagnosis two months ago, he did his best to sound upbeat on the phone with his parents, but the sight of their number on the call display hit like a smack in the gut. One day, the call would come announcing the chemo had stopped working and the lung cancer had spread out of control. "Have you seen today's paper?"

"Your mother say it is time."

Zol squeezed the handset. His knees gave out, and he slumped into his chair.

"Oh, Dad. No. Really?"

She'd looked pretty good yesterday. Her oncologist had virtually promised that chemo and radiation would provide a good eighteen to twenty-four months of remission. She still had sixteen months of good health left. Maybe more. She'd been making elaborate plans for Christmas with Max. Was she not going to make it to Halloween, her second-favourite holiday?

"She's wanting talk to you."

"About what?"

"She not tell me."

That was a bad sign. His parents had shared everything: their midnight escape from Hungary as young children in 1956, their years of low-paid agricultural labour, their pennies scrimped for the down payment on a farm, their worries over crop damage and tobacco market dips.

"She just say it is time, Zollie."

He wanted to ask "time for what?" but he couldn't force out the words. And he didn't want to hear the answer. He knew it would come to this. Mum had almost refused her last chemo treatment, insisting that her back pain, and the overwhelming nausea, exhaustion, and mouth sores of chemotherapy were going to steal her dignity. She hadn't fussed over the loss of her hair, but she had vowed never to relinquish her self-respect. She'd carved out her place in the New World and she was going to leave it on her own terms, proud of her family and her accomplishments. He pictured the stash of morphine behind the Bible in her bedside table. They both pretended he didn't know it was there. Her security blanket.

"Can she take the phone?"

"She say you must come. Must see you in person."

"But can't we talk for a sec?"

"No, Zollie. You come now."

CHAPTER 5

Zol glanced at his mother sitting beside him in the minivan. Katalin Szabo — Kitti to her family, to her friends at the Catholic Women's League and the hospital's volunteer association — fidgeted with the tissue wadded in her bony fist. Her eyes widened at the sight of the next set of potholes, and she braced against the armrest. He pumped the brake as gently as he could and eased onto Robinson Street. Simcoe General Hospital loomed at the end of the block like bits of mismatched Lego snapped together through the decades.

Mum clutched her handbag to her chest and leaned forward. Damn, here it came, another coughing fit. He swallowed hard, slowed to a crawl, and planted his hand on his mother's shoulder. As he rubbed her upper back, he felt the shuddering through her heavy cloth coat. When the fit stopped, the vehicle was eerily still. With heartbreaking grace, she pressed the Kleenex to her lips and deposited something undoubtedly nasty.

He'd never get used to her turban. It was supposed to hide her chemo baldness, but instead it drew attention to her cancer like a neon sign. It would not let him forget that though his mother looked encouragingly robust, she had a serious illness. He couldn't stop thinking of the impending weight loss that would steal the flesh from her soft round face and make a mockery of her high, Slavic cheek bones.

No matter how gently he tried to negotiate the county's neglected roads, she winced with back pain every time the vehicle rocked like a tractor on a stony field. "I'll drop you at the front door," he said, "and get you settled. I can park in the visitors'. Won't take me half a minute."

"No. We walk from car. I still have my good legs."

They used to be gorgeous legs. Everybody said so. A closet full of shoes was her only vice. That and a pack-a-day smoking habit she'd kicked about a year before her lung cancer diagnosis.

"No, Mum. Let me fetch a wheelchair."

"Certainly not."

"But, Mother, it's freezing."

"We walk. Together."

He parked in the visitors' lot, as close to the front door as possible. She took his arm against the heavy gusts blowing all the way from Chicago. He had no idea why they were going to this effort. Though she wasn't as strong as she liked to pretend, she didn't seem sick enough to need immediate admission to hospital. She hadn't packed a bag and she'd warned him to steer clear of the emergency department.

Why were they here?

Twenty minutes earlier, greeting him from the wingback chair in her living room, she'd looked surprisingly confident. Her breathing seemed comfortable, she was a good colour, and she'd thrown him a warm smile. Then she'd told him enigmatically that *Now is time, Zollie* and insisted he take her to the hospital. He'd asked what was wrong, but she wouldn't say. She had a handbag in her lap, but no suitcase.

"Is your doctor expecting you?" he'd asked.

"No questions. Take me to hospital."

"But don't you need a few things? What about your meds?"

She'd waved her hand dismissively, then extended it to indicate that he should assist her out of the chair. His dad helped her into her coat and made a face that said, *Your mother, she make up her mind, and I doing what she tell me.*

Now, as Zol walked her from the parking lot toward the hospital's main entrance, Kitti refused the wheelchair ramp and steered him to the steps. Three teenagers were lighting up, two paces inside the yellow line marking the tobacco exclusion zone, an exact nine metres from the front door. Of course, it was his health unit that was charged with enforcing the Smoke-Free Ontario Act, but only a jerk would hassle those kids over a couple of metres.

Two of the teens had ski jackets thrown over their flimsy hospital gowns. The third teen, a boy of about fifteen, looked like a visitor — black pea coat over a tee-shirt and jeans, piercings in his lip and eyebrows. Zol was getting used to the body jewellery kids sported these days, but he couldn't help being shocked by the boy's extreme obesity. The youth was a head shorter than Zol and weighed well over three hundred pounds. Diabetes, heart disease, and sleep apnea were lurking for him around the corner. The kids in the gowns, a girl and a boy, were attached to IV poles and puffing away. He couldn't see any obvious lesions on their lips. Were they jaundiced? He couldn't tell from this distance and didn't want them to think he was some weird guy leering at them.

Both kids were emaciated, weighing no more than ninety or a hundred pounds, that was obvious. He couldn't help eyeing the contours of their collarbones jutting above their open jackets. It struck him again that much of the world had lost its ability to correctly judge how much they should eat. Until half a generation ago, calorie consumption came naturally to almost everyone. Without thinking much about it, Zol's family had stayed trim because they balanced their food-energy input with their exercise-energy output. But nowadays, most people were too fat and a few were too skinny. And whose fault was that? He understood the urgency of the issue, but nothing in his training as a chef and a doctor had taught him how the fatness epidemic had happened so quickly and on such a grand scale. And no one seemed to know what to do about it.

He nodded to the smokers through their tobacco fog. He was struck by the harsh, tarry smell of the cheap, unregulated stuff from Grand Basin Reserve. Half an hour away, dozens of Native-owned smoke shops offered cigarettes they produced from locally grown tobacco and sold at one tenth the cost of the international brands available in town. The sale wasn't legal, but law enforcement had given up interfering with the trade. He despaired at the hopeless task of persuading young people not to smoke in the face of a ready supply of cigarettes sold in packs of twenty-five that cost less than a cup of coffee.

Ringo Starr jammed three bars of "Yellow Submarine" into Zol's brain as he fought the stench, the front door, and the blustery wind. Two steps inside, Kitti stopped and clutched her chest. Her face was ashen. She tried to speak, but nothing came out, not even a cough. Oh my God, was this the end? Had Mum known it all along and was putting on a false front?

His own chest tightened with panic. He scanned the lobby for a wheelchair. He spotted one and scooped her into it as her knees gave out.

He started wheeling her at top speed to the emergency department. When she realized where they were headed, she put up her arms and shouted, "No, Zollie. Stop."

He kept rolling. "Don't be silly. You're having a heart attack."

She waved her arms. "A little spell, only."

He stopped rolling and looked her in the face. "Mum, this is serious."

"I am fine. This happens. Sometimes. When I am doing too much . . . vacuuming."

"You've been vacuuming?"

"Who else? Your father, he doesn't even know . . . where I keep it."

"For God's sake, Mum."

"Zollie, is okay." She motioned to the bank of empty chairs in the waiting area at the far side of the lobby. "We wait there. A few moments only. Then we continue."

"No," he said, pushing the chair forward. "You're going to Emerg."

She scraped her boots against the floor and jammed them under the wheelchair's foot rests. He had to stop pushing before he broke her ankles.

"Good," she said firmly. "Now, let me catch breath." She felt her handbag as though checking to be sure the contents were intact. "And then I tell you where we going." She closed her eyes and bowed her head.

A few moments later, she opened her eyes. Her breathing had settled and she pointed to the hallway leading to the older section of the hospital, which housed the inpatient wards. "I'm ready. Take me to elevator."

"Not so fast. You said you'd tell me where we're going."

"Soon, you see," she said and waved him forward with an imperious flip of her fingers. "But now, you push."

Opting for peace, he rolled her toward the elevator, the route taking them past the cheery gift shop and the spartan library. Being Saturday, the gift shop was open, the library closed. Commerce trumped knowledge. He wondered whether these days anyone read printed medical texts and journals. Medical stuff was better online — easier to find, more up to date, and loaded with fantastic images.

They stopped in front of the twin elevator doors. "Up or down?" he asked.

Kitti thought for a moment, which surprised him. He thought she'd already worked this out. "Down," she said.

"The basement? Are you sure?"

"Yes, down." She slipped something out of her purse and palmed it so he couldn't see it. Whatever it was, it seemed to reassure her.

Against his better judgment, he pushed the down button. His chest was still tight. They should be in Emerg, not taking an elevator to God knows where.

The left-hand door opened, and he wheeled her forward.

"Stop. Not that one."

"For heaven's sake, Mother, they both go to the same place."

"No. Stop." He did as she asked and let the door close without them. She waited a moment, then pressed the up button three times. "We take next one."

They waited in silence.

Was she losing it? First down, now up. Maybe it was a lack of oxygen. He glanced at her lips. They were pink enough. But what was that in her hand? What the heck was she up to?

Her eyes flashed in satisfaction as the right-hand elevator opened.

"Okay, now?" he asked. He'd let a little sarcasm creep in. His mother was used to that. His sister had a Master's in it.

She looked from side to side, as if checking to be sure they were alone, then nodded. "Yes. This one."

"Which floor?" he said, once they were inside.

She hesitated, then told him to push number four, the top floor.

He pushed the button and watched the indicator numbers light up in succession. Two. Three.

Suddenly, she lunged forward, waved the thing in her fist over the elevator's control panel, and hit the large red button.

The car lurched to a stop, and so did Zol's stomach. "What the —? Mother, what are you doing?"

She sought his face, and held him tightly with her gaze, her lips quivering. She pressed her palm to her mouth, then took a slow, deep breath. Still clutching her purse, she said, "Know where you are, son?"

Yeah, stuck between floors three and four with a woman whose behaviour was becoming increasingly irrational.

She stared up at him with a faraway look, her eyes glistening, teardrops on each cheek. He took a step back, unnerved. He couldn't remember the last time he'd seen his mother cry. This wasn't the face of the practical, no-nonsense woman who, until a few months ago, had kept a spotless household and spearheaded half a dozen charity projects. It was downright frightening to see her this way.

"You born right here." She pointed to the scuffed linoleum that looked as though it hadn't been replaced in more than thirty-five years. "My first baby."

He fumbled in his pockets for a Kleenex, but realized she didn't want one. She wasn't tearing with sadness. She was indulging in a moment of nostalgia.

He knew the story, of course. And the graphic details of his sudden appearance on the elevator floor amid a gush of blood and body fluids.

"Your dad, he parking the car. I told him he should hurry, the baby is coming. But that man, he always behind. Like cow's tail."

"Come on, Mum. You're not supposed to interfere with the elevator. Security's going to —"

She showed him what she'd hidden in her fist. Her photo ID card from hospital. CODE ORANGE VOLUNTEER was printed across it in bold letters. "I'm on Disaster Team. They allow me control the elevator when necessary. And necessary now. A few minutes only."

"But —"

"No time wasting." She dug into her handbag and pulled out something the size of a couple of cigarette packs wrapped in blue gingham.

Without unwrapping the object, she raised it with both hands. "I must die in peace."

He grabbed the handrail and squeezed his eyes closed against the vertigo threatening to topple him. His own mother, delusional from the cancer now spread to her brain, was asking him to euthanize her. Right here in the exact spot she'd delivered him. Her sense of the poetic was in overdrive, and she was out of her mind.

He opened his eyes and held the rail with both hands. His mother's eyes were clear, the faraway look replaced by earnest practicality. Maybe she hadn't lost her marbles. Perhaps she'd come to a rational decision about ending her life. That would be just like her. Everything planned, micro-organized to a fault. She must have squirrelled away enough of her bedside morphine to do the job. And now here, where she'd brought him into the world, she wanted him to inject her with an overdose. She was asking him to end her life in the exact location she'd brought life to his. Rational perhaps, and clearly dramatic, but out of the question.

"Mum, I can't —"

"Quiet, Zollie. I show you something." She removed the gingham wrapping. In her lap was a small box. He recognized the logo and blue colour — a Birks jewellery box. She removed the lid to reveal the object inside, nestled in a bed of cotton batting. "This for you. Now your turn keep it safe."

Zol couldn't believe what his mother was holding. He rubbed his eyes and looked again. His heart was racing, his chest tighter than ever. "How did you get this?"

"You promise keep it safe? Don't tell your father?"

His tongue was as dry as a boxful of sand. "Um . . . well . . ." He'd never seen her look so vulnerable — her turban, her sunken cheeks, her grey eyes imploring with a new set of tears welling at the corners. At this moment he'd do almost anything she wanted.

He stared at the object in the box. Its eyes. They weren't red, they were black. How could this be?

She replaced the lid and the gingham wrapping, then handed him the box, the tears rolling down her cheeks. "Hide it in your pocket. Quickly."

She watched as he stuffed the box into his jacket. When she was satisfied, she wiped her cheeks on her coat sleeve and said, "Okay. Now we go."

"But —"

She pressed the green button on the elevator panel. "Take me home. I tell you story in car."

CHAPTER 6

An hour later, his hands shaking, Zol removed the gingham cloth from the Birks box and placed it, unopened, on his kitchen counter. All the way back to Hamilton from his parents' place, he'd been obsessed with keeping to the speed limit, terrified the police would pull him over and search his pockets.

Colleen padded into the kitchen and pecked him on the lips.

"Any news from Hamish?" he asked.

She shook her head. Her eyes narrowed. "Oh my God, you look awful." She squeezed his arm. "How's your mum?" She searched his eyes. "What's happened?"

He cocked his ear toward the computer room. "Where's Max?"

"Still with Travis. Swimming, then a movie. He was really keen on it, and I didn't think you'd mind. They promised to have him back before dinner."

"Perfect." He didn't want Max knowing about any of this. He pointed to the Birks box on the table. "I need you to open that."

Colleen raised her eyebrows, then scrutinized the box from several angles. She looked and listened, but didn't touch. "Birks," she said, finally. "The jewellers. What is it? Something of your mum's?"

"Please, just open it."

She grasped the lid and it eased off, then jumped back when she saw what was inside. She leaned in for a closer look. "How extraordinary. Zol, it's stunning." Her face tightened. "But it's hot. The police . . . The Native councils . . . However did she get it?"

"It's not what you think."

"It doesn't matter what I think. The police are going to —"

"It's never been in the ROM."

"You've lost me."

"It's not the loon in the newspaper. See? Her eyes are black, not red. It's the —"

"The mate? No. Don't tell me the second loon actually exists?"

He wiped his hands on his jeans and lifted the beautiful little loon from her cotton nest. He cupped her in his palms, stroked her smooth grey back, felt the sharpness of her beak, her heft, the fine balance of her tail. He held her to his face with the smoke hole opposite his lips, and stared into the creature's eyes. He could see that if you were stoned on its hallucinogenic tobacco, those piercing, black eyes would be mesmerizing.

"Your mother gave you this?"

"She didn't want anyone to find it accidentally when . . . you know . . . the time came to go through her things."

Colleen's eyes began to glisten. "Oh, Zol, I'm so sorry. But how touching." Her mouth twitched as she gazed at the loon cupped in his palms.

"Here," he said, "you hold her."

She held out both hands, then cradled the creature like an injured duckling. She seemed reluctant to hold her for long. "Let me put it away before either of us drops her."

She placed the loon in the box, then took Zol by the hands and kissed him on the lips. "You'd better sit down. And then tell me what this is about."

He poured himself a glass of water, took a few gulps, and sank into a chair at the kitchen table. "Turns out they've had that black-eyed loon for at least five years."

"Your mum and dad?"

"Dad found her, then gave her to Mum for safekeeping. She's the organized one."

"Why didn't they give it to the ROM?"

"Because of all the hassles and indignities they endured after finding the first one."

He told her the story of the Native land claim made against their farm as soon as word got out that the Szabos had unearthed a priceless First Nations artifact. The Natives were convinced the family was sitting on a sacred Iroquois burial site. For three weeks, a gang from Grand Basin Reserve — and a few imported rabble-rousers brandishing unregistered firearms — barricaded his family's driveway, built bonfires on their front lawn, and blocked access to their home. For Hungarian immigrants who'd fled the excesses of Soviet totalitarianism, the experience was terrifying. The land claim fizzled when his dad produced the English strongbox in which Zol had found the pipe and persuaded a group of moderate Native elders that the pipe came from a White man's cache and not a First Nations burial site.

"Do your parents know about the legend?"

"That's another reason why they hid the second loon. To keep the two of them apart."

She nodded, her expression solemn. "Had your mum and dad heard about the bombing at the ROM?"

"Oh yeah." He gestured at the little blue box. "I think that's what reminded Mum about our friend here."

"Where did your dad find it?"

"In the opposite corner of our property from where he found the first one."

"In another strong box?"

Zol sipped his water. His tongue was still thick. "Also made in Sheffield."

"So at one point, the same guy had possession of both loons."

"Looks like it."

"And chose to separate them. What does your mum want you to do with this second one?"

"Told me not to tell Dad I had her. He's terrified of another land claim and doesn't want anyone to know we've got it." He shrugged, then cracked his knuckles. "But otherwise, she told me to use my judgment."

"That's a bit heavy. Especially with the coppers looking for its mate as part of a potential terrorist attack and homicide investigation."

He was stuck in it deep. Up to his neck in the crap. If he presented the loon to the curator of the First Peoples Gallery at the ROM, the Assembly of First Nations would go crazy. They'd rail against yet another instance of a White guy, and a government agency, misappropriating their aboriginal heritage. Any goodwill between his office at Simcoe's health unit and his flock on Grand Basin Reserve would fly out the window barely two weeks into his new job as their medical officer of health. "If I hand the loon over the ROM, no one on Grand Basin will ever speak to me again. And if I hand it over to the cops, they'll accuse me of theft and being an accessory to murder. I can't see them believing I came by it honestly."

She answered without hesitation. "You do have a point. Police detectives are not in the business of crediting the innocence of coincidence. Your possession of this loon, at this moment, no matter what its eye colour, will be seen as highly suspicious."

"So, what do I do?"

"Give *me* the loon and keep quiet. I have a safety deposit box in the name of a numbered company. Absolutely no link to you. Even with a search warrant the police will never find it. And nobody else will, either, for that matter."

The corners of her mouth were twitching. "Something else has you worried," he told her. "What is it?"

She took a deep breath and paused as if debating what, or how much, to tell him.

"Colleen?"

Her eyes swept the room, she glanced at the loon, and then she said, "I spoke with my contact in the Toronto Police Service."

He wasn't sure whether it was creepy or reassuring that she had nameless contacts inside various police forces.

"Those three bodies they found under the rubble at the ROM? It wasn't the explosion that killed them."

"What do you mean?"

"They were already dead. Each shot in the head, execution-style."

"Before the explosion?"

She pursed her lips and nodded slightly. "Probably a matter of minutes."

"Who were they? Mafia?"

"I believe the current politically correct term is First Nations. The bodies have yet to be formally identified, or completely examined, but they exhibit certain features that lead the police to be quite certain they are Natives."

"Do the cops have any idea who did it?"

"Only speculating at this juncture."

He pictured a cigar-toting multimillionaire in a brocade smoking jacket, feeding a psychotic passion for two-thousand-year-old Native artifacts.

No, that was only in James Bond films.

"The police are concerned," she said, "that a rival Native gang got wind of the intended heist and intercepted it."

Zol looked at the black-eyed loon, nestled not so innocently in the Birks box. The creature had suddenly become tainted with a danger he couldn't quite get his head around. "A shootout between gangs at a museum? That's too freaky."

"Not a shootout, Zol. Something more calculated. There's no denying three bodies with neat holes in their skulls." She gave him a look that told him that in her line of work she'd seen stuff he didn't want to know about. "It's the apparent premeditation that has me worried. And I think you should be too."

He put up his hands. "Okay, I'm with you. Believe me." He nodded toward the loon, now almost afraid to look at it. "Please, bury it as deep as you can."

She set the lid on the Birks box and pressed it in place. "It won't be forever. When things cool off, you can decide what to do." She rubbed the back of his neck exactly where he liked it. "And I know you'll do the right thing."

At this point, the right thing was anybody's guess.

CHAPTER 7

Natasha Sharma hit the NEXT DISK button on the Honda's CD player. Given the potential pandemonium that awaited her down the road, five minutes of Bollywood on a Monday morning was as much as she could take. Her cousin Anjum had slipped the CD into the machine on Saturday during their drive to the wedding in Toronto. Anjum said the soundtrack from *Slumdog Millionaire* would get them into the mood. It hadn't worked. Without an escort, Natasha had a miserable time at the wedding; the older women kept eyeing her up and down, as if she were an ageing cow with bad teeth. Her mother had threatened to have one of her meltdowns in front of every person they knew in the Indian community from Niagara Falls to Toronto if Natasha arrived at the wedding with that Greek boy Kostos on her arm. She'd considered bailing, but the bride was a sweet girl and there was no way she could snub a friend. Besides, if she'd stayed away, her mother would have whined about it forever.

Michael Bublé came on crooning "Cry Me a River" as the fields of Norfolk County whizzed past. Most of the crops had been harvested, and the shaded ground below the ginseng netting was either bare or covered with mulch. Her GPS had offered her the scenic route when she'd typed in Erie Christian Collegiate, Simcoe, Ontario before starting her journey. The device was directing her along a series of respectable but minor roads.

As she drove deeper into farm country, she couldn't help noticing the identical, dilapidated wooden buildings clustered beside many of the houses. The caved-in roofs, weathered walls, and doors askew on rusted hinges gave the utilitarian shacks an artistic flare. She was reminded of the black and white photograph Dr. Zol used to have hanging in his office. The evocative image showed a pair of lonely buildings like these casting shadows in the afternoon sun. Dr. Zol had said they were tobacco kilns, as iconic to the Brant and Norfolk County landscapes as the grain elevators of Saskatchewan. He'd slogged summers and autumns as a teenager hanging tobacco leaves inside his family's stifling kilns, where the crop dried to precise levels of humidity under his father's exacting eye. In the winter, the tobacco was then sorted, baled, and sold to the cigarette companies. No one used the wooden kilns any longer, and many had fallen down, replaced by low, techno-efficient, unro-mantic constructions of boxy metal.

Now, an hour after leaving her office in Hamilton, and with Michael Bublé still belting out the tunes, the GPS directed her onto Highway 3 a few kilometres east of Simcoe. It soon warned that her destination, Erie Christian Collegiate, was coming up four hundred metres on the right. Her stomach did a flip as she pulled into the parking lot next to the spot reserved for the principal. She'd been to a principal's office only once in her life, a humiliating experience she hoped never to repeat. Yet here she was again, and though this time she had an appointment and not a summons, the cockroaches were nibbling the lining of her stomach.

She sat down in the chair indicated by the tearful secretary who greeted her at the front office and rushed into a back room, where cries and sobs punctuated desperate voices. Natasha was fifteen minutes early and glad of some time alone to review her notes and plan her strategy. She shuddered at the fear infiltrating this school like a poisonous cloud.

And no wonder. In the past few days, six students at this private Christian high school had come down with liver failure. Totally unexplained. Two sisters were only mildly affected and two kids had died on Friday. And that wasn't the end of it. Earlier this morning, a cheerleader for the basketball team — her eyes and palms said to be fluorescent with jaundice — had shown up in Simcoe General's emergency department.

While Natasha had been enduring the Bollywood wedding in Toronto, Hamish Wakefield had got to do something far more thrilling. He'd spent the weekend tracing the liver cases and discovered that all of them attended the same high school, Erie Christian Collegiate. Their blood, when tested for an alphabet soup of hepatitis viruses, came up negative, which ruled out the garden varieties of liver infections the health unit dealt with every week. Some of the hundred and fifty students at this school were into something dangerous, she was sure of that. But did their parents and teachers have the faintest clue what their kids were up to?

The principal's office door opened and out limped a tall man with a large paunch straining his shirt buttons. He looked like he'd forgotten to shave and had pulled his suit from the dirty laundry basket. His eyes were so close together he'd never be handsome, even with a properly pressed suit and a nice haircut. His mouth twitched as he greeted her with a sweaty palm and introduced himself as Walter Vorst, ECC's principal.

"I suppose you've come to close us down," he said as soon as he'd ushered her into his office and shut the door.

"Not at all, sir." She flashed the professional smile she'd perfected in the mirror for such encounters. "I've come to help."

He slipped off his loafers with a grimace that suggested they were too tight, then sank into the chair behind his imposing desk. He grabbed a pack of gum from a drawer and popped a stick into his mouth. He closed his eyes and chewed hard for a long moment. Soon the scent of spearmint mixed with the reek of tobacco and sweaty socks that had greeted her on the way in.

"To help?" he said.

"Discover why your students are getting sick, so we can prevent further cases."

"Seriously? Further cases?" He ran his hand through his hair. "You don't know what it's been like . . ."

"Mr. Vorst, Dr. Szabo and I need to go through your school and its students with a fine-tooth comb, and find out what the five students had in common. Something that looks quite innocent on the surface, but is actually . . . you know . . ."

The word hung in the leaden air between them, unspoken but understood. Deadly.

She looked down at her notebook until Mr. Vorst broke the silence.

"But this is a superior school, Miss uh . . ."

"Sharma."

"Sorry. I'm usually good with names. But today I'm . . . never mind." He tossed his gum wrapper into the waste basket next to his desk. "Miss . . . Sharma. Most of our graduating students go to university. They come from good Christian families. Dutch Reform and Baptist." He scratched the stubble on his chin and shifted in his chair. "And in case you're wondering, our kids don't smoke, their families are mostly teetotallers, and we don't have a drug problem."

She let go of her professional smile. Was there even one school in the western world that didn't have an issue with drugs? Kids everywhere used tobacco and alcohol, no matter what their parents said. Vorst was deluding himself. And in her line of work, delusions were dangerous.

She looked around the office. There was a photo of four smiling children on Vorst's desk and another, taken maybe a couple of years later, on the bookcase behind him. A formal family portrait of the kind produced by Sears or Walmart included Walter Vorst, but none of the photographs included a woman. He must be divorced, she decided. If the man were widowed, there would be at least one photo of his wife with her children. And clearly, this man was not living with a female partner. No one in possession of two X chromosomes would have let him out of the house in that suit. How did his marital status affect his role as head of a private Christian school? Families paid heavily out of their pockets to send their kids to this fortress, thinking it was a haven from drugs, premarital sex, and teachers with flexible morality. When it came to personal shortcomings, it had always seemed to her that fundamentalists of any religion were less than forgiving.

She'd promised Hamish she would include his cases of lip and finger lesions in her investigation of the liver failure cases. Small sores on the lips and fingers constituted a less emotional issue than deaths from liver failure and a good place to start with Mr. Vorst. She would try settling the principal's obvious anxiety and gain his confidence by first focussing on his students' skin. Hamish had told her that two Erie Collegiate students had presented to his clinic with lip and finger lesions that wouldn't go away.

"Here at ECC," she began, "has anyone noticed a number of students or staff with blisters on their lips? They might look like large cold sores. And perhaps something similar on their fingers?"

Vorst tugged at his tie. "What's that got to do with a hepatitis problem?"

"We're not sure. Maybe nothing. But there's been a cluster of something in Brant and Norfolk counties we're calling lip and finger eruption." Well, that was Hamish's name for it. Dr. Zol was reluctant to call it anything and insisted she stay focussed on the liver cases.

Vorst glanced at the Band-Aids partially concealing the yellowed tips of the index and third fingers of his right hand. "No," he said quickly, without giving his answer any thought. "No, no. Nothing like that."

"Are you sure, Mr. Vorst? Many of the cases come from the postal codes that surround your school." She shot him her *We're working on the same side* smile and added, "It's probably a harmless skin condition, but I've been told to check it out all the same."

Beads of sweats glistened above his eyebrows as he took his time formulating an answer. "Well . . ." He paused to loosen his tie, keeping the two bandaged digits hidden in his palm. "I don't know anything about finger blisters, but three girls missed a track meet because they were too embarrassed to show up with sores on their lips."

"When was that?" Natasha asked.

"A couple of weeks ago."

"Any others?"

"Maybe. I can't say for sure." He popped another stick of gum into his mouth and leaned back in his chair, the wrinkles less tight around his eyes. Something in that gum was having a calming effect on him. Nicotine? "Some students have been staying home, emailing their assignments." He sat forward, and his wrinkles tightened. "Midterms are coming up, and I'm not sure how we're going to manage the exam schedule if kids refuse to turn up for reasons of personal . . . vanity."

A bell sounded outside the office. Vorst looked at his watch and reached for his shoes. "If that's all, Miss Sharma, I've —"

"Actually, Mr. Vorst, this is just the beginning." She held up her checklist. "I've got a long list of questions for every student, every teacher, every employee at this school."

"But —"

"In outbreaks like this, especially when emotions are running high, I find it best to invite everyone concerned to a fact-sharing session."

"You mean —"

"Our team would like you to gather all your students, parents, and employees in one place."

"I can't think when we could do that. It would have to be at a convenient time and not interfere with the upcoming midterms."

She glanced at her watch. It was too late to get the parties assembled today. "We need to do this as soon as possible. No later than tomorrow. And as early in the day as possible."

"Tomorrow? Imposs —"

"Dr. Szabo says we should start at ten a.m. In your auditorium." It usually helped to drop her boss's name at the right moment.

There was a knock at the door and the tearful secretary who'd greeted her earlier padded in. A sheet of paper trembled in the woman's hand. At the same time, Natasha's mobile phone chimed the arrival of a text message from Dr. Zol: Simcoe General was reporting another ECC student admitted through emergency with jaundice, dark urine, bleeding gums, and confusion. They were sending the girl to Toronto General by helicopter.

Vorst glanced at the paper. He pulled a wadded Kleenex from his pocket and wiped his forehead. "Noreen," he said. "Activate the telephone tree. Emergency meeting in the auditorium. Tomorrow morning. Nine o'clock. Sharp."

CHAPTER 8

Hamish Wakefield strode into his academic office at the rear of his lab at Caledonian Medical Centre. He locked the door behind him and dropped his briefcase onto the desk. He fumbled with the key as he struggled to unlock the tall, custom-made wardrobe. He got the door open and lifted out the ironing board. He extended its legs, then removed the iron and filled it with distilled water. He set the iron on the board and plugged it in, then slipped off his lab coat and wiped his sweaty hands with a towel. As the iron heated up, his anxiety began to subside.

He opened his briefcase and removed the folded shirt he'd placed there this morning before breakfast. As usual, this was an exact match to the shirt he'd been wearing all day. He always bought dress shirts in pairs. One for the mornings, its identical twin for the afternoons. He washed and ironed on Sundays, preparing for the week ahead. He loved the feeling of a clean, freshly pressed shirt. The only way to sustain that crispness, especially in a line of work that confronted him with a steady stream of germs, was to change his shirt twice a day. But a folded shirt lost its freshness when tucked into a briefcase. Creases slashed its front and wrinkled its sleeves. He fixed that with the hot iron. Today, his morning clinic had run late and delayed his ritual, had made him feel edgy. No one at the medical centre knew about his two-shirt habit, or the ironing apparatus locked in the wardrobe. People wouldn't understand. They would think he was overly fastidious. Or plain weird. And he had no interest in defending himself over something as calming as a warm, perfectly pressed shirt.

Al knew. And understood. Over the past six and a half months, he and Hamish had grown closer. Not in spite of each other's quirks, but because of a mutual delight in them. They'd first met during karaoke night at the Reluctant Lion pub. Hamish, a choir boy until his voice cracked at age fourteen, had hidden behind the beer glasses piling up on the table. But Al Mesic, a *Hamilton Spectator* reporter with a toned body and a Frank Sinatra voice, raised the audience to its feet with his first three bars of "The Music of the Night." Since then, they'd been making music together. And not just in the living room with Al's karaoke machine.

Love of singing was not their only bond. Hamish reckoned they were both refugees. Hamish from the unrelenting attacks of the schoolyard bullies who never let him forget he was a . . . yes, a fairy. Al from the snipers, mortars, and hunger of the siege of Sarajevo in the nineties. They were both in the process of coming to terms with their pasts.

Hamish's pulse quickened as he buttoned the warm shirt. Al seemed keen that they move in together in the house Hamish's aunt had left him in her will. The old place had become vacant two months ago, after the tenant broke her hip and moved into a nursing home. It was a detached, two-storey fixer-upper in the wilds of North Hamilton, two blocks from Lake Ontario. Not an area he would have thought he'd ever live in. He and Al had toured the empty house together, then traded ideas with an architect who'd promised to deliver a set of preliminary sketches this week. With Al in his life, perhaps anything was possible. A renovated house, a renovated life, a part of town showing signs of rebirth?

He locked the wardrobe and opened the office door, then he sat at his desk and gave himself a few minutes to answer urgent emails waiting in his inbox.

Half an hour later, he was racking his brain again, thinking of those young people with galloping liver failure. Yesterday there'd been five of them. Today it was six. Until Friday, fifteen cases of strange-looking lip and fingers blisters had been an interesting medical puzzle. Now, with two teens lying in the Simcoe morgue with their livers kaput and those same undiagnosed sores on their mouths, the pressure to find the cause was excruciating. Natasha was convinced that the liver-failure cases, all students at Erie Christian Collegiate, had nothing in common with the lip and finger outbreak. She said that while the liver disease was highly focussed, involving a single school, the blister cases came from all over the region. But two puzzling outbreaks presenting simultaneously in the same part of Ontario? They had to be linked. There was no way around it.

He ran through the list of viruses he'd looked for in the skin samples of the fifteen blister patients he'd seen in the past six weeks. No sign of herpes simplex, the cold sore virus; no varicella zoster, the chicken-pox and shingles virus; no adenovirus, the ear-nose-and-throat virus; no Coxsackie, the hand-foot-and-mouth virus; no Echovirus, the causes-almost-anything virus; and no human papilloma virus, the culprit in warts and cancers of the mouth, throat, and genitals. He'd even checked for orf, a blistering disease goat farmers sometimes contracted from their livestock. It wasn't even syphilis, known through the ages as The Great Mimicker.

He'd asked for every test but electron microscopy. The local EM machine used for clinical samples was under repair, awaiting a part being manufactured to order. If he wanted EM results this side of Christmas, he'd have to send his samples to the federal microbiology laboratory in Winnipeg, half a continent away. Even then, the results would take ages. The kids at that school needed answers today.

A short bear lumbering along the corridor outside his doorway caught his eye. Striped suspenders held up the blue jeans hugging his ample hips. Despite his rounded, bent-over back, curly chest hair escaping through the collar of his red lumberjack shirt, and his booming baritone laugh, Wilf Dickinson was no grouchy grizzly. Not even a miniature one. He was more like a playful cub. Wilf had earned his Ph.D. in cell biology. As an undergrad he'd studied the oboe, which he continued to play in the university's orchestra. Hamish had no idea how Wilf got his stumpy mitts around the slender woodwind without choking it.

Wilf had an electron microscope, funded purely as a research tool for his studies of Alzheimer's disease. Could he be persuaded to run a few clinical samples that had nothing to do with brain disease? Probably not. Basic-science researchers never took kindly to invitations to go zebra-hunting, no matter how exotic and fascinating a diagnostic conundrum Hamish wanted to present them with. Non-clinical types weren't used to getting their emotions entangled with direct patient care. They'd chosen the purity, the detachment, the safety of the ivory tower and they weren't prepared to leave it. And, as Wilf often said, he wasn't licensed to handle clinical specimens and could not possibly comment on anything his investigative tools might turn up.

Hamish pulled his specimens from the freezer and set them on a tray. It had to be worth a try, and from the way Wilf was whistling, he might be in an accommodating mood.

"Come on, Hamish," Wilf told him a few minutes later, "you don't actually expect me to see anything but junk in those specimens?"

"I froze them immediately. In sterile containers."

"And what preservative did you use?

Hamish felt his cheeks flushing. The technical aspects of electron microscopy were alien territory. "Well . . . none."

"I rest my case."

Hamish lifted the small plastic jars containing the crusted blisters of two of his patients with lip and finger eruption. "See? The lesions are still intact."

"Look like decapitated zits to me. What do you expect me to find?"

"A virus, maybe. Or a fungus? Remnants of atypical mycobacteria, perhaps?"

"Don't tell me you're hunting for leprosy."

"I have an open mind."

Wilf gestured to the clutter that filled his laboratory: books, academic journals, glassware, pipetting tools, coffee mugs, centrifuges, water baths, bottles of every shape and size and colour. Despite the mess, he was known for his enviable publishing record. "And my mind is not?"

Hamish pointed to his tray of specimens. "Not if you're sure, without even looking, that every one of these is worthless."

Wilf stroked his chin with two stocky digits. "Where are they from, again?"

"A group of kids dying from liver failure." He was stretching the truth. As far has he knew, only two of the liver failure cases had exhibited the skin lesions. But that was enough. The two jaundiced kids brought to Simcoe Emerg this morning could easily have the lesions. He hadn't examined them yet.

"Drug addicts?" Wilf said.

"High school students. At a Christian collegiate. Norfolk County."

"Not that place on Highway 3, a few klicks shy of Simcoe?"

"You know it?"

Wilf's face darkened. "That's where they found Tammy's body. In that vicinity, anyway."

The air between them hung like an out-of-tune tuba. Dr. Tammy Holt, a research scientist working in the lab next to Wilf's, had been young, single, and vivacious. Always ready with a humorous anecdote and a kind word, Tammy was an expert baker who took cake decoration to a high art. She combined taste and whimsy to spectacular effect. Without fail, she brought in elaborate, personalized cakes for the laboratory staff on their birthdays. For Hamish — the *bug* doctor — she'd brought in his favourite carrot cake festooned with grasshoppers and dragonflies. For Mr. Singh, the Punjabi janitor, she replicated the Golden Temple in Amritsar in lemon pound cake. A bit over the top, but that was Tammy. A plant expert with a doctorate in genetics, she always seemed to have plenty of grant money for her projects. While most researchers at Caledonian were fairly forthcoming about the basic nature of their work, Tammy was tight-lipped to the extreme. She would talk about anything except her work. "Plants and genetics" was all she would say. And though her results never got published in academic journals, they led to numerous patents probably worth a tidy sum. No one was certain which plant species she worked with. And no one spoke of the irony that her life had met its end in a field full of plants. Tobacco plants.

On a Monday morning in August last year, Tammy didn't show up for work. The days went by. People thought she must have gone to a conference and had forgotten to tell anyone. When her family reported her missing, everyone started to worry. A few days later, a farmer in Norfolk County found her body dumped near Highway 3, about half an hour's drive from Tammy's home on Grand Basin Reserve. After the Ontario Provincial Police forensics team finished its cursory examination of her laboratory, a guy in a suit showed up with a couple of heavy lifters and two security guards. They stripped the workbenches clean and carted out everything but the curtains and floor tiles. And refused to talk to anyone.

The police wouldn't release many details of Tammy's death, but did admit she'd been sexually assaulted and suffered one or more gunshot wounds. There were rumours that it was an execution-style killing, and people speculated about Mohawk gangs and the Korean mafia operating on her reserve. In the research corridors at Caledonian University, the unresolved murder of a simpatico and accomplished colleague was still extremely painful. Staff birthdays felt awkward and tinged with sadness whenever a store-bought cake showed up instead of one of Tammy's creations. The subtext that no one dared mention played again in Hamish's mind: Tammy's murder was yet another setback in the long struggle of First Nations people to achieve full status as valued professionals.

Wilf blew his nose with a striped handkerchief then eyed

Hamish's containers. "They're skin lesions in there? Fingers and what else?"

"Lips."

"Hmm."

"Yeah." Hamish forced a smile.

"And you got nothing on culture or DNA testing?"

Hamish shook his head.

"What about blood tests?"

"Nothing."

"Have the pathologists had a look?"

"Didn't see anything diagnostic. Even with special stains."

Wilf's gaze swept his laboratory. Though it was cluttered, it was quiet. Perhaps Hamish had come at a good time. Wilf pulled back his sleeve and checked his watch. He seemed satisfied with what he saw. "That mean we're chasing another of your zebras?"

Hamish pushed the tray of specimens toward the smiling bear cub and allowed himself a restrained grin in return. "I knew you'd come through."

"Don't get excited. I'm not going to see diddly. But I guess I can't refuse that choir-boy face."

During the three years since Hamish had arrived at Caledonian, he and Wilf had traded stories of their days as boy sopranos. Unlike Hamish, Wilf had enjoyed his church choir experience. Probably because he was a natural-born musician and too burly to elicit sexual advances from his choir master. Or maybe he'd just been lucky. "How many samples you got there?"

"Twelve. I had three others but —"

"A dozen? That's an entire Serengeti full of zebras. Geez, Hamish, you can't be serious."

Hamish pulled his business card from his wallet. "Get me on my cell. Any time, day or night, soon as you're done. This evening, maybe?"

"Don't push it, Choir Boy. I've got orchestra practice at six-thirty."

CHAPTER 9

It was the end of a long day at the office. They'd given him more space here in Simcoe, but the view through Zol's window was an abomination. It confronted him with a string of obscenities scrawled onto a concrete wall behind a line of garbage bins. The town fathers and mothers had sandwiched their health unit between a muffler shop and a pizza joint at the back side of a strip mall. They'd awarded the prime riverside location downtown to the LCBO, the government-run liquor store. At least he knew the local priorities without having to ask.

All he needed to do now was gather the files he planned to review at home this evening with his single malt. Tonight, it would be a Balvenie, the Doublewood. In an hour, he'd be home with Max, who was usually at his best at the dinner table and a lively tonic against the workday's curveballs and nasties. An enthusiastic talker and eater, Max knew more about the herbs and spices of international cuisine than was probably seemly for a ten-year-old. They shopped together at Four Corners Fine Foods, across Concession Street from his old office. The lady at the confections counter handed Max a different assortment of European chocolates at every visit. The boy was now an authority on the differences between Swiss, Dutch, Belgian, and German chocolate.

Max was certain to be attentive at supper, thanks to Zol's no-electronics rule. As soon as the food hit the table, no cellphone, no computer tablet, no video games were allowed. Not for either of them. Nothing was permitted to inhibit the fine art of conversation. For tonight's supper, Zol had asked Ermalinda to prepare spaghettini with clam sauce. She was a fantastic nanny and housekeeper, but not much of a cook. She did do a nice enough job with tinned clams, and Zol had taught her how to cook pasta al dente. All he'd have to do was pull salad greens from the fridge, add toasted almonds and dried cranberries, and zap the clam casserole in the microwave.

The desk phone started ringing beside him. Who the hell was calling at five-fifteen? Probably someone with a complaint best left to the answering machine. He waited six more rings, but couldn't stand the noise any longer.

"Answering for Dr. Szabo," he said. Anyone who didn't yet know his voice would think they were dealing with an underling and might be persuaded to have their concerns addressed by the big cheese first thing tomorrow.

"Zol?"

That voice, even with some sort of commotion in the background at her end, was unmistakable. It had seared itself forever into his brain.

Shit. What did she want? Francine never called to chat. She'd never spoken to Max since she'd deserted the two of them nine years ago — with five minutes' warning. Zol had been a surgical trainee at the time, standing gowned and gloved in the operating room. Francine paged him to say she was on her way out the door and leaving for good, and by the way, Max was asleep in his crib and would soon be wanting lunch. Zol raced home, and while Max flung canned spaghetti at the walls, Zol called his program director. They arranged his immediate transfer to a public-health traineeship, where the working hours might be more predictable. That wasn't exactly the case, but he'd never looked back.

The last time she'd called was over a year ago, from an ashram in India, with a crazy plan to travel halfway across the planet to take Max away for a weekend. Of course she didn't show up. Sometimes she wanted money via Western Union. Never very much. It was faster to send a couple of hundred bucks than to argue.

He cleared his throat. "Where are you?"

"Cambodia."

Thank God. Half the world away. But what was she doing in a Buddhist country? Wasn't she hooked on Hindu mysticism? Well, she didn't stick at anything for long.

"Zol?"

"I'm still here."

"I'm flying into Toronto. For a conference and retreat."

Who was she trying to kid? Francine wasn't the conference type, and any retreat she might attend would be stoked with so much weed she'd never remember what happened.

"I have my ticket. October twenty-sixth. It's a Wednesday."

He rolled his eyes. Just in time for Halloween. How appropriate. Was she coming in on a broom?

"And I'd like to see Max."

His heart rate doubled. "Remember what the judge said."

Any visit had to be supervised. "I understand, Zol. I'll do whatever you say."

He'd never heard her so compliant. In the two years they'd been married she'd never agreed with him. Not even once. What was she on?

"They have ashrams in Cambodia?"

"Monasteries. I'm a Buddhist nun and have learned a lot about myself and my place in this life and the next. And I'm ready to see Max. All of him. And hug him. And hold his . . . you know."

Francine had freaked at the distortion of Max's left arm caused by the stroke at the time of his birth. The doctors blamed her cocaine addiction for Max's isolated brain injury. She'd never properly cuddled him, rarely changed his diapers, and flatly refused to touch his spastic left hand.

"Have you thought about where you're going to stay?" It didn't matter. Her plans were always half-baked.

"I'm not sure yet. Probably with Allie."

She'd said that last time and nothing happened. "Tell Allie to call me."

"You'll let me see Max?"

He couldn't stop her. But he wouldn't tell Max about the visit until he was certain it was going to happen.

They ended the call, and he pulled two loonies from his blazer. He flipped the coins and took deliberate, even breaths until his heart rate began to slow. It was amazing how quickly that woman got under his skin.

He was still flipping the loonies when the phone rang again. The call display showed a Toronto area code. His gut tightened when he recognized the number: the Ministry of Health head office.

"Szabo," said Dr. Elliott York. "I got a call from Jed Conroy. Reeve of Norfolk County. Holds Simcoe Health Unit's purse strings. That means, after me, he's your boss."

Zol squirmed on his chair. A complaint already? But what was the reeve of Norfolk County doing talking to Zol's boss in Toronto?

"Jed's in my brother-in-law's poker group," Elliott York continued. "Apparently six or seven kids in his county have come down with liver failure. A couple of deaths. All at —"

"Yes, it's six cases, all at one high school. Erie Christian Collegiate. Natasha Sharma, our best field epidemiologist, made a site visit there first thing this morning. We've got a big meeting planned with everyone concerned tomorrow, bright and early."

"Jed wanted me to pass along a little friendly advice." If Elliott York was impressed at Zol's command of the details, his voice wasn't showing it. "He says that school is in tiger territory."

"I don't think I understand, sir?"

"For heaven's sake, man. Do I have to spell it out?"

"Dr. York?"

"Lots of Native kids there. From Grand Basin Reserve. With parents who know their rights. And know how to work the system."

"And that makes a difference to our work?"

"I'm just saying . . . Be careful."

"I think I always work carefully."

"For God's sake, Szabo. I'm not talking science." York was now whispering into the phone. "You find anything implicating the shenanigans we all know go on at Grand Basin, you'd be wise to tread carefully. Very carefully." Zol pictured Elliott York dwarfed by the enormous rosewood desk he somehow kept free of clutter. The desk was legendary, as was his thing for blown-glass kitsch, which he displayed in his office on every other possible surface. "Sometimes it's better to turn a blind eye than to get the other one poked out."

The chief MOH for the province of Ontario was telling him to turn a blind eye to what had killed two teenagers and might kill who knows how many more? "I'm not sure I understand, sir."

"Jed doesn't want another standoff with the Indians. And neither do I. Not another bust-up like that business at Dover Creek Estates. Or another Ipperwash. One more unarmed Indian killed by a cop and the current government won't get re-elected for a generation."

Zol was too stunned to answer. How could the man talk like that? It was one thing to be realistic about the troubles facing Native communities across the country, but quite another to hold such blatant hatred and express it to a subordinate.

Elliott York had no trouble filling the silence. "Between you and me, I think Jed's twitchy after that explosion at the ROM. Those were Mohawk artifacts that got stolen. Jed Conroy seems to think they were repatriated to Grand Basin, a sign the Indians are restless. Not a good time for you to be doing a high-handed epidemiological investigation."

Zol felt his whole body flush with anger. His throat tightened.

He planted his feet on the carpet and felt the resolute firmness of the floor beneath him. "We'll be certain to be respectful, sir." He paused and swallowed hard. "But we'll be thorough. And don't expect me to be timid."

"As I say, you could be looking at a powder keg. Consider yourself warned. Officially."

Elliott York hung up, and two seconds later Zol's cellphone buzzed against his belt.

Now what?

"Hamish? What's up?"

"Let me put it this way. I'm hopeful."

Hamish was rarely hopeful about anything. "Seriously?"

"Went zebra-hunting this afternoon. We may have bagged a zinger."

"Bagged it with what?"

"EM."

"Plain English?"

"An electron microscope."

"And?"

"Let me set the stage." Hamish was the master of the grand entrance, even over the phone. Zol pictured his friend in his spotless white lab coat, his pompous finger raised to its professorial position.

Hamish recapped the scenario. Fifteen people, half of them teenagers, presenting with large blistering lesions on their lips and fingertips unresponsive to treatment. No fever, fatigue, malaise, or organ malfunction except for two Erie Christian Collegiate students who'd succumbed last Friday from lightning fast liver failure.

"Okay," Zol said. "I'm up to speed."

"You ready?"

"Zing me."

"Fragments of itty-bitty matchsticks. With helical elements."

"Hamish, you're toying with me."

"Not at all. Wilf Dickinson, a basic-science researcher down the hall from me, called me to his lab a few minutes ago. He spent this afternoon looking at the blisters from eight of my patients under his electron microscope. He was sure he'd find only junk, but there they were, clear as day. In all eight patients. Thousands of tiny broken matchsticks, each with a central spiral core."

"Does he know what they are?"

"He won't say. His expertise is Alzheimer's, not microbiology."

"Did he hazard a guess?"

"He won't go out on a limb at this stage. Says he wants to try a variety of tissue staining techniques and run the specimens again tomorrow. But . . ."

There was a lot of Oscar Wilde in Hamish's voice. He was bursting with something he could barely contain. "Hamish, I know you too well. You and your colleague have got a pretty good hunch. No point in denying it."

"We . . . we think they may be infectious particles."

"Bacteria?"

"Way too small for that."

"So you've seen them too?"

"Yes."

"So what do you think they are?"

"Nothing I've ever seen before. Not in a patient, not in a textbook. Something strange, but hopefully not contagious enough to become a plague."

A plague? Zol's heart catapulted into his throat. Was Hamish serious or grandstanding? Everyone was getting under his skin today. He warned himself to keep his tone measured. With the first hint of derision, Hamish would hang up and pout for a week. "For heaven's sake, man. Give it to me straight. I promise not to shoot the messenger."

"Microbiology class. U of T. Our second year. A Friday. You were snoring behind me. The prof was speculating about plagues and mutant organisms of the future."

Thursday nights at medical school had been pub nights, Friday mornings a write-off. But how could he have slept through a lecture on plagues? "We're dealing with a — a plague? Ebola? The Black Death? Germ warfare?"

"No, no. Put your loonies back in your pocket. At least until we've got more information. Sorry. I spoke too soon. But I didn't want to keep anything from you."

"These matchstick things, are they responsible for the liver failure?"

"Too soon to say. But probably not. Only one of the eight cases Wilf examined under his machine is a liver failure patient. That means almost ninety percent of people with those blisters have not come down with liver disease."

"I was hoping for a breakthrough on the liver thing."

"Stay tuned. We'll talk tomorrow."

They hung up. He grabbed his paperwork and car keys. Forget the spaghettini with clams, he'd be heading straight for the Balvenie. Well, after he'd made his daily check-in call to Mum. She'd seemed a lot stronger when they'd spoken yesterday. Had even made it to church for the first time in weeks. It was as if getting the black-eyed loon pipe out of the house had taken a huge weight off her psyche.

He paused as he reached for his coat. Was it a relief that ninety percent of Hamish's blister cases were showing no signs of liver disease? More to the point, was the electron microscopy report a critical clue demanding a thorough understanding, or a confusing confounder irrelevant to the primary investigation? He had no idea. And despite Hamish's expertise in the realm of microbiology, he wasn't certain, either. Zol hated the anxiety that churned inside him during the early days of an outbreak. Lives were at stake, dozens of questions hung unanswered, and there was too little information of substance. God, he hoped the team would mine some answers tomorrow at that Christian school.

CHAPTER 10

A tall, gaunt man greeted Colleen at the front door of Erie Christian Collegiate the next morning. He was wearing cream chinos and a corduroy jacket in warthog brown. He was also wearing a mauve striped shirt, black dress shoes, and a bright green belt. She reckoned he was either colour blind or the art teacher. Not even a maths teacher could be that sartorially challenged. He asked for her ID and checked her name against a list attached to the clipboard he was brandishing like a shield-bearing Zulu. Natasha had warned her to have her ID ready; this morning's meeting was restricted to teaching staff, students, families, and health-unit personnel. Good idea. People clammed up in the presence of strangers, and when you were prospecting for clues, the last thing you wanted were tied tongues.

Colleen had come early and alone so she could observe the audience arriving for the nine a.m. meeting. The most productive tidbits often came before proceedings started; people said the most revealing things as they took their seats and chatted with their neighbours, thinking no one was listening.

There was nothing wrong with her hearing, but she'd inserted a hearing aid into each ear before leaving home. They were top quality instruments and practically invisible, made in Denmark. And being medical devices, they were perfectly legal to wear. The remote control she kept in her purse allowed her to crank up the volume.

When she'd started as a private eye seven years ago, an old hand had suggested she learn to lip read. She took courses at the Hearing Society and didn't disabuse them of their assumption she was going deaf. Though she mastered the technique, she came to realize that even the best lip readers mistake half the words in a sentence because so many words look identical but sound different. On the lips, *lock the door* looks like *take the car*. But by supplementing lip reading with the Danish hearing aids, she could get an accurate gist of most conversations from a distance of ten metres.

Being the first to arrive, she picked a seat at the end of the third-last row. From there she would be able to see most of the audience and hear the throwaway comments from the back of the room, where people with the most to hide usually sat.

She pulled a partially knitted scarf from her handbag. She'd used the same coarse olive wool for the past seven years, ripping out and starting again each time she ran out of yarn. No one paid attention to a woman with her hair wound in an old-fashioned braid, sitting quietly in a grey housedress, wearing no jewellery or makeup, knitting a scarf.

She watched a trio who looked around the nearly empty auditorium then chose seats at the far end of a row halfway down. She didn't miss a beat of her knitting and they didn't acknowledge her. None of them was happy to be here. The mother held her lips tight across her teeth, the father kept turning around and looking at his watch, and the girl sitting between them texted on her mobile with the focus of a concert pianist. The bandage on the tip of her right index finger flashed in the overhead lights, but didn't slow her down. Every half minute or so she used the phone's screen like a mirror and fussed with a zit at the corner of her mouth.

"Stop touching it, Emily," said the woman.

"But it's so gross," said the girl, peering into her mirror.

"If you leave it alone, no one will notice. Keep fussing with it and you'll rub your concealer off."

The girl glanced around to be sure no one was looking, dug a stick of something from her purse, and dabbed it on.

The woman frowned at her husband. "I know it's the cafeteria," she said. "That new company they hired. They don't care about nutrition."

The father shrugged. "So? Neither do the kids."

"I'm serious, Bob. I heard they're using cheap ingredients imported from China. Doing the fries in some kind of tropical nut oil."

"Let's wait and see what the doctors have to say."

As the auditorium filled, the noise level increased and, between Colleen's hearing aids and her lip reading, she caught concerns about the safety of the science lab, complaints about a gym teacher, and more worries about the cafeteria. Anger and anxiety oozed from the parents. The students projected sullen hostility, as if mortified to be seen in public with the dorky adults beside them. Of course, with six of their classmates sick or already dead, the teens were bound to be frightened. But it seemed they weren't about to share their true feelings with anyone but their peers, and only via text messages.

As she observed the petty disharmonies playing out in the families around her, her mind wandered and she wondered how she would have coped with motherhood. She and Liam had three false starts — three miscarriages in as many years. If the babies had lived, by now she'd be a single parent to three kids under ten, with no living grandparents, aunts, or uncles to offer moral support or lend a hand. And she wouldn't be earning her living as a private investigator. Single mothers didn't do all-night stakeouts. Would she have been a patient mum, or would her overly practical nature have turned her into a nag, crabby and exhausted from obsessing over every little problem?

It was easy with Max. She wasn't his mother. Like a favourite aunt, her role was to be upbeat and understanding. When things got fractious, she could withdraw to her own space. Not that she felt the need very often, but it was wonderfully reassuring to know that her condo — her private retreat and emotional safety valve — was always waiting for her. She'd lose that flexibility if she gave up her place and moved in with Zol and Max, especially if Zol went so far as to ask her to marry him. What would be her answer? That depended on how she coped with the question that plagued her every day: why had everyone she'd ever loved — even those little lost babies whose hearts had barely begun to beat — been taken away from her?

As the minutes ticked toward nine o'clock, she realized she was witnessing a phenomenon that in South Africa had seemed so natural as to go unnoticed. The audience was segregating itself into a Canadian-style apartheid. White divided from Native. The Native families occupied the back left corner. There were fewer men than women among them, and they were quieter that the Whites, but she suspected they were no less anxious. The Native kids were texting with the same fervour as their White peers.

Shorty before nine, a florid-faced man in a baggy suit led Zol and Natasha to the front row. From Natasha's description, Colleen knew he must be Walter Vorst, the gum-chewing principal with the oversized painful feet. Zol turned and caught Colleen's eye as he took his seat, careful not to give her away.

At five past nine, Vorst stood up. He faced the back of the auditorium and studied the stragglers searching for seats, then pointed at several available places and invited them to sit down. His tone was halfway between friendly and authoritative. A moment later, he leaned toward Zol and told him they may as well get started. He spit his gum into a tissue and climbed to the stage. He grabbed the lectern with both hands and looked out over the audience, his expression grave, his forehead glistening with sweat. You could have heard a meerkat fart. She turned down the volume on her hearing aids with the remote hidden under her knitting.

Vorst introduced Zol and Natasha and motioned for them to stand. Zol looked particularly handsome in his black blazer, his hair fixed in that semi-dishevelled look she knew took longer to achieve that one might think. Natasha looked adorable in her pixie cut, black and white shift, and skin the colour of Darjeeling tea with a jot of Jersey cream. Natasha never wore pants. Always a dress or a skirt with darling shoes. A cute package that kept her intelligence non-intimidating and her government-initiated investigations non-threatening. If the girl didn't have such obvious chemistry with her surgical resident beau, Colleen might have worried she had designs on her beloved Dr. Zol.

Zol took the stage, cleared his throat, and reviewed the situation for the audience. He was suitably serious but not dour, clear without being condescending, and brief. Unlike Vorst, whose sincerity seemed manufactured, Zol's came across as one hundred percent genuine. He explained the importance of finding the hidden factors linking the students with liver disease in order that the cluster — he always avoided the e-word, epidemic — could be stopped and no one else would fall ill. Promising to provide plenty of time for questions in a few minutes, he passed the microphone to Natasha, who started with a warm greeting and explained the detailed questionnaire she needed everyone to complete at home tonight and return to the front office at nine tomorrow morning. She apologized for the short deadline, but said she knew that everyone wanted to get the liver issue solved as soon as possible. Like Zol, she never let the word epidemic cross her lips.

When the question period began, the tension in the room trebled. Colleen stowed her knitting and slipped through a side exit.

She'd heard enough from the audience — Zol and Natasha were hearing a good deal more — and it was time to have a look round for physical evidence.

It was clear that this school had little in the way of an outdoor sports program. The schoolyard was too small for rugby, soccer, or gridiron football. It was large enough for volleyball, but there was no sign of a net. The spotty field was mostly gravel with patches of withering grass and dandelions past their prime. Dozens of gum wrappers, a few pop cans, and the occasional sheet of discarded homework lay where they'd blown against the perimeter chain-link fence. She followed the fence to the northeast corner of the schoolyard, where she found a large gap through which a well-worn path led into an abandoned property. She followed the path as it wound to the far side of a stand of spruce. Beyond the trees, the trail led her to an empty clearing littered with broken beer bottles. This teen hangout wasn't visible from any of the school windows, but its existence would be obvious to anyone with more than a passing interest in the comings and goings of the student body. The ground was covered in cigarette butts and gum wrappers, the air heavy with the stench of tobacco and stale beer. She picked up a battered plastic box about the size of a deck of cards. The teens wouldn't be playing bridge here. Blackjack, perhaps? Dozens of empty cigarette packages, faded and muddied, lay trampled into the dirt. She picked up two and examined them. She'd never heard of the brand: Hat-Trick. She put the plastic boxes, the cigarette packs, and a handful of butts into the large resealable plastic bag she always had handy in her purse. She didn't bother with the beer bottles.

So much for the fundamentalist dogma expounded by this Christian school, which the principal had promised Natasha was free of drugs, tobacco, and alcohol. It seemed he was prepared to overlook Moses' commandment about bearing false witness. The ninth, was it? And his students were clearly disregarding the fifth, the one about honouring their fathers and mothers with respectable behaviour. What other lies were Vorst, his staff, and his students hiding here?

CHAPTER 11

Zol shut the dishwasher and turned it on. Bacon and eggs made for quick cleanup after a long day of collective nail biting at the Simcoe Health Unit. He'd spoken to Hamish, but Wilf Dickinson was still fiddling with the blister specimens and couldn't say if or when he'd have more definitive results from his electron microscope. The guy sounded like a perfectionist. Every time a phone rang at the health unit, the staff froze, fearing the call was from an Emerg doc reporting more teens with liver failure. So far, so good, but waiting until Natasha finished her analysis of this morning's questionnaires from Erie Christian Collegiate was killing him. She promised she'd have something to tell him by tomorrow. He didn't know what he would do if there was no beef in her results.

He was about to ask Colleen whether she wanted to finish off with a peppermint tea or a shot of Amarula when he heard the rumble of ten-year-old feet entering the kitchen behind him.

"Hey," he said. "You're supposed to be in bed."

Max made a face. "I can't sleep."

"Have you tried?"

Max cocked his head and pouted. "Why can't Colleen read me a story?"

"Because it's past your bedtime. What will Mrs. Rivers say when you start snoring in class?"

"Da-ad."

"You need your full ten hours."

"Awhhh, just a quick one?"

Zol checked his watch and threw Max a wink. "Tell her I said no longer than nine and a half minutes."

Max beamed and threw his arms around Zol's chest, the soft, pyjama-clad torso pressing into him with firm, exuberant warmth. In came waves of the same soothing energy, the same indelible connection, that had overtaken him, filled him with love, when he'd held Max for the first time at a minute of age. How long would it be before Max stopped wearing pyjamas, and teenage angst tore the two of them apart? This morning, Erie Christian Collegiate's auditorium had been raw with contempt and hostility. Was a cold war between parents and their teens an unavoidable by-product of impatience on one side and the craving for emancipation on the other? If he worked on being more flexible and less cranky than his own dad had been, would he and Max stay close, no matter what?

Max let go and swept the room with a tentative gaze. "And . . . and Daddy?"

"Careful, bozo. Don't push it."

Max's face clouded with sudden disappointment. He shrugged and the smile left his eyes. "Never mind."

This late in the day, flexibility didn't come easily. "Sorry, son. What is it?"

Max hung his head.

"Come on, you can tell me."

Max turned and stamped toward the sunroom. "I said, never mind."

Zol's stomach tightened. Something was on Max's mind and he'd blown it. Like his dad used to do. Would Max bring it up tomorrow, or had the moment been lost forever?

Fifteen minutes later, Max was hugged and kissed and settled.

He seemed happy enough despite whatever had been on his mind. He'd really taken to Colleen, no question about it.

Zol handed her a glass of Amarula and watched the light dance in rainbows through the crystal's pattern and onto her cheeks. From the other tumbler, a perfect match to hers, he warmed his throat with a generous swallow of Glenfarclas. He'd found the second Waterford glass on eBay to partner with the one left intact after Francine had smashed the others in a fit of pique. He'd hated the symbolism of the solitary crystal piece. Luxury and elegance were pointless unless they were shared.

"Is he okay?" Zol asked her.

"He's fine."

"There's something on his mind."

"He is a thinker, Zol."

"It's just that . . . well, he's been a bit moody lately. Almost secretive." And now spending time in his room with the door closed. He never used to do that.

"He needs his space. They all do."

"I'm scared of the teen years. You know, after the undeclared war we witnessed this morning."

"Which, by the way, is worse than you think."

Shit. Was that possible? "What do you mean?"

Colleen dug into her handbag and pulled out a plastic shopping bag. "Get me a newspaper, will you? Got something to show you. And it's going to be messy."

Zol retrieved today's *Hamilton Spectator* from the recycling box and spread it on the coffee table.

"Perfect," Colleen said. "I've been desperate to show you this all afternoon."

She dumped the contents of her shopping bag onto the newspaper, covering the table with squashed cigarette packs, fag ends, beer caps, and gum wrappers. The sunroom filled with the harsh smell of Native tobacco. Ringo Starr filled his head with an annoying chorus of "Yellow Submarine." He'd never liked that track.

When Ringo had finished, he asked her, "Where'd you get that stuff?"

"The smoking den at the rear of the school."

"Erie Collegiate provides a smoking den? But Vorst told Natasha —"

"It's unofficial. And not on school property." She described her discovery of the hangout behind the school, screened from view by a thicket of evergreens.

She put down her drink and held up a small plastic box. Her eyes twinkled below her puzzled frown. Colleen was at her most radiant — well, almost — when facing a mystery. "Do you know what this is? I thought maybe it was for holding a deck of playing cards."

Zol took it, looked at it quickly, then laughed. "It's for Rollies."

Her silvery earrings twisted and sparkled as she cocked her head. "And they would be . . . ?"

"Cigarettes manufactured on the rez and sold in bulk. In Ziploc bags, two hundred at a time. People who smoke Rollies don't go in for silver cigarette cases, so they carry a day's worth of fags in a plastic box the size of a cigarette pack." He took the box and slipped it into his shirt pocket. "Like this. See?" The weight of the plastic against his chest felt like a violation. He yanked the disgusting thing out and tossed it on the table. He wiped his hands on his jeans. "Smokers buy a dozen or so bags of Rollies at a time, store them in the fridge, and take them out as they need them."

"The refrigerator?"

"So they don't go stale." As if anyone could tell the difference between a fresh Rollie and a stale one.

"Is it legal?"

"To sell Rollies? Not the way the Natives do it. For starters, the Ziploc packaging breaks all the rules. And only fellow Natives are supposed to get them tax free. Status Indians are not required to pay taxes on tobacco, except for a token excise tax. Don't forget, they invented the stuff."

"But most of the kids at Erie Collegiate are not Native."

"Of course not. It's the biggest contraband game in the country. Billions-worth every year."

Colleen's pupils widened. "Anyone can purchase Native smokes tax free?"

"The government estimates that forty percent of the cigarettes smoked in Ontario come from Native reserves. Unburdened by government regulations, inspection, or taxes." A memo to the health units from the Ministry had reported a rate even higher among teen smokers.

"How much do they cost?"

"Rollies? Bought on the reserve? Ten dollars for two hundred cigarettes. Some shops throw in an additional twenty per bag."

He watched her doing the math in her head. Her amazement was obvious. "That's about a dollar for twenty-five cigarettes."

"Less than a cup of coffee, and ten times cheaper than premium, name brand smokes in an off-reserve store. They're made in clandestine factories that make no pretence of legitimacy."

"Extraordinary. How do you know all this?"

"Dad harps about it all the time. He may have given up tobacco farming, but he's still plenty pissed that the industry is forced to struggle on an uneven playing field where only the brand-name companies have to follow the rules. As Dad says, the tobacco pirates do whatever they like."

"Where do these pirates have their factories? In China, like practically everything else?"

"No, no. Right here. Grand Basin Reserve. The tobacco is locally grown and purchased under the table from willing farmers glad to have a ready market." He put his finger beside his nose. "Cash only. Undeclared farm income. No worries about income taxes, quotas, or a tobacco-grower's licence."

He pointed to the two empty Hat-Trick packs she'd dumped from the bag. "D'you know what a hat-trick is?"

"For goodness sake, Zol. I know my hockey terms. I earned my Canadian citizenship, remember?"

"Sorry," he said, his face reddening. "The Hat-Tricks are made on the reserve too. Supposedly higher quality than Rollies. Still local tobacco, but maybe better leaves and fewer floor sweepings. Not quite as harsh on the throat, but little government inspection or quality control of the factories that produce them."

"The packaging makes them look like normal cigarettes. Are they more expensive?"

"Hat-Tricks are two or three times the price of Rollies, but a terrific bargain all the same."

"And tax free?"

"Almost, but not quite. The Native producers of the nicely packaged cigarettes have an arrangement with the federal government. They collect the small excise tax the law says everyone, Native and non-Native, has to pay." He picked up a Hat-Trick pack and showed it to her. "See, that's the excise stamp they put on every pack. It keeps the feds happy and lets everyone delude themselves into thinking they've bought fully taxed cigarettes at a bargain-basement price."

"Only they haven't?"

"Not even close. Anyone without a Certificate of Indian Status has to pay all the other federal and provincial taxes — amounting to about fifty dollars a carton — whether they purchase cigarettes on or off a reserve."

Zol sipped his Glenfarclas. It slipped down his throat like warm honey. "Native smoke-shop operators figure they're doing business on sovereign territory, where they refuse to collect taxes on behalf of a foreign government. They leave it up to the non-Native buyers to own up and pay the various taxes owing when they leave the rez."

"Could honest smokers do that, pay the taxes due, if they wanted to?"

"That's the rub. The taxes are complicated and multi-layered. And different in every province. There are federal excise duties, federal tobacco taxes, provincial tobacco taxes, federal goods and services taxes, provincial sales taxes. Even if you wanted to be a model citizen, where would you go to pay the taxes on that carton of smokes you purchased on the rez?"

He pictured a guy with five bags of Rollies in one hand and a wad of ten-dollar bills in the other, standing in line with people renewing their drivers' licences.

"And of course," he continued, "the police don't set up check-points at the exits to the reserve and confiscate smokes from non-Natives as they drive out."

There were many reasons for such inaction on the part of the police. The Canadian Charter of Rights and Freedoms, for starters. You couldn't go searching people and their cars without a good reason. And a warrant.

"Can you imagine the hue and cry," he said, "if the police set up road blocks outside every Native reserve in the country?"

"Sorry, you've lost me. Every reserve in the country?"

"Sure, smokes get shipped by the millions from cigarette factories in large reserves like Grand Basin to tiny reserves located in every nook and cranny of the country."

"Rollies and Hat-Tricks are sold coast to coast?"

"Yep. In any of the six hundred First Nations reserves across the country. Quite the network, eh? Sort of like Walmart. Cheap Smokes R Us."

Colleen gathered her evidence and swept it back into her bag. "My God, this stuff stinks."

He dipped his nose into his glass and breathed deeply, erasing the stench of tobacco and stale mint. He closed his eyes and Joni Mitchell sang softly in his ears, "A Case of You." Sometimes, Joni was the best part of two fingers of Glenfarclas. He savoured a deep drink.

"But it gets worse," he told her. "A good portion of the tobacco trade originating from reserves isn't controlled by Natives."

"Do I want to hear this?"

"No one knows what really goes on, but my dad and the other tobacco farmers are convinced that the factories making most of the Rollies on Grand Basin are operated by Asian gangs."

Colleen swirled the ice in her Amarula and stared into the glass for a long time. Finally, she took a sip. "I suppose that makes sense.

The Asians put up the start-up money, pay the local Natives a roy-
alty, and reap most of the profits."

"Yep. Most of the local guys in the Rollies trade are factory
owners in name only. They could never finance such a large operation or have access to the expanded off-reserve market."

"Off reserve?"

"Korean and Middle Eastern convenience stores that sell rez
cigarettes under the counter. And pushers hanging around school-
yards and welfare offices. Even when middlemen take their cuts,
Native smokes are way cheaper than the brand names."

"And what about the Hat-Tricks? Controlled by Asians as well?"

Zol shook his head and told her how the best of the packaged cigarettes were made by Watershed Holdings, an outfit owned
entirely by a Native guy named Dennis Badger. "He's a smart fellow.
Well, cunning's more like it. And now insanely rich."

"You know him?"

"He was a year ahead of me in high school. That's where he
started calling himself the Badger."

"Tough guy?"

"No more than the other kids from Grand Basin who got
bussed to our school from the reserve."

"How well did they get along with the Whites?" Colleen asked.

"Hard to say. They mostly kept to themselves. But they did make
our hockey team the regional powerhouse."

"Which was good for their currency on campus?"

"Never thought about it that way at the time, but I guess you're
right."

"Was he a good student?"

"Heck, Colleen. It was a long time ago."

"Don't look at me like that. I'm just trying to put the story
together."

"You and Hamish. It's always about the story."

"Most certainly. The answer is embedded in the narrative." She
held his gaze. "Well, what sort of a student was he?"

"Can't say I noticed. But like a lot of the Native kids, he left school early. Didn't think it was worthwhile graduating. But that didn't hurt him." He shuddered at the image of Dennis Badger twenty years earlier, swanning around in a tee-shirt that showed four rifle-carrying Natives above a caption that warned, HOMELAND SECURITY: FIGHTING TERRORISM SINCE 1492. The slogan seemed clever until you realized that guys like the Badger were serious about the guns and the retribution.

"He went back to night school, then to college. Got a diploma in business. And now he owns one of the largest tobacco companies on the continent. With huge markets overseas."

"There's an international market for low-quality cigarettes?"

"Make them cheap enough, no one cares about the quality of the smoke. Still the same nicotine hit. One of Dennis Badger's biggest customers is the German Army."

"You're not serious."

"Exclusive contract. Europeans love strong tobacco. Ever smoke a Gauloises?"

She raised her eyebrows. "What would it take to shut it all down?"

"A major catastrophe that neither the police nor the politicians could ignore."

"Is that what we're facing here?" she said, gesturing to her bagful of evidence.

CHAPTER 12

Zol threw the door open to his Simcoe office the next morning and set his Starbucks mug on the desk beside the keyboard. When given a choice, he avoided the American monolith, but the mug was a Christmas present from Max, well insulated, and brimming with a competitor's Ethiopian blend. His second hit of the day. The Detour's eager barista promised he'd roasted the beans at six-thirty this morning. Where else could you get coffee brewed with beans a mere two hours out of the roaster? At least there was one upside to this Simcoe secondment.

He removed the lid from the travel mug and breathed the aroma. As soon as the java tickled his nostrils, Céline did her thing with "My Heart Will Go On." He took several swallows, savoured each one, and tried to remember the tasting notes chalked on the blackboard at the Detour Café. Hazelnut? Cherry? Dark chocolate?

His eyes caught the front page the *Simcoe Reformer*. Nancy, the keen-to-please secretary assigned to him, placed a copy of the community rag on his desk every morning as a way of introducing him to local issues. Two stories dominated today's headlines. The mystery liver illness killing students at Erie Christian Collegiate had local doctors stumped and families begging for answers.

In the second story, the national chief of the Assembly of First Nations was blaming the loss of irreplaceable Iroquois artifacts on the deplorably lax security at the Royal Ontario Museum. It wasn't just Zol's loon pipe that had been stolen. Among other artifacts missing were a pair of ball-headed, black walnut clubs, a wooden walking stick featuring an intricately carved human face, and an iron-bladed tomahawk that doubled as a pipe.

Was he doing the right thing by hiding the stolen loon's mate in Colleen's safety deposit box? She'd told him to put the bird out of his mind, but the damned thing might get more incriminating the longer he kept it to himself. Maybe there would never be a good time to present it to the authorities, and the loon would hang forever around his neck like the Ancient Mariner's albatross.

He scoured the first story for signs of dissatisfaction with the health unit's handling of the liver outbreak. So far, the honeymoon in Simcoe was holding. But he knew it wouldn't last long. Any more deaths, another couple of days with no answers, and the public would be ripping him apart. He opened the letters-to-the-editor section, usually a frank source of public opinion. Nothing about the liver outbreak, but there was one about the ROM bombing. The writer speculated that the RCMP should head straight for Grand Basin Reserve if they were serious about finding the artifacts and the murderers. Yeah, like that that was going to happen. Surprised that the *Reformer* had printed such an overtly anti-Native letter, he gulped his coffee and mentally shook his head.

The phone rang on his desk, surprising him once again with its Big Ben chime, the ringtone set up by the previous MOH. He wouldn't have chosen Big Ben, but found it wasn't as jarring as a regular ring and a nice touch for someone who hated the phone as much as he did.

"Yes, Nancy," he said.

"Sorry to disturb you, Dr. Szabo, but I think you're going to want to take this."

"Who is it?"

"Dr. Hitchin. He's calling from Emergency at Simcoe General."

"Did he say what he wanted?"

"He's very upset."

"More students from Erie Collegiate?"

"Please, will you talk to him?"

"Of course," he said, feigning confidence while his gut did a backflip. "Put him on."

"Dr. Szabo?" said a male voice, sounding somewhere between twenty and fifty. "John Hitchin here."

"I understand you've got something for me."

"It's spreading."

"Sorry?"

"That liver thing."

Here it came. "Really? How many?"

"Six new."

The honeymoon was over. He pictured yesterday's hubbub in Erie Collegiate's auditorium during the question period. With six more cases, he'd be facing it all again, only worse. Hitchin was still talking but Zol wasn't taking any of it in.

"How're the parents coping?" he asked.

"What parents?" Hitchin said.

"From Erie Collegiate."

"These aren't kids. They're first responders. Paramedics and fire-fighters. Showed up this morning. Jaundiced as hell. Doesn't look good for them."

"With the same thing as the students?"

"Dunno. We're assessing that now." Hitchin was more breathless with every sentence. He did manage to say that all six new cases, four firefighters and two paramedics, were barely coherent. The only woman among them was a paramedic and in the worst shape.

"What other details have you got for me?" Zol asked.

"It's trench warfare down here. You want details, you come see for yourself. Can you get that Wakefield guy in here? He's got a nose for this stuff."

"One more question," Zol said, remembering the bandage on

Walter Vorst's finger, and the lip lesions he'd noticed on several Erie Christian Collegiate students during yesterday's meeting.

"Gotta make it quick."

"Any scabby lesions on their lips or fingers?"

"A couple have cold sores. Doozies. Can't miss them. Haven't looked at any fingers yet."

A siren went off at Hitchin's end. "Gotta go. One of the guys is seizing again. Shit, he's coding."

Zol was left with a dead phone in his hand.

CHAPTER 13

Hamish removed the dinner plates from the kitchen table, wiped it down, and spread out the sketches. He'd heard the feces had hit the fan today in Simcoe, and he'd gone to hell and back with a family of four in Caledonian's intensive care unit. All of them — mother, father, and two pre-teen kids — were near death from the malaria they'd picked up in a school-building trip to Cameroon. A friend had told them that taking medication to prevent malaria weakened the body's immune system and played into the hands of the multinational drug companies. And now they were on life support, circling the drain with multi-organ failure. He was desperate for thirty minutes of down time before the hospital called him with an update, and before Zol arrived to brainstorm over the latest developments in the liver epidemic.

The sketches were preliminary, but impressive. The architect had transformed Aunt Gwen's dumpy cottage into a Nantucket-style captain's house. She'd left the place to him in her will, but probate had taken longer than he'd expected. Never mind, the design was perfect for the North Hamilton location near the lake, and it would be great to have a house.

"What do you think, Al? Pretty cool, eh?"

Al tossed the dish towel onto the counter and pressed his fore-arms on the table. His Bosniak eyes missed nothing and seemed capable of recording everything. He stepped back and eyed the sketches from a distance, framed the drawings with his hands as though viewing them through a camera. He dropped his hands and leaned in for a closer look, then frowned and rubbed his sideburn. "Not so sure."

"But don't you love the front veranda? The way it wraps around on two sides? Tons of space on it."

"For what? Staring at the neighbours across the street?" Al pointed to the map the draftsman had drawn of the immediate neighbourhood. "See? The veranda is looking the wrong way. It should be facing in the direction of the lake."

The house occupied a corner lot, and the front door faced Ferrie Street. Bay Street ran along the west side. "But that would mean moving the front door ninety degrees."

"As I told you before, the best thing about that house is you can tear it down and build whatever you want."

"But if the front door got moved, the address would have to be changed. To Bay Street. Is that possible?"

"Why not?" Al said.

"Sounds like a lot of hassle."

"Not when you have friends at City Hall."

"Friends? Who's got friends there?" As a staff reporter for the *Hamilton Spectator*, Al had exposed his fair share of back-room antics among city politicians. "Certainly not you."

"Hey. There are many people at the Hall who are grateful I got their stories out."

Hamish let that hang for a few seconds. "You mean? You're friends with people who can . . . you know . . . ?" He dismissed the thought with a flick of his hand. "No, I couldn't do anything illegal."

Al beamed his rakish smile. "Not illegal. Just efficient."

Hamish rotated the sketches and let himself imagine sitting on the veranda and admiring the harbour view. He pictured the morning sun sparkling over Lake Ontario, sails flapping on the bay. "The architect is going to have a fit. He seemed very proud of these sketches."

"He can swallow his pride. And hey — do we, two gay guys, really want to live in a house on Ferrie Street?"

Hamish felt his cheeks flushing. He loved the sound of that we. He'd never been we before, not even as a child. "And . . . and the contractor?" he said, suddenly almost tongue-tied.

"He won't care as long as the architect doesn't make the drawings too complicated."

"And the extra cost?"

"What does it matter? You got the house for free. With a few more renos in that block, values are going to skyrocket."

The intercom buzzed from the front lobby.

Hamish pressed the button on the speaker phone.

"Hey, Hamish." It was Zol.

Hamish looked quickly at his bare legs. Al's too. They had nothing on but tee-shirts and undies, matching Calvin Kleins. Low-rise, black bikinis. It was an intimacy Zol didn't have to know about, and wouldn't want to share anyway. Good thing the intercom didn't have video.

"Uh . . . Zol. Hi. Um . . . you're early."

"Sorry. Did I catch you at a bad time?"

"Of course not," Hamish said a bit too quickly. He and Al exchanged glances. "We're finished dinner." Al smirked and rolled his eyes. Of course, it wasn't dinner that Zol imagined he'd interrupted. Hamish returned Al's silly grin and pressed the door release. "Come on up."

Half a minute later, Al returned from the bedroom zipping up his jeans. He tossed a pair to Hamish.

Hamish pulled on the jeans, then scuttled around the living room, tidying what he knew was already a spotless apartment.

"It's okay, Choir Boy," Al said. "I hid the condom wrappers."

"Very funny." Their relationship had breezed safely past the condom stage months ago. "I should never have told you Wilf Dickinson called me that."

"You don't like it?"

"From you, it's fine. No . . ." He smiled. "Better than fine." He leaned forward for a kiss. "But only in private, okay?"

"Sure."

A second later, Zol was rapping at the condo's door.

"What'd you find out?" Hamish asked Zol once he'd poured him a drink. It wasn't one of those single malt Scotches Zol liked so much. It was a Jack Daniel's Tennessee whiskey. Hamish never touched the stuff, but kept it on hand for Al.

Zol took a gulp, then quickly took another and then practically fell into Aunt Gwen's wingback chair. It seemed he'd drink anything Hamish offered tonight without even tasting it.

Hamish sat beside Al on the small chesterfield Mother had nearly sent to the dump last time she redecorated. Al said the hodgepodge of old but respectable furniture was part of the charm of Hamish's otherwise spartan apartment. It reminded him of Sarajevo before the siege: modestly dignified and comfortable.

"God, Hamish. I wish you'd been there," Zol said. "After I called you from Simcoe Emerg, I tried to have a meeting with the families. It was a real struggle."

"Sorry. I couldn't get away."

"It was impossible to get logical stories from six sets of relatives talking at the same time. Natasha's going back to do a proper job of it."

"It couldn't have been a dead loss," Hamish said. "You must have got at least one useful tidbit."

Zol looked at Hamish, then at Al, then back at Hamish, frowning the whole time. He fixed on Al again. "Um . . . I'm not sure, you know, it's a good idea for me to —"

Hamish was in no mood for beating around bush. "You mean, discuss this in front of Al?"

"This is a hot one," Zol said. "Six first responders on the heels of those high school kids. Until we get this figured out, we can't afford any leaks to the press."

Al stood up. "No problem." He fished his car keys from his pocket. "I understand."

Hamish hated being tugged from two sides. It reminded him of his parents' relentless bickering when he was a kid. "Don't go, Al. Please. We haven't finished checking out the sketches."

Zol set his glass on the coffee table. "I'm sorry. I know I got here a bit early, but . . ." He paused, his expression embarrassed. He grabbed his glass and gazed long and hard into it as though hoping its contents might provide a solution to his dilemma. Finally, he said, "Dammit, this outbreak is snowballing out of control, and more than anything, I need your help, Hamish."

It was nice to be flattered, but expecting Al to leave, just like that, was completely unfair. Al Mesic was discretion personified. His delicacy over confidential matters had bought him the respect of the denizens who stalked City Hall's dark corners. And his insights were spot on, his perspectives fruitful and often surprising. Hamish picked at the lint of his tee-shirt and pictured the cases of liver failure piling up in Norfolk County. Today, the number had blossomed to twelve. "How about we speak off the record? We can do that, eh, Al?"

"Of course," Al said. He turned to Zol. "It's your call."

Zol still looked worried. "You can do that?"

"You mean, do we reporters have a secret pact like your Hippocratic Oath? A moral obligation to tell the world everything we see and hear?"

Zol squirmed in his seat and flushed from his neck to his ears. His eyes sought Hamish's, then darted to Al's, then back again. After a while, the tension in his face settled. His shoulders sagged. "I'm sure the three of us agree . . ." He paused for a gulp of his Jack Daniel's, then smiled as if tasting it only now. He coughed into his fist. "Agree that now, before we've put all the facts together, the situation would look alarming to the general public."

Al nodded. "No one will hear a word out of me."

"For sure?" Zol said.

Al returned his keys to his pocket, then folded his arms over his chest. "For sure."

Zol looked relieved. "Thanks."

Al sat down, stretched out his legs, and leaned backwards into the chesterfield. He closed his eyes.

"So, Zol," Hamish said, buoyed at the unexpected détente between his only real friend and his lover, "what's in that shopping bag?"

Zol lifted the Kelly's SuperMart bag from the floor and held it in his lap. "I did as you said. Examined the first responders for scabby lesions. Four firefighters and two paramedics."

"And?"

"I found scabs on two of them. One of the firefighters and the female paramedic."

"Lips and fingers?"

Zol nodded.

"Tell me exactly what the lesions looked like."

"Large crusts. Round, about a centimetre across. Like giant cold sores, but thicker and tougher."

Old crusts all looked the same, no matter what their underlying cause. It was much easier to identify micro-organisms in fresh, fluid-filled skin lesions. "Any fresh vesicles?"

"Nothing the least bit fresh. They'd had them for weeks. Thought they were cold sores that wouldn't go away." Zol dipped into the shopping bag. "I lifted them off with a scalpel and put them into sterile containers, exactly as you told me. Two from each patient." He held up four small jars sealed in a sturdy plastic bag marked BIOHAZARD.

"You labelled them clearly, like I told you?"

"Of course."

Hamish took the bag from Zol and studied the specimens through the plastic. It was impossible to make an eyeball diagnosis by looking at a few pieces of crust and ooze, but they did look more or less like the lesions he and Wilf had examined under the electron microscope. Wilf's latest manipulations hadn't revealed anything new or definitive, but the guy was beginning to lean toward suggesting the matchsticks were fragments of plant virus. Surely, there was little sense in that. Of course, Wilf wasn't a clinician. If he were, he'd know that plant viruses were not able to cause disease in humans or other animals. Only plants.

"I'll get Wilf Dickinson to put them under the EM tomorrow. See if they show the same particles we saw in the others. Even if they do, I'm not sure what that will tell us."

There was a major *but* to this. And Zol wasn't going to like it. "Even if these skin lesions are caused by some new or mutant infectious agent," he told Zol, "I can't see any definitive link between a bunch of lesions in the skin and galloping destruction of the liver. Out of today's six new liver victims, you found possible lesions in two of them. What about the other four cases? And most of the teens with liver disease had no blisters, either."

"But . . . hold on," Zol said. "We've got two discrete populations — high school students and first responders — with simultaneous outbreaks of two unusual conditions — weird skin lesions and galloping liver failure. There's got to be a connection."

"Then tell me about the questionnaires from Erie Collegiate." Frank reporting by the students and their families was now the best hope for discovering the link between the ailing teens and first responders. "Or is Natasha still fiddling with them?"

"She's not a fiddler. You know that, Hamish. She finished a preliminary analysis half an hour ago." Zol touched his briefcase. "Got it with me."

"Good. We can stop speculating and look at some hard evidence."

Zol lifted his briefcase onto his lap, but stopped short of opening it. Hamish had never seen Zol's face look so dark. "Afraid not," he said.

Hamish exchanged glances with Al, who hadn't moved a muscle since Zol had started sharing his evidence. What was Zol playing at? "Come on, Zol," Hamish said, his frustration building, "we've been waiting all day for this."

"Truth is, there's nothing to tell. A big fat zero."

"A computer glitch?"

"I wish it were that easy."

He was happy enough to concede that Natasha was smart, but she wasn't infallible. Not to the degree Zol liked to think. "Faulty questionnaire design? A confounding bias in her tool?"

Zol stiffened. "Nothing's wrong with Natasha's investigative tool. Or her computer skills."

"Well then?"

"The kids lied."

"You can't be serious. When?"

"On their questionnaires."

"You're sure?"

Zol explained how Colleen had found a teen hangout in the abandoned lot behind Eric Christian Collegiate. "Major drinking and smoking going on there," he said. "Yet only two teens — one White, one Native — admitted to smoking on their questionnaires."

Al stirred for the first time. "Did the questionnaire ask about drugs and alcohol?"

"Denied those, of course," Zol said.

"And solvents?"

"Those too."

Al opened his eyes and took his hands off his chest. He leaned forward in his seat. "If they're lying about beer and cigarettes," he said, "what else are they hiding? Were there liquor bottles with the beer bottles?"

"Colleen didn't mention any," Zol said.

"And there really were tons of cigarette packs?" Al said.

"Everywhere," Zol said. "Mostly Hat-Tricks from the reserve. Why?"

Hamish's ears burned, his palms itched. Why were those kids — and their parents — being so stupid about the questionnaires? Didn't they know how serious this was?

Al rubbed his sideburns, first the right, then the left. For a long moment he stared at the opposite wall. Finally, his eyes began to glow. He pushed himself off the chesterfield and marched into the kitchen.

"What . . . ?" Zol said.

Hamish shrugged and flicked his hand. He wasn't about to tell Zol that Al had run off for a Nicorette fix.

Seconds later, Al was standing in the doorway tapping his foot on the hardwood. Hamish's stomach lurched at the sight of his lover holding his nemesis, a cigarette in his hand.

"Come on, Al. You promised —"

"That these were only for show? A reminder that my former filthy habit was playing hell with my voice box?" He looked at Zol and explained, "It's okay. I haven't had a smoke in four months."

"Sounds great," Zol said. "So, what gives?"

"Watch."

Al put the unlit filter tip to his mouth and took a long pull. Then he waved the cigarette ostentatiously in his hand and pretended to exhale a huge cloud of smoke. He looked like a drag queen. Ridiculous.

"What was I doing?"

"Pretending to smoke a cigarette," Hamish told him. "With far too much drama."

"But what exactly was I doing?"

"Try it again," Zol said. "And I'll tell you what I see."

While Zol gave a running commentary, Al lifted the cigarette toward his mouth, pinched it between his lips, took a drag, then removed the cigarette by grasping it between the index and third fingers of his right hand.

"Shit," Zol said. "I get it." He slapped his forehead with his palm. "Brilliant."

What was so brilliant? Hamish felt stupid and left out. "Come on, guys."

Al threw him a reassuring smile. "It's okay. Let me do it again. You'll get it this time."

Al repeated the routine, but in slow motion.

Suddenly, Hamish could see them. The scabby lesions that had walked into his clinic. The worried teens and adults with sores on their lips and fingertips, exactly where a cigarette would touch them.

"Oh — my — God," Hamish said. "So why aren't we seeing hundreds of cases? A quarter of the population smokes."

"Maybe we are," Zol said, "but we haven't noticed. The two first responders I saw today thought they had cold sores. Herpes simplex virus lesions above the belt aren't reportable. No jurisdiction keeps track of them."

"The two cases you saw this morning, are they smokers?"

"Yes. Pack-a-day, at least."

"What brand?"

"I didn't need to ask. I could smell them. Rollies and Hat-Tricks. You know, from the rez. Of course, they may smoke other brands as well."

Hamish's mouth filled with sand. If cheap cigarettes from the rez were the cause of the outbreaks of skin blisters and epidemic liver failure, the consequences would be catastrophic. "You've got to do something, Zol. Immediately."

"What? Get on TV and scare every smoker off the habit with threats of ugly scabs and liver disease?"

"If that's what it takes."

Al was pouring himself a generous whiskey, his cigarette nowhere in sight. "Have you ever looked at a cigarette pack, Hamish? The government's been trying to scare smokers to death with threats of impotence and lung cancer for decades. Doesn't work."

"So what do we do?" Hamish said.

"The liver thing's the bigger problem," Zol said. "Our top priority."

"Gentlemen," Hamish said, "the kids at Erie Collegiate have to be forced to tell the truth. Spill everything that could possibly have a bearing on the liver outbreak."

"How're we going to do that?" Zol said. "Torture is against the law."

He didn't dignify Zol's sarcasm with a reply.

Al swirled his bourbon. "How about a non–authoritative approach? Empathetic interviews with someone close to their own age. One on one."

"Natasha's young. And empathetic," Zol said. "Those kids didn't respond to her."

A sly smile crossed Al's lips as he dipped his nose into his glass. "You need someone who's both hip and professional."

"Well, there's no question that Natasha is professional." Zol looked around as if to be sure no one else was listening, then lowered his voice, "And she's sort of hip. Well, hot is more like it."

Al chuckled at Zol's candid admission. "Hot or not, she's attached to your office. No offence, Zol, but no matter how hip or sweet she comes across, she's an agent of the Ministry of Health and all its baggage." He took a long swallow of whiskey, then ran his tongue along his lips.

"Come on, do I have to spell it out? Letter by letter?"

"You mean . . . ?" Zol said.

"You read the *Spectator*, don't you?"

"Of course."

"Catch the story of that Ponzi scheme operating out of a back room at City Hall?"

"Shameful business, but —"

"Who do you think coaxed that story out of the mortified victims?"

"Shit," Zol said. "Pour me another whiskey. Hamish can drive me home."

CHAPTER 14

"We still haven't settled on a game plan," Natasha said, struggling to keep her tone professional. Al Mesic was impossible to read. And driving her crazy.

"Holy crap," Al said, pointing out the window. He turned, and again she felt the power of his eyes aiming at her from the passenger seat. "Have you ever seen so many pumpkins?"

For the umpteenth time in the past hour, she thought her heart was going to jump out of her chest and she'd crash the Honda into the trees. Forget the potential for dogs and deer and God-knows-what leaping onto the road from the Norfolk County woods to her left, Al Mesic's intoxicating amber orbs were ten times more dangerous. And those shoulders . . . a pair of tigers barely restrained by his skin-tight shirt and light-blue linen jacket. She gripped the steering wheel until her nails bit into her palms. She couldn't believe Al was gay. He had to be at least bisexual.

"I mean, really," he continued, pointing to the right and filling Natasha's tongue-tied silence, "who could possibly eat all those?"

Dr. Zol was wrong about this fact-finding interview he'd arranged for this morning with the Vanderhoef twins. Al Mesic wasn't going to get any more reliable information out of those girls than her failed questionnaire had recorded from their peers at Erie Christian Collegiate. Al might be a reporter, but he was anything but focussed. And incredibly distracting.

"Those are for Halloween," she told him. "You know, jack-o-lanterns. Scary faces lit with candles."

She forced herself to focus on her personal cure for nervousness in anxiety-provoking situations: concentrate on the practical details of the environment around her.

And here, the practical details were pumpkins. Fields and fields of them. Half of Waterford's annual crop would've been shipped by now to supermarkets across the country and served at thousands of Thanksgiving dinners. She pictured the elaborate pumpkin pie she and her mother had baked two weeks ago for the holiday. As usual, Natasha rolled and crimped the pastry because her mother insisted "English" pastry was impossible to work with and not worth the effort. Mummyji did the filling, and of course her mother couldn't make a regular Canadian pie. She had to Indian it up with saffron and cardamom, and serve it with kulfi instead of whipped cream or Häagen-Dazs. Delicious, but why did Mummyji always have to flout the family's Indianness, even at Canadian Thanksgiving?

Before Natasha knew it, the highway was leading them into the village of Waterford, past an enormous sign that said HOME OF THE PUMPKIN FESTIVAL. Her body felt as tense as ever.

"Must be some good money around here," Al said, pointing to the yellow-brick Baptist church. "Takes a lot of coin to reno a building like that."

They'd done a beautiful job of restoring the church's Gothic revival detailing. The slate on the steeply pitched roof looked new, and the bargeboard scrollwork on the gables had been renewed to achieve the cheery gingerbread effect she loved so much. She'd seen this church four years ago, when the renovations had been half finished. Professor Lindley had taken their art history class on a Gothic revival field trip here to Waterford and several other nearby towns.

Her dashboard GPS told them it was ten-fifty-five, five minutes short of their eleven a.m. appointment, that they were driving along Main Street in Waterford, and the address they wanted was one hundred and fifty metres ahead on the right. She drove one hundred metres, signalled, and parked at the curb. She wasn't going any farther until they settled on a game plan.

She never operated unprepared and wasn't going to start now. She had no idea whether she was dropping Al off alone at the door or accompanying him inside. If they went in together, would he take the lead? Who was doing the introductions and explaining what they needed? She wished Dr. Zol had been more explicit about how this interview was going to work.

Al looked perplexed. "This can't be it," he said, pointing to a boxy red-brick bungalow that hadn't seen new paint on its shutters for decades.

"It's up ahead about a block, but I'm not going any farther until I know how we're going to approach this."

Al shrugged and for some strange reason looked relieved that the Vanderhoefs didn't live in the red bungalow. Perhaps he had something against peeling paint. "There'll be a story," he said, "and we'll get to the bottom of it. No problem."

But if they weren't prepared, there would be a problem. "You've got your questions ready?"

"How am I going to know what to ask until I get a feel for the place, the people, and what's happening between them?"

"So, I'm going to watch and you're going to wing it."

"Not quite. I'm going to charm them so thoroughly that they'll drop clues left, right, and centre and lead us to the heart of the story."

"Can I take notes?"

"If you do, they'll clam up." He turned and gave her a killer smile and dazzled her again with those eyes. "Use that brilliant memory of yours. Hamish doesn't like to admit it, but I know he thinks your grey cells are almost as highly developed as his."

She felt herself melting, foolishly. "Hamish said that?"

"Between you and me, he's a bit threatened by your intellect."

He pulled a pen and notebook from his jacket pocket. "Now relax, and together we'll get the story behind the story. How old are these girls?"

"Twins. Sixteen."

"Grade eleven?"

"With good marks."

"And they missed your show on Tuesday?"

"They were in the hospital. A mild form of probably the same liver problem as the other ten cases. Amelia was discharged home yesterday, Annabel the day before."

"So we're starting fresh with them. That's good."

Clearly, Al considered her failed questionnaire to be incompatible with his charm-the-story-out-of-them technique. She was just as glad not to mention it in front of the Vanderhoefs.

She put the car in drive and drove the final fifty metres while Al fussed with his hair in the vanity mirror, smoothed on some lip balm, and fluffed up his jacket collar. Suddenly, she couldn't wait to see him in action.

"I really like what you've done with this Gothic revival," Al was soon telling the four Vanderhoefs in their living room, where the family had lined themselves on their chintz-covered chesterfield.

Natasha watched him scan the room, as though fascinated by the decor. He turned to Mr. Vanderhoef, a ruddy man in his early forties, and asked him, "Did you do all that scrollwork on the bargeboarding?"

"You like it, eh? That was last summer's family project."

"Never seen finer. But you didn't turn those king posts and finials yourself."

"Sure did."

"Impressive," Al said, telegraphing his enthusiasm for Mr.

Vanderhoef's carpentry skills. "Especially in this day and age. Most people buy mass-produced pieces from Home Depot. Of course, only hand-turned finials have that look of authenticity."

Mrs. Vanderhoef leaned forward, eager not to be deprived of her share of the enormous pile of charm Al was heaping on her husband. "I found the bargeboard and finial patterns in the library. Like you said, they're authentic."

The couple beamed their proud smiles at each other, and then at Al. "Hans cut out the scalloping under the eves as well," said Mrs. Vanderhoef. "From a vintage pattern I found on the Internet. The girls painted it."

"I love the colour," Al said, his teeth gleaming, his eyes darting from one twin to the other. "Is it Williamsburg blue?"

"You've got a good eye," said Mr. Vanderhoef, his chest puffed out like a tom turkey's. "That was my choice."

"Alkyd paint makes such a nice job of exteriors," Al said, "but the clean-up is a terrible nuisance."

"You can say that again, eh, girls?" Mrs. Vanderhoef said. "My laundry room was a mess for weeks."

Al didn't take his eyes off the twins sitting there side by side on the sofa, flanked by their parents. They were an attractive pair, obviously sisters but not identical. One was white blond, the other more sandy; they were wearing narrow-legged blue jeans that highlighted their ultra-slim hips. "You girls did the cutting-in?" Al said. "Looks like a professional job."

The twins nodded, either too shy or too mesmerized to talk. If Al wasn't careful, they'd be too much in awe of him to say a word and he'd never get the story.

"What's your secret, Amelia?" Al said to the sandy twin. "An angle-sash brush? Natural fibre, I bet."

The girl looked to her dad for the answer.

"You did the work," said Mr. Vanderhoef. "You tell him."

Amelia's gaze dropped to her lap, where her fingers picked at an ugly crust on her right thumb. "We cheated," she mumbled.

"Yeah," Annabel said, "we used FrogTape. A ton of it."

"That's not cheating," Al said, "that's smart. Learned it from your dad, eh?"

"No way," Annabel said. "Figured it out for ourselves. From the Internet."

"YouTube," said Amelia. "You can learn anything there."

Mrs. Vanderhoef's face tightened. She didn't like the sound of what uncensored YouTube sessions might be teaching her daughters.

"The paint fumes bother you?" Al asked. "Me, I hate them."

The girls looked at each other, shrugged, and shook their heads. They seemed surprised to hear that paint could have a strong, unpleasant odour.

Mr. Vanderhoef straightened his back and clapped Amelia on the shoulder. "Good Dutch stock. They don't complain. Except about homework."

The girls rolled their eyes at their dad, then returned their gaze to Al. Clearly, he was a package they might like to unwrap. They were probably into urban fantasy and its vampire heartthrobs.

"I do a bit of painting myself," Al said. He reached into his jacket pockets and pulled out two small boxes. "Here," he said, tossing a box to each girl, "have a look at my hobby. I use acrylic paints." He smiled at Mrs. Vanderhoef. "No smell and much easier clean-up."

The girls caught the boxes and glanced at them with a guilty familiarity they couldn't disguise. They turned to each other in what could only be described as horror, and tossed the boxes onto the floor as if they were hot potatoes. Their faces shone beet red in their pastel hoodies.

"Goodness, girls," said Mrs. Vanderhoef, "what are doing?" She stared long enough at the boxes scattered on her ivory broadloom to get a good look at them, then turned to Al. "Sorry about that. Girls, that's no way to treat our guest. Those boxes are beautifully decorated."

"It's okay, Mrs.V.," Al said, picking up the boxes. He turned and winked at Natasha. She had no idea what he was up to. He aimed his reassuring gaze once again at Mrs. Vanderhoef. "No offence taken, ma'am. Not between us smokers."

"Smokers?" said Mrs. Vanderhoef. "There are no smokers in this house. And no drinkers, either. This is a Christian home, Mr. Mesic."

"Of course it is, Mrs. V.," Al said. With a solemn glance, he acknowledged the leather-bound Bible open on a lectern beside the front window. He held up the boxes and raised his eyebrows at the twins. "What do you say we tell your mum what these are for? Eh, girls? Bring her into the twenty-first century?"

Natasha watched Hans Vanderhoef's reaction — certain the burly man was going to throw her impudent colleague out of the house. But Vanderhoef sat calmly on the chesterfield beside Annabel, his hands clasped across his belly, a knowing look glowing on his face. He knew what was going down and seemed to be relieved to finally have it in the open.

"Annabel," Al said, "why don't you start. Tell your mum what Rollies are. I'm sure your dad knows already."

Half an hour later, they said their goodbyes at the front door, and Natasha followed Al to the street. Her head was spinning with the details he'd extracted from the Vanderhoef twins. Facts had poured out of them as easily as milk from the pair of Delft porcelain jugs displayed on their mantel.

"I'll drive, if you like," he said with a look of either warm concern or brash patronization for her obvious giddiness. She couldn't tell which, but figured it was probably the latter.

She didn't let anyone drive her car, not even Kostos. "No thanks, I —"

"What? You don't trust me?"

She was tired and had no energy for arguing. And there were

dozens of details to be scribbled into her notebook. "I suppose." She dug her keys from her purse and tossed them to him. "But please, no speeding."

Al started the car and headed back the way they'd come. He looked pleased with himself. "I'd say that counts as a pretty good scoop."

She hated to admit it, but once Al got the girls started, they hadn't shut up. Those few days in hospital with bright yellow skin had put quite a scare into them.

Al tugged at the collar of his linen jacket. "That dad was a straight shooter. A good guy. Made his girls feel safe about fessing up about the Rollies. And everything else."

"I couldn't believe how you schmoozed over his Gothic revival handiwork."

He shrugged and made no attempt to hide the smirk on his face.

"Honestly," Natasha told him. "King posts and finials? You actually know that much about nineteenth-century Ontario architecture?"

"I'm a reporter. I know about a lot of things."

"But those terms rolled off your tongue as if you used them every day. Don't tell me you're a closet designer."

"Closets aren't my thing. Never have been. Now, Hamish, he's another matter. Locked inside for so long it stunted his growth. But I'm working on him."

"You're changing the subject."

Al was smirking again. "You don't want me to spoil the magic, do you?"

"I can take it."

For a half a minute, Al's face was pensive as he drummed on her steering wheel. "If you must know," he said finally, "a little background research never hurts."

So much for his impromptu *we'll take the story as it comes approach.* He made a sheepish face.

"And somehow, you discovered the Vanderhoefs lived in a newly restored vintage house painted Williamsburg blue?"

He let out a sigh in mock defeat. "Facebook. The girls bragged about the gingerbread reno on their house and posted photos of their paint job."

And then, of course, Al had boned up on Gothic revival lingo: bargeboards, scrollwork, king posts, and finials. Clever.

"Mrs. Vanderhoef had no idea about the Rollies," Natasha said. "Did you see her face when the girls admitted that two-thirds of the kids at their school smoke cigarettes from the rez?"

"I was waiting for her to cover up that huge Bible while the girls were talking about buying two hundred Rollies at a time from the schoolyard pusher."

"She nearly fainted when the girls said they stashed their Rollies in the basement rumpus room behind the Encyclopedia Britannica."

Al laughed and Natasha snuck a peek at the speedometer. Seven points over the limit.

"So far, how many kids at that school have come down with that liver thing?" he asked.

"Six." The girls had said that every one of the Erie Christian Collegiate students who'd developed liver disease was a smoker. Sometimes Rollies, sometimes Hat-Tricks, all supplied from Grand Basin Reserve. Mostly, the kids smoked Rollies, because they were cheaper and the resealable plastic bags they came in were easy to hide. No incriminating packaging to dispose of.

"What about Hamish's lip and finger thing?" Al asked. "The girls weren't clear about the number of their peers affected."

"I expect most are keeping their lesions hidden, or passing them off as zits or cold sores," Natasha said. "Did you notice? Both twins had lesions that are probably Hamish's blister-rash thing. I wish we knew what was causing it."

"I'd say Amelia had at least one scab on her thumb," Al agreed. "And that was probably one on Annabel's lip."

"Her makeup didn't do much to cover it up."

Al set the cruise control and took his foot off the gas. She had to admit he was a smooth driver.

"Tell me, what was that about the twins not noticing the paint fumes?"

Al beamed. Like Hamish, he loved playing Sherlock. And showing it off. "That was my first clue that they'd been smoking Rollies. And had started sometime before last summer, when they'd painted the house."

"How so?"

"Cigarettes that strong do a number on your sense of smell. Believe me, I know." He dug into his jacket pocket and showed her a half-consumed pack of Nicorette gum.

But what else was rez tobacco doing to those kids?

CHAPTER 15

At three o'clock, Zol pulled open the front door of the Nitty Gritty Café across Concession Street from his old office. He was an hour late for the meeting and his hands wouldn't stop shaking. He could have been killed.

He waved to Marcus, the owner-baker-barista behind the bar, and headed to the back corner. Colleen, Natasha, and Hamish were sitting in their usual spot, which Hamish called their crisis centre. Hamish had been held up too, for some reason. His latte cup was half full. The women's cups were empty.

To be sure, the team did some of their best brainstorming here. He was anxious to learn if anything else had been gleaned from the Vanderhoefs. Natasha had called from her car to tell him how Al had charmed the twins into divulging the magnitude of the rez tobacco habit at Erie Christian Collegiate. So much for fundamentalist Christian values turning high school students into saints. But what did he care? Max would never be going to anything but a public school, and the tobacco lead was getting stronger and stronger.

"Sorry I'm late," he told them as he threw his coat over the back of the empty chair and dropped onto the seat, his knees buckling.

"A woman hit a deer. Right in front of me. A twelve-point buck. I didn't want to tell you on the phone."

Colleen's hands flew to her mouth. "Oh my God! Where?"

"Highway 24. On that stretch between Simcoe and Brantford."

Hamish glanced at the window. "Not surprising. You've got to expect it on an overcast fall day like this. Dusk brings them out, you know."

Zol rubbed the sweat from his forehead and looked away. He clamped his teeth into his tongue. Hamish could be so damned clinical in the face of a friend's distress.

Colleen leaned in to Zol, close enough for him to smell the jasmine on her skin. She knew it settled him. "Was anybody hurt?"

"I called 911 on my cell. The paramedics took her to Simcoe Emerg. Her nose was a mess. Not sure about the rest of her." He'd wiped the blood off her face and held her hand until the ambulance arrived. He hadn't let her move in case she'd injured her neck.

"Did she have any passengers?" Natasha asked.

"Luckily, no. Her car's a write-off, though."

Colleen squeezed his forearm. "What about you?"

"I'm fine." He wiped his palms on her serviette and willed his heart rate to settle below a hundred. "And — and so's my minivan." He still didn't know how he'd managed to swerve to a safe stop. He'd have to get his brakes checked. Did they get fried when you jammed on them that hard?

Colleen squeezed again. "Are you sure?"

"Yeah." He sensed a quiet presence behind him waiting to take his order. "Oh man, I need a hit of your best caffeine," he told Marcus. Actually, what he really needed was a Glenfarclas. But that would have to wait until he got home. You couldn't brainstorm with blunted senses. "Make it your largest latte with a double espresso on the side. Do I smell sticky buns?"

Marcus smiled through his ginger beard. "You bet. How about some extra maple glaze on that?"

"Sounds great."

Natasha rattled her spoon inside her empty mug, the frothy

milk long gone. He found himself remembering the time he over-heard her telling a girlfriend she lived in mortal fear of getting a milk moustache in public. He didn't know why she worried. It would take a lot more than a bit of froth on her upper lip to diminish that face, crowned as it was by such vibrant, intelligent eyes. He hoped her Greek surgical-resident boyfriend appreciated what a catch she was. Not quite the gorgeous, seasoned package that Colleen offered, but . . .

"Dr. Zol?" Natasha was waving her spoon in front of him. "Do you need a moment to — you know — catch your breath?"

"I'm okay. Let's get started. Now we know those kids, and the first responders, are heavily into rez tobacco." He turned to Natasha. "Good job, by the way. What else have you got?"

Natasha put down the spoon and opened her notebook. Yesterday's doleful embarrassment over her failed questionnaires had left her eyes. She was back on sound territory. "After our trip to Waterford and the Vanderhoefs, I spent a couple of hours in Simcoe Emerg. The first responders and their families were helpful." She paused, then added, "In the end."

Colleen was taking everything in, making her own set of notes. "Was there a problem?"

"Well . . . it took them a while to warm up to me. They're inde-pendent down there. Seem to enjoy their relative isolation. And . . ." Natasha paused and looked around, as if uncertain whether to speak frankly. ". . . and the only brown skin they're used to seeing is on migrant farmer workers with little education."

Zol signalled his understanding with an apologetic shake of his head and pressed through the awkwardness. "What d'you find?"

Natasha related the details she'd collected in what must have been an emotional setting. She'd memorized almost everything and barely glanced at her notebook.

Between them, the six first responders owned five dogs and two cats, an iguana, a parrot, and two guinea pigs. Two hunted locally. One had a hobby farm and admitted to using pesticides. Five of the first responders lived in apartments or condos with no contact with farms or gardens. Four had travelled to Florida last winter, and two to Myrtle Beach. None had ever visited Asia, Africa, or South America. None had hobbies that employed liver-toxic chemicals and none lived next to a dry cleaners.

"Dry cleaners?" Colleen said.

Hamish leaned forward. He started to raise his right hand, but dropped it to his lap like a stone. By the flushed look on his face, Zol reckoned someone had told Hamish to ditch the nerdy professorial digit. It must have been Al Mesic. No one else would have been brave enough to risk the consequences — a major pout — by offering such feedback. "Solvents can be hepatotoxic," Hamish said. He threw Colleen a patronizing lift of the eyebrows and added, "As in liver-damaging." He turned to Zol. "But as you must know, the agents used these days are . . . well . . . safe." He made a face. "Supposedly."

Natasha caught Zol's eye and acknowledged Hamish's intrusion with a perfunctory nod, then tapped her pen against her notebook. "The firefighter with the lip and finger lesions is a hobby taxidermist."

"Hmm," Hamish said. "Does he hunt?"

"No, his wife was clear about that. He doesn't shoot anything himself."

"What animals does he stuff?" Hamish asked.

"Mostly birds of prey."

"Anything else?" Hamish pressed. "Sheep? Goats?"

Natasha made a face. "Does anyone stuff those?"

"How about rabbits, then? Or foxes? Raccoons?"

"Not for a couple of years."

Hamish shook his head and narrowed his eyes. "No good. The timing's all wrong."

A pall of disappointment hung over the table and sucked the energy out of the air.

Natasha had gleaned an astounding amount of detail, but when it came down to it, she'd found nothing exciting beyond the link with rez tobacco. Was that enough? It was difficult to see how it could be. The health effects of tobacco had been studied to death. No one had ever suggested that it caused either blistering skin lesions or galloping liver failure. Al's performance last night with an unlit cigarette had been quite convincing, but what did it mean?

Damn.

Hamish picked up his mug, glanced inside it, and seemed surprised that he'd already emptied it. He threw Zol an incongruous smile. "I heard from Winnipeg today. They were cagey with me at first, but I could tell the boffins could barely contain their excitement."

"Sorry, Hamish," Colleen asked, clearly puzzled by Hamish's sudden change in demeanour. "Who or what is in Winnipeg?"

"The National Microbiology Laboratory," Hamish told her. He waved his empty mug in the air, flourishing it like a sceptre or a magic wand, dispelling the gloom. It seemed Oscar Wilde had entered the building. "The guys with the best toys in the country. Not bad on brains, either. Anyway, I got them to look at the photos Wilf Dickinson took of our blister specimens under his microscope. Ten cases in total." He was focussing on Colleen, bestowing her with the patronizing attention he used on his junior students. His enunciation was infuriatingly pedantic, but you couldn't fault his clarity, or his devotion to the investigation. "Wilf took the images from his electron microscope and loaded them onto his website. Then I emailed the address to the guys in Winnipeg. Gotta love the Internet." Hamish's pupils were now so wide his blue eyes looked almost black. "At first, they did some strategic stalling and warned me that this was an informal opinion they couldn't put in writing. For a proper opinion, they'd need the original specimens so they could do their own set of tests."

"Come on, Hamish," Zol told him. "The suspense is killing us."

The guy was glowing. He'd been a child soloist at his church and thrived in the limelight. And always insisted on presenting last, for the most dramatic effect.

"Okay," he said, putting down his mug. "I'm coming to the good part. But remember, this is only a preliminary opinion." He swept the table with his gaze, making sure he had everyone's attention. "Based on our images, they say the matchstick particles in the skin lesions from my eight outpatients — and the two first responders with hepatitis — look like a rare and novel type of infectious particle. No getting around the e-word now, guys. We have ourselves an infectious epidemic. At least as far as the lip and finger blisters are concerned."

Natasha bit on her lower lip and pulled on the curls at the back of her neck. "But . . . but what do they think they are?"

"Wait for it — Winnipeg says the particles have some of the hallmarks of a hybrid virus reported once before in the medical literature." With every sentence, Hamish's tone was more triumphant. "The patient was a Mongolian sheep farmer and local political celebrity. And he got infected with something never seen before. An infectious particle that was part plant virus and part animal virus."

Colleen looked like she could barely speak. "What happened to him?"

"Scabs and blisters spread all over his hands and face and drew a lot of local attention. He was convinced he had leprosy, locked himself in his home, and committed suicide."

"Anybody else get sick?" Natasha asked.

"His wife and three kids. He killed them too. Then, no more cases." Hamish shrugged. "If the family was shunned by the local community, the mini-outbreak — and the disease — would've died out on the spot."

Natasha's cheeks were a pale contrast to the red blotches on her throat. "I'm almost afraid to ask," she said. "But did they get hepatitis or liver failure?"

"Negatory. No mention of jaundice or liver involvement in the case report. Purely skin."

Colleen, looking pensive, clasped her hands together, then dropped them in her lap. "How did it happen?" she said. "The plant-animal hybrid thing?"

Hamish was loving this. "Nobody knows for sure, but there's

speculation that orf virus — which infects sheep, goats, and sometimes humans — and turnip mosaic virus — which infects Mongolian cabbage among other vegetable crops — somehow got together and produced mutant offspring contagious to humans."

Colleen looked around to be sure no one at other tables could hear her, then lowered her voice. "And you think something like that has happened here?"

Hamish nodded. "We've got to face that possibility. Of course, Winnipeg may be overstating things a bit. I couriered a set of blister specimens to them this afternoon. Their formal opinion may take awhile. A few weeks, even. They're going to be more than method-ical about testing anything this unusual." He peered at Natasha's notebook open beside him. "Hey, does that say Donna Holt?"

Natasha stiffened. "Well, yes."

"Hmm. Tammy Holt was a plant virologist," he continued, oblivious to the pall his previous comments had cast over the table. "She worked down the hall from me at Caledonian. In the research wing. She was murdered last summer. Her case is still unsolved. Had a sister. I'm pretty sure her name was Donna. I do know she was a paramedic. Visited the lab a couple of times." He turned to Natasha. "Is she Native, the Donna Holt on your list? Tammy's sister taught figure skating on the reserve. Had been Ontario pro-vincial junior champion or runner up. Something like that. Got a medal, anyway. Tammy was very proud of that."

Natasha tapped her notebook with her ballpoint. "This Donna Holt does live on the reserve. Works for the Norfolk County ambulance service. Her mother's a magistrate."

Hamish snapped his fingers. "Must be her, then. How sick is she?"

"Dr. Hitchin says he's more worried about her than any of the others."

Zol's chest was so tight he could hardly speak. "What . . . what did you tell Winnipeg? Is . . . is this mutant virus thing going to be all over our newspapers by the morning?"

Hamish still looked pleased with himself. "I told them they

were from a family I encountered on a recent trip to the Namibian desert."

"Namibia?" Colleen said. "What have you got against Namibia?"

"I figured the boys in Winnipeg would barely know where it was, and treat the images as an academic curiosity and not a front-page story."

Zol's relief was almost as palpable as his panic had been. "Brilliant. Hamish, I could kiss you."

"Zol, a little decorum, please." Hamish's eyes were positively twinkling. "Save that for the Reluctant Lion. The guys who frequent that establishment are used to that sort of thing."

CHAPTER 16

It was well into the evening by the time Hamish pulled the Saab into the doctors' lot at Simcoe General. He took a ticket from the machine and steered toward the lamppost closest to the Emergency entrance. Someone in a Seven Series BMW — probably a specialist whose medical practice was stacked with lucrative procedures — had beaten him to the brightest spot, directly under the security camera. Second brightest would have to do.

Inside the emergency department, he introduced himself to Breanna, the young receptionist behind the front desk. He had to tell her his name three times before some sort of dim light bulb went on in her head and she remembered they'd spoken only an hour ago. That was when he'd phoned to arrange this meeting with the Holts. Finally, she shot him a stupid smile and told him the family was waiting in the quiet room.

He stopped at the vending machine down the hall, put in a toonie, and took out a ginger ale. Those Nitty Gritty lattes of Marcus's always made him thirsty, as had the stress of watching for skittish deer on that stretch of Highway 24. No bucks or does on the roadway, and only three dead raccoons and a groundhog, and of course their countless worms and bacteria — ascaris and leptospira — spattered across the asphalt. The undercarriage of the Saab would be teeming with animal pathogens.

He spotted the sign that said QUIET ROOM and stopped in front of the door. He straightened his tie and took two swigs of ginger ale before knocking and walking in.

He was greeted by three anxious faces and the smell of chewing gum and stale tobacco.

"I'm Dr. Wakefield. Are you the Holts? Tammy's — I mean *Donna's* — family?" His cheeks burned at the slip.

A tallish young man — mid-twenties, a handsome round face, wavy dark hair gelled back off his forehead — rose quickly from a chair. Blue jeans hugged his slim hips. He was wearing a dark sweatshirt and a matching nylon windbreaker featuring automotive logos. Embroidered on the front of the jacket was MECHANICALLY SOUND: MATT HOLT. He looked exhausted and didn't speak, just shot out his hand, gave Hamish's a quick shake, and sat down again.

The older couple, mid-fifties or a bit beyond, grimaced and creaked as they shifted in their chairs. Between them, they were packing an extra hundred pounds, and wore them with subdued dignity. A large, dark handbag sat on the floor at the woman's feet. Dangling from the handle was a miniature pair of white figure skates along with an embossed metal disk of some sort. It was several centimetres across and whether it was bronze or deep gold, he couldn't be sure. He wasn't good with colours. Was that Donna's provincial skating championship medal?

"We're Tammy's *and* Donna's family," the woman said. There was a kindness to her eyes, but worry and fatigue were trapped in the wrinkles and dark circles. "I'm their mother, and this is their father," she said, gesturing to her husband seated beside her. She glanced across the room at the younger man. "And Matt there, he's their brother."

The older man raised his eyebrows and touched his chest. "Vernon," he said. "She's Leona." His voice was flat, barely more than a murmur, his accent straight off the reserve.

"How's Donna doing?" Hamish asked them.

Matt shook his head. "They're transferrin' her. To Toronto."

"Tonight?"

Matt raised his eyebrows. The rest of his face was impassive.

"But, Doctor," Leona said, "where did Donna get this from, this liver coma? She's always been active and healthy. And we don't drink. None of us."

Vernon's eyes narrowed. "Must've got it from a patient. They don't protect their paramedics, you know. The gloves they give 'em don't fit right."

"Those scabs around her mouth," said Leona, "are they gonna leave scars?"

Draped across Leona Holt's lap was what Hamish now realized was her daughter's skating-coach jacket. GRAND BASIN FIGURE SKATING CLUB was embroidered on the back.

The maternal way that Mrs. Holt was caressing the garment reminded him of something he'd seen before. He couldn't place it, and of course he'd never experienced such motherly tenderness directly. The frustrating vagueness of the image at the back of his memory nagged at him. What was he thinking of? A painting? A statue?

Matt was out of his chair again, his face taut. "You gotta tell us *somethin'*, Doc. No one's givin' us no answers."

"That's because they don't have any. It's as simple as that."

Vernon heaved himself from his chair and strode forward, almost stepping on Hamish's shoes. "There's teenagers with this liver thing," he said. "White kids. I'll bet you're doin' a better job for them."

Suddenly, the tiny room felt like a coffin, its dingy walls pressing inward. The anxious trio in their heavy fall clothing were sucking every molecule of oxygen from the air. Hamish stumbled backwards. He felt for the door handle behind him and grabbed it like a lifeline. He took three yogic breaths and willed his shoulders, his spine, his gut to relax. Then he asked everyone to sit down and dropped into the remaining chair himself.

His tongue was too dry to form any words. After a swallow of ginger ale he was able to say, "We're trying our best for everyone, Mr. Holt."

Vernon laid his arms across his oversized belly and stared at his sneakers.

Hamish took another steadying swig. "Actually, I was hoping . . . to get some answers from you."

"We told the doctors everythin' already," Leona said.

Vernon's round face was a stone mask. "I'd say we're done answerin'."

Hamish found himself counting the jagged nicks and scratches in the wall behind the senior Holts. Why were hospital rooms often so desperate for a fresh coat of paint? "Can we talk about Tammy for a few minutes?"

"This has nothin' to do with her," Vernon said. "She left us more'n a year ago."

"You said you were a doctor," Leona added, "not a detective."

Matt leaned forward and caught Hamish's eye. "My parents have had it up to here with police officers," he explained. "And their endless questions."

"Well, I *am* a doctor," Hamish said. "In fact, Tammy and I worked on the same floor at Caledonian Medical Centre. Our research labs were practically side by side."

Leona looked surprised. "So . . . you knew our Tammy?"

"Saw her almost every day."

"She bake you one of her famous cakes?" Leona said. "You know, for your birthday?"

He nodded. "Covered in dragonflies and grasshoppers. Maybe you saw it?"

Leona thought for a moment, as if trying to picture a cake crawling with icing-sugar insects. She threw her husband a look that seemed to say *This guy's okay*, then turned back to Hamish. "So, what d'you wanta know 'bout Tammy?"

"Careful, Mother," Vernon told her.

Careful about what? Did the family have a theory about their daughter's death? "I'd like to know what you think happened to her. Tammy's death was a terrible shock to everyone at Caledonian."

"Then you know she were murdered,"Vernon said. "And that's pretty well it."

"Do you have any idea why she was killed?"

"Nope," said Vernon. "And no idea who done it, neither."

Leona glanced at her husband, hesitated, then told Hamish, "But whoever done it stole her . . ." her face crumpled and her shoulders heaved, "her . . . great-grandma's pendant."

Hamish felt sick. He knew how Tammy had cherished that antique, beaded medallion, the centre of which featured an eight-pointed star. He'd never seen her without the Native heirloom suspended from a leather thong around her neck.

Anger flashed into Matt's previously well-controlled face. "Stealing Great-Grandma's pendant wasn't the only violation she . . ."

"Stop it,"Vernon said. "Not in front of your mother."

"No, Dad. We have to tell him." Matt turned to Hamish. "She was raped, Doc. There's no other way to say it."

"I said stop it,"Vernon said. "You know how your mother hates that word."

Leona stiffened and gave her husband a look that said *Don't pin your hang-ups on me*.

"Do you have any ideas about a motive?" Hamish asked.

"That's police business,"Vernon said. "Got nothin' to do with you."

"I don't like coincidences," he told him, "unless I can explain them. And what I see here is a huge, unexplained coincidence."

"What do you mean, Doctor?" Leona said.

"Let me put it this way," he said, not certain how to proceed in the face of such pent-up emotion. "Donna is suffering from a serious and unexplained liver condition. And . . . and last year, her only sister was killed shortly after her principal research project was cancelled."

"What's one got t'do with th'other?"Vernon said. "Except we made sure they both got fine educations and good jobs off the rez." He gaped at his son, as if terrified that Matt was headed for the same fate as his sisters.

Leona adjusted Donna's leather jacket weighing heavily on her lap and took a tissue from the table beside her. As she quietly wiped her nose, Hamish remembered the source of the half-forgotten image. A postcard from Rome. Saint Peter's. The Pieta. Neither the Madonna nor Leona Holt could hide her tears.

He had to press on. "Did any of you learn why Tammy's research got cancelled? Or why some mysterious heavyweights came and cleaned out her lab?"

"At the university," Leona said, "she was Dr. Holt. And on the rez, just plain Tammy. We didn't know nothing about her work."

Something about the way Matt's lips twitched said he didn't agree with his mother. Did Tammy's brother know more about her research projects than her parents?

Hamish held Matt's gaze and said, "There was a rumour going around Caledonian — maybe you heard it — that a drug Tammy was testing ran into problems."

"She wasn't testin' no drugs," Matt said.

"Are you sure about that? I know her research was being financed by a large pharmaceutical company."

"She wasn't testing nothing," Matt repeated.

"No?"

Matt stared at his hands in his lap and offered nothing more.

"I need some help here," Hamish said. "If you know she wasn't doing any testing, you must know what sort of work she *was* doing."

Matt's clam-shell face opened a crack. "I promised not to tell."

"Why?"

"She signed a confidentiality agreement and was scared of the big company she worked for."

Hamish paused and forced himself to think. With the father angry, the mother in tears, and the brother holding back, he was going to lose them all unless he chose his words carefully. "If . . . if something about Tammy's cancelled project led to her death, wouldn't it be perfectly appropriate to talk about it?"

"Not if it got me killed too," Matt said.

Hamish took another swig and let that sink in. "Surely you can tell me *something*. I'd be grateful for *anything* that put me on the right track."

Matt flashed a glance at his parents, as if asking for permission to open up.

Hamish leaned toward Leona, who was trying to dab her eyes with a shredded tissue. He handed her a fresh one from the box. Five centuries of broken promises stood between them, but he hoped she could feel that his sincerity was genuine. "What we all want to do tonight is help Donna," he said. "And if there's something important you're not telling me . . ."

Matt exchanged another glance with his mum and paused as if debating with himself. A moment later, he narrowed his eyes and stood up. "Doc, we gotta step out into the hall. Just you and me."

Matt led him away from the buzz of the emergency department and into the hospital's front lobby. Soon they were standing opposite the gift shop, dark and deserted at this time of night.

Matt looked around, then relaxed his shoulders, apparently satisfied they were alone and out of earshot. He smelled of aftershave, auto-shop grease, and just the right amount of manly sweat. "Okay — Tammy was working with a virus that attacks tobacco plants."

"Tobacco mosaic virus?"

He shrugged, and a curl of his thick, black hair dropped onto his eyebrow. "I forget the name, exactly."

"What was she doing with it?"

He pushed the errant lock back onto his scalp. "Some sort of genetic engineering. Molecular biology. I'm not intimately familiar with the details. I'm a mechanical engineer, not a biologist."

Matt was now speaking like a high-priced professional. He'd dropped the rural dialect and flat Native accent he'd used in front of his parents, probably in deference to his dad. His mother seemed a lady of considerable refinement.

"Tammy was infecting live tobacco plants," he continued, "with a genetically modified virus that induced the plants to produce some new wonder drug."

Hamish pictured the sandy loam fields of Norfolk County

covered with tobacco plants stirring in the breeze as far as the horizon. It was ingenious. Tobacco grew with little encouragement, didn't belong to a union, and could be programmed to fill its stalks and leaves with wonder drugs by the tonne. The technology to grow drugs in plants had first been devised to produce a vaccine against Norovirus, the diarrhea demon that spread like wildfire among cruise-ship passengers. The vaccine was a promising innovation and rumoured to be close to a marketable product.

"What was the drug?" Hamish asked, unable to suppress the excitement in his voice.

"A derivative of nicotine. And if you can believe it, it wasn't addictive."

"Who'd want that? Certainly not the tobacco companies."

"We're not talking smoking. Or chewing."

"Oh?" Hamish said.

"Appetite suppression." Matt looked around to be sure they were still alone. "You know what our rezes are like." He mimed a big belly. "Most of us are way too fat. Diabetes is killing us. This could have been a breakthrough. Take a pill a day and you get a nice slim body without any work."

"What went wrong?" Hamish asked.

"I don't know. I tried to talk to her research assistant, but he went underground after they found Tammy's body."

"Do you have any idea why she was killed?"

"My parents think it was personal. Motivated by hatred. You know, because of the . . . the brutality of the rape. There's a lot of domestic violence on the reserve and . . . and hell, you almost come to expect it. As a rez magistrate, my mother has to deal with it almost every day." Matt's face flashed with shame and guilt, then quickly became neutral. "Except Tammy didn't have a boyfriend. She lived quietly with Mum and Dad. Her work was her life."

"You think her murder was related to her research?"

Matt nodded.

Something had gone terribly wrong in Tammy's experimental tobacco fields, and there'd been a major cover-up, no doubt about that. Why else would anonymous heavies be allowed to strip everything from her laboratory in a single afternoon?

Matt was living in two worlds — that was clear by the way he'd switched dialects so readily. Tammy had led two lives too: Dr. Holt at the university, plain Tammy on the rez. What about Donna? What double life had she been living? And had that secret life destroyed her liver? Had she got hold of Tammy's problematic wonder drug? And had she, or someone close to her, been supplying it to the students at that Christian high school? Unlikely. It didn't make sense that Donna and the others got sick more than a year after the door was slammed on Tammy's project.

Hamish massaged the back of his neck and took a couple more yogic breaths. In through the nose, out through the nose. If they were going to solve this liver thing and stop further deaths, they had to discover exactly how Tammy's failed research with tobacco mosaic virus intersected with her sister Donna, the other first responders, and the kids at Erie Christian Collegiate.

It seemed everything focussed on cheap tobacco from Grand Basin Reserve.

CHAPTER 17

Hamish took Matt's business card and headed back to the Saab. He circled the car twice to be sure no one had taken a key to the new paint job, then got in and punched Zol's home number into his phone.

He counted the rings.

Zol picked up on the sixth.

"Zol. Glad I got you. We've got to go shopping."

"Okay?" Zol sounded suspicious. "For anything special?"

"Rollies and Hat-Tricks. And whatever other tobacco products they sell on the reserve."

"And you need me to carry your shopping bag?"

"Give me a break. You grew up next to Grand Basin and went to high school with Native kids. You know the protocol. I've never been on a reserve."

"It's just a rez, Hamish. There's no protocol."

"You mean, you're allowed to drive in unannounced, any time you like? Without an invitation?"

"Yep."

"What about a permit?"

"For God's sake, Hamish, there are no border guards. It's not a foreign country."

"All the same, I'm not driving in alone. Not in the dark. I've heard stories."

"Never mind the stories. They're normal people, same as us. But it's almost nine, kind of late for a shopping trip, don't you think? Why do you want to go now?"

"We've got to keep moving on this. Matt Holt says the smoke shops on Grand Basin stay open until eleven or midnight."

"Matt Holt?"

"Tammy Holt's brother. And Donna's — the female paramedic they medevac'd to Toronto General's transplant unit. Matt says Tammy was working with tobacco mosaic virus. Right before . . . you know . . ."

He told Zol about Tammy's secret diet-drug project that went haywire. And he shared his theory that the experimental drug, or the engineered virus, must be somehow tied to the liver cases. And the blisters. Winnipeg had said the lip and finger lesions he sent them contained what appeared to be a plant virus hybrid. It was no stretch at all to implicate Tammy's strain of tobacco mosaic virus as having a role in the lesions. They could prove it if they knew exactly what to look for. For that, they'd need specific details about Tammy's research and a comprehensive analysis of rez tobacco.

Zol scratched at his five-o'clock stubble and said nothing. For an awful moment, Hamish pictured his late father pawing at his cheeks and making that same sandpapery sound before flying into one of his rages.

Finally, Zol stopped scratching and said, "Exactly what are you looking for tonight?"

"I won't sleep until I've got a good idea of what rez tobacco actually is. What it looks like. How it's packaged and labelled." The closest he'd ever been to a Native smoke shop was two summers ago when he was driving along the highway near Grand Basin Reserve. He'd been on the way to Lake Erie for a picnic and spotted a cluster of three roadside smoke shacks flying Mohawk flags. He'd wondered briefly what went on in those places, then forgot about them. Until this week.

Zol was muffling the receiver with his palm. And talking to someone. Colleen? Oh no, they must be in bed. With their clothes off? He could feel himself blushing.

"Tell you what," Zol said, after several moments. "I've got to stay home with Max, but Colleen knows the reserve. Sometimes her work takes her there."

"You're kidding."

"You know, misplaced cars? And other, shall we say, lost property?"

"Oh."

"In fact, she was there this morning. Doing a little professional sightseeing. For our side."

"All I want to see is a smoke shop."

"She says meet her in Caledonia. The town, not the university."

"That much I guessed. But where, exactly?"

"The Canadian Tire parking lot. On the main drag. A few blocks south of the Grand River. Think you can you find it?"

"Sure." He hit SEARCH on the dashboard GPS. "When?"

"Half an hour."

"They take Visa?"

Zol scratched his chin again and chuckled loudly into the phone. "Everything but Monopoly money, good buddy. Have at it."

CHAPTER 18

Colleen spotted Hamish standing under a lamppost, polishing the front grill of his beloved Saab with a handkerchief. He looked innocently boyish. His perfect, not overly short, blond flat-top shone like a beacon of wholesomeness in the sharp glare of the Mercury lamplight. She honked lightly and turned into the parking lot. The Canadian Tire store was dark, the shoppers now home and parked in front of their TVs, their DIY resolutions postponed for another day.

Hamish gave his car an anxious backward glance as he climbed into the passenger seat beside her. He was right to worry. This region lamented the highest rate of car thefts in the country. Somehow, vehicles got sucked into Grand Basin Reserve and were never seen again, or they were found as burned-out hulks, the good parts long gone. She'd done surveillance on a couple of the chop shops on the rez; funny how the cops studiously ignored them.

"Thanks for coming," he said. "I was expecting your Mercedes."

She glanced at the anti-theft club at Hamish's feet. "Zol thought his minivan would be less conspicuous."

Hamish forced a half smile that faded quickly. "Not too many Mercs pull up at smoke shacks, eh?"

"Well, not with their rightful owners behind the wheel," she said and killed the radio. She steered onto Argyle Street and headed south. "I think it's extraordinary that you've never set foot on an Indian Reserve. Especially with Grand Basin practically on your doorstep."

He was clearly uncomfortable, and more than the integrity of his vehicle was worrying him. "Wasn't sure how to go about it. Or whether it was even kosher to visit it uninvited."

She felt unsettled too. But that had nothing to do with their shopping trip. "You may be disappointed at how ordinary it is," she told him. "Except for the smoke shops, of course."

"They won't mind us browsing?"

"Why should they? I understand you're armed with your Visa card."

"And the cops?"

"Don't worry, you won't see any of those. The provincial police only venture onto the rez under the most extreme circumstances. And the Native officers on the Grand Basin force know that their presence anywhere near the smoke shops is bad for business."

The Canadian Tire was now a minute behind them. As always at this spot, she was apprehensive. But ready for it.

Right on cue, her right foot lifted away from the accelerator. All by itself. As it did every time she drove along this stretch of the road out of Caledonia. It was a reflex she couldn't control. Her body simply refused to let her whiz past this wretched intersection at high speed. She was compelled to slow down and let the sad story play in her mind like a tragic movie.

"Look," Hamish said, pointing to the flames leaping out of the oil drum that was always there beside the flags. "Are bonfires allowed so close to the highway?"

"Depends on who you talk to."

He braced his right elbow against the door. "Why are you slowing down like this? I don't like the look of those guys."

"They won't hurt us. Not physically, anyway."

Hamish stiffened. "Those are Mohawk flags." He pressed his

arms against his torso, as if trying to make himself invisible. "I know where we are. All that brouhaha with the Natives. What was the name of this place? Something Creek Estates?"

"Dover. Dover Creek." Now the locals called it No Man's Land, or Sovereign Indian Territory. Again, it depended on who you talked to, and on which side of the Great Divide they were born.

There it was, in the darkness beyond the barricade, that desolate expanse of weeds and dirt and heartache at the edge of town. By now, it should have been a pretty bedroom community of single-family homes surrounded by proudly tended gardens. The Canadian parallels with the Apartheid legacies that still troubled her African homeland were nauseating. It seemed humanity's tribalism was a fact of life in every part of the globe. Conflict between Them and Us was hardwired into us all.

Two men, red bandanas hiding their chins, were standing between the flaming oil drum and a solitary pick-up truck. They were warming their hands. They'd parked their battered vehicle sideways across the potholed side road leading to the site. Did they realize how strange they looked defending a short dirt drive to absolutely nowhere?

"Do they man that barricade 24-7?" Hamish asked.

"Don't know why they bother. No one's going to take back the land from them now. The place is tainted with too much bad blood."

Six years ago, a developer had bought the acreage from a White farmer, apparently in good faith on both sides. Shortly after the developer erected his first couple of houses, a modern-day Mohawk war party seized the site at gunpoint and claimed the land as Indian territory. They cited a three-hundred-year-old treaty, which the federal government claimed was bogus and not worthy of a millisecond of discussion. With the feds officially ignoring the situation, and the provincial government too timid to send in its crackerjack Ontario Provincial Police, the Natives retained control of the land. No Native was arrested, though many taunted the police by openly committing assaults, weapons offences, property damage, and dangerous driving. Tempers flared, animosity smouldered into hatred, and heated clashes erupted between the Mohawks and Caledonia's townspeople. Finally, the provincial government bought out the developer, but made no attempt to extricate the Indians from the land. And though the Mohawks had made a big show of claiming the few acres as their "sovereign territory," they'd done nothing with it in six years. They just kept guarding their sad and useless trophy. Day and night.

What bothered Colleen about the Dover Creek situation, and the chop shops on the rez, was the failure of the rule of law. Two levels of government stood idly by while a gang from Grand Basin Reserve behaved as they pleased and lived above the law. As a Native, you could try to seize your neighbour's farm in a trumped-up land claim, steal his car for parts, and sell cheap cigarettes to his kids. Not the image that Canada liked to project of itself on the world stage.

She felt a shudder pass through her shoulders as the oil drum faded from view and her foot pressed itself back onto the accelerator. The car regained highway speed, and a few minutes later she turned right onto Side Road 4, where a faded tin sign said GRAND BASIN INDIAN RESERVE.

"And there they are," she said, after they'd driven two hundred metres along the side road and into the rez. "The pride and joy of modern Native culture."

"And so many?" Hamish pointed through the windscreen and counted the smoke shops under his breath. "Five, six, seven. Practically on top of each other."

"Conveniently located for the smokers of Hamilton, Hagersville, Jarvis, and Caledonia."

Smoke shops crowded the rez's northern and western entrances as well, providing ready access for the good people of Brantford, Waterford, Simcoe, Woodstock, and the four adjacent counties of farm country. Most sovereign nations posted border guards at their frontiers and checked your passport. Canada's First Nations posted tobacco sellers and eagerly swiped your credit card.

"Funny little buildings, eh?" Hamish said. He pointed at a beaten-up camping trailer that barely qualified as a shack, and a tiny but respectable shop made from a corrugated steel shipping container, the kind carried on cargo ships around the world. In Africa, she'd seen those abandoned containers strewn all over the place, housing everything from health centres to drinking dens. This one was painted bright pink and called itself Aunt Minnie's Tiny Smoke Shop.

"Don't need a fancy place to sell smokes," she told him. "A few shelves, some overhead lighting, and a credit card machine."

She drove twenty metres beyond Aunt Minnie's and pulled up at Smoke Depot, a shop that had caught her eye on other trips to the rez. Constructed of two mobile homes side by side, it had white siding and fuchsia trim, and usually a seasonal decoration at the front door. Tonight it was a jack-o'-lantern carved from a large orange pumpkin. Real, not plastic. And as always, three flags were flapping on the same pole: the Stars and Stripes, the Maple Leaf, and the Iroquois Confederacy. Though she'd never been inside, the place looked about average size for a smoke shop, orderly, and most importantly at this hour, well lit.

"We stopping here?" Hamish asked, looking more anxious than ever.

"As good a place as any. I imagine they'll have a full selection of what you're looking for."

"I guess," he said, glancing around suspiciously. He still looked worried about the cops.

"Cold feet?"

"'Course not. It's just that . . . well . . . I've always been such a rule follower."

She couldn't help cracking a smile. "You won't get caught, Hamish. And you shan't go to jail, even if you do."

He rolled his eyes. "Gee, thanks."

She opened her door and climbed out of the minivan. Hamish hesitated and looked pointedly at the anti-theft club still on the floor.

She waved her hand dismissively. "The car is safe here. These are good, savvy business people. They don't steal from their customers. And look at the flags. This establishment promotes harmony."

She led him inside and said hello to the two young Natives watching TV behind the counter. The boy — he didn't look older than sixteen but he could have been twenty — flicked her an indifferent glance and went back to his show. A smile seemed to come naturally to the large round face of the girl standing beside him. She waved and said, "Lemme know if yous need any help."

Hamish scuttled to the far end of the trailer, out of earshot of the teens. In the process, he had to dodge the heavily loaded displays of potato chips, corn chips, candy bars, pork jerky, and Mexican salsa that crowded the front third of the store.

"This is incredible," he whispered, gawking at shelf after shelf piled with brightly coloured cigarette cartons. He swept the room with his gaze and relaxed a little, apparently relieved there were no other customers in the shop.

They browsed together for a couple of minutes. Most of the cigarettes came from the same manufacturer, similar in style to the empty Hat-Trick packs she'd found behind Erie Christian Collegiate. They came as twenty-five cigarettes to the pack, two hundred to the carton, as Lights, Kings, Golds, and Menthols.

Hamish glanced at the kids to make sure they weren't watching him from their counter, then picked up a clear, resealable plastic bag stuffed with neat rows of individual cigarettes. "These are Rollies, eh? And look at the price. Only ten dollars. For two hundred? This many cigarettes should cost at least seventy or eighty bucks."

She spotted a discount table piled with more bags of Rollies. At first glance, they looked like all the others. "Look, these are seven bucks for two hundred."

"Only seven?"

"The little notice says they're seconds. Rejects, I suppose." She loved the irony of some cigarettes failing the grade, being somehow worse than others. She lifted one of the bags, and together they examined it closely. "I'd say these don't look quite as neatly rolled as those in the ten-dollar bags." Some of the cigarettes were bent, others a bit crushed. But still readily smokeable.

Hamish raised his eyebrows, then turned to another table and picked up a carton that was a different shape from the most of the others. It was long and narrow. "These look different. Got a different name. Trackers. Reminds them of the old days, I guess. Pre-contact."

"American-style," she told him. "See — narrower packs of twenty instead of twenty-five. Still two-hundred smokes to the carton. And have a read of what it says."

He nodded and found the message printed on the side of each pack. "SURGEON GENERAL'S WARNING: QUITTING SMOKING NOW GREATLY REDUCES SERIOUS RISKS TO YOUR HEALTH."

After studying the warning, he turned the carton over several times and scanned every surface. His frown deepened. "There's no French on here anywhere. And we don't have a Surgeon General. That's an American designation. These are totally illegal."

"That is the point, Hamish." She spread her arms and did a half turn. "Everything about this place is illegal. Even the snacks, which they sell without collecting sales tax. What you are holding are either American cigarettes smuggled in from the U.S., or a product made right here on Grand Basin and made to simulate American smokes. Probably the latter. A lot easier and more profitable — no border guards or middlemen."

Hamish cocked his head toward the teens, who were now munching from giant bags of chips and clearly absorbed in their TV show. "Those kids are too young to be working here."

"Ya think?"

"And in Ontario, cigarettes aren't allowed to be displayed for sale on open shelves. Or sold to minors. Or sold without a Health Canada warning in both official languages. Or sold free of all kinds of federal and provincial duties and taxes."

"You've been doing your homework."

He looked pleased with himself, then handed her the Trackers and examined a professionally shrink-wrapped eight-pack carton of Hat-Tricks. "This one has a bilingual warning from Health Canada. And a thing like a postage stamp that says Duty Paid Canada Droit Acquitté. Are they legit?"

"Zol says they're semi-legit. The result of a deal between the manufacturer — that's Dennis Badger who lives and operates here on the rez — and the federal government." She explained how Zol had told her that Badger's company, Watershed Holdings, was allowed to sell his excise-duty-paid Hat-Trick brand to Natives on reserves anywhere in the country without charging them extra taxes. And to export them overseas. And to sell them to non-Natives who were willing to pay the additional taxes.

Hamish voiced the obvious conclusion. "But no one collects those taxes from non-Natives,"

"Of course not."

"What would they total, those missing taxes?"

"In Ontario, about fifty dollars a carton. Closer to seventy in some other provinces."

"No wonder Dennis Badger does such a booming business." He held up the Hat-Trick carton and looked for the price tag. "So, how much are these anyway?"

"Thirty dollars."

"For two hundred cigarettes? Still a good deal. One third the normal price."

"These American-style Trackers are a few dollars cheaper still, because they don't have the Canadian federal excise tax on them." She turned the carton over several times. "See . . . no stamp on this one anywhere."

The girl up at the cash had finished her chips and was scrunching her empty bag. She threw Colleen a puzzled look, as if wondering why this well-dressed White couple was spending so much time deciding which cigarettes to buy.

She touched Hamish's arm. "I think we should go soon. Have you decided? Which of these shall we take with us?"

Hamish looked flustered, like a boy who couldn't make up his mind at an ice cream counter. "We know the kids at Erie Collegiate smoke Rollies almost exclusively," he said. "We better get a couple bags of those. And . . . and the firefighters smoke mostly Hat-Tricks."

"Kings, Golds, Lights, or Menthols?"

"Did anyone think to ask?"

"Better take one of each," she suggested. "And a carton of Trackers. In case some of them like the American-style brand."

"And a bag of the seven-dollar reject Rollies. They could be the whole problem if they're in some way substandard or made of bad tobacco. Do you suppose Erie Collegiate kids smoke the rejects?"

"I can't see the firefighters putting up with them. Not when the other cigarettes are such a bargain."

"Still, I think I'll get two bags of the rejects. That's, um . . . five cartons and four bags. Sound about right?"

She told him that sounded fine and helped him load them into the shopping cart.

Halfway to the front counter, Hamish stopped dead. Pearls of sweat had broken out across his forehead. "Those kids will know we're up to something," he whispered. His tone bordered on frantic. "No one ever buys this many cigarettes at a time. They're going to rat on us, for sure."

"You kidding? I understand the average order is twelve cartons per person. Between the two of us, we've got less than half that."

"Really?"

"Zol says don't forget to keep the receipt."

"Yeah, sure. Like the health unit is going to reimburse me the cost of almost two thousand contraband cigarettes."

CHAPTER 19

Zol put down his book and glanced at the bedside clock. Ten-thirty. Colleen would be back any minute. It shouldn't take her long to nip over to the rez and buy a few smokes. Of course, it would be Hamish's luck to be caught in a rare OPP blitz against contraband tobacco leaving the rez. Or would he escort Colleen back to his lab for a longwinded lecture on plant viruses? Either way, Colleen should be home soon or checking in on her mobile.

The floor outside the bedroom door creaked under tentative footsteps as an approaching shadow crept across the carpet. "Dad?"

"Max? Something wrong?"

"I can't sleep." Max took one step into the bedroom and stopped, his hands at his sides. Standing there in his Star Pirates pyjamas, he looked vulnerable. And worried. Not frightened or angry, but anxious. His face showed the same concerned expression as the other evening when Zol had stupidly blown him off.

Zol tapped the duvet beside him. "Come sit with me. Tell me a story. That might make you sleepy."

Max marched into the room and crawled onto the bed. He didn't burrow down and he didn't want to snuggle. He sat cross-legged on top of the duvet at the foot of the bed, his hands on his knees, his face set for business. He opened his mouth, but nothing came out. He tried again. Not a word. He bit his lower lip and gazed at his toes.

What was he being shy about? He was never shy. Art Greenwood, Max's great-grandfather, a polished gentleman himself, said the boy was the most serenely confident youngster he'd ever encountered. Of course Art was biased, but a good judge of character all the same.

Was this about the facts of life? Was Zol going to have the birds-and-bees talk with his ten-year-old son at ten-thirty on a Thursday night, ten days before Halloween? Why not? The parenting magazines said you were supposed to talk to your kids about love and sex when they gave you the entrée. It wasn't like the old days when Zol had learned most of it at the hockey arena from the grossly misinformed older boys. But surely Max was already a man of the world when it came to sexual plumbing. They'd covered it in health class last year, and he'd come home with a number of matter-of-fact questions that Zol had done his best to answer. On the other hand, romantic love was a complicated topic. Max would have plenty of questions about that for decades to come. Hell, Zol certainly did.

"Maybe I should start, then," Zol said. He closed his book and tossed it onto the bedside table. "When your mother and I decided it was time —"

"Really, Dad? You mean it?" said Max. His eyes were as wide as hockey pucks. "Francine can come for a sleepover when she comes for her conference in Toronto?"

"What? Max? How? I mean . . ." He had no idea how to start this conversation.

"Can she, Dad?" Max had his hands together. He was praying, for God's sake. Where had he learned that? "Please, please, please?"

Zol wiped the sweat from the back of his neck and took a deep breath. He patted the bedclothes beside him and said, "Come and sit here. I need you right next to me."

Max leapt over the covers and snuggled close. "She says she can come for two days and one night. Isn't that great?"

"How . . . ? How do you know about her conference?"

"She told me."

"Francine phoned you? Told you she was coming to Toronto?"

"She lives in Cambodia, Dad. And her name isn't Francine any-more, it's Soksang. It means peace. And she doesn't have a phone. Her religion doesn't believe in them. Isn't that cool?" He jumped off the bed and raced out of the room. "Be right back."

In a flash, he returned with a heavy book under his arm. He pounced into Zol's lap and in the process nearly bashed him in the balls with the National Geographic atlas. "Hey, careful with those, bud. A guy only gets one set, you know. They have to last a lifetime."

Oblivious to anything but the atlas that Art Greenwood had given him last Christmas, Max turned to a page he'd flagged with a bookmark. A detailed map of Indochina: Vietnam, Laos, Thailand, and Cambodia. He pointed to a smudge roughly in the middle of Cambodia. Chocolatey fingers had been here before. "That's where she lives. Siem Reap. It's near a big lake."

"How do you know that?" Zol didn't even know where she lived. All he knew was that her last phone call had come from Cambodia and that she'd changed religions.

"She doesn't believe in normal clothes or hair that you have to brush and comb. She loves being bald."

"I thought you said she doesn't have a phone."

"She doesn't."

"How do you talk to her, then?"

"We write."

He had to process this. His ten-year-old son, who to his knowl-edge had never spoken to his mother since she stormed out of the house when he was an infant, was now communicating with her across the world? Email and the Internet made almost anything possible. But this was a total shock. How long had it been going on? And why didn't he know about it?

"Francine . . . um, your mother . . . has access to a computer?"

"She doesn't believe in them."

"No?" It seemed Francine didn't believe in a lot of things. "So how do you communicate?"

Again, Max jumped off the bed and ran to his room. Zol heard doors banging and things clunking on the floor. This time, Max padded back with a shoebox. He was holding it reverently in front of him with both hands, like a communion chalice.

He climbed back onto the bed, assumed the Buddha position, and held the box in his lap. His left hand, though spastic from birth, had been given the job of guarding the lid. His right index finger wiggled high in the air as he enquired, "Are your hands clean, Dad? These are very special." He had Hamish down to a tee.

"Um . . . yes, I think so."

"Lemme see."

He showed Max his hands, front and back.

Max shook his head. "Sorry. Not good enough. Soap and warm water, please. And dry them properly." Like father, like son. That hand cleanliness thing had actually stuck. Who knew?

Zol set his jaw to maintain an earnest face he hoped matched Max's and washed his hands in the ensuite bathroom. He made a modest show of drying them thoroughly, taking care not to overdo it. There was no way he was going to trivialize this delicate moment by mocking his son.

Max nodded his approval of the hand washing and invited Zol to sit beside him. He opened the box, no more than a crack, and stole a peek inside as if to be certain the precious contents were still in prime condition. And then he removed the lid, cradled the box in his lap, and beamed with pride.

Zol sniffed the air. He half-expected to see a furry pet jump onto the bed and scurry under the duvet. A gerbil or a white rat. But there was no smell of wood chips. No urine or feces. Had Max been collecting beetles or butterflies on the sly all summer? No, Francine hated bugs of any kind; he wouldn't be collecting them for her. And there was none of that earthy smell insects carried with them. Just the faintest smell of lavender.

"May I have a look?" Zol asked.

"Yes, but don't touch yet. You have to hold them in a special way. I'll show you first."

Zol directed the reading lamp into the shoebox for a better view. The box was almost half full of picture postcards, all about equal size, but varying in style, subject, and quality. It took Zol a moment to realize what they were. Max had stacked them into four groups, image side up, and now he reached in with his favoured right hand and gingerly lifted one by the edge. He clamped his tongue between his teeth as he concentrated.

"Hold it like that, Dad, okay?" he said, handing the card to Zol without touching the glossy surface.

"I got it," Zol said, and followed Max's instructions. In his hand was an elaborate stone temple surrounded by lush jungle. The place looked like somewhere famous he should recognize. He didn't have to look far for the answer. It was written in bold blue letters in the bottom right corner: Angkor Wat Temple.

"May I read it?"

"Yep. Turn it over. That one's got a wicked stamp. And my name and everything. It's from . . . you'll see."

CHAPTER 20

Hamish placed the three shopping bags of contraband into the back of the minivan. Before he'd stepped out of the smoke shop, he'd got Colleen to check there were no cop cars hanging around. Now he stood back. No good. Anyone could see the bags from the outside of the vehicle and guess what they contained. What if Colleen got dinged for speeding, or they ran into one of those clampdowns on drunk driving where the cops stop every car and gawk inside? The OPP would find all those smokes, for sure.

He spotted a greasy blanket and a pair of booster cables in the pile of crap Zol always kept in his vehicle. This thing hadn't seen a carwash in a year. And the rear licence plate was missing. Granted, this was only a minivan, but Zol should be more respectful of his vehicle.

Hamish placed the blanket over the bags and secured it with the cables. He stood back again and looked at his handiwork. It would do.

"What are you doing, Hamish?" Colleen called from the driver's seat. "Sampling the merchandise? I thought you were hungry."

He closed the cargo door and climbed in beside her. "I am starved. How did you know?"

She started the engine and made a three-point turn. "Remember, I observe people for a living too."

"Come on, how did you know? Lucky guess?"

"Does your stomach always growl as loudly as it has for the past half-hour?"

"Touché. I haven't eaten all day. What I wouldn't give for a pizza. Bacon, mushroom, and green pepper."

"I know just the spot."

She threw the minivan into Drive and turned left. Right would have taken them back to the highway.

He didn't like the look of this. There were no street lights, the moon was barely a sliver, and she was heading deeper into the rez. "Hey. Where're we going? Let's get out of here. Forget the pizza."

"This is the safest place in the world for your contraband. You can be certain no one on the rez will look at it twice. Especially not the members of the Grand Basin Police."

His stomach betrayed him by growling again.

Colleen threw him an understanding smile. She looked like Cameron Diaz in a ponytail, and had a way of making you feel that everything would be fine no matter what. Zol was a lucky guy. Max too. But what was Zol waiting for? He should have proposed to her by now. Maybe he had, and they were keeping it quiet.

"Iroquois Pizza is only a few minutes up the road," she told him. "In the heart of the village."

"It better be worth it."

"No worries there. I've had their pizza during a couple of all-night stake-outs."

"Do I want to know the gory details?"

"I wouldn't tell you anyway."

Ten minutes later, they left the dark, semi-wooded country-side and entered the village of Grand Basin, a crossroads of low-wattage street lamps lighting an assortment of two-storey buildings arranged in strip malls. There'd been no attempt to coordinate the architecture or the paint jobs, and nothing looked particularly new or prosperous.

They passed a mobile home with a sign out front that said GRAND BASIN WELFARE AND INNOVATIONS OFFICE. Colleen turned right into the strip mall beyond it. She parked directly in front of Iroquois Pizza, the only place along this stretch with the lights on. It was a small takeout joint, flanked by the Ancestral Voices Healing Centre on one side and Grand Basin Counselling Services on the other. A large sign in front of the counselling place listed a sad but impressive array of services available: men's addiction program, women's addiction program, domestic violence advocacy, sexual assault counselling, emergency shelter.

They got out of the vehicle and Hamish looked around. Across the street, beyond a parking lot that looked like it should have been repaved a decade ago, stood a long, boxy building that had been probably thrown up by a government agency. It housed the Taking Care of Our Own Social Services Centre, the Grand Basin Housing Centre, the First Nations Nursing Clinic, and the Free Legal Clinic. Down the road about a hundred metres, a well-lit sign marked the entrance to Healing Hands Dialysis Centre and Nursing Home. It seemed the small population living here required a lot of support. The reasons behind that would fill an encyclopedia.

They ordered a large bacon pizza to go and waited at one of two tables across from the counter. A grizzled guy with one milky eye turned blindly outward was sitting — and swaying — at the other table, muttering to himself. His good eye oscillated between the half-empty bottle of Coke and the pack of Hat-Tricks in front of him. He didn't touch either, just kept fidgeting with the disposable lighter in his fist. The two cooks behind the counter paid the man no attention. Did he ever order a pizza, or did he simply come in here to get out of the cold when they tossed him out of the shelter?

Hamish was so famished that the smell of roasted garlic and freshly baked pizza dough was driving him crazy. Colleen raised her eyebrows each time his stomach growled, but they didn't talk. They were outsiders here, and both knew that at times like this you held your tongue and waited patiently for your pizza.

Finally, it was ready. As he paid the bill, he noticed that the amount owing was $10.99, exactly what the sign on the counter said it would be. Anywhere else, there would have been an additional dollar and a half in unadvertised taxes courtesy of two levels of government.

They each ate a slice at the table, then Colleen suggested they bring the rest to the car. It seemed Zol wouldn't mind if they added to the patina of food already adorning the minivan's upholstery.

Outside, two heavyset guys in their twenties were leaning against a Silverado, waiting for them. Hamish stiffened. He held the pizza box in front of his chest. He knew it looked lame and was useless as a shield or a weapon. Still, he found himself holding it like a lifebuoy. He glanced at Colleen. He would take his cue from her. She'd know whether these guys were thugs, undercover cops, or a couple of nice fellows asking for . . . for what?

Directions?

No, they looked like locals, and when the shorter guy spoke it was clear he was from the reserve. "Hey," he said, looking up at the tiny moon and the cloudless sky. "Nice night, eh?"

"Certainly is," said Colleen. "What do you think, will we get some frost before Halloween?"

Both men looked her up and down, then glanced at each other as a glint of recognition — and appreciation — lit their deep-set eyes. Wouldn't they love to have their way with Cameron Diaz. Hamish's pulse shot up twenty-five points as he spread his feet and held his ground.

The shorter guy turned to him. "Did yous spend all your money in there?"

"Um . . . no. Just picked up a pizza. Bacon and mushroom." He waved the pizza box to indicate what he was talking about. Then felt foolish again.

Colleen gave him a look, as if he'd said the wrong thing. But it was too late. He couldn't take it back. Now these thugs knew he still had cash in his pocket. But would they actually rob him on the brightly lit sidewalk in front of a wide-open pizza place?

"Thought yous might be interested in a deal, that's all," said the shorter guy. He had thick spiky hair cut by an amateur into a modern version of a Mohawk. And an eagle tattoo on the side of his neck.

Colleen stepped in close beside Hamish. "Don't think so," she said.

"It's just that we got this TV. Belongs to a buddy a' ours, eh? He don't want it no more and it's practically brand new."

"Yeah," said the other man. "It's a forty-inch. Flat screen. HD 'n' everything."

"Yours for two-fifty." The shorter guy jerked his thumb toward the Silverado. "Got it right here. Only take a sec to load it from the truck to your minivan."

"No thanks," Hamish said, the pizza box growing increasingly hot in his hands. The cloying smell of bacon was now nauseating. "I don't have that much cash."

"That's okay," said the first guy. He took a step forward and nodded toward the pizza place. "They got a ATM in there. Always lotsa cash inside it. How 'bout an even two hundred?"

Hamish exchanged glances with Colleen. She gave him a look that said he should walk to the car *now* and get in. "Thanks, anyway," he said, relieved to hear the door locks clunk open in response to her key fob.

They hopped in, and she locked the doors. She made another of her three-point turns, but instead of turning east toward the city on Side Road 4, she turned west.

His heart rate jumped another ten points. "Where are we going now?"

"Eat your pizza. You'll feel better. And ready for one final adventure before I drop you back at Canadian Tire."

Ten minutes later, they were well out in the countryside, but still on the rez. He hadn't seen a smoke shop since they'd left the village. He placed the pizza box at his feet. He couldn't face the last two slices. He'd had his fill of greasy bacon.

He wiped his hands on a paper serviette and tossed it into the box. "Okay, so I've had my supper. Now will you tell me where we're going?"

"Up here on the left. But I'll turn right and we can have a look at the operation from there."

"What do you mean?"

"I found this place this morning when I was doing my reconnaissance. It must be a Rollies factory. I saw four Asian men pull out in an S-Class sedan. Dark suits."

"How do you know it's not one of Badger's operations?"

"His place is two roads over. Same sort of shiny new buildings with no windows. But much bigger. At least half a dozen eighteen-wheeler lorries parked in the lot. And a helicopter pad to the side."

"Dennis Badger has a private helicopter?"

"And a business jet parked at Hamilton Airport. He keeps one of those narrow, extraordinarily fast speedboats on Lake Erie."

"A cigarette boat?"

She shrugged. "I guess that's fitting."

"I used to love watching them race off Toronto Island when I was a kid. They make a heck of a lot of noise."

"Seems he's not afraid to advertise his money, or his business. He's posted a large Watershed Holdings sign on the front gate of his Hat-Trick factory, next to the Restricted Entry warning. The Rollies people are more subtle."

As he was coming to understand it, the Rollies guys made no pretence of being anything but outlaws. There'd be no sign in front of their operations. But probably as much security, maybe more.

"I don't like this, Colleen. We shouldn't be skulking around a criminal operation in the dark."

"I do it all the time."

Yes, well.

"But don't worry," she insisted. "We won't get overly close."

"Come on. Please. Let's go home before we get shot at."

She slowed down and turned right onto a gravel road opposite an impressive compound surrounded by a ten-foot barbed-wire fence. If the owners were looking for privacy, they'd chosen the right spot. The woods closed in on three sides. Behind the fence stretched two long, windowless buildings clad in metal siding. Halogen security lamps had been fastened to the eaves at regular intervals. It looked new, professional, secure, and forbidding.

"Okay," he told her, "I get the idea. We can go now."

She ignored him and continued along the gravel road, putting them at right angles to the compound. After two hundred metres or so, she stopped and killed the ignition, and then the lights.

"We sit here for a moment, while our eyes adapt to the dark. Then we use this." She pulled an expensive-looking device from the console beside her. It looked like a pair of binoculars, but with more bells and whistles.

"What if they see us?"

"They won't. Look at those ash trees. They make a nice distraction. We shall be able to see all we need through the rear windscreen. Thank you for polishing it, by the way."

"Force of habit."

She unfastened her seatbelt, then knelt on her seat and faced backward. She activated the binoculars, held them up to her face, then peered through them out the rear window.

For the longest time she said nothing as she scanned back and forth.

"Anything happening?" he asked, wishing she'd hurry up and they could go home.

"Extraordinary. This was certainly the time to come. These punters are nocturnal." She passed him the binoculars, quickly explained the infrared mechanism, and showed him what to do.

It took him a while to get the hang of aiming the binoculars and looking at the night-vision screen, but once he did, the pizza turned to stone in his stomach.

CHAPTER 21

It was about midnight when Zol heard the garage door lumbering on its track below him. It made a hell of a noise here in the bedroom. Maybe you were supposed to grease the bearings from time to time. Or replace them? Dad would know. Before Mum got so sick, all it took was the hint of a home maintenance question and Dad would be over, his truck loaded with tools and his head full of know-how. Funny how you expected so many things in life to stay exactly the same. But they never did, so why would you expect it? Like Max and Francine. Who'd have predicted they'd reconnect and carry on a lively correspondence via snail mail?

He turned on his bedside lamp as Colleen ran up the stairs. When she pushed through the doorway, he could see she was flushed in a way that only guns, death, and sex could provoke in her.

She dropped her purse on the floor and tossed his keys on the dresser. "It's worse than we thought," she said, her tone breathless.

"What happened?" Those smoke shops were pretty tacky. "Did Hamish balk at the decor? Don't tell me he embarrassed you by giving them pointers on cleanliness and pest control?"

She tossed her ponytail over her shoulder and kicked off her shoes. "He purchased his smokes, no problem. Two thousand of them."

"What's he going to do with them? He doesn't have a clue what to test them for." Until they had concrete information about the murdered woman's research project, any scrutiny of rez tobacco would be a stab in the dark.

"We did some sightseeing after the smoke shop." She removed one earring, then the other, and placed them on the dresser.

"On the rez? In the dark? Hamish would have been thrilled with that."

"Oneida Road. A Rollies factory." She described the forbidding compound in detail.

"Did they see you? Rough you up?"

"I was discreet. We stayed well back and . . . hey, don't look so worried. I removed your number plates before I set off."

"There were guns, weren't there?"

"Two armed guards. Maybe a third guy by the gate. It was difficult to be sure."

"Guarding what?"

"Forklifts. Loading a fleet of cube vans. All white and unmarked."

"Could you see any of the cargo?"

"Cardboard boxes. Quite light, by the way the punters were tossing them into the vans."

Sounded like Rollies in their flimsy packaging. "I see what you mean, it's a bigger operation than we thought."

She shook her head and the flush drained from her cheeks. "That's not what I meant."

"A fleet of cube vans loaded with smokes, all in one night? Sounds to me like they're servicing quite the network of off-rez sellers."

She dropped her clothes on the floor, revealing the last of the bikini tan that looked so hot on her. She grabbed his navy bathrobe from the closet and threw it on. There was something particularly sexy about a petite woman in a man's robe.

"It's the AK-47s that have me worried," she said. "Both guards were packing them." She pulled the tie around her waist and knotted it with a sharp tug. "Look, Zol, I know you have to do the right thing by your liver epidemic, but this is a major criminal operation. When one of the guys with the AK-47s picked up his night-vision binocs and aimed them at us, I suddenly felt like an amateur."

Ten minutes later she stepped out of the shower looking one hundred percent delectable. But, given the look he'd seen on her face when she described being sighted by organized criminals packing AK-47s, he figured she'd be in the mood for no more than a reassuring cuddle. But no, as she slid in beside him she made it clear that his task was to dispel her thoughts of guns and gangs. Completely.

He was happy to oblige, accompanied at first by Marvin banging out a few bars of "I Heard It Through the Grapevine" to the alluring scent of bergamot on her skin.

And now, with her head nestled on his chest, and her left hand stroking that scar on his right shoulder, she said, "Okay. I unloaded my latest on you. Tell me about yours. What happened while I was out with Hamish?"

"How do you —"

"Your breathing. It gets that little hiccup when you're doing one thing and thinking of another."

Shit. He'd failed when it counted most. Made her feel second fiddle when she deserved to be treated like . . . well, like the woman of his dreams. "I'm sorry, sweets. Was it that bad?"

"Not in the least. It was wonderful. Exactly what I needed." She lifted her chin and gave him a reassuring kiss on the lips. "Now, who called?" Her eyes widened. "Oh, heavens, I'm so sorry. How thoughtless of me. Is it your mum?"

"Yes and no. But not what you think."

He told her the story of Max's shoebox of postcards, mailed one-by-one from Cambodia starting eight months ago. The first had been addressed simply to Max Szabo, care of Kitti Szabo, Scotland, Ontario, Canada. No street address or rural route. The message was simple:

Dear Max, I think of you every day and hope you are happy, healthy, and learning forgiveness and compassion from your loving father. If this card reaches you, please write back with your proper address and tell me about your friends, your hobbies, and your dreams. Your loving mother.

Either Max or Kitti, must have answered that first card. Three weeks later, Francine sent a second card, this one to Max at the farm's full address on Jenkins Road, including the postal code. According to Max, his grandma thought it was natural that his mother wanted to write to him. And wasn't he lucky to be receiving wicked stamps and pictures from so far away.

It seemed Kitti had agreed to be the go-between. She'd reviewed the mechanics of snail mail with Max and encouraged him to send a reply each time a card arrived. It was Max's idea to keep them in the shoebox. And apparently Kitti's to keep the correspondence from Zol.

When had they been planning to tell him? Time was running out for Mum. She'd made her peace with the black-eyed loon, but was she afraid there could never be peace with Francine if Zol got in the way? Mum had never thought Zol had done enough to make his marriage work. For a few minutes last night, he'd burned with resentment over his mother's secrecy, but the pride on Max's face told him to let it go.

"What's a lost art, Dad?" Max had asked. Zol had chuckled and held Max close. Though Kitti Szabo could acknowledge that the Internet made itself indispensable — especially for organizing her Catholic Women's League events — she insisted email was for business purposes only. Well-mannered ladies and gentlemen sent handwritten cards and letters to their friends and loved ones.

"And now," Zol told Colleen, "he wants Francine to come for a sleepover."

"That's very sweet. When?"

"A week tomorrow." He told her about Francine's phone call and her plan to attend some sort of Buddhist retreat thing in Toronto next week.

"Not much notice, but that doesn't matter. She has to come."

"You think it's a good idea?"

She pushed herself off his chest and held his gaze. "It's the *only* idea. Francine is Max's mother. No matter what happened in the past, no matter how poorly she took to mothering him as an infant, she's an essential part of his life. And it took guts to make the first move."

"You don't mind if she stays here, in my guest room?"

"Of course not. I'll make myself scarce."

"I don't want her chasing you away. Please stay."

"We'll see, Zol. It might be better for Max if I'm not here." Her eyes danced with a cheeky smile. "You don't want him caught in the middle of two women competing for his attentions," she laughed, pinching his belly, "like his kind and compassionate dad."

CHAPTER 22

Zol took two swallows of the Detour's finest Guatemalan blend, his second coffee of the morning, then proofread the email a second time. He indulged himself in an epic sigh and pressed Send. Allie would make sure that Francine received the invitation, in which he'd given her a choice of Friday or Saturday night next week. He hoped she'd pick Saturday for the sleepover. Zol was always exhausted on Friday nights, especially with all this driving back and forth to Simcoe and watching out for deer. How did people commute like this for decades at a time?

Today's *Simcoe Reformer* lay on his desk. The front page was reporting that though the "mystery liver plague count" was holding at twelve, the number of deaths had risen from two to three. A twenty-year veteran of the Simcoe fire brigade had died late yesterday in the liver unit at Toronto General Hospital.

The paper didn't mention it, but two other victims were sitting atop the transplant list: Donna Holt and an Erie Christian Collegiate cheerleader.

According to the *Reformer's* city desk, the regional council passed a resolution late last night expressing its extreme concern for the safety of the citizens of Norfolk County. Reeve Jed Conroy was quoted as urging everyone to remain calm while the Health Department sorted out this terrifying epidemic.

Great. Comforting words from the rational souls who controlled Zol's budget and doled out his salary.

Nancy buzzed from her post in the outer office. She had Jed Conroy on the line. Speak of the devil. Anywhere else, he'd be called the mayor, but here in Norfolk County he was known as the Reeve, which people around here seemed to think meant the Revered.

"Dr. Szabo," barked Conroy. "I got a call from Grant Dyment the fire chief first thing this morning. He's findin' it damn near impossible to cover his shifts at the fire station. Three more of his guys called in sick today. One of them thinks he's down with the yellow jaundice thing. But who knows? Maybe they're all of them incubating this plague and it's gonna show up for real on them tomorrow."

Conroy had switched from the e-word to the p-word. The man had read his *Reformer* — or at least the headlines — and seemed in no mood to be either gracious or logical.

Zol was careful with his tone. He knew he had a thing about politicians and could not afford to show it in his voice. He'd strive for equanimity. "I'll call the chief and arrange to have his men checked out in Emerg without delay, sir."

"All I'm sayin' is you gotta get to the bottom of this before we lose our fire service. Because, as I said earlier today to the *Reformer*, I'm afraid our Norfolk County Detachment of the provincial police will be next." There was a pause, and Zol could hear the reeve dragging on a cigarette. After a short cough and another quick drag, he said, "You got somethin' new to report?"

"Well . . . as a matter of fact, sir . . . yes."

How much should he tell Conroy? Nothing of substance, he decided. Not when the reeve and his council indulged in the propagation of inflammatory resolutions.

"We do have an important lead," Zol ventured.

"Tell me about it."

"I'm afraid it's too soon to say."

"Come now, man. It's about time you guys got this problem out in the open. I won't have any secrets on my watch."

"We're getting there, but the situation is rather delicate. I wouldn't want to be premature in my comments."

"Delicate, eh? I hear you've got it in for our First Nations brethren."

"Mr. Conroy, I don't have it in for anyone."

"Didn't Elliott York pass on my warning about venturin' into tiger territory? You better speak to that hotshot specialist friend o' yours from Hamilton. You know, the blond fellow who's a little light on his loafers."

"Sir?"

"My sources tell me he's been sniffin' around, trying to pin this liver business on Native tobacco. The idea is ridiculous."

How had such a boor managed to get himself re-elected so many times?

Dumb question.

But had Hamish actually said anything about Native tobacco and the liver epidemic? Nothing quotable, Zol was sure of that. It was too early in the investigation; Hamish's pride made him guard his opinions until he was certain he had all his germs in a row. Somehow, Hamish's tête-à-tête with the Holts had been shared with a neighbour, then broadcast via the Grand Basin grapevine.

The real puzzle was how Native gossip had arrived so quickly at Conroy's ears. It was only last evening that Hamish had interviewed the Holts and learned something of Tammy's tobacco virus project.

Conroy swore under his breath and coughed heavily from lungs long steeped in death smoke. His two-pack-a-day habit was common knowledge. As was his contempt for provincial legislation that now kept him from smoking inside any building except his own home.

"Dammit," Conway said, once he finally finished coughing. "When will you guys give the tobacco industry a break? You know how important tobacco has always been to our local economy."

Zol knew from his dad that Conroy was tight with the local growers and counted on their support at election time. And though a property developer himself, Conroy had remained absolutely silent on the debacle over Dover Creeks Estates. Dad said that Conroy was terrified that any of his numerous properties in Norfolk County could be the object of the next Mohawk land grab. Did the reeve have informants stationed deep in the rez?

The call ended with Conroy telling Zol to get the damned lead out, leaving Zol pondering his cold and lifeless coffee.

Conroy was right, of course. This liver thing wasn't going to stop at Erie Christian Collegiate and the Simcoe Fire Service. Police officers, teachers, bus drivers, power plant workers — any of them could be next.

Nancy slipped in with a message. Dr. Hitchin had called from Simcoe Emerg while Zol was on the other line. A school principal had arrived in Emerg this morning — weak, delirious, and jaundiced. His name — Walter Vorst.

Zol put his head in his hands. Was this ever going to end?

He looked up and stared out the window. He hated the gangster rap scrawled on the wall behind the parking lot. At the muffler shop next door, a cube van pulled in with a delivery of auto parts. Last night on the rez, Colleen had watched five cube vans take delivery of a large shipment of Rollies. Those hundreds of thousands of smokes could be anywhere by now. How many of them were contaminated with a liver poison?

Whether Dennis Badger admitted it or not, he held the key to the epidemic. Zol was sure of that now. But until the team discovered how Native tobacco was poisoning some livers but not others, he had nothing concrete to take to the Badger. No evidence to confront him with. Just an empty plea for cooperation.

Concrete evidence or not, he and the Badger had to meet face to face. If not today, tomorrow. Dennis had to be persuaded to withdraw his tobacco products from the market until the liver thing got sorted out. And the Badger needed to pressure the Rollies barons to do the same.

Zol knew that asking for a temporary shutdown of the smoke shops was one thing, but what would the Badger have to say about the dozen eighteen-wheelers Colleen had spotted outside his Hat-Trick factory? Did he care how many livers that cargo might poison? Maybe he'd care if he could be persuaded that killing off livers was bad for his business.

As Zol gazed through the window, he imagined his former schoolmate swooping in aboard his private helicopter. Was there anything that anyone could do or say that would get the guy to listen?

CHAPTER 23

The shadows were beginning to lengthen as Zol got into the minivan and headed for his six o'clock appointment. Too bad there wasn't enough time to pick up a tall one at the Detour on the way out of town. He could do with the hit.

It had taken all day to set up this meeting with Dennis Badger. The tobacco don kept himself guarded by layers of administrative armour. No one at Badger's Watershed Holdings appeared concerned that the region's medical officer of health needed to speak with Mr. Badger on a matter of the utmost importance. Clearly, the Native cigarette enterprise didn't know what to do with a call from a government official; it seemed they'd never heard of the Federal Tobacco Act of 1997, which said inspectors may enter any place in which they believe a tobacco product is manufactured.

Zol had finally given up on Watershed Holdings and phoned the office of the chief of Grand Basin Reserve. The secretary, speaking in flat-toned monosyllables, agreed to ask Chief Falcon to return Zol's call "sometime later today." Surprisingly, the Chief called back in under an hour and agreed to do his best to contact Mr. Badger and see whether he might be available.

Several more phone calls and a couple of emails made it clear that the Badger was reluctant to cooperate, but then something changed his mind and he agreed to a meeting. Zol asked for a venue outside the rez, but the Badger was insistent: the chief's office on the reserve. Clearly, even the medical officer of health who had attended Simcoe Composite High School with the Badger would not be permitted entry to the holy of holies at Watershed Holdings.

And now, as Zol turned off the highway onto Side Road 4, he was greeted by the colony of ragtag smoke shops that crowded the entrances of so many reserves. Looking like they'd dropped from the sky onto an undeveloped section of bush were Aunt Minnie's Tiny Smoke Shop, Grand Basin Smokes, Log Cabin Qwik Mart, Smoke Depot, Smokes R Us, and two scruffy shops whose signs he couldn't make out. He smiled inwardly at the thought of the fastidious Dr. Wakefield perusing the shelves of Smoke Depot last night and being shocked at the blatant volume of contraband smokes on offer.

Ten minutes later, he reached the centre of the village and drove past the Counselling Services, the Ancestral Voices Healing Centre, and the Healing Hands Dialysis Centre. Two blocks along, he spotted the brand new Dennis Badger Arena. With the blue-and-gold helicopter parked on its roof, the flood-lit structure was impossible to miss. He turned right at the sign for the Grand Basin Band Council and steered toward the new, two-storey box whose brickwork and trim matched the arena looming beside it.

Inside, he stopped at a waist-high counter running the length of an open office. Behind it were two desks, a photocopier, several filing cabinets, and a couple of computers with the usual peripherals.

A Native woman, seated at one of the desks, ignored him until he cleared his throat to catch her attention. The look she gave him suggested there must be dog shit clinging to his shoes. "Yes?"

He sniffed and checked his brogues. Clean soles and shiny uppers. Ermalinda made sure of that. "Dr. Szabo. From the health unit. Chief Falcon is expecting me."

She nodded toward the small waiting area to his right. "If you want, you can have a seat."

He sat there for twenty minutes, wishing he'd stopped at the Detour after all. Twice, he took out a loonie but pocketed it immediately. Never let them see you sweat.

He looked at his watch and for the thousandth time felt grateful for Ermalinda. When he'd called home to say he had an unscheduled meeting and wouldn't be back until well after supper, she'd replied with her characteristic, "You do whatever you have to do, Dr. Zol. Me and Max, we take care of things here. You drive safe." The stars had been perfectly aligned that day, now nine years ago, when she'd walked into their lives. To call her a nanny didn't begin to describe the vital role she played in their household.

"Okay, Doctor," the woman called from behind the counter. Without leaving her seat, she indicated a dimly lit hallway to his left. "First door. On the right."

The brass doorplate said Chief Robert Falcon. Zol felt his heart rate accelerate about twenty beats. His stomach felt as if he'd stuffed it with a potful of cold porridge.

He knocked and heard some sort of muffled response. He knocked again, waited for a moment, then walked in. No posse. Just two men standing in the middle of the generously sized office drinking from Tim Hortons cups. Beside a large desk stood a Native man in his forties — thick dark hair, cut short, classic smooth round cheeks high in his face, a few thin whiskers struggling to sprout on his chin. He was wearing blue jeans and a plaid shirt. Standing in front of a small sofa was Dennis Badger, looking much better dressed than he had in high school. He was as tall as Zol and a good forty pounds heavier. His white dress shirt looked fresh and crisp beneath a charcoal waistcoat in what looked like fine Italian wool. His dress pants were cut from the same material, and he was wearing a handsome deerskin jacket. The perfectly tailored garment had a touch of fringe along the shoulders and hand-laced trim outlining the collar. A narrow band of beading accented each cuff, and three deer antler buttons finished off the front. It was exquisite, obviously Native, and anything but folksy.

"Well, well," said the Badger, his steel-blue eyes surveying Zol from head to toe. "Zollie Szabo." He swept the pinstripe fabric of his made-to-measure trousers with the back of his hand. "We clean up well, eh?"

Zol shook the Badger's outstretched hand, then turned to the chief and said pointedly, "Dr. Zol Szabo, from the health department." No one had called him Zollie since high school. Well, sometimes his parents. "We spoke on the phone."

The chief nodded and mumbled something Zol didn't catch.

The Badger took a seat on the sofa and invited Zol and the chief to each grab a chair. "Now, what's all this about? You didn't come all this way just to admire my jacket." He lifted his eyebrows, paused, then cracked a slight smile. "Dr. Szabo?"

Where to begin? Though he'd rehearsed in the car on the way over, he felt flustered. He told himself to take a page from Hamish's book and lay out the facts one by one. But he'd leave out the professorial finger and the Oscar Wilde flourishes.

He proceeded step by step. The string of liver failures. The agonizing wait for organ donors. The deaths. The undeniable link to rez tobacco and the need to stop its sales and shipments until they figured out what was wrong and how to fix it.

When he'd finished, the Badger looked almost amused. And certainly sceptical. The big man put his hands together — was that the shine of lacquer on his nails? — and summarized what he'd heard. "So . . . you put two and two together, and because you got no proof, you get five. And then . . ." His eyes looked like he was ready to shoot fire out of them. ". . . and then you expect me to bring my multimillion-dollar operation to a standstill?"

Zol swallowed hard. "The proof will come, Mr. Badger. Though it might take some time to show exactly what extremely toxic substance has contaminated your tobacco."

"This is another stunt, isn't it?" said the Badger, his face rigid. "Another attempt to shut us down. We kept the feds happy by letting them license our factory, and then complying with all their foolish labelling regulations." He looked at the chief as if summoning official validation. "And we pay their excise tax on our cigarettes, like everyone else." He slapped his thigh. "But you guys still aren't satisfied."

"No, that's not it. Not at all."

"Come on — I know you got sent here by a government looking for more money. Which one was it this time? The feds? The provincials? Or all the fuckers together?"

"No, Dennis, please. I came here because we've both got to do the right thing. Before any more young people die of whatever it is that's destroying their livers."

"I don't buy it. You were sent here to put the damned Indians in their place. Stick them in their teepees with no visible means of support and criticize them when they get drunk out of boredom and low self-esteem."

The chief, who'd barely moved a muscle until now, stood up and wiped his mouth with the back of his hand. He pointed out the window. "See that arena? Built with tobacco profits. Dennis Badger gives back to our reserves ten times what the government steals from us with their excise tax."

The Badger smiled at the chief, managing to look defiant and proud and insincere, all at the same time. "And don't forget about my three hundred employees here on Grand Basin. That's three hundred families off the welfare rolls." He reached into his jacket and tossed a pack of cigarettes onto the coffee table in front of him. "Here," he told Zol, "have a look at this. And, goddammit, tell me what you see."

Zol picked it up. It was an unopened pack of Hat-Tricks. Canada Duty Paid was written on the cellophane wrapper. "Well, it's a pack of twenty-five cigarettes. King-Size. Filter-tip. There's a Health Canada Warning about impotence —"

"In both English and French. Go on."

Zol turned the pack over in his hands, summarizing out loud the notices printed on every surface. "There's a bilingual list of the toxic emissions, a notice that they're made by Native enterprises on Native territories, a declaration that says 'FOR SALE ON NATIVE TERRITORIES,' and a DUTY-PAID stamp. Did I miss anything?"

Badger grabbed the pack from Zol's hand and pointed to an outside edge. "Read this. Go on, read it."

"The Original Tobacco Traders."

"That's us. For two thousand years. Get it?"

This wasn't the time to quibble, not the time to point out that although these Native-made cigarettes seemed to follow the letter of most of the federal tobacco laws, they were only semi-legit. Without saying it in so many words, these smokes purported to be for sale only to Natives on their reserves. But anyone, Native or non-Native, even minors, could buy them and avoid the hefty sales and tobacco taxes the law said was payable by non-Natives. And of course, the tobacco in them was purchased under the table from the local growers at bargain prices, and no government inspector ever ventured inside the factories that produced them.

"Dennis, the tobacco laws and taxes are not my concern. If it weren't for this liver thing, you could sell cigarettes to anyone who wanted them at any price, and I wouldn't care."

The Badger looked surprised. No government official would've ever told him they didn't care about lost taxes. His features hardened. "You're playing with me, Szabo. It has come to my attention that some visitors attempted to make a late night inspection at one of my fellow enterprises. Know anything about that?"

Zol felt sick. Colleen and Hamish had been seen. The sweat trickled down the back of his neck as it dawned on him. They'd been spooked by the cube vans and AK-47s at a Rollies factory, not at Dennis's Hat-Trick operation. The Badger's ties to the Asian gangs were more intimate than Zol had imagined. Though Dennis Badger played the role of the ultra-successful businessman running a legitimate international operation he called Watershed Holdings, maybe he was also a criminal kingpin, as deep into the Rollies as the Asians. Hell, was he their boss?

"You can't hide from me, Szabo. You White guys show every one of your emotions on your faces. Including guilt. It was you or your cronies sneaking around last night. You can't deny it."

No wonder the Badger had been able to parlay a noxious weed into an empire. The guy had savvy to burn.

The sweat was now pouring into the back of Zol's shirt. "I'm . . . I'm greatly concerned about the liver epidemic. We have to stop it. You and I."

The Badger frowned and waved his hand. "There's nothing wrong with my tobacco. Find some other scapegoat for your liver plague."

"I'm not looking for a scapegoat, Dennis. I'm here about the lives of real people. Firefighters, for God's sake. And high school kids."

Dennis stood and gazed out the window toward his namesake arena. He stroked his chin. After a while, he turned, appeared to contemplate the Hat-Trick pack on the coffee table, then said, "You said firefighters and school kids?"

Zol nodded.

"No one else out of the thousands of people who smoke my cigarettes?"

"So far."

"Doesn't make a lot of sense to me, Doctor Szabo. You've got more homework to do." He stared through the window again, as if scrutinizing every rivet in his helicopter parked on the roof next door. "Tell you what. You show me proof it's my tobacco that's the problem. Give me real McCoy proof without any government bullshit. And then . . ." He hesitated, as if surprising himself with his own words. "And then . . ." He coughed into his fist. "Maybe we'll talk."

Dennis drained the last of his coffee and set the cup on the table, then straightened the creases in his trousers and looked around the room as if signalling that the meeting was over.

Zol stood up.

"No, no. Don't go, Zol. Please, not yet. Despite what you think, I've enjoyed our little reunion. And now it's time to seal it with a traditional indulgence."

Zol sat down, too surprised by the Badger's change in tone to say a word.

Dennis took his seat and told the chief, "Bob, bring out the special pipe." The chief gave Dennis an icy look that suggested he must be out of his mind.

Dennis ignored the silent admonition and turned an unctuous smile on Zol. "A special pipe for a special occasion. It's okay, Chief. Zol's an old friend."

The chief shrugged and looked anything but happy. But he stood up, unlocked a drawer in his desk, and with both hands pulled out a wooden box. He presented it to Dennis with care bordering on reverence.

Dennis set the box on the small table in front of him and pulled a leather tobacco pouch from his jacket. Zol felt himself smiling inside; Dad used to have a similar pouch, in the old days when he smoked cigarettes during the day and a pipe in the evenings. By the delicate aroma escaping from the Badger's pouch, it was clear he didn't smoke his own product.

When Dennis went to place the tobacco on the table, he hesitated. It seemed the disposable coffee cup, now a piece of trash with ugly teeth marks on the chewed-up rim, was offensive to the upcoming ritual. Zol grabbed the cup, crushed it in his fist, and stashed it in his pocket.

Dennis smiled as though he appreciated Zol's gesture and the intuition behind it, and opened the lid of the finely crafted box. He reached inside with both hands. Whatever was nestling there made the Badger's pupils widen as he touched it.

He lifted his hands and concealed what lay on his palm by cupping one fist over the other. "Of course, you've held this little fellow before. I remember when you found him."

Zol felt like he'd been kicked in the solar plexus. No, it couldn't be. Even the Badger wouldn't be that bold.

Dennis Badger opened his hands and beamed a huge, beatific smile. "See? It took him a long time, but he's made the trip back home. I believe the biologists call that nest-site fidelity."

CHAPTER 24

It was almost eight when Zol threw the minivan into park and hit the button to close the garage door behind him. Ermalinda greeted him at the door with a smile and helped him out of his blazer. Her face went from round and sunny to flat and serious as she sensed his mood. He used to feel guilty that she treated him with such gracious deference, making him feel like the village squire coming home to his butler. But she was so sincere, so genuine in her love — yes, it felt like love — for Max and him, that he'd stopped feeling guilty long ago. After all, the love — at the least the deep respect and appreciation — was returned in spades. By both Max and him.

"Your supper, it in the fridge, Dr. Zol. That chicken curry you made, I cook basmati to go with it. Ready for the microwave. Sorry . . . Max, he finish the naan. Just one piece left anyway."

"Thanks, Ermalinda. Sounds great." He glanced out the window. It was dark, and had been all the way back from the rez. "Let me drive you to the bus."

"You tired." She looked at her watch. "It still early. And the bus, it come in ten minutes. I'll be fine." She pulled off her apron.

"Mr. Art, he call. Asking if you coming for brunch." Her dark eyes danced in their sockets. "He say be sure bring Miss Colleen."

"Is it this Sunday?"

"Yes. Day after tomorrow. Twelve-thirty." She'd added administrative assistant to her duties and knew his schedule by heart.

"I'll call him."

Brunch once a month at Camelot Lodge with Francine's irrepressible grandfather had become a tradition. But this tobacco-versus-liver case threatened to consume every second of the weekend. At the table would be Art Greenwood, his girlfriend Betty, and their friend Phyllis, who peppered her conversation with Latin swear words. He hated to miss them. The silvery threesome, full of charm and pithy anecdotes free of political correctness, provided a lift from the everyday struggle. And Max sure loved the attention from the thirty spritely old folks in the residence, especially when he went to their rooms, helped them with their computers, and got paid in chocolates and jelly beans. The converted mansion now had Wi-Fi in every room, but needed a ten-year-old consultant to keep things running smoothly.

As Ermalinda headed off to her bus, he resolved to do his best to squeeze an hour and a half out of Sunday afternoon for brunch at the lodge.

"Hi guys," he said to Max and Travis, busy in the den at what Ermalinda had said was a school project. Only a computer assignment would have them working so enthusiastically at schoolwork on a Friday night.

It was good to see Travis looking so well after his bout in the hospital. It had been touch and go for him — septic shock, intensive care, a protracted coma, the whole ball of wax in a business that had seen them all entangled in the plot of a revengeful madman operating at Camelot Lodge. Art, Betty, and Phyllis had borne the brunt of it along with Travis. Phyllis still had to steady herself with a cane occasionally, but not even a fractured femur could stop her driving her '72 Lincoln. Public health was supposed to be a sane, logical specialty with family-friendly working hours. Why did the worst of the cases land flat on his doorstep?

He steadied himself against the doorjamb. He'd nearly had a stroke when the Badger had brought out the red-eyed loon and insisted they share a smoke. What should he have done, stormed out in a huff, lost all semblance of rapport with the Badger, and risked catching a bullet in the head on the way to his car?

He'd kept a healthy distance from the Badger in high school, but now he was deeply entangled with the guy. And with the Badger came contraband tobacco, the liver epidemic, the explosion at the ROM, and the apparent execution of three Native rivals in a clash for possession of the legendary loon. The guy was more than a canny businessman, he was a pirate in a pinstripe suit and a deerskin jacket. And Zol had shared a ceremonial smoke with him from a hot, two-thousand-year-old artifact.

Max waved distractedly without looking away from his screen. "Hi Dad."

Travis ventured a shy smile, the briefest flash. He was an unusual kid, but completely loyal to Max. A purple birthmark, a flame nevus, covered the right half of his face. He was clumsy on the soccer pitch because he often lurched to the left. The two boys had been drawn together since kindergarten, each with a physical distinction that set them apart: Max with his spastic left arm, Travis with his birthmark. Neither considered himself sick or handicapped, but between them was the bond of the outsider. Calling the mark on Travis's face "the map of Norway" was Max's way of describing it in complimentary terms, especially since Travis claimed his mother was descended from the Vikings. There didn't seem to be a father in the picture. The boy was a great gamer and pulled his weight when he and Max did school projects together.

"Did you phone Grandma?" Zol asked Max.

"Yep."

"And?"

"She's fine. Said she's having a good day."

"Did you actually call and speak to her, or just send a text?"

"I called. Like you said." Max looked at Travis and rolled his eyes. "My grandma is old fashioned. She thinks texting isn't polite."

"She didn't sound too tired?"

Max kept clicking at the keyboard. "Nope. She had rocky-road ice cream for lunch."

At least she was eating. But then, she always put on a good face for Max.

He left the boys to their project and zapped the rice and curry in the microwave. He managed a few bites, then poured himself a Glenfarclas. He slumped into his recliner chair in the sunroom and closed his eyes.

In a flash, something grabbed his arm. A giant bird had his wrist in his beak. It was flapping its wings, smoke was billowing from its nostrils, and it was trying to sever his hand from his arm. He struggled to scream but nothing came out.

"Zol. Zol . . . wake up. Come on, wake up."

The giant loon took off across the water.

Colleen's face appeared from behind the smoke.

"There, now," she was saying. "That's better."

"Oh . . . thank God. I'm so glad it's you. That was so . . ."

She kissed him on the forehead and caressed his cheek. "Take a deep breath. It was a dream."

He scanned his surroundings and was surprised to find himself in the sunroom. A glass of whisky was sitting on the table beside him, mostly untouched.

"Back so soon?" he said, rubbing his eyes.

"It's gone nine o'clock."

"Everything okay?"

She leaned in for a kiss, a proper one this time. "I got what I needed."

Sometimes, she had to stay out most of the night on a case before she got what she needed. He'd learned not to ask for the details.

He took a swallow of his Glenfarclas and asked her if she'd eaten. She insisted she was fine and pressed him to tell her about his meeting with the Badger.

"Dennis Badger reckons he's got you where he wants you," she said, once he'd finished the story. "That's how criminal gangs operate. They use fear, debt, and obligation to manipulate their rivals and associates."

The reheated curry was sitting unhappily in his stomach. "I guess I'll have to manipulate right back."

There was a sly smile on her face.

"What?" he said. "You don't think I can be as manipulative as the next guy?"

"You're too honest."

"Thanks."

"Actually, in you, I'd call it cunning." She helped herself to a shot of Amarula Cream from the liquor cabinet. "It happens that I might be able to help with that concrete proof Dennis Badger says he may be willing to hear about."

"Really?"

"I reckoned there had to be a smart guy in charge of operating those factories on the rez. You know, a mechanical genius who'd worked for one of the big-name cigarette manufacturers. Someone well familiar with the shop floor, after years of experience in the industry."

She'd made a good point. Dennis Badger and his cronies could never have set up those factories on their own. Nor could they be the ones keeping the equipment so finely tuned it churned out thousands of cigarettes every hour. "You're thinking a scientist of some sort? An engineer?"

"Exactly."

"But why would he talk to us?"

"I can't see how else we're going to suss out what's unique to the rez operation and makes their cigarettes vulnerable to — let's say — contamination by something more noxious than normal?"

He let go a cynical chuckle at the irony and pulled the loonie from his pocket. "Yeah, but any smart guy would know that the first rule of working for organized criminals is keep your mouth shut."

She no longer looked so confident. "I'd hoped the person might be in some way disillusioned. Or have an Achilles heel."

"Or kids who smoke Rollies and have a classmate dying of liver failure?"

"Our person doesn't have kids."

"What? You found him? The Badger's mechanical genius?"

"At this juncture, a name. And a home address."

"How did you do that?" When she gave him her *you know you're not supposed to ask me that* look, he took another mouthful of Glenfarclas. He let the warmth of the whisky linger for a moment, then pressed, "Are you going to trust me with the name?"

"Colborne. Olivia Colborne."

"A wo—"

"Yes, Zol. A female mechanical genius is working for the tobacco mob."

"Sorry. It's just that . . ."

She raised her hand to stop him. "Don't dig yourself in any deeper." She sipped a mouthful of Amarula Cream — she called it the taste of her African homeland captured in a bottle — then held him with her steely green gaze.

When she was sure he'd got the message, she rolled her eyes and cracked a smile. "She lives in Simcoe. Norfolk Avenue. In a nineteenth-century mansion that looks like it's tumbling down."

"You've seen it?"

"And the two dozen Southern Comfort bottles in the recycling bin."

"She doesn't sound too happy."

"Perhaps she has a conscience that needs to be soothed — so she can sleep at night."

He eyed his whisky and felt a pang of guilt. Too much of this stuff could soothe a conscience into oblivion. Or reduce it to tears.

"Dad?" said Max, shuffling across the carpet and staring into his cellphone.

"Hi Buddy. Travis still here?"

"What are obli . . . oblig . . . obligations?"

"That's when you owe someone a favour because they did something special for you. Why?"

"Someone sent me a weird text about you smoking a pipe. But Dad, you don't smoke, do you?"

Zol glanced at Colleen. She'd put down her drink and had stiffened her shoulders.

"Of course not."

"It says I'm supposed to remind you about your . . . obligations."

"Let me see."

The message was blazed across the screen.

The second time through it, the Glenfarclas turned to nettles on his tongue.

MAX: REMIND YOUR DAD THAT SHARING PIPE SMOKE CARRIES CERTAIN OBLIGATIONS.

CHAPTER 25

The next morning, Colleen gunned the Mercedes along Iroquois Road, through the centre of Grand Basin Village. By the look of the car park at the Helping Hands Dialysis Centre, Saturdays offered no truce in the war against kidney failure. Further on, she shuddered as she passed the neoclassical facade of Dennis Badger's arena. What a wicked man. He must have spies everywhere. It was the only way to a control a criminal empire of such magnitude.

She glanced at her handbag. It contained a tiny piece of him — his DNA on the Tim Hortons cup that Zol had stashed in his blazer pocket toward the end of their meeting. Zol had jokingly said they should stick pins in it, voodoo style. But she had other designs. The police lab would never fingerprint Dennis Badger's DNA without probable cause and a six-month waiting list. But there were private labs who would, for a reasonable fee, look for matches between samples of DNA you submitted to them — for instance, they could compare the DNA on the well-chewed rim of Dennis Badger's coffee cup with the DNA recovered from the assailant's skin beneath Tammy Holt's cold, dead fingernails. Her savage attacker had been scrupulous about his condom and not left behind a single drop of semen.

Sometimes, a homicide detective with whom one had a mutually cooperative relationship — and who was desperate to solve a case now a year old and looking hopeless — could be persuaded to use private-lab DNA evidence to get her case back on track. On the hush-hush, of course. Such results could never be admissible in court — the samples lacked any semblance of integrity in their chain of custody. With luck, the informal lab findings would point out the guilty party to the police, who could collect and test samples of their own. One would hope they could then obtain a search warrant for other evidence they might need to secure a conviction, all by the book.

Poor Zol — he'd tossed and turned all night, more certain than ever that his only choice was to take on the Badger, but worrying himself sick over Max's safety. They'd talked about hiding Max at the farm, but Kitti's cancer treatment had become a full-time occupation that left the senior Szabos little room in their lives for an active pre-teen. As adorable as he was, Max needed a fair bit of feeding and watering. For today and tomorrow, Zol wasn't going to let the boy out of his sight. But then what? With her track record, she certainly wasn't going to try hiding someone she loved at her place. And she did love Max; she hoped it was safe to admit that now.

Two hundred metres farther on, she turned right at the entrance to Mechanically Sound, Matt Holt's garage. She wasn't worried about parking her Mercedes here, even for the entire day if it came to that. Waiting their turn to be serviced were a Lexus sedan, two Cadillac SUVs, an E-Class Mercedes, and a herd of battered Fords and Chevys. Matt ran an equal opportunity repair centre. Colleen had seen his books when she'd investigated Grand Basin's chop shops. Her client at that time was a Hamilton dealership whose cars were being stolen with alarming regularity. Though she hadn't made much headway with the chop shops, she'd seen that Matt Holt kept his place in perfect order: the workmanship, the accounts, even the sales taxes. He ran the Vehicle Identification Number of every vehicle he serviced; this was no place to bring a hot car for a makeover.

Today was her first time back since the fire. They'd done a nice job of the rebuilding, even added a fourth work bay. Perhaps the chop-shoppers had done him a late-night favour with their petrol and rags. It could have been worse, but Matt's fellow firefighters on the Grand Basin volunteer brigade had rallied quickly. They'd contained the damage to the right-hand side of the building. And now everyone knew that Matt Holt was under the protection of the big shots on the rez who appreciated an honest and gifted mechanic as much as anyone. Perhaps more.

As she entered the shop, he acknowledged her from behind the counter with a flick of his eyebrows. Though he couldn't muster a smile, understandable under the circumstances, he'd gussied up for their meeting. Freshly laundered blue jeans hugged his slim hips, and a blue-and-white dress shirt looked smart under his black leather bomber jacket.

He held up his keys. "I'll drive, okay? I know the place."

So did she, after scouting it yesterday, but she was happy to let him drive.

They climbed into his Ford-150. He must have special-ordered it or had the paint job done in his shop. She didn't think she'd ever seen another one this rich a shade of British racing green.

"You're sure you're up to this?" she asked him.

"Better than pacing outside Donna's room at Toronto General." He explained that the transplant unit's visiting hours were restricted and they let only two family members in at a time. "I'm better doing something positive, like helping you guys nail the bastards who did this to her."

As long as the truck was moving, he seemed in his element. Distracted, perhaps, by thoughts of his sisters — one murdered, the other in a coma — but confident, born to control a turbo-charged machine. But whenever they stopped at a turn or a crossing, anxious crinkles puckered near his eyes. He kept looking in the rear-view mirror, as if worried they were being followed. Frequent glances in her side mirror told her they had the road to themselves.

"Half of me is driven crazy by my own people," he said, wiping a sweaty palm against his blue jeans. "The other half is worried about being an Uncle Tom, you know, a stoolie."

"I don't think —"

"Dennis Badger keeps harping on about the three hundred jobs his Hat-Trick factory brought to Grand Basin. They're low-level positions, and he should be paying his workers better, but if he'd stopped there, things would've been fine. He'd have made a lot of money and thumbed his nose at the government." He ventured a chuckle. "Can't blame us for that, after hundreds of years of White guys stealing our land, our lives, our buffalo, our artifacts, our kids, and especially our dignity." He turned to her and softened his tone. "No offence, but you know what I mean."

Like every South African, White or Black, she knew exactly what he meant. And she didn't have to say it; he was bound to see it in her face.

"White people look at me and automatically see a drunk who beats his girlfriend, abandons his kids, and gets unlimited government freebies. They refuse to let themselves see a university-educated engineer with a bonus built in." He paused, saw the puzzled look on her face, and made a sweeping motion over the landscape with his arm. "Twenty thousand years of intimate knowledge and understanding of these lands."

She hadn't looked at it that way before, but a man like Matt Holt did embody modern expertise imbued with traditional intuition. Intellect and instinct could be a powerful combination. "It's going to take guys like you to demonstrate that Natives can run clean and reliable businesses as well or better than anyone else."

He turned to her and slapped the steering wheel. "You know what really pisses me off? People who come to my shop and give me that look that says *Nice to see an Indian doing well for a change.*"

She felt herself blushing and looked away. Was it possible to show that she was on his side without appearing patronizing? Perhaps the gulf between Whites and Natives was so wide that any attempt at bridging it could seem false.

"I'm sorry, Colleen. I didn't mean to unload years of cultural baggage on you. I appreciate what you and Dr. Szabo and the team are doing. And don't think I kid myself. I'm still in business only because Dennis Badger, Chief Falcon, and their cronies don't trust their cars to anyone else. Not because I'm a good mechanic — though I am that."

"Nothing wrong with being good at what you do, is there?"

"You mean like Dennis Badger? He had a nice business going there, with his Hat-Tricks. Really nice. Then he got greedy and brought in Asian gangs to distribute his smokes not to other reserves, but to stores and street corners in every city and town in the country."

Zol had told her about the Asian angle. Their presence in the business was like a fire accelerant that turned a campfire into a conflagration.

"Those guys are super-organized," he continued, "and they've got no right to be profiting from our land and our special status. They brought in their assault rifles, their hard drugs, their hookers, their loan sharks, and who knows what else. And now, after five hundred years of being victimized by White colonialists, my people get hard-ons when Asian criminals promise them easy money."

She let Matt simmer for a while and watched the speedometer slowly fall after peaking at one-thirty, fifty kilometres over the limit.

When Matt got it down to one-oh-five, she said, "Did you tell Olivia what this meeting was about?"

"Said you were a client."

If he meant her to play a role, she'd better get it right. "What sort of client?"

"My guys installed a home theatre system in her basement. Custom job. The works. I told her you were a fussy client who was thinking about getting something similar."

She wasn't so good at fussy, but she'd do her best to fake it. "So, I'm having a look to see if your workmanship is up to scratch?"

"That'll do it."

It was going to take some creative talking to move the conversation from home theatres to home-grown cigarettes. She'd faced tougher assignments, such as persuading a Baptist minister to seek help with his Internet porn addiction after she'd supposedly shown up to redecorate his office and caught him red-handed.

She came up with an idea as they were approaching Highway 3. Matt said it sounded fine, and that no, it didn't trivialize the danger his sister Donna was facing.

At the outskirts of Simcoe, Erie Christian Collegiate appeared on the right. The place was deserted, and had been since yesterday. She could imagine the panic that had consumed the place when the paramedics arrived to cart the delirious principal, yellow as mustard and raving like a lunatic, off to Emergency.

Once they reached Simcoe proper, Matt turned left onto Norfolk Street. A few blocks later, he steered to the curb and stopped opposite a café. It had a crunchy-granola, fair-trade look.

The penny dropped. "We're not meeting her here, are we?"

"Just picking up some fuel. Olivia's pretty rough in the mornings. How do you take it?"

"Black, thanks."

It took fifteen minutes for the aficionados at Zol's infamous Detour Café to produce three hand-crafted coffees and a small bag of pastries. Did Zol wait this long every time he came in for a fix? Well, why not? Better caffeine than tobacco or Internet porn. And the walk from the health unit was good for him. Well, she hoped he was walking.

She held the coffees in her lap as they continued south on Norfolk Street, turned right at James, and then a quick left onto John, which was little more than a lane opposite the fairgrounds. According to the billboard bordering the large grassy field, they'd missed the Norfolk County Fair and Horse Show by a couple of weeks.

Matt killed the engine, took the coffees, and led her back the way they'd come. The streetscape looked tidier now that yesterday's garbage bins and recycling boxes had been put away.

"Hope you don't mind a short walk. It's just around the corner. No need to advertise our visit."

Olivia Colborne's house was around two corners, in fact. On

Norfolk Street. It looked like three floors of a haunted mansion on a movie set, standing well back from the road on a half-acre lot. Matt may have performed some mechanical magic inside, but Olivia had neglected the neo-Gothic exterior. The place was desperate for a repair job on its sagging eaves, a new coat of white around the windows, and anything to cover up the hideous purple on the massive front porch. And that would only be a start.

It took awhile for Olivia to come to the front door, but she seemed glad to see Matt and pleasant enough behind a face that looked somewhere between thirty-five and fifty. Her eyes were red and puffy, there were wrinkles around her mouth, and she'd smeared her lips with a cherry-red gloss that was popular two or three years ago. Her long, wavy hair looked almost black, and naturally so, and she was tall even in her slippers. She'd braced herself for the meeting. A hint of Southern Comfort betrayed itself on her breath.

They drank their coffees in the living room at the front of the house. Not bothering to fetch a plate for the pastries, Olivia smoked three cigarettes in rapid succession, lighting each with the glowing butt of the one before it. No wonder her voice sounded like a cement mixer and the wallpaper was covered in a dull grey residue. She favoured a premium brand of king size filter tips, not for sale on any rez.

When Olivia offered to show them Matt's basement handiwork, Colleen caught his eye, then dipped her gaze and confided she felt a bit guilty contemplating extravagant renovations as her niece lay in Toronto General, in a liver coma. "She goes to Erie Collegiate," Colleen added. "The one where that liver plague is picking off one cheerleader after another."

"Like my sister." Matt said, his voice grave. "They're both waiting for liver transplants."

Olivia rose to the bait, appearing genuinely stricken. "Oh, I'm so sorry. Your sister, Matt? Isn't she a nurse or something?"

"A paramedic," Matt said. "Works her butt off on the front lines. Then this. My parents are with her now. My turn's tonight."

When they'd finished their coffees, they trooped downstairs, and

Colleen made a show of studying the home theatre in detail. Olivia went on about the layout, the decor, the plush seating. Colleen was far more impressed at the sharpness of the seventy-two-inch flat screen and the opera-house quality of the surround sound. Dennis Badger must be sharing the wealth. At least with his senior management.

Colleen caught Matt's eye again and said, "It's all very nice, but I can't help feeling guilty. My niece was going to apply to film school in Toronto. Of course, now our lives are on hold. And to think it might be caused by something as ordinary as smoking cigarettes."

"Yeah," said Matt, gazing at his wingtips and shaking his head. "One of the doctors from the health unit told me that every one of the liver cases is a smoker. Doesn't seem fair, but he's blaming the cigarettes they make on the rez."

Olivia stiffened her back and narrowed her eyes. "Who said that?"

Matt shrugged. "Don't remember his name. Some specialist from Hamilton."

"Why is he blaming Native tobacco?" Olivia said.

Matt should have been an actor. He had the looks and the natural grace. "Can't say for sure. I guess because everyone whose gotten sick smokes it regularly. But around here, that's pretty well standard behaviour, eh?" He scratched the back of his neck and put on the small-town boy look. "There they go, blaming us Indians again. But tobacco is tobacco, eh? No one said it's supposed to be good for you. No matter where it comes from."

Unable to hide the pained looked on her face, Olivia took them back upstairs to the living room. She snatched her cigarettes from the coffee table and wasted no time in lighting up.

Colleen tried to sound as breezy as possible. "Matt tells me you're a mechanical engineer, a whiz at machinery."

Olivia shrugged. "Don't know about the whiz part."

Colleen gestured to Olivia's pack of premium smokes. "Is there a difference between the tobacco you're smoking and the tobacco in the cigarettes from the reserve?"

"Not really."

"Then why is it that they smell so different? My niece says Native tobacco is harsher on the throat. "

Olivia looked away. "I guess it's the type of tobacco. What we use in our factories is one hundred percent locally grown."

The woman had said factories. Plural. Olivia Colborne had let it slip. She was involved with the production of more than Dennis Badger's nicely packaged, excise-duty-paid Hat-Trick brand, produced in a government-licensed facility. She managed the machinery in several factories. But the only other factories within commuting distance were located on the rez, both of them informal, and neither of them licensed. Olivia was working in the Rollies trade. As Colleen contemplated the complexities of the criminal network they were facing, she pulled out her knitting and hoped the face that went with it was a picture of innocence and sincerity.

Today, she'd chosen the front panel of a winter sweater. A snowflake pattern in white, teal, and fuchsia that she'd been working on for ages. "I started this for my niece. And I'm going to keep going with it. No matter what."

Matt covered his confusion by helping himself to the last muffin. She'd forgotten to tell him about her knitting.

Olivia said nothing.

Colleen held up the panel and showed Olivia the design. "I'm quite pleased with this pattern. It's from *Canadian Living*. I love that magazine. It covers everyday life in such fascinating detail." She completed a row of moss stitch, then added, "Like peanut butter, for instance. Did you know it can be toxic to the liver? There was an article not long ago about mouldy peanuts from China causing — what was it? Cancer? Yes, that was it, some sort of cancer of the liver." She shook her head as if to say it was a crazy world.

Matt fidgeted with his empty cup and took his time on the muffin. Olivia shot him a look that said *Okay, you two have had your look, now it's time you got going.* When he showed no sign of reacting, she dragged on her cigarette as if desperate for every molecule of nicotine it could possibly deliver.

After another half row of stitches, and with as much treacly innocence as she could manage, Colleen ventured, "Come to think of it, we did have a rather wet summer. Was it bad for your business? I mean, does *tobacco* ever go mouldy?"

Olivia's bloodshot eyes flashed with revelation, which morphed into anxiety. Or was it terror? She looked down, stubbed the half-smoked cigarette in the already littered ashtray on the coffee table, and grabbed her Bic. "No. Not the tobacco we use."

The word *mouldy,* had struck a nerve, there was no doubt about it. Knit one, purl one. Knit another, purl another. "Of course not."

Colleen looked at Matt and smiled. "You certainly do fine work, sir. But we've taken up enough of Ms. Colborne's time. I think we should be going." She stowed her knitting in her handbag and stood up. "If I could use the facilities for a moment."

Olivia looked uneasy and conflicted, as if she didn't want her guests to see the rest of the house but knew she couldn't refuse to let Colleen use the toilet. "Better use the one at the top of the stairs. Third door on the left."

Colleen closed the bathroom door loudly enough to be heard downstairs. She removed the plug from the hand basin and turned on the tap. Then she opened the door without making any noise and only wide enough for her to slip through it. It was an acquired skill, but she was good at it. She crept along the edge of the corridor, where the floorboards were less likely to creak, and found Olivia's bedroom. What a mess. No wonder she didn't want visitors up here.

She wasn't sure what she was looking for, but knew where she'd find it. Women were embarrassingly predictable when it came to hiding things.

She went straight to the drawer, and there it was. Olivia's Achilles heel. It made the poor woman far more vulnerable than her addictions to nicotine and Southern Comfort.

And Colleen knew how she was going to use it.

CHAPTER 26

As Zol expected, they had the place to themselves. The Nitty Gritty Café catered to Concession Street's weekday lunch and after-work crowds, so it was never busy on Sunday afternoons. Especially in weather like this. The rain pelting the windows and the mist climbing the Escarpment wiped out all traces of the lake, the steel mills, and the lower city. Not a bad spot for a team meeting, nicely cocooned from prying eyes.

It had been misty at noon on Jenkins Road when Zol dropped Max at the farm. Kitti and Gaspar had Scrabble, Clue, and Monopoly out and ready to play. Mum insisted she'd always loved Clue and was up for a game. Zol told himself a computer-free afternoon would be good for Max, who'd keep Mum and Dad amused with his lively company. All they'd have to do was feed him until Zol collected him after supper. Max would be driven everywhere now, and Ermalinda had strict instructions not to open the door to any visitors. They'd agreed that Zol would take him to school in the mornings and Colleen would collect him in the afternoons.

Art Greenwood had sounded terribly disappointed this morning when Zol called to say they couldn't make it to Camelot Lodge today for brunch. The gang would be having coffee and dessert by the fire about now, and Phyllis would be having them in stitches over a recent escapade in her '72 Lincoln. He hated cancelling on Art and Betty. Every moment spent with them was precious.

Something flashed at the front of the Nitty Gritty. It was Colleen, striding through the entrance and struggling with her umbrella. As he watched, he knew she'd never get it collapsed. Though she was a whiz with the electronic gadgets of her PI trade, she was hopeless with simple tools like umbrellas and corkscrews. That's what came, he supposed, of growing up with a houseful of servants who did everything for you. Marcus took charge of her wayward umbrella and stowed it in the stand with the others, then helped her out of her soggy coat. She gave him her hat, a fisherman's large-brimmed thing only she could make look chic. When she unwound her ponytail, it was bone dry. She beamed appreciatively as Marcus took her order for something undoubtedly warm and soothing, then joined them in the back corner of the café, sinking into the empty chair between Natasha and Hamish.

She flashed Zol a serious look that said she had something important to tell him. Something she didn't want to share with the others. His pulse shot up until he checked his phone for a text or a missed call. Nothing from the farm. Whatever was on her mind didn't involve Max. Hell, he hated being this jumpy.

Maybe she'd managed to squeeze something important out of Olivia Colborne. Last evening, she'd told him the trip to Olivia's house had unearthed some serious suspicions and a nefarious little something Colleen was hoping would persuade Olivia to cooperate. The matter sounded so close to extortion that he stopped the conversation there. Anything further would be TMI, too much information. It was tricky having a private investigator working as a consultant for the health unit. Especially when he was making love with her several times a week.

He threw her a look that said he'd be all ears later and told the team, "We might as well get started. Natasha, you first."

"The liver outbreak continues to . . ." Natasha hesitated, as if looking for the right words. "To gradually expand. But it continues to involve only the two populations — students at Erie Collegiate and Norfolk Fire and Rescue Services."

"How many are we up to?" Hamish asked.

"Fifteen. Seven first responders and eight from the school."

"Eight?" Hamish said. "Last I heard it was six."

"That was Thursday," Natasha told him. "But then on Friday, the principal, Mr. Vorst, took sick. And a member of the boys' basketball team. They're both still at Simcoe General. I think they're talking about transferring Mr. Vorst to Toronto."

"Can you tell us about the three firefighters who called in sick on Friday?" Zol said.

"Only one has liver disease."

"And the others?" Hamish said. "What was wrong with them?" He craned his neck and inched Natasha's notebook toward him. Something about this case had captivated Hamish more than any other they'd worked on together. Maybe it was the murder of his coworker. Or was Dennis Badger putting the screws to him as well?

Natasha stirred her latte, then retrieved her notebook. She wasn't going to let herself be rushed. "Dr. Hitchin, who saw them in Simcoe Emerg, called it contagious anxiety."

"Hmm. Any more deaths?" Hamish asked, still trying to read her notes.

Natasha bit her lower lip. "One. A firefighter. Died yesterday, in the transplant unit at Toronto General."

"How many's that?" Hamish said.

"All together, three."

"And . . . and Donna Holt?" Colleen seemed afraid to be asking.

"I understand she's holding her own, but her only hope is that a liver becomes available very soon."

"Anything else for us, Natasha?" Zol asked.

Her eyebrows went up. "Some interesting biopsy results. There's a doctor Zeiter in Simcoe who has an interest in liver disease."

Zol had spoken with him briefly on Wednesday, before he had any results.

"He deals mostly with alcoholics who've developed cirrhosis,"

Natasha continued, "and injection drug users with hepatitis C. He arranged biopsies for our first eight cases."

Hamish opened his mouth, but closed it and sat on his hands when Zol shot him a look that told him to let Natasha finish.

"All the livers show the same thing," she said. "I'll read you one of the path reports." She glanced at her notes and quoted, "The basic liver architecture is preserved, but there is widespread centrilobular necrosis of hepatocytes and complete absence of any inflammatory infiltrate."

"May we have the plain-English translation?" Colleen asked.

"The pattern of liver damage visible under the microscope is typical of chemical poisoning," said Natasha. "The toxic substance could be any of a variety of chemicals including chloroform and carbon tetrachloride."

"So there's no infection?" Zol asked. "No virus, no strange parasite?"

Natasha shook her head. "The pathologist sounds definite in his report. These livers have been poisoned, not infected."

Hamish looked sceptical. "What would a bunch of high school students and firefighters be doing with old-fashioned chemicals no one uses anymore?"

"How does this fit with the hybrid virus thing in the lip and finger lesions?" Zol asked. "You recovered those matchstick particles from a couple of the jaundiced firefighters? Don't tell me that's a coincidence."

Hamish straightened in his chair. "You know I don't believe in coincidences. I spent half of yesterday and most of today in Wilf Dickinson's lab. And guess what we found?" He looked around the table, but didn't get any takers, just anxious faces. "More matchstick particles." He turned to Colleen. "The tobacco you and I purchased at the smoke shops is riddled with them."

"Similar to the thingies in the Mongolian case you told us about on Thursday?" Colleen asked.

Hamish looked triumphant. "Wilf's been glued to his electron

microscope since Friday morning. Even missed an orchestra practice. He found the particles in at least one sample of everything I
gave him from the smoke shop. Rollies, reject Rollies, and Hat-
Tricks. Plains and menthols. King-size and regular. Even the mock
American-style Trackers."

"Could it be an artifact?" Zol asked. "You know, something
you'd see in tobacco everywhere, even in off-rez premium brands?"

"That's what Wilf thought," Hamish said. "So I bought packs of
Players, Belmont, Export A, and du Maurier." A triumphant twinkle
flashed in his eyes. "All were negatory on matchstick particles."

It wasn't an exhaustive study, of course. And there was no proof
that the particles were causing more than nuisance blisters in people
smoking contraband cigarettes. It could almost be called perverted
justice. But at least they were getting closer to the sort of "concrete
evidence" he'd need if he was going to confront the Badger again.

"What about the toxin angle?" Zol said. "Any ideas, team?"

"The couldn't be sniffing solvents, could they?" Colleen said.

"Firefighters sniffing solvents?" Hamish said. "Really, Colleen, I
don't think so."

"And not the Vanderhoef twins," Natasha said. "For them,
lighting up in that vacant lot so close to their school was pushing
the rebellion envelope as far as they dared."

"Don't forget Tammy Holt's project," Hamish said. "You know,
the wonder drug that went sour?"

"And got cleaned up without a trace," Natasha added.

"Expunged is more like it," Hamish.

"You think that's our poison, Tammy's wonder drug?" Zol said.
Had it made its way into Grand Basin's tobacco fields?

"But it was more than a year ago that they closed down her
project," Colleen said. "Why would we be seeing the effects all
these months later?"

"Last year's tobacco crop is this year's cigarettes," Zol said. "The
kiln-dried leaves sit and age for a few months. The longer the
better, actually. Like wine. I'd say the timing is perfect."

"The matchstick particles could be merely a marker," Natasha said, "telling us that tobacco from the smoke shops is contaminated with something. Why don't we test rez tobacco for a liver toxin?"

"Because technically," Hamish said, "the stuff is toxic already. Full of hundreds, if not thousands, of chemicals. Look at the warnings on a pack of cigarettes. We're looking for a brand new chemical and we have no idea what it is. Where would we start?"

"Yeah, we need targeted testing," Zol said. "That's how the guys at airport security examine your laptop for traces of explosives. Those people know what they're looking for, and their machine tells them when it finds it." The team, on the other hand, hadn't the faintest clue what they were looking for. It seemed hopeless.

"Not everything was expunged from Tammy's lab," Hamish said.

"No?" Zol said.

"We still have Jovan Ligorov. Well, sort of."

"Who's he when he's at home?" Colleen asked.

"Tammy's research assistant," Hamish said. "Her number-one guy. He was a surgeon in one of those Yugoslavian states or provinces or whatever they call them. Kind of a strange guy. Used to wear a huge, ornate cross around his neck. Over his lab coat. It gave Tammy the creeps."

"He still around?" Zol said. Ligorov could be anywhere; when research projects folded, the assistants dispersed to find work wherever they could.

"Directly below my lab, as it turns out," Hamish said. "In the morgue."

Natasha's hand flew to her mouth. "Murdered? Like Tammy?"

"Alive and kicking." Hamish paused, then added, "He's a diener."

Zol answered Colleen's puzzled frown. "A morgue attendant. Helps with autopsies." He turned to Hamish. "You talked to him?"

"It wasn't a conversation. He clammed up as soon as I mentioned Tammy's name."

"But at least we've still got him," Zol said.

"Good luck," Hamish said. "This morning, he looked like I'd

invoked the devil. Clutched his cross and told me to leave the past in the past."

When they'd finished the meeting, and the others headed ` toward the door, Colleen held Zol back.

He'd been expecting this.

"My contact in Toronto called me at noon," she whispered. "The three guys they found executed under the rubble at the ROM were from Misty Shores First Nation."

"Where's that?

"A couple of hours northeast of Toronto. The Trent River watershed."

"They're not Mohawk up there," he said.

"So I've learned. Anishinaabeg."

"Yeah," he said. "Related to the Ojibwa and Algonquins. Never have been on exactly friendly terms with the Iroquois down our way." Actually, it was worse than that. The Iroquois were at war with the Ojibwa and Algonquins when the Europeans first arrived. Did hundreds of years of enmity ever get resolved?

"I did a little research," Colleen said. "Misty Shores sits on a rare and historically rich burial mound built two thousand years ago by the Middle Woodland People. Most of the site's sacred treasures have disappeared. Appropriated by scholarly collectors or stolen by thieves, depending on your point of view. "

He chewed on that for a moment: these days, special interest groups saw museums not as palaces of shared history, but as plunderers of cultural icons.

"Whatever we might think about museums," Colleen continued, "the people of Misty Shores have become militant about reclaiming their artifacts. Some inflammatory statements on their website."

"They figured the loon pipe was theirs? Stolen from their mound and not from a similar one in Ohio?"

"I'd say so. Enough to break into the ROM and attack the First Peoples Gallery with the sledgehammers and crowbar the police found near their bodies."

He pulled on his raincoat. "And then the Badger gets them popped off, snatches the goods before their corpses are even cold, and tries to cover his tracks by blowing up the White Man's folly."

And having seized one of the legendary pipes, he'd be looking for the second. It seemed the Badger had no more liking for the Anishinaabeg than he did for the Whites. All his wealth was not satisfying his greed. The Badger was on the march for political power, and not just at the local level.

Colleen tugged her hat down over her forehead. "The bugger has eyes and ears everywhere."

He pictured Max stashed at the farm, playing Clue with Gaspar and Kitti. "Don't remind me."

CHAPTER 27

"I'm afraid that's the law, Mr. Cheeseman," Zol told the indignant farmer on the other end of the phone, first thing Monday morning. "You and your family can drink as much unpasteurized milk as you like, but you're not allowed to sell it."

"Our family's been dairy farmin' in Norfolk County back four generations. Hell, that's how we got 'r name." As Percy Cheeseman's voice rose to a shout, Zol pictured the man's face getting redder and redder. "I'm not lettin' none of your stupid, new-fangled laws interfere with seventy-five years of tradition. For God's sake, man, our product is completely natural. And hund'erd percent pure."

Natural, yes. Pure, too. Pure salmonella, E. coli, campylobacter, and listeria, the lively quartet of unpasteurized milk.

"When's the other doctor coming back?" Cheeseman continued. "You know, the guy who took sick. He was the right man for the job down here in Norfolk County. Left us alone."

"I'm afraid we'll have to agree to disagree . . . sir," Zol said. "And —"

"Those city ways o' yours got no business down here in God's country. You'll be hearin' from my member o' parliament."

That cosy little promise ended the call, and Zol made a note to send one of the health inspectors to the Cheeseman farm. The job needed someone tall, broad, and blessed with a good-old-boy manner. He hadn't met all the inspectors yet, so no one came to mind. He'd have to ask Nancy.

Cheeseman's call had come through before Zol had a chance to look at his overnight emails. He was turning to read them when Nancy knocked twice and entered.

The light had disappeared from her shiny brown eyes.

"You better have a look at this, Dr. Szabo. Out here. I'm not touching it."

"What is it?"

"Please, come see for yourself." She led him out of the office toward her desk in the reception area. She stopped two paces from the desk and pointed to a packet sitting beside her in-basket. "See? Bad news pasted right across it."

It was a large, brown envelope addressed to Dr. Zol Szabo, Health Unit, Simcoe. The address was neither handwritten nor typed. It had been crudely cut and pasted from the pages of a newspaper, probably the *Simcoe Reformer*. That wouldn't have been difficult; his name had been all over it lately. Without a stamp or a return address, the thing did look menacing. And oddly melodramatic.

"Any idea how it got here?" he asked.

She wrinkled her nose. "There's an outside mailbox. Sylvia checks it at nine-thirty every morning before she starts sorting the mail, in case there's been an overnight external delivery. The mailman comes right to her office, so the outside box rarely has anything in it."

"Sylvia put this here?"

Nancy nodded without taking her eyes off the package. It was as if she was trying to control the villain inside it with her gaze.

Zol leaned over the desk and sniffed. Nothing. He sniffed again. Suddenly, Ringo was jamming those too-familiar bars of "Yellow Submarine." The odour was faint and Ringo's session correspondingly brief. But there was no denying the stench of rez tobacco.

He lifted the manila packet from the desk. It was lightweight but stiff, as if it contained a piece of cardboard cut to its exact dimensions. "Got a letter opener?"

Nancy pulled in her arms. "Our policy is not to open anything that doesn't have a return address. One time we had a stink bomb."

"Really?"

"From a disgruntled parent. Unhappy that her child got dismissed from school for not being properly immunized. During a German measles epidemic, for heaven's sake."

Zol returned the envelope to the desk. Very slowly. And with two hands. "So, what do we do with it? What is the policy?"

She looked puzzled for a moment, as if trying to remember. Then her lips tightened into a shy smile that seemed to catch her by surprise. "Notify the medical officer of health."

"I guess that means I get to use my judgment."

She maintained her stare at the envelope and said nothing. It was clear she wasn't going to sit at her desk until the manila menace had been dealt with.

He picked it up, again with both hands, and took it into his office.

He closed the door.

He held the envelope to his ear. It wasn't ticking. He turned it over. The simple flap had been secured with a length of wide, transparent tape. Nothing on either side indicated where it had come from or who had sent it. The odour of rez tobacco brought the Badger to mind. Was it another warning from him? In the form of a written message or something more drastic? Dennis wasn't a prankster. It wouldn't be a stink bomb.

The easiest thing would be to call the police. Let them handle it. Did the Simcoe detachment have a bomb squad? Probably not. They'd send it to Hamilton or Toronto, and he'd never see it again. The police blew up anything they remotely considered might be a bomb. But if they destroyed this envelope, he'd never know what was in it.

And that could be a problem.

Maybe the Badger hadn't sent it. Maybe it was someone wanting to be helpful. Matt Holt, for instance. He had every reason to want to see the liver epidemic cracked, and every reason to stay in the shadows. He'd stuck his neck out before and the chop-shoppers had torched his garage.

Zol brought the packet to his ear again. He planted his feet and shook it. Nothing. He tried it again with a bit more force. Something rustled, and not with the tinkle of metal or the clunk of plastic. What did it sound like? Styrofoam? Paper?

This was silly. He had to know what was inside, but also be assured it wasn't a bomb. He had to get it X-rayed. Not at the hospital. He couldn't bring a potential bomb into Simcoe General and casually ask the radiologists to put it under their machine. He'd be out of a job by the afternoon.

Who else had an X-ray machine?

Eddy Pakozdi. At his veterinary clinic. He also had a lively curiosity about everything that crossed his path. Zol pictured Eddy as he'd seen him last, on his snowmobile flying across the snow-covered fields of Norfolk County, dashing from farm to farm and tending to cows with infected teats, horses with colic, and nannies with whatever troubled milking-goats.

Veterinary medicine. Curiosity. Milking-goats. It was slowly coming back to him. A couple of years ago, maybe longer, Eddy had told Zol about this weird thing called orf virus infecting milking-goat herds under his care. Lots of goats, but only a couple of farmers, had developed the characteristic blistering lesions that took weeks and weeks to heal. Acting on advice from the Veterinary College in Guelph, Eddy controlled the outbreak by culling the affected herds. Zol forgot about the incident because he hadn't been responsible for Norfolk County at the time, and orf virus was a relatively harmless human pathogen that health units never concerned themselves with.

When Hamish had described a possible orf hybrid in Mongolia, Zol knew the strangely named virus sounded familiar. But at the time, he was so rattled from seeing that woman hit the deer on Highway 24 that he wasn't thinking straight.

He looked at the envelope in his hands, made a mental note to ask Natasha to contact Guelph and see what details she could dig up regarding orf activity in Norfolk County, then banished the virus to the back of his mind. The big question for today: would either a vet or a public-health doc recognize the X-ray image of a letter bomb staring back at them?

CHAPTER 28

An hour or so later, Zol followed his perennially industrious father out of the kitchen door and into the yard. They hadn't told Mum what they were up to. She'd fuss and tell Dad to *put that stupid thing away, Gazsi. All it does is cause trouble.*

It was good to see Mum up and dressed today. Her cheeks lacked colour and that turban never let you forget she was in the throes of chemotherapy, but her smile was genuine when she told Zol how much she'd loved Max's visit yesterday. She'd made Zol promise to stay for lunch today, and yes, she was more than strong enough to heat up a can of tomato soup and make him a nice sandwich to go with it. They had yet to discuss her role in connecting Francine with Max. Bringing up the postcard correspondence didn't seem necessary at this point, and no matter how Zol might broach the subject, no matter how careful he was with his tone of voice, his mum would think he was being petty and bitter about Francine. Yesterday, over their rounds of Clue and Scrabble, Max had undoubtedly told his grandmother all about his mother's impending visit. Poor kid, he was getting set for an epic fall; Francine had yet to answer Zol's invitation, so it was anyone's guess whether she was actually coming.

With his dad now four paces ahead, Zol strode past the six tobacco kilns that had consumed his teenage summers. He rubbed his right clavicle, suddenly aching where he'd fractured it falling from the rafters of kiln number one. Age fourteen and exhausted, he'd been upended by a heavy bundle of freshly tied leaves. Now the buildings were abandoned and barely standing, but evocatively weathered and more photogenic every year. Like so many other tobacco farmers, Dad couldn't bring himself to pull down the old kilns, though it was difficult to imagine Gaspar Szabo having even one nostalgic bone in his flinty body.

Dad undid the workshop padlock, pulled open the door, and flipped on the light. He pointed to his spotless workbench. "Put it there," he said, meaning the mysterious envelope that had barely left Zol's grasp since he'd first touched it two hours ago.

With the care of a surgeon handling an endoscope, Gaspar lifted his metal detector from its place on a shelf. He'd created the instrument from an old hockey stick, a round metal disk that once had been a pie plate, and a bunch of electrical stuff Zol didn't pretend to understand. Gaspar took a fresh packet of batteries from a cupboard he'd rescued from a neighbour's kitchen renovations and inserted them into the device.

He fiddled with the detector, tuning it like a radio. It screeched like an indignant seagull when he passed it over a pipe wrench he'd set on the worktop. But it didn't so much as peep over a stack of newspapers piled on the concrete floor. When it squeaked over a bundle of rags in a cardboard box, Gaspar looked perplexed until he found a length of electrical cord buried underneath. Finally, he took a dime from his pocket, covered it with about twenty pages of the Simcoe Reformer, and passed the detector over it. When the thing whistled softly but clearly, he beamed.

"Looks like it's working," Zol said.

"Of course." The wink said it all.

He told Zol to move his envelope to the middle of the workbench. Then he raised his eyebrows, drew in a deep breath, and passed his instrument over it. Nothing. Not a hiss, not even a whisper. He lowered the device so that it was practically touching the envelope, then passed the detector over it again, systematically. Up and down, side to side.

The thing made no sound at all.

"No metal, eh?" Zol said.

Dad's face was serious. With his tongue clamped between his teeth, he looked like Max concentrating on a tricky video-game sequence. "One more test."

He switched off the detector and handed it to Zol, then turned to a box of electrical stuff. He rifled through switches, fuses, connectors, and bits of wire. From somewhere in there he pulled out a piece of copper wire a handbreadth in length and the thickness of a few human hairs. He tucked the tiny wire under the right-hand end of Zol's rectangular envelope, then threw the switch on the detector and started a pass from the left.

The gadget made no sound. Not even a chirp. No matter how slowly or how quickly Gaspar passed his detector over the envelope and the copper wire he'd hidden beneath it, the thing stayed silent. Beads of sweat collected on his forehead, and he began to look like an anxious inventor trying not to lose his cool in front of an important patron. He tapped the detector's metal disk, checked the position of the batteries, and readjusted the tuning knob. He tried another pass over the envelope. When he got to the spot where he'd hidden the wire, the gadget woke up and screeched enthusiastically.

Still not satisfied, Gaspar moved the wire to another spot, this time beneath the other end of the packet. When he tried the detector again, the thing stayed quiet until it got to the wire, then chirped like an angry robin.

Zol had to shout over the racket. "What's the verdict, Dad?"

Gaspar killed the switch. "You have to ask?"

Two tests were telling Zol the same thing, but uncertainty was making his heart beat overtime. Eddy Pakozdi's X-ray machine had revealed no interpretable shapes or shadows inside the envelope.

No wires, no bits and pieces made out of metal. And now, Dad's homemade device seemed to be saying the same. Could he trust it? Trouble was, neither Eddy nor Dad could promise there wasn't a wad of plastic explosive waiting to blow them from here to Lake Erie. Or a fine, dispersible powder teeming with enough anthrax or bubonic plague to infect the entire county.

Dad laid the detector against the wall and picked up the envelope. He shook it next to his ear, held it up to the light, sniffed it.

"Pirate smoke inside here," he said, finally. "From the rez. And not properly cured." He took a penknife from the shelf above the workbench and waved it toward the door. "Outside, son. This, I do alone."

"No, Dad. It's my problem, my responsibility."

"And this my workshop. You — you have Max and Colleen to thinking about. And your important work that — that makes me so — proud. Yes, I never say, but I am very proud." He put his left hand on Zol's right shoulder and gave it a long, hard squeeze. Was he aware that his thumb was pushing against Zol's old collar-bone fracture? No, but there were tears glistening in his eyes. "Soon, I will not have . . . well, you know what we facing . . ."

Zol squeezed his dad's arm, held his watery gaze for a long, quiet moment.

"It's addressed to me, Dad. I should be the one to open it."

Gaspar closed his eyes and turned away. Zol had seen that manoeuvre a thousand times before and knew there was no breaking through it.

Now he was blinking back the tears as his dad closed the door behind him with a resolute clunk. Zol plodded across the yard, stood beside kiln number one, and focussed on the work-shed door.

The moments crept by, and nothing happened. What was Dad doing? How long did it take to slice open an envelope?

An explosion tore from the back of the workshop. Zol dove behind the kiln and shielded his eyes as he hit the ground. He crouched motionless on the grass, his heartbeat hammering at his throat.

What . . . ?

He looked around. Nothing had changed.

Oh, for God's sake.

What a skittish idiot he'd been. It was only a Harley, misfiring as the driver gunned down Jenkins Road.

He jumped up, swiped at the telltale mud and grass on his slacks, and squinted at the shed.

Dad was standing at the open door, still in possession of the penknife and four intact limbs. And beaming a satisfied smile.

"You come see this, Zollie."

"What is it?"

"You will see."

"Nothing dangerous?"

"Not for us. Not anymore."

Gaspar had opened the envelope and removed its contents. Displayed on the workbench were an unmarked piece of corrugated cardboard roughly the dimensions of the envelope and a zippered food storage bag of about the same size. Sealed within the transparent plastic was something that at quick glance was thin, brown, and crinkled.

Gaspar swung a gooseneck lamp over the bag. "In old days, that blight in there bring tobacco farmers big trouble."

Zol looked through the bag without touching it. It contained a single tobacco leaf. At least, the major part of one. It looked aged to some extent, cracked in several places as if fairly brittle, and discoloured in a strange way.

"Looks like it's got a rash, Dad. Our crop didn't looked like that, did it?"

"Never. TMV spoils yield and selling price." Gaspar Szabo's tobacco had enjoyed the best of reputations. If he'd wanted, he could have bought himself a new car every year on the bonuses his crop earned from the brand-name tobacco companies.

Zol picked up the bag and examined the leaf on both sides. A healthy plant at this stage of curing would be an even, caramel brown. This one looked diseased. The top side was mottled with irregular swirls of yellow, grey, and brown. The underside was covered in red spots.

Zol pointed to the spots that looked like dried blood on sun-weathered skin. "What are those?"

Gaspar fished a pair of reading glasses from his shirt pocket. "Never seen those red marks before. Not with TMV." He turned the bag over. "The top side, that's TMV, tobacco mosaic virus. Stunts plant growth and gives bitter taste. Dark spots underneath? I do not know. Maybe it's from — What you call it? — a mutant?"

He pulled a sheet of letter-size paper from the envelope and handed it to Zol. "I didn't put my glasses. Maybe there is message?"

There certainly was, laser printed in capital letters at the top of the page:

OKAY, OKAY.

A LOT OF REZ TOBACCO LOOKS LIKE THIS.

BEST I CAN DO. BALL'S IN YOUR COURT.

Zol's cellphone chirped on his belt. It was Colleen.

"Hi," he said. "I'm here with Dad. What's up?"

"Oh Zol. I feel terrible."

"What's wrong? You sick?"

"It's all my fault."

"For pity's sake, tell me — what's wrong?" He could barely formulate the next words, but he had to get them out. "Is it Max?"

"Olivia. They got her in the parking lot. At the LCBO."

Anyone who drank as much Southern Comfort as Olivia Colborne was bound to get dinged for drunk driving sooner or later. "On a DUI?" Getting nabbed by the cops in the parking lot of the government liquor store sounded like karma.

"A drive-by. Asian faces with a high-powered rifle."

"Is she going to be okay?"

Colleen's voice dissolved into a flood of sobs. "She's on her way — to the morgue. And — and I put her there."

CHAPTER 29

Zol ushered Colleen into his office and asked Nancy to rustle her up a cup of tea. It wouldn't be Colleen's favourite, South African rooibos, but at this point any hot drink would probably do.

He'd never seen her look like this. Puffy eyes, blotches on her neck, shaky hands clutching at her handbag. He closed the door.

"I might as well have shot her myself," she said, her voice cracking. "If it weren't for me she'd still be alive."

He knew that could not be true. But there was no point in arguing.

He eased her purse from her grasp and set it on his desk. He took her hands in his. Their clamminess surprised him. "Tell me the story from the beginning," he said, hoping his unease at her agitation wasn't registering on his face. "You found something incriminating in Olivia's house when you and Matt Holt were there on Saturday?"

"We got so little out of her at the house that I phoned back a couple of hours later — threatened her with exposure and criminal prosecution if she didn't cooperate with our investigation."

"What could you have exposed?"

"The pad of blank prescriptions she stole from a doctor in Hamilton."

"You found them lying around?"

"In her underwear drawer."

Of course. That's where Francine used to hide her cocaine. Not that she ever held onto it for long. "Olivia filled them out herself?"

Colleen nodded. "I found the remains of a bottle of two hundred OxyContins — and three others like it, empty."

"Alcohol and opiates, eh?" It would be difficult to keep the neurons firing properly with all that in her system.

"And nonstop nicotine." Colleen described how Olivia had lit one cigarette on the butt of the other in an almost unbroken chain.

"What did you pressure her to do?"

"Tell us what had poisoned the rez's tobacco supply. And how it got there."

He was amazed at Colleen's directness. She was usually much more subtle, a master at finesse.

"I know what you're thinking," she told him. "But it worked. She got edgy and defensive. And no matter how much she tried to hide it, she knew we were on the right track with the contamination angle."

Nancy knocked and said she had Colleen's tea ready.

Zol let go of Colleen's hands and quickly relieved Nancy of a steaming teacup and two digestive biscuits.

He handed Colleen the cup and said nothing until Nancy was on the other side of the closed door and — hopefully — well out of earshot. "You figure Olivia had a word with her bosses?"

"She must have. Sometime after my call." Colleen's face crumpled. "And clearly, they didn't like what they heard."

A wave of shivers slammed his shoulders. Was the Badger that cold-blooded, or was the hit on Olivia the work of his Asian partners?

"Your little talk with Olivia got her to do more than contact her colleagues on the rez," he said.

"What do you mean?"

"I think she sent me a parcel."

"When?"

"I got it this morning."

He pulled the packet from the bottom drawer of the filing cabinet and set it on the desk.

Colleen sniffed at the envelope and made a face. "Reeks of rez tobacco."

"You got that right. Drives my dad crazy that they don't process the tobacco properly before turning it into cigarettes."

She sniffed at the open end of the envelope and cocked her head to the side. "There's something else trying to come through. Several scents, actually."

"What do you get?"

She thought for a moment. "Hmm. Mandarin peel. Oil of bergamot. And something else." She put her nose in the envelope and sniffed again. "Sorry, can't place it."

"Oak moss?"

"Maybe."

"Adding up to?"

She looked puzzled for a few seconds, then answered. "Of course. Calvin Klein."

He raised his eyebrows and ventured a smile. "Good on you."

"I should have nailed it immediately. I saw a bottle of Obsession in her upstairs bathroom. She'd sprayed it on rather too generously before our visit. Probably trying to hide the smell of her Southern Comfort." She warmed her hands on the teacup for a moment, then asked, "What's in her envelope?"

He held up the note and read it out loud. "Okay, okay. A lot of rez tobacco looks like this. Best I can do. Ball's in your court."

The first line made sense now that he knew Colleen had pressured Olivia over the forged prescriptions.

Colleen closed her eyes and shook her head. "Poor thing, I did put her in a bind."

His eyes strayed to the packet. "I hope what she sent us is more than a riddle."

"Zol! The woman just got herself killed by doing the right thing. It wouldn't hurt to give her the credit she deserves."

He wasn't sure about that, but let it go.

He slid his hand into the manila packet and pulled out the mottled tobacco leaf, still in its resealable plastic bag. "This is what she included with the note."

Colleen put down her tea, and as she scrutinized the leaf under the desk lamp, he could see the wheels turning inside her head. "If," she said, "those spots and swirls are even close to what I think they are, this was Olivia's way of telling us her factories use blemished tobacco."

"Hell, it's not merely blemished. It's infected." He summarized his discussion with his dad and explained the significance of the two sets of markings. There was the mottling caused by tobacco mosaic virus infection, classic in appearance and harmless to humans. And there were the mysterious blood-red spots Gaspar had never seen before and suggested could be caused by some sort of mutant microbe.

"Mutant?" she said. "Could we talking about the matchstick particles that reminded Winnipeg of that weird virus in the facial blisters — a hybrid, was it? — in the family from Mongolia?"

"Finding matchstick particles in those red spots would explain Hamish's cluster of lip and finger lesions, all right. But not the liver failures." He reminded her that the pathologist who examined the liver biopsies was categorical when he excluded infection as a cause of the liver damage. "To explain the liver failures," he told her, "we need to find a poison, not a germ."

"That brings us back to Tammy Holt's research, doesn't it? As I understand it, Tammy was genetically engineering a tobacco mosaic virus to produce an appetite-suppressing wonder drug. Was the project shut down because the virus morphed into something that behaved more like a human toxin than a plant infection?"

"But why was Tammy murdered?"

Colleen chewed on that until she'd swallowed her last bite of digestive and drained her tea. She put down the cup. Her eyes were less puffy, the red blotches on her throat starting to fade. "Because Tammy knew the virus had escaped her controlled laboratory conditions and was infecting the lucrative tobacco fields of Norfolk County and —"

"She confronted Dennis Badger, warned him he couldn't use any of the infected tobacco in his cigarette facilities."

"And he pictured his empire going —"

"Up in smoke?" Zol said.

Colleen gestured toward Olivia's leaf, now another indictment against Dennis Badger. "By sending you that bit of evidence, and admitting that much of the tobacco processed in her factories looks like that, Olivia is telling you what happened: Tammy's drug-making virus did escape. It got into the open tobacco fields of Grand Basin Reserve and surrounding Norfolk County, and is now being turned into Native cigarettes."

"That's a great theory, but how do we prove it?" He knew the answer to his own question, but maybe Colleen had a better idea.

"Hamish said Jovan Ligorov, Tammy's chief research tech, seemed scared to death. You're only that frightened when you're hiding something dangerous."

"He needs to give up the whole story," Zol said. "Every last detail."

Something had changed in Colleen's face. Today, her moods were impossible to keep up with. First, she'd been almost inconsolable over Olivia's murder. Then, she'd seemed excited at interpreting the blemishes on the tobacco leaf. Now, she looked wary. No, more than wary, terrified.

"Zol — no!" she said. "Ligorov's position is extraordinarily dangerous. He knows far too much." She squeezed his arm. "And if he tells you what he knows about Tammy Holt's project, then you'll know too much."

"But I'm supposed to be in the know. Getting to the bottom of all this is my job."

She shook her head and squeezed harder. "It's time to call in the police. Let them get the story out of Ligorov. And protect him from the Badger."

"You serious? I thought you private-eye types never —"

"There's nothing wrong with calling in the cops at the appropriate stage of an investigation."

"Come on, you go up against bad actors every day without involving the cops."

"Not like this. Dealing with criminal gangs is no cricket match. It's a very dangerous game. There are no gentlemen and no rules of fair play."

"You didn't seem to mind going after the chop-shop guys."

"I didn't go after them, Zol. I just watched them. And reported what I saw to my client."

"The car dealer guy?"

"Who then called the police." She lifted her empty cup and tapped at it absently. "And when the chop-shoppers thought it was Matt Holt who'd ratted on them, they tried to burn his place down."

He chewed on that for a moment. Had Colleen dodged a much bigger bullet on that case than he'd imagined?

"But hell," he said, "what are the cops going to do with our theories and empty allegations? Unless we hand them solid proof that rez tobacco is contaminated with a particular poison or lethal virus, they'll laugh us out of the station. Native reserves are forbidden territory as far as the cops are concerned — too politically hot for the provincial police and the RCMP. Nothing short of a national catastrophe will ever get our nation's finest to poke their noses inside Grand Basin Reserve."

She looked inside her teacup, seemed disappointed it was empty, and dropped it onto the saucer. A stew of emotions was simmering on her face. "I'm sorry, Zol, but at this point, this case is too hot for us to handle. The way things have been going, I feel like a bloody amateur. The Badger knows Max's phone number, he threatened you in no uncertain terms, and look what his lot did to poor Olivia."

She didn't have to spell it out for him any more clearly, especially the part about Max.

But still, he needed hard evidence. Without it, this case was going nowhere. Should he give it up? Leave the Badger and his gang to the police, which amounted to the same thing? Or could he get the information he needed some other way, by a completely different route? One that didn't involve Ligorov.

Tammy Holt's project had been bankrolled by an American pharmaceutical company, that was common knowledge. U.S. drug companies answered to the U.S. Food and Drug Administration. The FDA would have a record of every human study Tammy's sponsoring company had conducted. If pushed, the FDA could force Tammy's backers to cooperate with Zol's investigation, tell him why they'd shut her project down. That was it — he'd get the information he needed through the front door.

But then it hit him: the international paperwork would be a nightmare. It would take months to grind its way through multiple layers of bureaucracy on both sides of the border. He couldn't bear to think how many livers would be destroyed and how many lives would be lost along the way. And Erie Christian Collegiate wasn't the only school that was going to be affected. Any day now, the phone was going to ring with news of a string of liver failures erupting in another school on his patch.

He had no choice. He had to lean on Ligorov. The man knew the chemical composition of Tammy's wonder drug and the reason the project was abandoned so abruptly. When Ligorov coughed up that information, Zol could run the appropriate tests on Olivia's blemished tobacco leaf and the cigarettes Hamish and Colleen had purchased on the rez. If any of the rez tobacco contained the problem drug, he would call in Health Canada, the Ontario Ministry of Health, the Grand Basin cops, the provincial cops, the RCMP, the Ministry of Aboriginal Affairs, and whoever else it would take to shut down Dennis Badger's trade in poisoned cigarettes.

"Before we call the cops," he said, "I've got to have one more go at Ligorov. Get him talking. There's no other way."

Colleen shook her head. "Please, Zol, no. It's too risky for all of us. Besides, you won't manage it. Ligorov knows what danger he's facing. He'll not let you near him."

"Come on, I can make the guy understand what a serious situation we're in."

"Don't you think he knows that already? He reads the papers, watches TV newscasts. He must be terrified the tobacco mob will pop him off before he can finger them. Promise me you *will* leave him alone."

"No, I gotta talk to him. Myself."

The phone buzzed from Nancy's office.

"Sorry to disturb you, Dr. Szabo," Nancy said. "There's a gentleman here from Escarpment Cable. Needs to make an emergency adjustment to your phone and your Internet cable connection."

"Sorry, Nancy, this isn't a good time."

"I'm only bothering you because he says you have a critical privacy breech. Some sort of computer virus from Kazakhstan."

He had no idea what that might be, but it did sound important. "You trust him?"

"Really, Dr. Szabo, you're not in Hamilton anymore. Here in Simcoe we trust pretty well everyone with an honest face."

"You know the guy?"

"Not personally. But I've seen him around town and he looks legitimate. He's got lots of equipment with him, and he gave me his business card. Would you like to see it?"

"How long is it going to take for him to get the job done?"

There was a pause as Nancy conversed with the cable guy. "He says twenty minutes, max."

"Okay. We'll go out for a coffee." He needed some fresh air anyway. "But keep his card handy in case he screws up my computer. You know what these guys are like — always adding bells and whistles that make simple tasks a helluva lot more complicated."

As he strode with Colleen toward Norfolk Street and the Detour Café, neither of them said a word. Truly annoyed at his veto against calling in the police, she bristled when he tried to take her arm.

He left her to her thoughts, unable take his own mind off Jovan Ligorov. He pictured the man as Hamish had described him, heavy set, bent over a corpse in the autopsy room, thick rubber gloves on his hands, a plastic bib over his clothes, an ornate cross hanging from his neck.

The image gave him an idea. Colleen would think it was crazy, misguided, and dangerous. And it would make her even angrier.

He'd keep it to himself.

CHAPTER 30

It was after eight that evening by the time Zol kissed Max goodbye, got a frosty peck from Colleen, and checked twice to be sure the front door was locked and all the outside lights were on before he climbed into the minivan. He wasn't sure which was feeding her iciness with great vigour, anger or fear. Probably both in equal measure. Anger that he was not following her professional advice to call in the cops — after all, he'd hired her as a consultant on the case. And fear for their lives — the Badger was showing little reluctance to eliminate anyone standing in the way of building his empire.

It was becoming increasing clear that the Badger was on a quest for political power. He was no longer satisfied with the untold millions his tobacco empire had earned him. Seizing the loon pipe after executing his rivals and destroying the ROM's Crystal could have two motives: repatriation of a Native power symbol and proclamation of an anti-White manifesto. Dennis Badger's tobacco business was no longer a piggy bank for funding expensive toys, but a war chest. Was he planning to use the country's six hundred Indian reserves as guerrilla bases? He'd already consolidated them into an efficient and lucrative retail network for cigarette sales.

How much would it take to hide arms and explosives under the cash registers of his tobacco franchisees?

Zol shuddered and forced himself to think of the case purely as a public-health issue. His job was to bring the liver epidemic to a halt, and that was what he was going to do. It wasn't helping to allow his personal and deep-seated apprehensions about the Badger's intentions to turn fanciful.

As he backed out of the driveway, he satisfied himself there were no strange vehicles lurking on the street. Nothing but a cable company van was parked outside the neighbours' house. He turned left on Scenic, right on Garth, and ten minutes later was heading east past the industrial estates at the far end of Stone Church Road. He was keeping his eyes peeled for the crosses.

Why the heck had the Macedonians built their church way out here? The land must have been cheap before the city spread its tentacles this far south. He'd checked out Saint Naum of Ohrid on the Internet and knew what to look for: a beige stucco building with two square towers and a hexagonal dome, each topped by a simple but conspicuous cross. Its banquet centre — a popular venue for weddings and charity functions — extended from the rear and wouldn't be visible from the street.

He spotted the crosses about a half a kilometre in the distance as he passed a plumbing store on the left and a carpet showroom on the right. Two blocks later, when he could see the approaching towers, he braked opposite a self-storage depot surrounded by a chain-link fence two or three metres high. Beyond the depot, and immediately past an automobile windshield repair centre, a brightly lit sign indicated the right turn into Saint Naum of Ohrid Macedonian Orthodox Church and Banquet Centre. He followed the driveway into the church's expansive, unpaved car park. The lot was empty except for one car, and behind it a vacant field yawned in the darkness. The long, flat-roofed banquet centre was clad in the same beige stucco as the church. Most of its lights were off.

He swung the car around a hundred and eighty degrees and found a spot with a good view of the church, the banquet centre, and the street. The clock on the dash said 8:23. He was early by seven minutes, plenty of time to keep his promise to the priest by ensuring that no one followed him. He killed the engine, hit PLAY on the CD player, and selected track two of Ray LaMontagne's "God Willin' & the Creek Don't Rise."

At this time on a Monday night, there was almost no traffic on Stone Church Road. One small car, a Kia or a Hyundai, had been driving eastward behind him, but was long gone. There was no activity at the self-storage place or the windshield repair centre next door. Both businesses were closed and the lights were off. The Tim Hortons kitty-corner across the street was open but quiet. No cars in the drive-thru and one parked out front. As Ray LaMontagne and his Pariah Dogs belted out a mournful ballad about New York City, one car left the Tim's, another arrived, and then an Escarpment Cable repair van pulled in. These days, it seemed, society ran on three essentials: coffee, gasoline, and cable.

At eight-thirty, he said goodbye to Ray and stepped out of the car. His shoes crunched on the gravel as he headed toward the door marked BANQUET CENTRE AND CHURCH OFFICE. An illuminated sign advertising SUPER SAUSAGES AT WHOLESALE PRICES winked at him from a prefab hut across the street. He couldn't help wondering when the last time a health inspector had visited that seedy-looking place. He hated informal butcher shops; you never knew what they were hiding in their wieners and cold cuts.

From a distance, the church had looked impressive with its bright red roof, polygonal dome, and stately towers. Up close, the building looked as if it had been thrown together by volunteers whose budget and enthusiasm had flagged near the end. There were no railings guarding the front steps, the paint around the windows either had peeled or was missing in the first place, the stucco was flaking off in chunks, and the front door looked like it had been purchased from a local building supply centre during its annual scratch-and-dent sale.

He tried the door, but it was locked. No surprise without a banquet in progress. He couldn't find a buzzer, so he rapped with his knuckles. He knocked twice more before heavy footsteps approached, and the door was pulled open by a tall, young, pale-eyed man beaming a circumspect smile through a thick red beard.

"Dr. Szabo, good evening to you. Come in, my good man. I recognize you from your photograph in the newspaper." The priest touched the large silver cross hanging from a heavy chain around his neck and threw Zol an infectious smile. "I'm Stoyan Murphy, and you can see by my get-up that I'm the parish priest here at Saint Naum's."

The cross, which looked like it weighed a ton and appeared more garish than holy, was dominated by a high relief of a crucified Christ, naked and agonal; a knotted-rope design, oddly Celtic and also high relief, embellished each of the cross's four arms.

He led Zol across a utilitarian, low-ceilinged foyer, his black cassock swooshing heavily against his ankles. He opened a door that said FATHER D. STOYAN MURPHY and invited Zol in.

The first thing Zol noticed inside the priest's office were the framed photographs of fireworks. Nearly two dozen of them blanketed the walls. Some had been staged locally at familiar venues such as the Burlington Skyway Bridge, the Dofasco steelworks, and Dundurn Castle. Others showed the Eiffel Tower, the Egyptian Pyramids, the Washington Monument, and landmarks he couldn't place. A church seemed a strange place to hang photos of pyrotechnical displays. Maybe they were meant to symbolize the ephemeral power of the Lord.

"You don't play poker, do you Doctor?"

"Sorry?"

"Your thoughts are written all over your face. You're wondering what in the name of everything that's holy an Orthodox priest with an Irish accent is doing with so many photos of fireworks. Is he going to blow something up?"

Zol felt his ears flush. "Well . . . I don't think I'd say that."

"Just think it?" said the priest, a teasing smile on his face.

"It is a fascinating collection," Zol said, concentrating on a bouquet of fiery peonies dazzling the sky over Toronto's CN Tower.

"It's my hobby. One of my healthier passions. My wife would call it an obsession."

"You do it competitively?"

He shook his head. "Not so much. But I am a certified pyro-technician. I do holidays and special events. In Hamilton, Oakville, Brampton, Mississauga. Sometimes Toronto, but they have their own set of enthusiasts there in the Big Smoke." His chest puffed as he pointed to what looked like a layer cake and birthday candles floating atop the expansive arch of the Skyway Bridge over Hamilton Bay. "I think that's my best work. Canada Day last year. Weeks in the planning."

"Impressive. Do you ever do the burning schoolhouse?"

"A favourite of yours, is it? Mine as well. I have a special version of it. Do it at birthday parties."

He tugged at his clerical dog collar, as if pyrotechnics and the clergy weren't supposed to mix. Perhaps fire and brimstone weren't important elements of the Macedonian church.

"Last summer," he continued, "I did a party at a tobacco farm. Used one of those abandoned kilns as the schoolhouse. The kids squealed in delight when it seemed the entire building was engulfed by flames." He paused and threw his arms out for the dramatic effect he probably used in the pulpit. "And they were clearly amazed — and perhaps a little disappointed — when the smoke cleared and the schoolhouse emerged completely untouched."

"Sounds like magic."

"That's the fun of it. A bit of the blarney. Especially when I do it by remote control, and the fire appears to start all by itself, out of nothing."

He pulled at the cuffs of his cassock as his ruddy face turned serious. He indicated that Zol should sit in one of the four folding metal chairs in the room and took one for himself.

He closed his eyes for a moment and touched his cross with his broad palm. Then he fixed Zol with a stern gaze and said, "Doctor, this liver plague, as they're calling it, now that's a terrible business. Two more deaths yesterday, I'm given to understand."

Zol's stomach tightened at the reminder. Two more kids from Erie Christian Collegiate. Both cheerleaders. That school had become a train wreck in slow motion. Was he ever going to be able to stop it?

The priest shook his head in recognition of their shared remorse. "Is it true that you people have no idea what's causing it?"

"At this stage, I can't say anything quotable, uh, Father Murphy."

"Please call me Father Stoyan. The Murphy part comes from my late father, and doesn't sound the least bit Macedonian, does it?" His eyes, which Zol now noticed were shamrock green, twinkled briefly. "The Irish make their mark wherever they find themselves, and that is pretty nearly every corner of the world. But don't let me interrupt."

"As I explained on the phone, we're reasonably certain the liver deaths have to do with a research project at Caledonian University that — let me put it this way — spun out of control."

"That's putting it mildly, Doctor. I understand Jovan's boss — a young woman with a promising future — was murdered last year about the same time as the project was shut down. Near Grand Basin Reserve." He crossed himself. "Another terrible business. Jovan reminded me of the details."

Zol nodded.

"You can't blame the man for being terrified," the priest continued. "I would be too, in his position. Especially after that poor woman was shot this morning in Simcoe. Jovan seems convinced she was connected with your case." He shifted on his chair. "Is that the truth, Doctor?"

How much should he tell him? If he held back, he'd lose the man's trust. And without Father Stoyan's encouragement and support, Jovan Ligorov wouldn't sing.

He had to go for it. "We think it must be."

"This Dennis Badger fellow?"

Ligorov had briefed his confessor thoroughly. "Or his associates."

"If Jovan agrees to talk to you, tell you everything he knows about the research he was doing with Dr. Tammy Holt, how can you protect him from . . . certain irreversible reprisals?"

Zol hesitated. He couldn't give the answer Father Stoyan wanted to hear.

"As I thought," said Father Stoyan. "You are in no position to offer protection. The tobacco crime syndicate is too large, too complex, and too dangerous."

"Our team will use any information Mr. Ligorov gives us without attributing it to him."

"Mr. Badger will know where you obtained it."

"Not if we appear to discover it for ourselves."

"What do you mean?"

"If Mr. Ligorov tells us what compound Tammy Holt's tobacco plants were producing, we can have Dennis Badger's tobacco products tested for it."

"How do you do that?"

"Mass spectrometry."

The priest looked puzzled.

"I don't understand it, either, Father," Zol admitted. "All I know is it's the same technology they use in airports when they screen luggage for illicit drugs and explosive residues. You know, that little wand thing they wipe over laptops?"

Father Stoyan examined his hands. His face hardened into an anger he couldn't hide. It was obvious he knew exactly what Zol was talking about. He'd likely been snared by an airport-security sniffer machine, guilty of no more than handling fireworks in the preceding day or two. Zol pictured the tall, bearded man hauled off to a windowless side room, interrogated as if he were a terrorist.

"If we find Tammy Holt's toxic drug in Badger's cigarettes," Zol continued, "I can take the evidence to Health Canada."

"Surely you have enough suspicions already to interest the — relevant authorities."

Yes, the priest had been on the wrong side, felt the force of abused power.

"In a normal case, certainly," Zol said. "But anything involving our First Nations Peoples is never normal."

Father Stoyan closed his eyes and nodded slightly. "Hmm." He let out a long, slow sigh that said so much without being quotable or politically incorrect. Zol had seen that response so many times before. Political niceties superseded definitive action when the problems of Canada's Native Peoples were on the table.

"With concrete evidence of a toxin in the Grand Basin cigarettes," Zol explained, "and a clear story telling why Tammy's project was abruptly terminated by the American drug company, we should be able to overcome the . . ." How could he say this politely? ". . . the thick wall of political inertia."

"And force the authorities to act?"

"That's the idea."

"How many deaths so far?"

"Five."

"And counting?"

That was the reality they were facing. "I'm afraid so."

"And the police?" Father asked.

"The cops consider Native reserves to be alien territory where law enforcement is governed not by the rule of law but by political agendas and expediencies. Remember the troubles over Dover Creek Estates?"

"Some of my parishioners live in Caledonia. I understand the heartaches there."

"The police are not going to act on the mere suspicions of a guy like me, a public-health official with . . ." he raised his hands and mimed quotation marks, ". . . an overactive imagination."

"Jovan Ligorov is a good man. He was a pediatric surgeon in Macedonia, his homeland. He wants to do the right thing." Father Stoyan paused. He tugged again at his collar and rubbed the back of his neck. "But he's terribly afraid for his family."

Zol fingered the loonie in his blazer pocket. "This case is calling on all of us to do the right thing, Father." Sweat pricked the back of his neck. "Dennis Badger has threatened me personally. And my son."

The priest looked surprised, then shocked. "That's terrible, Doctor. But — but, obviously, you're pressing on." A warmth seeped into his eyes. "God bless you." He stroked his beard and looked pensive for a long moment, then brightened as if struck by a bright idea. "What about approaching the drug company that Jovan and Dr. Holt were working with? Surely, the company can give you the details you need without putting Jovan and his family at risk."

"I've already thought of that, believe me. But the truth is, the project was done so secretively that it would take months of paperwork, and probably a Freedom of Information request, to worm the information out of them."

The priest looked skeptical. "But surely, when it comes to issues of safety, drug companies act in the public interest."

"Their first allegiance is to their shareholders, who are interested in profit, not altruism. This may come as a surprise to you, but pharmaceutical companies have more lawyers on their payrolls than researchers."

"Blimey." This was clearly a revelation to a man who, the last time he stopped at the drug store for a bottle of headache tablets, hadn't thought about patent violations, intellectual property disputes, and exaggerated allegations of debilitating side effects. "Is that really the name of the game?"

"Afraid so."

"And you're sure the liver epidemic hasn't burned itself out?"

Zol shook his head. "No sign of it even slowing down."

Father stood and swept at the wrinkles in his cassock. Head down, gripping his cross in his fist, he paced the office several times. Suddenly, he stopped and stood erect. He let go of his cross and spread his arms. "The choice is clear. I need pray about it no longer." His face was aglow. "I will support Jovan in his decision to do what is right, what Our Lord expects us to do." He paused, fixed Zol's gaze, and held up his right hand. "But without coercion."

"Certainly."

"Let me go and have a private word with him. He's waiting next door in the sanctuary. Make yourself comfortable." He opened the door and looked back over his shoulder. "I won't keep you long."

Thirty seconds later, the priest came crashing through the door. His face was ashen. Spittle foamed on his lips. "Doctor, come quickly. Jovan has collapsed. I found him on the floor clutching his chest. I think he's had a heart attack."

CHAPTER 31

Zol ran out of the office behind the priest and followed him into the church through a side door. On the floor of the centre aisle, about halfway to the altar, Jovan Ligorov was lying on his back. Perhaps he'd only fainted and needed a couple of minutes to recover.

"It's kind of dim in here, Father. Can you turn on some lights?"

Father Stoyan dashed to the rear of the church, pawed at a bank of switches, and soon had every corner of the church and its gilded icons dazzling from the overhead lights. As Zol approached Ligorov, the first thing he noticed was the terror in the stocky man's eyes. The second was the large cross around his neck, similar to Father Stoyan's without the Celtic motif. Ligorov's face was ashen and his breathing laboured and raspy, but at least he was conscious. He looked late forties, early fifties at most. His grey hair was thinning on top and deep wrinkles slashed his forehead. His jowls wobbled with every gasp, and his nose had grown bulbous on generous doses of alcohol, presumably vodka and slivovitsa.

Zol knelt beside him, touched Ligorov's arm, and peered into his stricken face. "Mr. Ligorov, I'm Dr. Szabo. Do you have chest pain?"

Ligorov lifted his head from the stone floor and winced. He

tried to speak, but nothing came out. He touched the front of his chest, a little left of centre, then winced again.

Zol removed Ligorov's cross and handed it to the priest. He took the man's wrist and assessed his radial pulse — it was fast and weak, what the textbooks called thready. This was no simple faint. He was either having a heart attack or there was something seriously wrong with his heart rhythm. Or he was scared out of his mind. There was no indication he was hemorrhaging, at least not externally, another textbook cause of a thready pulse.

"Do you have heart problems?"

Ligorov frowned and shook his head.

A quick look revealed no obvious bruises or abrasions on his scalp. "Did you fall? Hit your head?"

Ligorov squeezed his eyes closed for a couple of seconds, then patted his chest again. Clearly frustrated at being too weak or too breathless to talk, he yanked at the front of his shirt, then extended his left index finger and stabbed it angrily toward his chest.

"Yes, I understand," Zol said. "You have severe, stabbing chest pain. We're calling an ambulance."

Ligorov grabbed Zol's wrist. His face filled with frustration as he pointed again to the front of his shirt.

Zol looked closely at where Ligorov was pointing. There was a rip in the cotton near the left front pocket of his shirt. There was a small stain there too. Zol touched it. It was wet. And sticky.

He opened the buttons and exposed Ligorov's hairy chest. A dark spot of fresh blood was glistening on a groove in the skin, halfway between the left nipple and the breastbone. Zol dug a tissue from his pocket, dabbed at the blood, and saw it was oozing from a laceration — a hole in the skin that was fresh, deep, a centimetre long, and startlingly surgical.

Could it be? He felt foolish even asking, especially after suggesting to the man he had stabbing chest pain. "Did somebody jab you with a knife?"

Ligorov relaxed his shoulders and nodded, relieved at finally being understood.

"When?"

He tried to speak, but when the most he could manage was a harsh whisper, he shrugged his shoulders and widened his eyes in exasperation.

"In here? In Saint Naum's?"

Ligorov nodded.

Zol scanned the cavernous church. The assailant could still be inside, hiding in the shadows behind a banner or crouching behind the high altar.

"Doctor, I think it's high time we call 911," said Father Stoyan, striding toward the side door.

Terror lashed at Zol like a rogue wave. The guy with the stiletto could pounce again any second. "Father, don't go. Please." Safety in numbers. Zol tossed him his phone. "Use my cell."

As Father Stoyan was dialling, Ligorov began pawing at his pant leg, struggling to reach below his right knee.

"Your leg hurts?"

He shook his head and made stabbing motions at his shin.

"They stabbed you there too?"

"N–no," Ligorov rasped.

"But something's bothering you there? They hit you?"

"L–look."

Zol examined the fabric of Ligorov's pants. No rips, no blood. He cradled Ligorov's entire right lower limb and rocked it back and forth, testing the integrity of the ankle, the knee, the hip. The joints moved smoothly, the bones felt solid, the muscle tone seemed normal, and Ligorov didn't grimace with the movement.

Why was he so fussed about a leg that seemed perfectly normal? What was the man trying to say? He might do better in his native tongue, but Father Stoyan was still talking to the 911 dispatcher.

Ligorov tried to stab at his right leg once more, but he quickly lost steam, and his arm flopped to the side. His neck muscles tightened as he made a supreme effort to lift his head. He took a deep breath, but what he mouthed was unintelligible.

"Say again?" Zol said, putting his ear to Ligorov's mouth.

"L–look. Un–under."

Under what? His back? His butt?

"Where do you want me to look?"

"Un–under s–s–sock."

"Okay, but if it's not hurting there . . ."

Zol grabbed the bottom of Ligorov's chinos and tugged the hem up toward the shin. Ligorov was a big man, the chinos were tight, and his leg was a dead weight. Zol pulled on Ligorov's black sock and noticed the edge of something white wrapped around the shin higher up the leg. At first it looked like a large bandage, but no, it was a piece of paper with something printed on it. He pulled the pant leg up higher still, and more of it came into view.

"What's this, Jovan? Should I —"

Father Stoyan swooped in, and crouching low, dug into Zol's right shoulder with his thumb.

"Father? I was only —"

The priest elbowed Zol firmly in the ribs, put his finger to his lips, and shook his head. Then he straightened his back and made a stop and freeze motion with his right hand. When he appeared satisfied that Zol wasn't going to move a muscle, he slowly scanned the church. After completing the full 360°, he leaned forward and whispered in Ligorov's ear, then cupped his own ear in front of Ligorov's mouth. He listened, then nodded as if understanding Ligorov's Macedonian mumblings and pulled the man's trouser leg higher, exposing more paper. The priest peeled the sheets away from Ligorov's shin and slipped them inside his cassock without looking at them.

Father fixed Zol with his gaze, then cleared his throat and said pointedly in a strong voice, "The ambulance is on its way. They promised it would be less than six minutes in coming."

That sounded like forever, especially as Ligorov was now fading rapidly. Zol took the man's hand and squeezed it with both of his, willing him to stay alive until the paramedics arrived with their intravenous fluids. By now, Ligorov had lost so much blood from internal bleeding that if his heart stopped, no amount of CPR would save him. He needed large bore intravenous needles, massive infusions of blood and saline, and a talented surgeon who could rip open his chest and sew up the tears in his heart and great vessels. But none of that was going to happen. The man would have to settle for the grasp of a compassionate hand and the comfort of not dying alone.

Father Stoyan knelt down and made the sign of the cross on Ligorov's forehead. He removed the man's cross from his cassock pocket, bent his head over the figure of Christ, and began praying.

As Father Stoyan recited his holy ritual, Zol felt Ligorov's pulse growing weaker and weaker. Soon, there was nothing left to feel. The man's jowls stopped wobbling as his breathing slowed to a stop and his dry lips took on the colour of cinders.

The wail of sirens shattered the moment. Brakes squealed and gravel crunched under tires. Zol let go of Ligorov's hand with some reluctance and scrambled to open the church doors.

The paramedics were too late, of course, but it wasn't their fault. It had been over for Ligorov as soon as the stiletto had pierced his heart. Everyone would do their best, but in the end they'd be returning him to the morgue where he'd worked. Would he be given special attention there, as one of their own?

CHAPTER 32

With the paramedics come and gone, and Jovan Ligorov now almost certainly Dead On Arrival at Caledonian Emerg, Saint Naum's felt more like a mausoleum than a sanctuary. Zol shivered as he realized how cold he'd become kneeling beside Ligorov on the raw concrete floor.

The flurry of activity   determining that Ligorov's heart had shown electrical impulses on the ECG but wasn't actually beating, jabbing him three times and failing to get an IV running, slipping on an oxygen mask that was useless because he'd stopped breathing, deciding he stood a better chance if they stopped fussing and rushed him to Emerg — had given way to the oppressive emptiness of absolute silence.

And overwhelming guilt.

"Oh Father," Zol said. "I'm so sorry. If only I hadn't —"

Father Stoyan held up his hand and shook his head. His face was solemn but commanding, his body taut. He put an arm around Zol and led him out of the church.

In his office, Father motioned for Zol to take a seat, then pulled a bottle and two glasses from a drawer in his desk. The bottle was half full of something clear and colourless. The label said SLIVOVITSA above a drawing of two dark plums. Father reached for the bottle, then stopped. He took a pen from another drawer, wrote three lines on a pad, and handed it to Zol.

Careful what you say.

You must be bugged.

How else would they know Jovan was meeting you here?

Father was right, but what was bugged? His house? His office? His car? His phone? His computer? All of them?

He took the glass from the priest and took two gulps of the Yugoslav brandy. It didn't have the finesse of a Balvenie or a Glenfarclas, but it did feel good going down. Nosing the remainder, he caught a strong whiff of plums, which launched Freddie Mercury and Queen into a high-volume version of "Bohemian Rhapsody." And dammit if Freddie's lyrics about killing a man didn't stab right at the heart.

There was obviously more to this synesthesia thing than random crossed wires. His sense of smell was tapping somewhere deep into his subconscious. Where was it going to take him next?

As Queen faded, he mused about the Badger. How had the bastard done it? Wiretaps? Scanners? Ultra-sensitive microphones? The guy would need a truck full of sophisticated equipment and a team of accomplices.

He grabbed Father's pad and scribbled a line: *Ever heard of Escarpment Cable?*

Father shook his head.

Got a phone book?

The priest looked through four drawers before finally fishing it out of the bottom of a filing cabinet. Zol flipped through the white pages. No listing for Escarpment Cable. He pawed at the Yellow Pages until he got to Cable Television Companies. Again, Escarpment Cable wasn't listed.

"Can I use your computer?"

"Be my guest." Father jiggled the mouse and the screen sprang to life. It showed fireworks crackling in a dark sky above Niagara Falls.

Zol called up Google and typed in *Escarpment Cable*. The top hits were a tourist spot in Portugal, a laundry in Kenya, a documentary TV show out of Toronto, and a vacation rental property in Australia. Next, he called up Canada411.ca and searched under Find a Business. Again, nothing.

Escarpment Cable didn't exist. At least, not as a legitimate business. But he'd seen their vans everywhere — outside his house, at the Simcoe Health Unit, at the Tim Hortons right here, across the street.

He pulled his phone from its holster and stared at the bloody thing. Not a mark on it, except for the dent from where he'd dropped it at the Detour answering a call while juggling two hot lattes. Yesterday, the cable guy fiddled with it when he'd shown up at the office to fix a privacy issue. Goddamn privacy, all right — bugged his phone and probably added some sort of tracking device. Maybe even a miniaturized video cam.

How could he be so trusting?

He turned the damned thing off and dropped it into the darkness of his jacket, where a video cam would see nothing but pocket lint.

Father Stoyan poured himself a second slivovitsa and swirled his glass. "This is Croatian. Not as good as Macedonian, but easier to get. Hits the spot, eh?" He closed his eyes, took a sip, and relaxed his shoulders. Two seconds later, he sat bolt upright in his chair and threw Zol a look that said *I almost forgot*. He undid a couple of buttons on his cassock, slipped his hand inside, and pulled out Ligorov's papers.

He scribbled on his pad: *Look at these before the police get here and want to confiscate them.*

Without a word between them, Zol took the two sheets of letter-size paper and began reading.

The first page was a typed, single-page executive summary of Tammy Holt's project entitled "GB Study TZ-4347: Commercial Production of 5-Fluoronornicotine (5-FNN) by *Nicotiana tabacum*." The project's objective was to induce greenhouse tobacco plants

(*Nicotiana tabacum*) to produce a derivative of nicotine (5-FNN) by infecting them with a genetically engineered strain of tobacco mosaic virus. 5-FNN was described as a well-tolerated, non-addictive, nicotine-like substance that caused neither cancer nor heart problems. Its claim as a wonder drug came from its ability to suppress the appetite continuously for twenty-four hours after ingestion. The project summary included the detailed molecular formula of 5-FNN and a schematic drawing of its structure. The final paragraph was printed in boldface type: *It is of the utmost importance that the TMV-infected tobacco plants remain confined to a greenhouse. The escape of infected plants into farmers' fields could have far-reaching negative consequences.*

The second page was from Genophy & Browning Pharmaceuticals, headquartered in Chicago. It was a letter to Dr. Tammy Holt dated fifteen months ago. The sender was the company's vice president of regulatory affairs. In terse sentences that left no ambiguity, he explained that researchers in Indiana had encountered several cases of liver failure and three deaths among university students taking 5-FNN under the controlled conditions of a clinical trial. In the vice president's words, the project was "hereby and irrevocably terminated and the company reminds all parties involved that it is essential they abide by the confidentiality agreement duly signed before they embarked on this project. Anyone found in violation of said agreement will be subject to vigorous litigation."

Holy shit. This was exactly what they'd been looking for. The chemical formula of Tammy's experimental drug and a frank description of its toxicity. The papers trembled in his hands. Three people had been murdered because they knew what was written on these sheets. If the Badger found out Zol knew this stuff . . .

He grabbed Father's notepad and copied down the formula and molecular structure for 5-FNN. Everything else on those sheets he'd already guessed. He stowed the formula in his wallet and handed the papers back to the priest. Father Stoyan nodded and raised his eyebrows, then pulled a red-leather tome from a shelf crowded with what looked like religious texts. On the front cover was a single word, embossed in gold in a foreign script. Did they use Cyrillic in Macedonia? The only Russian he knew was the CCCP on the hockey jerseys of the teams from the former USSR. This word started with a letter resembling an elaborate lowercase b, and there was another elaborate b in the middle. The priest slipped the two sheets of paper inside, brushed the holy book with his lips, and returned it to the far end of the shelf behind a much larger, black three-volume set.

"I've got to use your phone," Zol told him. "Mine's broken."

"Are you sure that's wise?"

He shot the priest a knowing look. "Don't worry. It's not long distance." He punched his home number into the desk phone. Colleen answered in three rings.

"You guys okay?" he asked her.

"We're reading a story. What's wrong? You sound anxious."

"Ligorov's dead. Stabbed in the church before I could talk to him."

She gasped. "Oh my God, Zol. I told you. I bloody told you. And you bloody well wouldn't listen."

What could he say? He let her words hang in the cavern between them.

"Zol? You still there?"

"Yeah."

"Are you okay?"

"We're waiting for the police, but we've got nothing to tell them. The priest knows nothing. And neither do I."

"I told you we should be calling them. But who —"

"They'll be here any minute. I might be quite a while."

It was killing him to imagine them alone in the house, and the Badger watching and listening to everything they were doing. Should he tell her to get Hamish and Al to come over for safety in numbers? No, they'd end up talking, putting themselves in greater jeopardy by revealing things that would make the Badger even more determined to get rid of them. She was right, they were amateurs facing seasoned professionals. But they were in it now and had no choice but to keep going.

"I need you to do something," he told her.

"A bit late now, isn't it?"

"Get Max to practise his silent reading. Lemony Snicket." What the hell was the name of the story that opened with a villain eavesdropping on a bunch of kids? "The . . . um . . . The Gruesome Giant."

"Are you out of your mind?"

"He's got a spelling test tomorrow, and that's a good story with plenty of challenging words. Start on page one and read along with him so he doesn't cheat. But remember, his teacher says it's his spelling and his silent reading he needs to practise most."

"He's almost asleep, Zol. He'll have to practise tomorrow."

"Please. The teacher says if his reading doesn't improve she'll have to put him in with the slow learners. You know how he'd hate that."

She'd know that was a boldfaced lie; Max was at the top of his class in every subject except French. Would she twig he was speaking in code?

"If you say so." There was a slight change in her voice. "But I don't know how far we'll get." Yeah, she'd twigged.

"Oh, and I dropped my phone," he said.

"Again?"

"This time it's toast. If you need me, call me back at this number."

"Got it. And Zol . . . take care."

As he hung up, his body stiffened at the sound of car doors slamming. Two thunks and a thud. How many cops had they sent? They'd be wasting their time. He'd be telling them nothing. Not with the Badger staking out his family.

CHAPTER 33

An hour and a half later, at the front door of Hamish's condo building, Max felt like a dead weight in Zol's arms. Pyjamas, slippers, Game Gadget, Harry Potter, Lemony Snicket, pillow, blanket, duvet, a box of cookies, and a bag of chips. The kid was set for a week. He'd fallen asleep in the taxi on the way over. In fact, at Colleen's suggestion, it had been two taxis. They'd changed at the Day-and-Night Pharmacy. If the Badger's thugs were still on their tail, it was impossible to tell. The headlights of one small Japanese import looked the same as another. He'd called Hamish from the pharmacy and warned him the three of them were on their way over. Who knew it cost fifty cents to use a pay phone?

Hamish buzzed them in and told them to come up to the sixth floor. Apartment 601. The condo tower was bulky — plenty of concrete and bricks — and this being Hamilton, there'd be lots of local steel in the framework. Colleen said the chances of the Badger being able to listen to anything they said inside Hamish's apartment was almost zero to zilch. Zol didn't like the sound of that almost. Of course, they'd ditched their cellphones and checked their pockets for electronic bugs.

Max and his paraphernalia weighed a ton by the time they made it to the elevator, up to the sixth floor, and along to Hamish's door at the far end of the hallway. Colleen pressed the doorbell and three seconds later Al and Hamish were at the door, clearly surprised by the child sleeping in Zol's arms and the two wheeled suitcases in Colleen's grasp.

"Sorry about this," Zol said, running out of breath. "We must look like refugees. Can I flop Max down somewhere? On a bed, maybe?"

Hamish hesitated for a second, obviously unsure about having a kid disturbing his perfectly made bed. "Um . . . sure. No problem." He turned and scurried across the living room. "The bedroom's this way."

Max moaned softly as Zol settled him onto what looked like a vintage Amish quilt on Hamish's king-sized mattress; he burrowed into his pillow and duvet without opening his eyes. Out for the count, thank God.

Back in the living room, Zol whispered to Colleen, "Did they turn their cellphones off?"

"No worries," she said, "had them off already. Put your feet up. We'll be okay here." She'd given up her anger and was as game to make the best of a bad situation as he was.

He dropped into the old-lady wingback chair. It looked out of place against Hamish's IKEA-inspired decor, but it matched Zol's mood, and what a relief to finally sit down. Al came out of the kitchen holding a tea towel. He looked like a busboy on the *Titanic* — anxious to please, but aware that no matter how well he did his job there was big trouble ahead. "What can I get you guys? Decaf? Herbal tea?"

"Nothing for me, thank you," Colleen said.

He turned to Zol. "How about a Jack Daniel's? You look like you could use it."

Not after the slivovitsa. "I'll stick with a decaf, thanks," Zol said.

Hamish kicked off his slippers, sank onto the chesterfield, and tucked his feet underneath him. "So, what happened?"

Zol looked around, realized he was checking for strangers

that couldn't possible be there, and felt foolish. "Well, basically, I went to Saint Naum's, the Macedonian church on Stone Church Road, to meet Ligorov. He'd agreed to tell me everything we needed to know about Tammy Holt's tobacco plant research, provided his priest thought I was trustworthy. I met the priest, Father Stoyan, in his office. Father figured I made the grade, but when he went to get Ligorov, the guy was virtually dead."

"What do you mean virtually?" Hamish said.

"He'd been stabbed. Through the heart. Inside the church — you know, where they hold the services."

"The sanctuary?" Al said.

"I feel so awful about it," Zol told them. He caught Colleen's eye and was relieved it held no reproach, maybe even a little encouragement. "Ligorov didn't want to come," he continued. "He seemed to know that Olivia Colborne worked for Dennis Badger. And knew what happened to her. But he did the right thing, and then . . . shit. I hate this. Oh God . . ." He held his breath and blinked back the tears.

"It's not your fault, Zol," Colleen said softly.

Her tone was sincere but it *was* his fault. And now they were all in it. Even Max. Up to their necks. He pulled a tissue from his pocket and wiped his face.

"And you figure Dennis Badger has tapped your phone, and maybe your cars and your house?" Hamish pressed. "Even your office?" He never seemed to notice tears, which at the moment was good.

"Certainly seems like it," Colleen said. "A guy like Badger has access to the very best gadgets."

"He even knows Max's cellphone number." Zol told them about the Badger sending the warning to Max's phone.

"No," Hamish said. "What are you going to do?"

"Not give in," Colleen said and threw Zol a look that said she was now backing him one hundred percent. "Before this all happened, I told him to call the police, let them handle it. But now it's too late. If we show the police the evidence we have linking rez tobacco to liver disease, the Badger will know we're onto him for all three murders — Tammy's, Olivia's, and Ligorov's."

"They must have quizzed you at the church," Hamish said. "It *was* a murder scene, Zol."

"They interrogated me. Thoroughly. For an hour. And warned me not to leave the province. But with an orthodox priest vouching for me, they knew they wouldn't be pinning Ligorov's murder on me."

"Did you tell them our suspicions about Dennis Badger and his tobacco?" Hamish said.

"You kidding? The Badger's got Max's cellphone number, friends in high places, and knows our every move. If he found out we'd fingered him to the cops, his guys would do to us what they did to those other three. Have Glock, will eliminate inconvenient witnesses."

Hamish turned to Colleen and narrowed his eyes. "Wait a sec. Did you mention new evidence linking rez tobacco to liver disease? Did you guys stumble on something I don't know about?"

Zol explained about the papers taped to Ligorov's shin.

"But that's great news," Hamish said, now beaming. "Now we know what toxin to look for in Badger's cigarettes. When we find it, we can join the dots, get the police to arrest him on the spot, and close down his operation."

"If he doesn't kill us first," Zol said. He could hardly believe they were involved in yet another public-health investigation where their lives were on the line.

"So, Dennis Badger doesn't know about Ligorov's papers?" Al said.

Zol shook his head, relieved he'd done something right. "No. Father Stoyan and I made damn sure of that."

"That means you're safe, right?" Hamish said. "I mean, as long as Dennis Badger figures you have no actual proof of toxins in his tobacco."

"I guess . . ." The weight of that uncertainty hung in the silence like a bad smell.

Zol fished out the crumpled piece of paper he'd slipped into his pocket at the church. It made him shudder, remembering how Jovan Ligorov had given up his life for these few scribbles. "Here's the formula. You think there's someone at the university who can use it to help us?"

Hamish stared at the paper as if he were looking at the Rosetta Stone. "I'll get on it tomorrow."

Several moments later, Al padded back from the kitchen with a mug of coffee and handed it to Zol. Al scratched at his sideburn. His face was grave, as if he was remembering scenes from the siege of Sarajevo he'd endured as a teenager. "Whether or not Badger knows about Ligorov's papers, you guys can't go home. It isn't safe. The guy didn't build his empire on fair play. He's ruthless."

Zol put the coffee on the table beside him. His stomach couldn't take it. There was an anaconda coiled in there, squeezing the life out of him. Where could he stash Max and Colleen? Not at her townhouse. Not at his parents' farm. And not here. The Badger's guys would trace them to Hamish pretty quickly, if they hadn't already. Zol pictured the boys transferring their scanning equipment to a new, unmarked van and setting up shop all over again. They would know the jig was up on their Escarpment Cable scam.

"What about the Sheraton?" Zol asked.

"No," Colleen said. "We'd be there two minutes, and the Badger would find out."

Al took a seat beside Hamish on the sofa. "What about your mother's place?"

"Which one?" Hamish said.

"The house in Toronto. She's away, isn't she?"

"For a few weeks." Hamish turned to Zol. "She's golfing in Myrtle Beach. Has a condo there. Stays in it every fall and spring." Hamish paused. Zol could see the wheels turning as he pondered. Hamish turned to Al and shook his head. "Sorry. I don't think so."

"Why not?" Al said.

"She's fussy about her stuff. I'm supposed to use the key only in an emergency."

"I'd say this qualifies," Al said.

"But what if Max breaks something?" Hamish caught himself and looked apologetically at Zol. "You know, by accident, of course."

Hamish could be a real shit sometimes, and ridiculously selfish. But you had to be cautious with him — he never took well to criticism. If he wasn't handled carefully, he could go into a sulk that lasted a week. "Never mind," Zol said. "It's okay. They wouldn't be able to get there without being followed, anyway."

Al launched himself off the sofa. "Sure they could." He glanced at his watch. "We've got half an hour. The car rental places at the airport close at midnight. Hamish, call me a taxi. Tell them I'm going to . . . I don't know . . . anywhere but Hamilton airport." He shoved his feet into his sneakers. "The hospital. That's it, tell them we need a cab right away. To Emerg at Caledonian." He grabbed his jacket from the front closet and said, "I'll redirect the driver en route."

"I'm not sure I follow," Zol said. "You're picking up a rental car? At this time of night?"

"The Badger's watchers have no idea who I am," Al said. "Just some guy getting into a taxi. And then another guy driving home for the night. The parking garage downstairs is secure and the elevator takes you directly into it from here. No one will see them. It's perfect. But I'll need that electronic thingie for the garage door."

"It's in the Saab," Hamish said, now standing in the middle of the living room, looking bewildered.

"You've got an extra one," Al told him. "I'm sure I saw it a few days ago. Look in your junk drawer."

Hamish shrugged, seemingly content, relieved even, to be letting Al take over. "Okay. I'll see if I can find it." He disappeared into the kitchen.

Zol heaved himself to his feet. Everything was happening way too fast, and it wasn't even clear that Hamish was completely on board. He put his arm around Colleen. "Do you understand what's going on?"

"Max and I are driving to Hamish's mother's house. Tonight.

In a rented car. Thanks to the smarts and kindness of these terrific gentlemen."

"You okay with it? You need to think about it?"

"It won't be for long. I have fake glasses and a black wig in the suitcase. After you phoned from the church and told me about Ligorov, it seemed an eternity before you returned." She turned to Al. "Where in Toronto does his mother live?"

"Forest Hill," Al said. "Quite the place. You'll like it. She's got a fantastic record collection. All the great baritones and tenors. Caruso to Bublé and Groban."

Colleen drew in close and squeezed Zol's waist. "You'll have to explain to Max what's happening, and why he has to lie low on the back seat until we reach Toronto. And don't forget to call Ermalinda first thing in the morning."

He'd make some excuse for their sudden absence and tell Ermalinda to take a mini holiday. Until Monday at least. "How will I contact you?"

"There's a 7-Eleven on Upper Wellington. Stop there in the morning and get one of their pay-as-you-go phones." She squeezed him again. "And never let the blessed thing out of your sight."

CHAPTER 34

Zol woke up with a start. Where the hell was he? On yeah, on Hamish's chesterfield. What time was it? Six-thirty by his watch. And still dark. His rubbed at the sharp ache in his neck. This sofa was too damned short for a proper sleep. And how could he have slept, anyway?

He hadn't heard from Colleen. She should have called as soon as she and Max got to Forest Hill. Rosalind Wakefield's phone would be secure. Colleen could have made at least a quick call to let him know the two of them were safe. The sound of her voice, her distinctively musical accent, would have been good enough. She needn't have said anything substantial or compromising.

When he'd heard nothing by one o'clock, he'd phoned the Wakefield mansion, but no one answered. A woman's voice on the machine — private-school Toronto accent, halfway between plummy British and nasal New York — invited callers to leave a message and informed them that "calls will be returned in due course." He'd got the same response at two a.m. and at four. What the hell was going on?

He groped for the switch on the lamp beside the chesterfield, gave up, and stumbled to the bathroom for a leak. He found the kitchen phone and punched in the Forest Hill number again. As before, five rings, six, then the machine clicked on. He nearly hung up, but decided to wait for the uppity voice and leave a message, though he wasn't sure what he'd say. But this time, the greeting was different. He must have punched in the wrong number. He glanced at the display on the phone. No, he had it right.

Five words into the recording, it hit him. The voice was Colleen's, apologizing for being away from the phone and asking the caller to please leave a message. It was a short greeting and the beep took him by surprise, left him too flummoxed and tongue-tied to leave a message. He hung up, his mind spinning. Should he be relieved that they'd made it to the house or shitting his pants because something terrible was going on? He downed a glass of cold water from the tap, racked his brain for a plan, and dialled again.

After Colleen's greeting, he said, "This is Daniel Handler trying to reach Ms. Beaudelaire. Sorry I missed you. I'll try again between seven and eleven." Colleen and Max would understand the cryptic message. As fans of the Lemony Snicket series, they'd know that Daniel Handler was the author's real name — it appeared nowhere in the books — and Beatrice Beaudelaire was the woman Lemony Snicket loved from afar. Colleen would get the 7-Eleven reference too. Of course, it wouldn't mean diddly if Colleen and Max were . . . he couldn't let himself think what could be going on in that house if the Badger had followed them there.

He showered and shaved, hoping the morning ritual would make him feel a bit more human. It didn't. He dug through his suitcase for a clean shirt and underwear while Hamish took his turn in the can. Al, in tee-shirt and bikini briefs, was preparing breakfast in the kitchen.

"Coffee and waffles okay?" Al asked.

The waffles sounded like a stretch, even if they were smothered in real maple syrup. He might manage the coffee. "Sounds great. Thanks. Can I help?"

"Got it covered."

A few minutes later, Hamish stabbed at a second mass-produced waffle from the plate in the centre of the table. He turned to Zol. "Know where these are made?"

Zol was halfway through the mug of instant Al had handed him. He found breakfast conversation impossible until he'd drunk at least one full cup of coffee. How could anyone live like this, no grinder, no coffee apparatus anywhere in sight?

When Hamish got no answer, he supplied it himself. "In Simcoe," he told them. "A huge factory, just for waffles." He looked at Zol, "Know how I know?"

Zol threw him a look that said *Not a clue.*

"A patient of mine. Truck driver. Every week he makes the circuit to Arkansas and back. A tractor trailer full of frozen waffles destined for Walmart."

Zol forced down another swallow of the liquid in his mug that was masquerading as coffee. "They must eat a lot of waffles in Arkansas," he said. It wouldn't be authentic maple syrup they put on them, but something horrible and synthetic.

"No, no," Hamish insisted. "Once Walmart receives them at their international headquarters, they repack them and send them off to every town in North America. Back here, even."

Zol pictured freeways crawling with eighteen-wheelers hauling waffles from Simcoe to Arkansas to Yukon.

Al held his fork above the half-eaten waffle on his plate. "You mean this waffle was made in Simcoe, sixty minutes down the highway from here, trucked all the way to Arkansas, only to be trucked back again?"

"Dumb, eh?" Hamish said.

The caffeine was starting to kick in. "What was wrong with your patient, the trucker guy?" Zol asked. "He choke on a waffle and come down with some exotic infection?"

"Scrotal abscess," Hamish said seriously. He hadn't gotten the joke. "His testicles were floating in a bag of pus the size of a grapefruit. Group B Streptococcus."

Waffle, syrup, and saliva spewed out of Al's mouth. "Shit, Hamish," he said, spluttering. "Not at the table."

Hamish looked at Zol as if to say *What's the big deal? Pus is a natural biological substance.*

Sometimes the guy just didn't get it. As Zol's mum liked to put it, how could someone so smart be so dumb?

Mum and Dad! He'd been incommunicado since last night. Mum could have taken a turn for the worse and Dad could be trying to reach him, the same way he'd been trying to find Max and Colleen. Getting that phone from 7-Eleven was now number one on his to-do list.

He put down his fork. "How did your guy get the infection?" He imagined these things started as ingrown hairs or innocent little zits on the privates.

"From driving a big rig for hours on end, stuck to a sweaty seat. I call it truckers' balls. Especially bad for diabetics. Sometimes the infection gets so brutal they lose their boys to gangrene."

Al had his hand clamped over his mouth. His face had turned pea-soup green.

"All that," Zol said, "so we can pop a waffle in the toaster for a quick breakfast. How nice is that?"

Al scrambled from the table and scraped the remains of his waffle into the garbage. "You two can talk about all the gross things you like, I'm having a shower."

"I haven't told you about Winnipeg," Hamish said after Al was out of earshot. He leaned in close and lowered his voice. "They're threatening to report me to the College of Physicians."

"Who? Not the guys at the National Microbiology Laboratory?"

Hamish nodded.

"Why'd they do that?"

"They know I lied about the samples from . . ." he made quotation marks with his fingers, ". . . Namibia."

"How so?"

"Docs in Swift Current, Saskatoon, and Prince Albert have been seeing cases of non-healing blisters on hands and faces."

"Anything like your lip and finger disease?"

"Identical. Winnipeg sent me photos."

"And the EM findings?"

"Matchstick particles. Identical to ours. That's what got them suspicious."

Zol leaned back in his chair and massaged the painful crook in his neck. Things were starting to make sense. Winnipeg realized it was too much of a coincidence that the ultra-rare, hybrid virus that Hamish had sent them last week was now turning up in three Saskatchewan cities.

"It didn't take a genius to figure out that my specimens didn't come from Namibia."

Hamish's problem with the national laboratory aside, there was one question that mattered more than anything else. "Do any of these Saskatchewan blister cases have acute liver disease?"

Hamish shook his head. "Believe me, I asked right away. As far as Winnipeg knows, no outbreaks of jaundice, hepatitis, or liver failure in any of the prairie provinces." He paused and made a dismissive gesture with his fork. "Except for a minor outbreak of hepatitis A traced to bean sprouts from a hydroponic operation near Moose Jaw."

Bean sprouts. They got you every time. If it wasn't viral hepatitis, it was salmonella or E. coli.

Zol took another bite of mass-produced waffle. Not so bad, considering its cross-continental perambulations. "Are they any closer to fully characterizing the particles?"

"They're not saying. But they will. And when they do, they'll hog the academic limelight."

"Look on the bright side," he told Hamish. "Winnipeg tipped you some important information we could never have proven on our own."

"Like what?"

"Dennis Badger's contaminated tobacco has made it halfway across the country. At least as far as Saskatchewan. Those matchstick particles prove it."

Hamish rolled his eyes. "Terrific."

"Did you tell them about Wilf Dickinson finding those same particles in cigarettes manufactured on our local rez?"

"Of course not. I'm not crazy."

Zol swallowed the last of his so-called coffee. It was cold and tasted like charcoal, but he could feel the effect of the caffeine. "Why the complaint to the College of Physicians?"

"The guys in Winnipeg take their public-safety mandate very seriously. My less than truthful story about the blister specimens I sent them got their director onto his high horse."

"Did you come clean?"

"More or less, but it was too late. By then, the guy was ready to burst a gasket. Gave me a thorough blasting on the phone. Said their institution is built on trust, which I had subverted."

"Subverted? That's stretching it, for crying out loud." He put his hand on Hamish's shoulder. "Don't worry about it. The College won't take away your licence. The worst they might do is send you a stern letter that demands a response."

"Not according to the man in charge of our nation's premier reference laboratory."

Zol looked at his watch. Seven-forty-five. "I know you've got to get to work. But a couple more things before you go."

Hamish raised his eyebrows.

"Can I use your study today? My Simcoe office is bugged and I don't dare go home. Badger's probably blanketed the place with microphones and scanners."

"Sure, the computer's login password is on the underside of the keyboard. And there's an extra set of house keys in the top drawer of the desk." He folded his serviette, pushed away from the table, and set his dishes in the sink.

"How quickly will you be able to get our samples tested for traces of Tammy's 5-FNN?"

"I've been thinking about that. There's a mass-spec genius in our building. He's got a federal grant to build the next generation explosives detector for use in airport security — something passengers can walk through without stopping. He's usually up for a challenge."

"Can he do it today?"

Hamish held up both hands defensively. "I haven't the faintest idea how long these things take. Could be an hour, could be a week. How will I find you?"

"Email me. My Google account."

"It hasn't been hacked?"

"If the Badger is that good, we're screwed."

He'd change the login password first thing, just in case.

CHAPTER 35

Shortly after ten-thirty, Natasha helped Marcus set the table back on its legs. They'd been looking under it and under the chairs. And inside the sugar bowl. For bugs. Not germs, of course; Marcus kept the Nitty Gritty spotless. The other kind, which were a lot more sinister. "Sorry about this," she told him, "but we have to be sure no one can eavesdrop on our conversation." She wasn't prepared to share the information Guelph Veterinary College had faxed to her a few minutes ago with anyone but Hamish — and Dr. Zol, when he got his new phone working.

Marcus's eyes danced above his ginger goatee. "I never realized you guys discussed such top-secret stuff back here." He polished the table top with the tea towel he always carried slung over his shoulder, then stopped and pretended to look serious for a moment. "You need me to swear an oath of secrecy to the health unit?"

"Just keep feeding us treats."

He smiled again and touched her arm. "Who will be joining you, Dr. Szabo?"

"Just Dr. Wakefield."

His hand darted away after the briefest of seconds, but his eyes didn't stop twinkling. "Should I rustle up a couple of lattes?"

Hamish was unpredictable when it came to beverages. He was as likely to order a lemonade as a latte.

"For now, just one, please."

"How about a slice of lemon loaf?" When he saw she was hesitating, he teased, "Just took it out of the oven . . ."

She could smell the irresistible aroma from here, and she had skimped on breakfast. And now that Guelph had come through with its surprising goat-farm data, she was in a mood to celebrate. "Sure. Sounds great. Thanks."

"Coming up."

Had Marcus been flirting, or was he like that with all his female customers? A bit of both, she decided, then watched as he greeted Hamish at the front door with a wide grin. Hamish waved his hands dismissively and didn't smile back when Marcus took his coat. Hamish looked anxious and hyper-focussed as he strode toward her and slid into the chair opposite. As usual, he didn't bother saying hello. It would be nice if some day a little of Marcus's manners rubbed off on the brusque Dr. Wakefield.

"You checked for bugs?" he whispered. "I trust you *do* know what I mean?"

"Marcus and I made a careful sweep. And I left my phone at the office."

"Mine's in the car. And I didn't see any vans parked nearby."

"I think we're okay."

Ordinarily, this cloak and dagger stuff would seem silly, embarrassing even, except that when Dr. Zol had phoned her a couple of hours ago he was majorly upset. And rightly so. It was awful not knowing whether Dennis Badger had apprehended Colleen and Max on their way to the safe house, or if they were fine and Colleen was being super cautious about their location.

"Any news about Colleen and Max?" Hamish asked, no longer whispering.

"Nothing, I'm afraid."

"If he doesn't hear from them in the next hour or so, he'd better call the police. The longer people are missing, the less like they are to be found aliv —"

"Please, Hamish." How could he talk like that? "I'm sure Dr. Zol will do the right thing. He always does."

"Did he give you the number of his new cellphone?"

Natasha opened her purse, wrote the ten digits on a slip of paper, and handed it to him. "Here you are. It's not working yet."

"Why not?"

"Apparently, 7-Eleven has some sort of glitch that's slowed down their registration system."

If he'd noticed her hands were trembling, he didn't show it. Heck, she could be wearing only a bikini and he wouldn't notice. He scrutinized the number, as if committing it to memory. "This new one better be bug free," he told her, as if getting a phone from 7-Eleven had been her idea, and a poor one at that.

Marcus arrived with her latte and slice of cake. He set them in front of her and took Hamish's order for a club soda, no ice. As Marcus headed back to the bar, he dragged a lip-sealing finger across a little smirk on his mouth. He wouldn't be smirking if he knew the dangers they were facing. There was a lot more to this job than lemon loaf and lattes, no matter what it looked like.

She turned back to Hamish. Making small talk with him was practically impossible at the best of times. Today, he was clearly pre-occupied, as if he'd rather be anywhere than sitting across from her at the Nitty Gritty, waiting for a club soda. "Any news from your colleague with the mass spectrometer?" she ventured. She knew it was too soon to expect any results, but she had to say something to fill the void.

He frowned and studied his watch. "Give me a break, he's only had the samples for an hour."

"Can he process them today?"

"Going to try." His eyes met hers and darted away. "But if you knew anything about chemistry, you'd know these things do take time."

She churned her latte with the spoon, destroying Marcus's artistic frothy swirls. "Organic chem was my minor in undergrad."

He looked surprised, as if she'd never seemed smart enough for the intricacies of organic chemistry, then he tightened his lips and made that my-opinion-is-the-only-one-that-matters gesture with his hand. "The guy has assayed nicotine before, so Tammy's 5-FNN, a close molecular cousin, should be easy for him. Unless 5-FNN is unstable, of course."

She put down her spoon. "Actually," she told him, "the fluorine at the five position makes the molecule quite stable. The readings should be more reproducible, and the results more reliable, than would be the case if the fluorine were, say, in the three position." She was careful not to smirk. As her mother would say, it would be unseemly.

"Whatever," he said flatly, "let's hope he comes up with useful results by the end of the day."

She returned the spoon to her latte and stirred slowly. Hamish had called at eight-thirty this morning and told her he had something important to discuss, but only in person. He demanded she drop everything and meet him at the Nitty Gritty. But now he was staring out of the window as if there was so much in his head he didn't know where to start. Maybe he expected her to keep breaking the ice on their conversation until he was ready to burst forth with some startling revelation. Fine. She'd kick things off by telling him how she'd solved his lip and finger outbreak. Thanks to Dr. Zol's tip from his friend the vet, and today's fax from Guelph, she had fit the pieces together. Though she was thrilled to hand Hamish the solution to the origin of the blister lesions on a platter, she had no delusions that he'd congratulate her on her handiwork.

"I got a fax from Guelph today," she told him. "From the vet school."

"What did they want?"

"It's the other way round. They're helping us explain the origin of those intriguing matchstick particles in our rez tobacco samples and in your lip and finger lesions."

"I don't know why you're calling them *my* lesions. They're from my patients, not from me personally."

She let that pass and waited for his next question. She could tell by his dilating pupils that she'd piqued his curiosity.

"What does Guelph know about hybrid viruses?" he said.

"They're experts in epidemics involving farm animals. They sent me detailed data on an outbreak of orf virus infection on three goat farms in Brant and Norfolk counties."

"No way," he said, aiming his frown at her. "That can't be true. We confirmed there's been no orf virus activity in Ontario any-time this year. I made calls to vets' offices, and you were supposed to make a thorough check through your sister health units. Didn't you do it?"

"I did. And indeed, there's currently no evidence of orf activity anywhere in the province. But —"

"But what?"

"There *was* a significant outbreak two years ago. Among dozens of milking-goats."

"Why didn't you know about this until today?"

"Orf infection isn't on the list of reportable illnesses. No one is obligated to tell us when they've diagnosed a case. More to the point, it's primarily an animal pathogen. Either way, our public-health database has no record of it."

"Sounds like a hole in the system. Were there human cases along with the goats?"

"Guelph knows about four goat handlers who developed orf lesions on their fingers during the farm outbreak. There could have been others. Guelph keeps detailed data only on animals." She pulled the fax from her briefcase along with the annotated map she'd made of Brant and Norfolk counties. She'd highlighted all the tobacco-growing areas in blue, and the orf-infected goat farms in yellow. She hadn't used red and green because she knew that Hamish was colour-blind and couldn't distinguish crimson from chartreuse. His shirts and ties were all some shade of blue.

She spread the map on the table and watched while he examined it. "Do you see what I see?" she asked him, half afraid he was about to blow her nice little theory out of the water.

"Of course. I'm not blind. Well, maybe colour-blind, but . . ." His face flushed a deep scarlet. She wondered how he'd interpret the colour of his cheeks if he looked in a mirror at this moment. He buried his nose in the map for a good minute before he said, "Gotta admit it. This *is* pretty cool. And the timing is perfect." He was on the verge of smiling, and even looked intrigued by her efforts. Now, it was her cheeks that were blushing. "Look," he said, his voice rising as he ran his fingers over her map, "every orf-infected goat farm is surrounded by tobacco fields."

"Are you thinking what I'm thinking?"

"A set-up for microbiological high drama?" he said. "Highly improbable, but . . ."

She pictured orf virus from Dr. Eddy Pakozdi's goats colliding with tobacco mosaic virus escaped from Dr. Tammy Holt's experimentally infected tobacco plants. Something similar had happened in Mongolia. Why not in Ontario? "Do you suppose an orf-infected goat handler did some moonlighting on a TMV-infected tobacco farm at harvest time?"

"And transferred orf virus from the blisters on his hands to the tobacco he was picking? It's a long shot."

"The literature says that orf virus is very hardy. Remains alive and infectious in the environment for prolonged periods."

"True enough," he admitted. "And of course that does increase the likelihood that the two viruses could combine to form the matchstick hybrid Wilf Dickinson's electron microscope keeps turning up."

Hamish stared at the map again. He shook his head, his face full of disappointment. "But we're still a long way from explaining the liver failures. Blisters, maybe, but liver failures, no."

He was right, of course. There was no indication that the matchstick hybrid virus caused anything more serious than blisters on the lips and skin of people who smoked the tobacco it contaminated. Her clever bit of epidemiological sleuthing had revealed something academically fascinating, but not the breakthrough the case demanded. "So it's back to the drawing board?" she said.

"Forget the goats, it's the demographics of the liver cases that's bothering me."

The geographic distribution of the people suffering liver failure had been puzzling her too, especially after the fax from Winnipeg had reported matchstick-positive blister cases from three cities in Saskatchewan. It was now obvious that all across the country people were smoking Dennis Badger's contaminated cigarettes and contracting Hamish's lip and finger eruption. But, as Dr. Zol said this morning, no one outside Norfolk County had been stricken with liver failure. There had to be a rational explanation of why Dennis Badger's tobacco was poisoning the livers of local students and firefighters and leaving everyone else's liver untouched.

Hamish removed the lime wedge, which Marcus had balanced on the rim of his club soda, and made a face as he discarded the thing on a napkin as if it were a cockroach. He wiped his fingers thoroughly, his way of saying he knew all about the bacterial contamination of limes in bars and restaurants. Then he ventured a sip. Thirst clearly trumped OCD. "Something in addition to rez tobacco is linking Eric Collegiate with Norfolk Fire and Rescue," he told her. "There's a cofactor out there somewhere in Norfolk County, and it's activating Tammy's tobacco toxin. Once we find that cofactor, we can take the pressure off Dennis Badger."

"He's a creature and a half. Why would we want to ease the pressure off him?"

"So he'll leave Zol alone."

"Sorry?" she said.

"Look, if we find the cofactor that's making Erie Collegiate students and Norfolk first responders susceptible to the toxic effects of Tammy Holt's drug, Zol can put out a health-unit alert warning the public to avoid the cofactor."

"We're not positive Tammy's 5-FNN is actually in Dennis's tobacco," she reminded him.

He made that dismissive flick with his hand again. "We will be soon."

"But why would we want to help Dennis Badger stay in business?"

"We can't stop him. He's going to carry on, regardless of what anyone says or does. There's no way he can be prevented from selling his cigarettes across the country and around the world."

"Is there not something we can do?"

"Take control of the cofactor. Whatever it is, it's bound to be easier to contain than Dennis Badger and his Native tobacco racket."

"Surely the lip and finger lesions are bad for his business. I can't imagine that his biggest customer, the German Army, would find it acceptable to have its soldiers infected with some sort of mutant virus."

"Come on, Natasha. Everyone knows cigarettes cause emphysema, heart disease, impotence, lung cancer, and other bad things. What's a few blisters that look like cold sores taking longer than usual to heal?"

"Okay then, how do we find your cofactor?"

"Those students were a bust. You found that out the hard way." His face softened. "They wouldn't tell the truth if their lives depended on it. No matter how professional your questionnaire."

Was that a back-handed compliment? She'd take it as such.

"What about the first responders?" she said.

"They're almost all men."

"So?"

"Most men are terrible historians. It's women who spot the details that produce a comprehensive medical history. And of course," he said, "many gay men."

She'd never thought about it that way. "Is that why you're so good —"

"At clinical diagnosis? "A smile crossed his lips. "Maybe."

Al had the same gift. She'd watched him notice the freshly restored bargeboarding on the Vanderhoef's Gothic revival house and use that detail to charm an entire family into spilling crucial information. But what about Dr. Zol? He was pretty good at detail. Though now that she thought about it, he was better at synthesis — making sense of the bits of information other people collected.

"What about their wives?" she said. "I bet if we gathered them in one room, got them racking their brains, we might come up with something."

"A room full of anxious women, one of them a very recent widow? All talking at the same time? Better you than me."

"But you'll come? And bring Al?"

He hesitated, as if more from surprise than uncertainty. "I don't know. I should leave you to it. Couldn't take that much concentrated estrogen."

"Come on — the existence of a cofactor was your idea in the first place."

He grinned, rolled his eyes and cocked his head to the side, like Oscar Wilde basking in the attention. Hamish did love to be complimented. But it took a fair chunk of chutzpah to get close enough to peer through his shell and glimpse the man inside.

"Well," he said. "Okay, sure. But only if Al can come too. Bosniaks are used to taking it from all sides."

CHAPTER 36

Zol shook the mouse on the desk in Hamish's ultra-tidy den and watched the monitor spring to life. At least something was working. He pulled the new 7-Eleven phone from his shirt pocket and stared the damn thing down. When he'd tried it five minutes ago, a recorded voice had thanked him for his patience and said his service on their crystal-clear network would be operational in a few minutes. A few minutes? What the hell did that mean? What a stupid idea to get a phone from a convenience store. What was Colleen thinking? And where was she? His knees trembled as he thought of Max — frightened, tired, and mixed up in something no kid should have ever to go through.

He called up Simcoe Health Unit's email program and waited for it to load. Until the phone started working, he might as well check his email. He had to do something useful. He'd called Rosalind Wakefield's house from Hamish's landline a couple of minutes ago, but again Colleen hadn't answered. He'd got her recorded greeting, which by now he'd heard five times. Natasha was pretty certain no one would've fiddled with the home phones of the health-unit team, but he'd decided if Colleen answered he'd make sure neither of them said anything the Badger could make use of.

Why hadn't she picked up? She and Max must have reached the house. Or had she manipulated Rosalind Wakefield's answering machine from another location? If so, where were they now? Not in a suite at the Royal York, that was for sure. Tied up in a closet? Cowering in the dark in a soundproof warehouse? Or had she understood his coded Lemony Snicket message, was keeping her eye on the incoming call display, and was going to answer calls only from a 7-Eleven phone? God, please make it that last option. Please.

He typed in his username and password. Thirty new emails since yesterday. Once Simcoe got to know him better, it would be more like two hundred. He scanned the list for anything that might not take much effort or brain power.

There was a message from Allison Sparling. The name didn't mean anything at first, but the subject line certainly did: "Francine arriving today YYZ." He opened the message and read it quickly. It was from Allie, Francine's BFF since elementary school. As far as he knew, Allie was still single and working as an intensive-care nurse at Sick Kids in Toronto. How she'd hung in through Francine's multiple breakdowns and hysterics, he never knew. Allie was hard-wired that way, he guessed, just as Francine had been hay-wired. When he allowed himself to think about it, the two of them were like Yin and Yang. And the fact that Francine was actually following through with a promise and arriving from Cambodia tonight, at 6:25, Cathay Pacific, into Toronto Pearson via Hong Kong . . . ? Well, he was reserving judgment. He'd have to see it to believe it.

He was about to type a brief reply to Allie's message, but remembered the "Escarpment Cable" guy screwing with the computer in his Simcoe office. The health-unit email service couldn't be trusted. He scribbled Allie's email address on a Post-it note — Hamish didn't tolerate stray bits of scrap paper — and logged out. He logged back in, this time to Google Mail, and scanned his inbox for a new message from Max or Colleen — nothing — then composed a brief note to Allie. He requested that she reply only to this Google address and included his new cellphone number — was the damn thing ever going to work? — and asked her to get in touch as soon as Francine landed. Before hitting Send he read the message twice to be sure it sounded cordial enough. Of course, he didn't mention he had no idea where Max was at this particular moment. The tables had turned — who was the flaky parent now?

He logged out, patted the phone in his pocket, and heaved himself out of the chair. He was desperate for a caffeine hit. He should have had the taxi driver take him to a Tim's on the way back from Natasha's office. What a hassle not being able to drive his own vehicle.

He went through four cupboards before he found the jar of instant. He tossed a mug of water in the microwave, set it for a couple of minutes, and rustled up some milk and sugar. The only way to get that stuff down would be with a couple of heaping teaspoons of sucrose. When the water boiled, he threw the concoction together — there was no way you could call it a coffee — and took it to the living room.

When was this damn flip phone going to work? He forced himself to drink half the coffee before he tried it again.

He flicked to the contact list, found Rosalind Wakefield's number he'd entered earlier, and pressed Call.

Four rings, five . . . "Good morning. Beaudelaire residence."

It was her. She'd picked up. He could hardly believe it.

"Yes?" she said when he didn't reply. "May I help you?"

"You're okay?"

"I'm fine, thank you. And so is Mr. Snicket."

Why was she speaking so formally? Was she using a code? Was there someone with her, threatening with a knife or a gun? Maybe she suspected the line was being tapped?

He had to be certain she was speaking freely.

"This is the LCBO calling," he said. "We have a case of your favourite nightcap ready for you."

"Good. A shot of Amarula and the world feels perfect." He adored the way she always said it: purrhfect.

"Oh, my Sweets. You really are fine? And Max? I've been so worried. Why didn't you pick up?"

"Until a few minutes ago, I wasn't sure the line was safe."

"But you are now?"

"Yes," she said, then told him a complicated story — to which he was able to only half listen, he was so frazzled — about a catering van following them last night from the Spadina exit off the Gardiner Expressway to the house in Forest Hill. The van had parked all night on the street, between the Wakefield's house and the neighbour's. A few minutes ago, a woman dressed like a chef (minus the tall hat) had left the house by the front door, kissed goodbye to a well-dressed elderly woman on the doorstep, and driven off in the van.

"Zol? You still there?"

"Yes," he said, pawing away the tears on his cheeks. "Still here."

"How are you, my love?"

"A lot better now."

"Did you get any sleep? That sofa of Hamish's didn't look too promising as a bed."

It wasn't the uncomfortable chesterfield that had kept him from sleeping. "It was okay."

"Have you called your mum today?"

"Not yet. But I will. This new phone started working only a few minutes ago."

"Anything new on the investigation?"

How much should he say? How secure were these phones? "Hamish has a guy who's going to run some tests. I think you know what I mean."

"And get results soon?"

"I'm hoping for today."

"And then what?"

That was the million-dollar question. Did he go to the Badger first, give him a chance to shut down his entire operation until the contaminated tobacco was out of circulation? The Badger would refuse, of course.

Zol did have something that might sweeten the deal. He pictured the second loon's bright, onyx eyes staring at him, pleading for his loyalty. Could he give her up? Could he surrender the second loon to Dennis Badger and risk emboldening the Badger to try making a giant land grab?

Or did he go straight to the authorities and let them deal with the mess? But which authorities would that be? The cops were so reluctant to go onto First Nations territories that he'd have to drag them onto Grand Basin, kicking and screaming. Could he even do that? And what did cops know or care about obscure poisons in tobacco? Health Canada was supposed to regulate the tobacco industry, but what did office jockeys know about reining in criminal gangs?

"I don't know," he admitted. "I haven't been able to think straight since you and Max drove off in that rented car."

"I'm so sorry, my love. I was terrified that the Badger's men had followed us, and —"

"I know, I know. You did the right thing." He paused, wondering whether to even bring it up. "Um . . . our little friend. Is she under lock and key?"

"If you mean the dear little creature with the shiny black eyes, the answer is . . . not exactly."

The tension gripped his neck again. "But she is safe, eh?"

"Certainly. No worries there."

"And . . . where is she, exactly?"

"What are you going to do with her?"

He wasn't sure, and he wasn't going to brainstorm about it over the phone. "Probably nothing. But I'd feel better knowing where she was."

"Mary Poppins has her. I gave her to Mary for safe keeping. It seemed appropriate."

"Mary Poppins? What the heck — ?"

"Long story. But I think you know what I mean."

"Max's friend?"

"Exactly. But do be careful. No rash decisions. Promise?"

She was right. Involving the black-eyed loon in any negotiations with Dennis Badger could be a huge mistake. It would be best to let nesting birds lie. Trouble was, that might be impossible.

"Look," he said, glad to change the subject, "I heard from Allie today. You know, Francine's friend?"

"Is she all set for her arrival?"

He told her the details.

"Tonight? That's wonderful," she said. "Max will be pleased."

"Can I speak to him?"

"If I can tear him away from the television. There's a home theatre in the basement that's fully loaded. Sixty-inch flat screen, movie channels galore, and an entire library filled with video games. Rosalind's grandchildren must love it here. How many does she have?"

"None," he told her. "Hamish is an only child." And he'd never heard him mention the words video and game in the same sentence.

But really, who cared? Max was safe. Nothing else mattered.

Unless . . .

Was Francine going to insist on traipsing all over Toronto with Max in tow, while the Badger's men were on the prowl?

Hell.

CHAPTER 37

At one-thirty, Zol couldn't keep his eyes open any longer. He needed a nap. He'd spent most of the morning glued to Hamish's desk, running through his To Do list from Simcoe. He'd opened a new Google Mail account just for work, forwarded the most pressing messages to it from his health-unit email account, and got back to work, hoping the new set-up was secure.

Now, as he studied the chesterfield in the living room, he was amazed how short it was and surprised that he'd attempted to sleep on it last night. His neck wouldn't take it again. Would Hamish mind, or even notice, if he stole forty winks in his bed? As he stood at the bedroom doorway, something kept him from entering. It was Al's bed now too. Something stronger prevented him from taking off his clothes and slipping under the duvet. Was he afraid it would seem like a threesome? Or did it run deeper than that? Was he afraid he might get a buzz out of sharing their sheets?

He decided he'd better go home to his own bed. If the Badger's team was listening on the landline, or trolling with their scanners near his house, it didn't matter: Max and Colleen were safe.

He called a taxi on his new phone, was surprised how quickly it came, and jumped in. Minutes later, they were coming up on

Kelly's SuperMart. On a whim, he asked the driver to turn in and wait. He wouldn't be long. The cabbie, who hadn't said a word since Zol had got in, pointed to the meter and shrugged — no problem.

Zol had never been inside the tobacco shop that occupied the front corner of Kelly's supermarket, but he'd walked passed it and glanced through the window countless times. The intriguing shapes of pipes, lighters, and other paraphernalia displayed in the glass cases had often caught his eye, as did the swashbuckling images on the tobacco tins.

Today, he was ready to do more than look at the pipes and tobacco. He was prepared to make a purchase. As he stepped into the shop, and the door closed behind him, he was instantly enveloped by a gorgeous, complex aroma. The odours flooded his mind with countless memories — summers hanging bundles of leaves to dry in his dad's stuffy tobacco kilns, evenings courting Francine over too many cigars and bottles of red wine, and nights entwined with Colleen, loving her and savouring smoky whiskys.

He steadied himself at the counter as Andy Williams crooned a private, dreamy rendition of "Days of Wine and Roses." It was far from his favourite style of music, but he had no control over this crossed-wires, odours-music thing. He had no choice but to give into it and hope it was brief.

If the stocky, middle-aged lady behind the counter thought Zol was behaving strangely by staring blankly at the ceiling, she didn't show it. She was too busy peering into a handheld device and checking her inventory. Her plain, fleshy face and drab grey blouse reminded him of the librarian at Max's school. Not someone you wanted to get on the wrong side of. After Andy had finished crooning his way through a dozen or more bars, Zol gave a slight wave to catch the woman's attention and ventured a tentative smile. "I'd like the finest pipe tobacco you have in stock."

She removed her reading glasses and let them dangle across her bosom from the silver chain around her neck. "Domestic or imported?"

Anything but Dennis Badger's local crap, he wanted to tell her. "Imported," he said.

"Mild, mellow, or full-bodied?" she said.

"Um . . . mellow?"

"I'd say you're after something full-bodied. I have a nice Davidoff, the Blue Mixture."

"What sort of aroma does it have? A hint of vanilla by any chance?" He had happy childhood memories of the whiffs of vanilla escaping from his dad's tobacco pouch. When Dad sat down to smoke his pipe, he was usually in his best mood; he sometimes told stories about the pranks he got up to as a kid back in Hungary.

The clerk's face softened, as if she sensed Zol was actually going to spend some serious coin. She took a packet from a locked case, put her glasses back on, and, reading from the label, told him, "It promises a rich, chocolaty smell in the tin and a smooth smoke offering a sweet, woodsy taste and . . ." she thrust out her bosom and grinned, ". . . a hint of vanilla."

He raised his eyebrows and chuckled. "Almost good enough to eat."

"I wouldn't do that. Not at these prices."

"You say it's imported?"

"From Denmark."

If Danish pipe tobacco was half as good as the butter cookies the Danes shipped all over the world in those large blue tins, he knew this would be okay. "How much is it?"

"Ninety-two twenty-five," she said without blinking.

Ninety-two dollars? This stuff was more expensive than Scotch. He swallowed hard and did his best to keep a straight face. "For how many grams?"

"Two hundred and fifty." She held up the bundle of five small tobacco tins presented together as elegantly as a lifetime investment from Birks or Tiffany's. "This is the minimum I can sell you, I'm afraid. Because of the way it's packaged."

He slid his credit card into the machine and punched in his PIN. He knew this was going to be worth it.

The taxi driver tooted at Zol as he exited the store. He hopped in. Again, the cabbie still didn't say a word. The midday traffic was light, and they got to Scenic Drive and Zol's street in a matter of minutes. The house looked okay. He could see through the window that his minivan and Colleen's Merc were still in the garage. There were no vans parked on the street or at the neighbours' on either side.

He went in the front door, turned off the alarm, and set his purchase on the kitchen counter. The house felt strange. Eerie. Alien. Something was wrong. He flipped on the halogens, froze, and listened. Then he realized what was different. The dead quiet. It was his house, but he never got to experience it like this — alone. Ermalinda always greeted him at the door with a string of chatter. Max was usually clicking on the computer, or banging around the kitchen making himself a snack, or up in bed snoring the place down.

He scanned the kitchen. Colleen had left everything spotless. Nothing looked out of place.

He jumped and nearly knocked the shopping bag onto the floor as something snapped, then whirred, beside him. He wasn't alone after all. His heart pounded in his ears. He turned, arms up in defence, ready to fight. But no one was there. Two seconds later, another snap, and the whirring settled into a familiar hum.

How stupid — it was just the fridge coming on. His heart fell back into his chest, but it took awhile for the pounding to fade.

Excited by his purchase, he looked at the bag. The clerk had wrapped her best tobacco in white tissue paper, sealed it with a gold sticker, and placed it in a hunter-green paper bag a manly man wouldn't be embarrassed to carry. He chuckled at the irony. The makers of fine tobacco got men to part with serious money because they were selling them a lot more than shredded leaves and nicotine. They were selling a dream. Single malt distillers played the same game. It wasn't ethyl alcohol they were peddling, it was prestige. Trouble was, all three — nicotine, alcohol, and prestige — were addictive.

He dropped his jacket on a chair and went into the computer room. He'd lined one wall completely with bookshelves and loaded it with DVDs — movies, TV shows, and video games. Mostly for Max. He couldn't let himself think about the money those disks represented. Was this a collection or another addiction? Or were they one and the same?

The DVDs were not in any particular order, though Max was careful they were returned to their proper cases. In the early days, he hadn't looked after them, left them strewn all over the place. He'd learned the hard way that the most exciting part of a video game could get ruined by careless gouges on the disk.

It took awhile, and Zol's back ached as he perused the shelves peering at the fine print, but he finally found *Mary Poppins*. And behind her, the blue Birks box.

He brought the box to the kitchen, paused for a deep breath, then lifted the lid. He took out the loon and couldn't help smiling. He caressed her with both hands and felt a warmth gathering in his chest. He lifted the little creature, held her nose-to-nose with his, and stared into her unwavering onyx eyes. What scenes had they witnessed in the past two thousand years?

He turned the silky-smooth pipe in his hands and examined it from every angle. The bird and the rectangular block she was nestling on, the size of half a deck of cards, had been carved from a single piece of dark grey pipestone. The whole thing fit perfectly in the human palm and balanced there gracefully.

The magical thing about fine art was you knew it when you saw it. Actually, you didn't see it, you beheld it. You succumbed to its presence. Moisture stung his eyes. It took quite a while to blink away the mistiness.

The carver had fashioned a large cavity, the tobacco chamber, into the loon's back. The chamber appeared empty but charred. He turned the bird on her back and tapped her against his palm. Nothing fell out of the cavity, no bits of tobacco, no pieces of dirt, not even a dead spider. He went nose-to-nose with the little bird again and put his lips over the small draw hole in the base. A bitter, flinty taste met his tongue, which he wiped away with the back of his hand. The bitterness faded, and he blew gently through the hole. A few motes of dust puffed from the chamber. He blew twice more, then inverted the bird again and tapped a few tiny bits of debris into his palm. Should he save those for the archaeologists? They could be hundreds of years old. He set them on a saucer, raised the pipe again to his lips, and made one final blow before inhaling through the draw hole. It was amazing how easily the air flowed, and with the right amount of resistance. This pipe was going to give a very nice smoke.

He opened the packet of Davidoff's finest, taking care to damage as little of the packaging as possible. It seemed wrong to rip the elegant wrapping. He removed a tin and slit its seal with his fingernail. He pried it open and breathed deeply. Delicious! The woman at the shop had promised chocolate, but that was only the beginning.

As he started itemizing the aromas, Warren Zevon took over the kitchen, belting out "Werewolves of London." When Warren's ebullient howls reached their peak, Zol knew he'd hit the jackpot with this Davidoff stuff.

He fished a paperclip and a disposable lighter from the junk drawer and carried them with the loon, the saucer, and the tobacco tin into the sunroom. He set them on the table and eased into his recliner. The buttery leather never failed to soothe.

He'd never been a pipe smoker, but when he was little his dad taught him how to pack his after-dinner pipe for him. There was a knack to it, which Zol mastered at an early age. Tobacco had to be trickled, not dumped, into a pipe's chamber. Then it had to be tamped to the proper density. If you tamped the tobacco too hard, the pipe wouldn't draw. Too lightly, and the tobacco would burn too quickly — all flame and little smoke. The novelty of preparing Dad's pipe, without being allowed more than an occasional puff, wore off by the time he became a teenager. But it was a skill you never forgot, like stringing tobacco leaves by the thousands, hanging them on wooden laths, and hefting them day after day into the stifling drying kilns.

And now, he was packing an heirloom calumet and tamping it with a paperclip he'd adapted for the purpose. He tried drawing on the pipe before lighting it. It gave the perfect amount of resistance, like sucking through a drinking straw. He flicked on the lighter and waved the flame in a circular motion over the tobacco surface while taking short puffs. No smoke yet, only a brief glow as a few strands of tobacco swelled and unravelled in the brief flame of this the customary "charring light." He extinguished the lighter and tamped gently once again, this time with his finger. Now the loon was ready for a proper lighting.

He applied the flame and drew short puffs, like his father used to do. The Davidoff and the loon did the rest.

Now this was a smoke. Richer, smoother, sweeter than he remembered his father's ever being. All the same, it was the by-product of incomplete combustion, so it made him cough and stung his eyes and throat. He puffed again and again, and gave into the seduction. The loon's eyes winked at him through the blue haze, and an orchestral version of "Rêverie" by Claude Debussy filled his brain with its glorious, sinuous melody. He sat back, breathed deeply, and let his mother's favourite musical piece waft through him. He really should give her a call.

As the orchestra played in his head, he puffed contentedly. The pipe went out twice, which was par for the course. Fiddling, re-tamping, and re-lighting were integral to the ritual. This pipe drew nicely, its smoke flowing in an effortless stream.

The Debussy lasted longer than his usual crossed-wire snip-pets of synesthesia, and by the time the piece had finished he'd smoked down to the dottle. He cleared the spent tobacco from the chamber and repacked it with fresh Davidoff. He set the pipe in his lap, then pecked at the keypad on the 7-Eleven phone.

"Hi, Mum," he said. "What's new?" She'd told everyone to stop asking her how she was doing. The short answer was that she had early lung cancer and chemotherapy wasn't such a big deal. The long answer was filled with a host of side effects, indignities, and future worries she wasn't prepared to discuss.

"Your father, he going crazy with that metal detector thing again."

"What's he doing?"

"Walking beside road, checking ditches for stray coins and other stuff."

"That's harmless. And, hey, he might find something valuable."

"He look ridiculous."

He lifted the pipe from his lap and held it in his palm. Should he tell her what he'd been doing? She wouldn't approve. But what the heck. "You know our little friend with the shiny black eyes?"

"Shhh, Zollie. I hope you not tell anyone. Is it safe?"

"Safe and warm, right here on my lap."

"Your lap? You supposed to hide it, so no one will see."

"Don't worry, she's fine."

"Did you say warm? What do you mean warm?" Her tone betrayed her alarm. "Like from smoking?" She never missed a trick.

"Just a little."

"Zollie, how could you?"

"I was curious. It's not every day you get to smoke a two-thousand-year-old pipe." Come to think of it, he'd done it twice in the past few days.

"I gave it to you for safekeeping only."

"Mum, it's okay. I'll take good care of her." He did his best to sound reassuring before they said their goodbyes.

What would Mum have said if he'd told her he'd puffed on the red-eyed loon with Dennis Badger and Chief Falcon? She and Dad would be apoplectic that he'd touched the now infamous stolen artifact, tainted by theft, murder, and wanton destruction. His parents had an unfailing belief in the power of honesty, though that sometimes clashed with their morbid fear of authority fostered by their upbringing behind the Iron Curtain.

He closed the flip phone and set it on the table beside the pipe. They looked good together, about the same size, but separated by two thousand years of technology. A lot of heartbreaks in that time, in both the New World and the Old. Wars, famines, plagues, wildlife extinctions, environmental disasters, superstitions, addictions, unspeakable pedophilia in residential schools. The two worlds shared it all because heartbreak went with being human, whoever you were.

A strange clanging woke him up with a start. He looked around, but it was too dark to see much. What? Oh, the phone. It was ringing and buzzing beside him. And flashing. Six-forty. He'd slept a good three hours, maybe more.

"Hello?"

"That you, Zol?" It was Hamish.

"Yeah?"

"You weren't asleep?"

"Didn't get much last night."

"I talked to Colleen. They seem comfortable in the house."

"Thanks."

"That's not why I called."

Zol rubbed his eyes. "Yeah?"

"The mass-spec results. Just talked to my guy. They're in. And looking good."

Zol shook the cobwebs from his head and pushed his heels down, stowing the recliner's footrest. "How good?" His feet were now firmly on the floor, his head surprisingly clear.

"He's calling them probably positive for 5-FNN."

Probably? What did that mean?

"Pending confirmatory testing," Hamish continued. "He says there's a fluorinated nicotine derivative in the leaf Olivia sent you and in eight of ten samples from the cigarettes I got at that smoke shop on Grand Basin."

"Did he run controls?"

"Of course," Hamish said. "We did do a proper job of it."

"And?"

"Nothing remotely resembling 5-FNN in ten brand-name samples."

That sounded good. "And?"

"Here's the good part — it's in the Rollies and Hat-Tricks from the rez."

"That's amazing."

"Actually, Zol, it's science."

An awkward silence hung between them.

"Zol? You still there?"

"Yeah."

"What are you going to do now?"

He had no answer. But he did know the hard part had yet to begin.

CHAPTER 38

On Thursday morning, Zol worked from home. He'd enjoyed a second smoke last night and almost had another this morning, but when he'd lifted the lid on the Davidoff, he realized that, like his dad, he was not a morning smoker. Before noon, coffee was his drug of choice.

He'd had his breakfast, and now he was in the computer room using the 7-Eleven phone and his new Gmail account to stay in touch with Nancy at the Simcoe Health Unit. Max had sounded fine enough on the phone this morning, but very disappointed that Francine's Hong Kong flight was being delayed for twenty-four hours. Mechanical difficulties with the aircraft, according to Allie. He hoped that was true and that Allie wasn't covering for another of Francine's deceptions.

The landline in the kitchen started ringing. He looked at his watch. Ten after ten. It was probably him, so if the phone was still tapped it didn't matter. He walked to the kitchen and looked at the caller ID — number withheld. It was either him or a telemarketer.

He planted his feet, closed his eyes for a sec, then picked up.

"Hello?"

"Zollie? Dennis. You're looking for me?"

He'd called back surprisingly quickly. Chief Bob Falcon hadn't wasted any time passing on the message and impressing Dennis with its importance. A good sign.

"I need to talk to you."

"Then talk away."

"Face to face."

"You White guys never learn. Face to face isn't good for you. No matter what comes out of your mouth, your body language betrays what you're really thinking. You're better using the phone. Shoot. I'm all ears."

"Sorry, Dennis, this isn't the sort of conversation I want to have on the phone, especially one that might not be secure, if you know what I mean."

"I'm busy, man," said the Badger without missing a beat. "Don't expect me to see you today. I'm three hours away."

"There's plenty of time left in the day."

"But I'm in Manitoba, for God's sake."

"I've got something to show you. It'll blow your socks off."

"Yeah, sure."

"Think of your wildest dream, and then think of it sitting in my pocket. Just for you."

"Why would you — ?"

"A little horse trading. Between former schoolmates. Because in my other pocket is something you don't want your German customers to see."

"Sounds like a threat, Dr. Szabo. I don't take kindly to those. Besides, I've got business to finish here. And then the flight home."

"I know you keep the Lear at Mount Hope. I'll make it easy for you. The Tim's at Duff's Corners."

"I don't do meetings at Tim Hortons."

The loon pipe was staring at Zol from the counter, telling him to stand his ground. Or was that terror in those onyx eyes, the little bird pleading not to be given up to the Badger? Zol picked up the frightened creature and cupped her in his hand, like he used to do with the chicks on the farm. Was he doing the right thing? God, he hoped so. "You will if you want to see what I'm holding in my hand."

"Shit, Szabo." There was a long pause, which Zol had no intention of filling. The Badger coughed, then cleared his throat. "I might be able to make it at five." He'd blinked. His contract with the German army was a gold mine he couldn't afford to give up.

Five o'clock was too close to sunset. This time, he was going to face the Badger in the full light of day. Besides, there'd been too many delays in this case already. "Two o'clock, Dennis."

"Two-fifteen. It'll take me twenty minutes to get from Hamilton airport to Duff's corners."

"It's twelve minutes, Dennis, even if your driver keeps to the speed limit." He'd checked out the route on Google Maps after Chief Falcon had told him Dennis was out of the province, but due back later today. "But okay," Zol told him. "See you at two-fifteen."

For a moment, hanging up on the Badger felt great.

But when it sank in, it felt terribly foolish.

CHAPTER 39

Natasha drew to a stop in front of the single-storey brick box that called itself Norfolk Fire and Rescue Services, Simcoe Station. The only open parking spot was beside a red fire-and-rescue minivan. She checked three times, but couldn't see a sign telling her not to park here. It must be okay. Hamish had arrived already. Who else would have a gleaming, burgundy Saab without a speck of dirt on it?

He greeted her in the vestibule with a nod, his eyes cold, his mouth tight across his lips. He was angry, anxious, or distracted, she could never tell.

"They know you're here?" she asked him.

"Just arrived. Not a soul around."

"Where's Al?"

"Had to work. You know, newspapers and their deadlines."

"Shall we go in?"

He shrugged. "Guess so. We said twelve-thirty, and it's almost that now." He hesitated, then added, "You get the meeting started, okay? That room's going to be full of wives and girlfriends, all anxious and tearful — as I told you before, way too much unbridled estrogen for me."

She flashed the Tin Man her gentle, concerned-professional

smile. It was the secret weapon she used with anxious relatives who were turning hostile in a nursing home closed by a flu epidemic. People said they were calmed by her natural sincerity. She knew that deep down, Hamish appreciated it too.

"No problem, Hamish. You'll be fine."

It had been Al's show at the Vanderhoef house. Today it was hers. She liked that.

Immediately ahead on the right was a reception area, no more than a wall-mounted window opening onto a single-desk office. She imagined that visitors were normally required to sign in — a logbook was hanging on a chain next to the window — but there was no one in the office. Were they out for lunch? Or were they with the others, waiting for the nerd team from the Ministry of Health? It was strange there was no one waiting to greet them. Maybe small towns worked on more casual terms than larger cities. She hoped the 911 line was being handled by a dispatcher located somewhere offsite.

In keeping with the casual flavour, there were no signs indicating what was where, but when she'd arranged this meeting last evening with the fire chief, he told her the group would be waiting in the lunch room, through the first door on the left.

That door took them into a short hallway lit with fluorescent tubes. Behind the closed door marked LUNCHROOM was one heck of a hubbub. She couldn't tell what was coming through loudest — anger, fear, or grief. There was certainly sobbing. Perhaps they were consoling the widows. Overnight, a second woman had lost her husband, a paramedic. He'd died at Toronto General before they could find him a liver. She didn't like getting morbid about it, but the death count was now standing at six. The team was running out of tricks.

She knocked. No one answered. They probably couldn't hear through the commotion. She knocked again, then tried the door handle. It was locked.

"Who ever heard of locking a lunchroom?" Hamish said. "You sure you got the time right?"

She ignored the barb. "Maybe the room serves a second purpose. This isn't a big building."

They looked around, but the hallway was empty. Hamish tried the other three doors off the corridor, but they were locked too.

Applause erupted from behind the door, and a few seconds later it opened. A slim woman slipped out, looked surprised to see them, and stuck out her hand. Her salt-and-pepper hair was cut in a striking page-boy, and she stood almost six feet in her Stuart Weitzman ankle boots.

Although the woman's skin was photo-shoot flawless, her eyes were bloodshot. She'd been crying. "Ms. Sharma?" she said, "I'm Joanna Dyment, my husband's the fire chief. I'm sorry, we weren't expecting you so soon."

Hamish looked at his watch and made a face. "We are only ten minutes early," he told her.

Natasha introduced Hamish, hoping Mrs. Dyment wouldn't be overly put off by his manner. She hadn't seen anything yet.

"You may have heard us," Mrs. Dyment confided without hesitation. "What started as a prayer vigil ended up as a free-for-all." She closed her eyes and wiped the tears from her cheeks. "Forgive me, this past week has been difficult. For all of us. But especially for my husband. The stress is killing him."

Natasha handed her a tissue from her purse and waited while the poor woman dabbed at her face then stowed the Kleenex in the sleeve of her Simon Chang jacket.

She'd noticed Natasha checking out her boots. "Don't you love the animal-print lining?" Joanna Dyment said, lifting her foot and turning it side to side. She pointed at Natasha's pumps, also Stuart Weitzmans. "I see we share the same designer." A spark of conspiracy gave a lift to the sadness in her eyes. "And the same indulgence. You must know Miller's in Hamilton, on James Street North?"

Natasha nodded. She could feel herself blushing. "My mother calls me Imelda. Says I have far too many shoes." She didn't look at Hamish, didn't need to see him rolling his eyes at this frivolous interlude in the gravitas.

"It never bothered me that the Marcos woman had so many pairs," Joanna said. "Except I heard she didn't wear most of them." She paused, and let out a sigh. "Lucky her, she didn't have to drive for an hour and a half to find a good shoe store. They probably came to her."

She straightened her back and tugged at the cuffs of her jacket. "I hope you're ready for this. They're not an easy crowd at the best of times."

CHAPTER 40

The lunchroom was crammed. It looked to Natasha like a TV news clip of an airport departure lounge in the middle of a blizzard, where stranded passengers were strewn about like dirty laundry. The windowless room — meant to accommodate eight people at a rectangular table, three more on a sofa, and one in a recliner — was packed with at least thirty bodies. And it looked like half of them had been crying.

A tall, uniformed man with a red face, broad shoulders, and a broader paunch introduced himself as Grant Dyment, the fire chief. He looked rattled, almost overwhelmed.

"Thank you for coming," he said. He swept the room with his arm. "As you can see, we're kind of in a bad way. But . . . but doing our best to pull together."

And they had pulled together. Three quarters of the faces in the room belonged to women. She knew that Donna Holt was the sole female first responder in Norfolk County, which meant that these women were the anxious wives, mothers, sisters, partners of the men who worked out of this station. The two widows were easy to spot: they'd been seated on chairs at the table and were surrounded by solicitous "sisters." It was a relief, and heartbreaking, that this micro-community had responded so quickly to Natasha's appeal.

Chief Dyment introduced them to the group, and in the process stumbled over her last name and Hamish's first. It happened so often it felt almost natural. She'd found out by accident that Hamish's middle name was Ulysses. The schoolyard razzing that must have caused him was too much to contemplate.

She thanked everyone for coming and told them she appreciated that this was a frightening time for them all. She explained that she and Dr. Wakefield were going to need their help in finding the key pieces of information that would unlock the puzzle and prevent further cases of jaundice and liver failure. She had learned to avoid four words in these situations: victim, stricken, quarantine, and epidemic. They were far too effective at pushing emotions passed the boiling point.

"So I hope you brought your thinking caps with you," she said as she turned her secret-weapon smile on the shy smiles that responded from a few of the faces in the middle tier. There were no smiles from the women in the front row, who looked like time bombs set with high-octane anxiety. The four men standing at the back, dressed in dark blue uniforms that matched their chief's, shifted on their feet and studied their highly polished boots.

She didn't recap the narrative of the epidemic. These people were living it, for heaven's sake. But she wanted them to understand that she and Dr. Wakefield were searching for all the threads that bound the affected first responders together. One of those threads, she hoped, would lead to the solution.

She looked at Hamish for reassurance, but saw only Tin Man diffidence in his stance and on his face. "There must be several threads," she continued. "Some we know already, and one or two crucial ones we need to discover together."

"As soon as possible," Hamish added flatly.

"And we have to keep in mind," she said, "that the most important threads will include the students at Erie Christian Collegiate."

She didn't have to remind them that four kids at that school had died and more were getting sick almost every day. It was front-page news.

She decided to start by itemizing the threads they already knew and writing them on the flip chart someone had set up at the front. "Thread number one," she said, "is working at this station." She wrote that down, then turned to the fire chief. "Is that true, all the affected firefighters and paramedics work here? This is their base?"

"Every one," he said, puffing his chest like a proud father.

"Their only base?" Hamish asked. "None of those with liver failure worked part time at another station?"

The chief scanned the room, looking for dissent. There wasn't any. "Only here."

"Number two," Natasha said, "they all smoked cigarettes manufactured on Grand Basin Reserve."

"Rollies and Hat-Tricks, and varieties of such," Hamish clarified.

There were reluctant nods among the women. The men at the back kept their arms crossed and faces fixed.

"Number three is exposure to chemicals," Natasha said, and wrote that down. "Chief Dyment, do the paramedics ever use the fire extinguishers, and do they ever help fight fires?"

He gave that some thought. "No. Never."

"Good," she said, "neither do the kids at Erie Collegiate." She threw Hamish a knowing look. "At least, that's what we've been told. It looks like we can rule out firefighting chemicals."

One of the uniformed men at the back put up his hand. "So you're ruling out all the toxins we're exposed to?" He shot daggers with his eyes first at the chief and then at Hamish, then snapped his fingers. "Just like that?"

"Put it this way," Hamish said, "it's not something that links the majority of the affected people together."

Clearly unhappy with the answer, the man shook his head and crossed his arms again. He muttered something to the man beside him.

One of the women seated at the table stopped picking at her lips and put her hand up. Her sloppy, mint-green tee-shirt said FORT MYERS, FLORIDA, CITY OF PALMS. "What about the new appliances?"

Natasha looked at the chief and raised her eyebrows.

The chief looked stumped, then threw a questioning look at his wife. Mrs. Dyment pointed toward the kitchen counter on her right, but the room was so full of bodies that Natasha couldn't see what she was pointing at.

"Sorry? What appliances?" Natasha asked.

"Let me see," Joanna said. "We wives got together and purchased a new electric kettle, a toaster oven, and a microwave. I think that's it."

Natasha turned to the woman with the Fort Myers palm tree sprawled across her boobs and asked her, "Is something about them bothering you?"

"I guess not. It's just that they're new."

"Do people usually bring their own lunches, or do you have a caterer come in?" Hamish asked.

The men at the back scoffed and chuckled. One of them, a bit shorter than the others, said, "A caterer? In here? Yeah, sure. Every day."

One of the women turned and threw the man a *behave yourself* look. "But they do have takeout," she insisted. "Several times a week. Pizza, Chinese, Thai. You name it."

"But no waiters or fancy dishes, and we clean up the mess ourselves," said the man at the back.

Natasha tore a blank sheet from her notebook and handed it to one of the women in the front row. "People," she said, scanning the crowd and catching as many eyes as she could, "would you please list the names of the takeout places you've ordered from in the past couple of months. And the phone numbers, if you have them."

The woman stared at the paper in her hand as if it were a piece of nuclear waste. The chief took it from her, asked his wife for a pen from her handbag, and instructed one of the men to get busy with the list.

Natasha glanced at her notebook. Had she turned up any other common threads when she'd spoken to the families of the affected first responders last week in Simcoe Emerg? No, none. She looked at the flip chart. It was awfully bare.

"I'm wondering," she said, "are there any events that brought the affected first responders in contact with kids from Erie Collegiate?"

The room filled with muttering and perplexed faces, but nothing that looked like an answer.

Hamish was beginning to look impatient, as if exasperated at having to do the thinking for a room full of ninnies with no ideas of their own. Natasha was beginning to feel the same but hoped her body language didn't betray her.

"For instance," Hamish prodded, "do all the affected firefighters go to the same church?"

One of the men at the back said, "Can't think of a single one who does go to church."

"Yeah," said the man beside him. "Working shifts means we're either at work or sleeping in on Sunday mornings."

"How about sports?" Hamish said. "Do you guys play on the same teams as a lot of people from Erie Collegiate?"

"Not with the kids," came a comment from the back.

"Any of the jaundiced guys coach kids from that school?" Hamish said.

"Our shifts kinda put the kibosh on that," said the talkative guy at the back. He looked pointedly at the chief. "Much as we'd like to."

The woman in the Fort Myers tee-shirt stood up. "What about Fire Prevention Week?"

"When was that?" Natasha asked.

"A couple of weeks ago," someone else said.

"Actually," said a woman wearing a chunky Juicy Couture necklace. Natasha had noticed the pavé heart glinting in the overhead fluorescents. Now, as the woman raised her hand, Natasha saw Band-Aids on two of her fingers. "It was a few days before all this started," the woman said.

The room went quiet.

Natasha's tongue went dry. Her heartbeat quickened in her chest. "Did your station visit Erie Collegiate?" she asked the chief.

He straightened his shirt collar and stepped forward. "We certainly did. Spent a full morning there."

Natasha's pulse was now racing at her right temple. Maybe they were getting somewhere. "The exact date would be very helpful," she said. "Anyone remember?"

The chief's face showed he was drawing a blank.

Joanna Dyment pulled her phone from her Coach handbag and started tapping on the screen. "Here it is," she said. "The day after Thanksgiving." She looked at her husband and touched his arm. "You dropped me off at the dentist on your way to that school. I remember, because you said the principal was a bit odd and you wondered how such a scruffy guy got on in a school full of demanding parents from the Christian Right."

Natasha wrote thread number four on the flip chart: Firefighters visit Erie Collegiate six days before first students come down with jaundice.

"What exactly did you do there?" Hamish asked the chief.

"I spoke to them at an assembly," the chief said. "You know, the dos and don'ts of fire safety. And . . . and I explained how to draw up — and practise — a home fire-escape plan."

"Did you demonstrate your equipment?" Hamish asked.

The chief chuckled. "That's the only thing that holds their attention."

"What did you show them?" Natasha asked.

"Our boots, suits, helmets. That sort of thing. They won't let us bring our axes into schools."

"Did you demonstrate the fire extinguishers?" Hamish asked.

"There'd be a riot if we didn't shoot off an extinguisher," the chief confided.

Hamish swept his hand over his flat-top. "Interesting. Did anybody get sprayed?"

"No, no," said the chief, looking embarrassed by Hamish's

suggestion. "We're careful about that. We spray at a bucket full of logs. Makes a lot of noise, mind you. And all that white CO_2 gas looks impressive." He looked for reassurance from his wife, but her attention was elsewhere. "For about a couple of minutes anyway, and then it disappears."

"Aren't you forgetting something, Chief?" said the smart aleck among the uniforms at the back. "Couple of twin girls in the front row got their high heels sprayed. Remember how they shrieked?"

The chief turned as red as a traffic light. "But — but only for a second," he stammered. "Didn't hurt them or nothing. And they were laughing about it by the time the assembly was over."

Was this the link they were looking for? The next question was crucial: "Were any of your paramedics there?" Natasha asked.

The answer came back quickly. "No. Only firefighters. We don't take paramedics away from the station."

Hamish looked colossally disappointed, arms tightly at his sides, eyes aimed at the linoleum. Was he even breathing? Then suddenly, his arms came up. "Did you give the kids anything? Or take anything from them?"

"Just a little booklet," said the chief. "On fire prevention. Comes from Toronto. The Ontario Fire Marshall's office. Given to kids throughout the province."

"Nothing else?" Hamish pressed. "You're sure?" He was waving in that camp way that overtook him when he got excited about a diagnosis. He'd finally warmed up. Oscar Wilde had broken free of the Tin Man.

The chief looked puzzled, uncertain, but shook his head all the same.

"Think carefully," Hamish pressed again. "As I'm sure you understand, Chief, this is very important."

Dyment raised his arms, palms up, and looked out at the audience. "What do you say, guys? Did we give them anything else?"

"Nah," was the consensus from the uniforms at the back.

"Sure we did," said a lone, male voice. It came from the side, from a well-built Adonis in a firefighter's jumpsuit. He was perched on the counter in front of the microwave. He looked about twenty-two. He'd rolled up his shirt to reveal his impressive biceps. He had a cute, freckled face, like Ron Howard as Richie on *Happy Days* reruns. "Remember?" he said. "The cheerleaders?"

A smirk slid across the face of the short guy·at the back. "Couldn't forget them."

"They wanted our special gum," said the Richie lookalike. "Their supplier wasn't sure when his next shipment was coming in. The kids' stock had run out and they'd heard we used it too."

What a funny choice of words, Natasha thought. Normally you chewed gum, you didn't use it. And why did it require a supplier?

"Good man," Hamish said. "What sort of gum?"

Richie dug into his pocket and pulled out a small packet. He tossed it to Hamish, but he fumbled it, and it dropped to the floor. Natasha picked it up.

The label said PRODUCT OF CHINA and called Snooze-Free Gum: KEEP YOU FROM DOZING WHILE IT FRESHEN YOUR BREATH. Though she'd bought lots of gum in her time, she'd never seen anything like this. The wrapper was the sort of beige that would never attract attention on a store shelf, and the printing was in a plain typewriter font. She turned the packet over. The active ingredients were listed as caffeine, taurine, and ginkgo biloba. A warning caught her eye: THIS PRODUCT CONTAIN NATURALLY BOOSTED GINKGO AMENTOF-LAVONE. NOT MEANT FOR PROLONGED USAGES. ASK DOCTOR BEFORE USING FOR MORE THAN THREE DAYS IN ROWS.

"I need to see that," Hamish barked, as if it were her fault he'd dropped it. He grabbed it and studied every surface. By the time he'd read the warning, his eyes looked like dinner plates. He turned to Joanna Dyment and pointed to her cellphone. "That a smart phone?"

She nodded, obviously taken aback by the abruptness of his tone, especially in front of her husband's subordinates.

"You got it connected to the Internet?" he said. "I mean, right here, immediate access?"

"Yes, Doctor," Joanna said, handing him her phone. "Be my guest."

Hamish tapped the screen, waited a few seconds, then began tapping again, oblivious to the absolute hush that had come over the room. Every eye was focussed on the pink device in the eccentric doctor's hands.

A minute went by, then a second, maybe even a third. No one moved. One person stifled a cough, but no one spoke, not even the smart aleck at the back.

Finally, Hamish looked up and realized he had a captivated audience. He held up the phone with a Wilde flourish and beamed at the crowd.

He punched the screen. "Gotcha!"

CHAPTER 41

Hamish handed the cellphone back to Joanna Dyment and addressed the crowd. "Okay," he said. "We're going to break new ground together. Field epidemiology by show of hands. And let me tell you, this is going to get a tad personal."

Natasha didn't like the sound of that. And what had he found on the Internet that had made him shout gotcha? He must have discovered that some ingredient in that gum could be the cofactor they were looking for — the agent that turned Tammy Holt's 5-FNN into a liver toxin. Why wasn't he letting her in on it? Why was he making her stand here uselessly like Vanna White?

She wanted to pull him aside, tell him there were rules and conventions they had to follow as agents of the Ministry of Health. These days, personal privacy was paramount, the ministry's holiest of sacred cows. But the guy was on a roll, a train that couldn't be stopped without a huge scene.

"So — are you with me?" Hamish continued, searching the faces, almost daring them to oppose him.

Chief Dyment shoved his hands in his pockets, then pulled them out, as if unsure what to do with them. He threw a shrug at

Natasha, then told Hamish, "Don't exactly know what you have in mind, Doc, but I think you should go for it."

Hamish turned to Natasha. "Get out your notebook. These people are going to give us some answers we won't want to miss."

Hamish held up the packet of Snooze-Free gum. "Hands up, who among you chews this stuff?"

People started looking at each other as if knowing they should raise their hands but not wanting to be the first.

Hamish aimed his now wild-eyed gaze at the Richie Cunningham lookalike who'd tossed the gum to him just minutes ago. He waved the packet in the air. "You chew this stuff, right?"

Richie nodded.

"Then put up your hand," Hamish said and looked around the room for other takers.

Slowly, the hands went up: three of the four uniformed guys at the back, a man standing by the refrigerator in a paramedic's uniform, four men in civvies who must be off duty today, two of the wives/sisters/girlfriends, one of whom was the woman with the Juicy Couture necklace.

"Good," Hamish said. "Now leave your hands up until Ms Sharma has taken your names."

Natasha realized she had three choices. She could refuse to cooperate, she could flounce through the room like a ditzy secretary with a steno pad, or she could act like this was a perfectly normal, high-priority epidemiological investigation.

She put on her professional face, walked confidently through the crowd on her three-hundred-dollar Stuart Weitzmans, and took down the names under the heading *Snooze-Free Herbal Gum Positive*.

Hamish looked at Richie again. "What about Donna Holt and the other first responders with acute liver failure?" He waved the packet. "Did they chew this stuff?"

It was clear that Richie didn't like being singled out. "Don't know for sure," he said. "Maybe."

"Maybe doesn't cut it." Hamish scanned the room. "Can anyone else be more definitive?"

Several of the wives huddled together, obviously conferring, their faces earnest and intense. A spokesperson emerged. "That gum has been a big hit around here," she said. "It's safe to say they all chewed it. You know, to help them cope with the night shifts?"

"I guess it works, then," Hamish said.

The two widows burst into tears. The woman with the pavé necklace looked stricken, as though she saw her future flashing ahead of her, and it was going to be short and bleak.

"Anyone who doesn't chew it?" Hamish asked.

Lots of hands went up. Most of the women, in fact. And the smart aleck firefighter standing at the back with his three mates.

"With husbands who work shift, our problem is getting enough sleep," said the woman in the City of Palms tee-shirt, "not staying awake."

"No way I'd touch that herbal stuff," Smart Aleck said. "It's from China. You never know what shit they put in it."

"Back to the rez tobacco," Hamish said, while Natasha was still scribbling names in her notebook. "Rollies, Hat-Trick brand, in fact, any kind of Native tobacco. We know the liver victims all smoked it. What about the rest of you? Hands up — who smokes rez tobacco?"

"You mean regularly or from time to time?" asked Smart Aleck.

"Let's say at least one pack in the past month," Hamish said.

Hands went up all over the place. Natasha wasn't surprised to see that Mrs. Juicy Couture and Mrs. City of Palms had their hands in the air. Having got a closer look at the two women, she'd already guessed that the partially hidden blisters on their fingers and lips would be positive for matchstick particles by electron microscopy.

Richie Cunningham was a non-smoker. So were the three gum-chewing firefighters in uniform at the back, the four first responders in civvies, and the gum-chewing paramedic standing next to the fridge. Mr. Smart Aleck now had a name, Roger Marshall, which she wrote below the heading *Rez Tobacco Positive Gum Negative*.

Smart guy to be suspicious of the Chinese gum, especially in such a dodgy wrapper.

When she'd got all the names down under the appropriate headings, Natasha walked to the front of the room and drew Hamish aside.

"There's one first responder unaccounted for," she told him. "All the others are either here, sick, or — you know," she dropped her voice, "never coming back. We need to find out whether the missing guy is one of those who smokes rez tobacco and chews the gum."

Hamish looked at Mrs. Juicy Couture, then dipped his eyes and whispered, "Like that woman with the flashy necklace."

Hamish looked up, cleared his throat, and addressed the group again. "We need to know who supplies you the gum. Not to get them in trouble, but we need more information about it."

Every eye turned to Richie Cunningham, perched on the counter.

"Is it you?" Hamish asked.

"No," Richie said. "My cousin. But it's not like it's a secret or nothing."

"Your cousin's name?" Hamish said.

"Ian Bell," Richie said.

Natasha flipped through her notebook. Ian Bell. The name sounded familiar. There he was. Admitted to Simcoe General four days ago. A Norfolk County paramedic with jaundice and moderate liver damage. Expected to recover.

"Where does he get it?" Hamish asked.

"A guy," Richie said.

"This is no time to be coy, son" said the chief. "Tell the doctor what he needs to know."

Richie looked uncomfortable, as if he wished he'd never let the Snooze-Free out of his pocket. "Orders it off the Internet. Directly from China. One of those sites where you have to know somebody who knows somebody before they do business with you."

"And exactly who is this guy?" Hamish said.

"A teacher."

"A teacher?" The chief made it sound like the strangest thing he'd ever heard.

"Gets them the gum so they can stay up late," Richie said. "You know, write their essays, study for midterms."

"Does this teacher have a name?" Hamish asked.

Richie picked at his well-bitten fingernails and mumbled something under his breath.

"Sorry?" Hamish said. "Didn't quite catch that."

"Mr. Vorst."

"Walter Vorst?" Natasha asked, the puzzle pieces fitting together in her mind.

Richie nodded and went back to his fingernails.

The room erupted into the disorganized hubbub that had been so obvious an hour ago behind the locked door.

Chief Dyment approached Hamish and Natasha, his wife by his side. Their faces were grey. "Gotta tell you something," he said.

"Yes, Chief," Natasha said, putting on a brave face for them. She could guess what was coming.

"I smoke that damn tobacco from the rez. Harsh as blazes on your throat, but I just can't give it up." He stared at his boots.

Natasha touched his arm.

Grant Dyment lifted his head and looked at his wife like a man about to leave on a long, lonesome journey. "And for the past week, since we've been short-handed, I've been chewing that gum like it's going out of style."

CHAPTER 42

At one o'clock, it was time to get ready to meet the Badger. Zol planned to arrive at the Tim's at Duff's Corners a few minutes early. There was never any strength in arriving late and breathless for a meeting, especially if it was going to be a showdown.

At noon, he'd had what he thought might be his final smoke from the black-eyed loon pipe. Then he'd removed the charred dottle from the chamber and let the stone cool down before wrapping the loon in a handkerchief and stowing her in his blazer pocket.

The pipe had felt clunky there, and her sharp beak dug into his hip. It seemed the little bird, so recently liberated, wasn't happy in the dark. He took her out, unwrapped the hankie, and looked into those enigmatic, onyx eyes.

What were those eyes telling him? To bring the pipe with him or to leave her at home? If he was going to trade the precious creature for the Badger's full cooperation in suspending sales of contaminated tobacco, was it essential that the pipe be at the meeting? Would the Badger believe that Zol had possession of the black-eyed pipe — until now, no more than a legend — only if he saw her with his own eyes?

But what if the Badger's goons strong-armed the loon away from him? It was one thing to give up the bird to a noble cause, but another to lose her in a foolish gamble that gave him nothing in return. And of course . . . if they did make a deal, would the Badger keep his word?

He took off his blazer and glanced again at the front page of today's *Hamilton Spectator*. The press was making a big deal of the latest revelations about the robbery at the Royal Ontario Museum. Now the whole world knew that the three men found under the rubble were Anishinaabeg from Misty Shores Reserve and had been executed before the explosion. Politicians of every stripe were wading in with nonsense statements about intertribal conflicts that showed how little they understood Native history and concerns. There would be a lot of noise for a while, a thorough clean-up of the ROM's demolished Crystal, a load of hotheaded rhetoric from the chief of the Assembly of First Nations, and no changes in the shameful living conditions on the reserves.

Or could things turn out differently? What if Dennis Badger agreed to trade his cooperation for the pipe and became inspired by the reunion of the two legendary loons? What form would such inspiration take? Would it be chaos and bloodshed as Natives across the country settled scores that had been festering for centuries? Or would the descendants of the continent's original inhabitants acquire newfound confidence, stop acting like helpless victims, and break into the twenty-first century not aboard birchbark canoes and stolen vehicles, but private business jets?

And then Zol pictured the bodies. Tammy Holt in the farmer's field, the three at the museum, Olivia Colborne at the liquor store, and Jovan Ligorov at Saint Naum's. They'd been killed on the Badger's orders. Zol shouldn't be trying to kid himself. The guy was ruthless.

He got his camera from the computer room and flattened the *Spec* on the kitchen counter. He set the loon on the newspaper beside today's date and the lead story about the ROM. He took three shots and previewed them to be sure they turned out as he wanted:

two close-ups that showed the loon with the date and one from farther away that showed the ancient pipe sitting in what was obviously a modern kitchen.

He slipped the bird into the Birks box, apologized for banishing her to the darkness again, and went to return her to the shelf behind Mary Poppins.

Looking at Max's long line of DVDs, it was obvious they were sitting on a case custom made for books that were much taller and wider than DVDs. What if the Badger, tantalized by Zol's possession of his wildest dream, sent one of his guys to search the house? Even the dumbest goon would find the loon behind those DVDs in a matter of seconds.

No, Mary Poppins wasn't going to cut it. But where in this house could he find a proper hiding place? He'd always meant to have a wall safe installed, but had never got around to it. What about the basement? Plenty of clutter there to hide something in plain sight.

He ran down the stairs and into the workshop. Hell. Ermalinda had tidied it. It looked like an operating room suite. Not a thing out of place. No good for hiding anything, not even a finishing nail.

The laundry room. Again, immaculate. A few socks and underwear arranged on the energy-saving drying rack. Ermalinda had requested the rack when she'd first arrived. He eyed the washer, then the dryer. Would that work? He opened the dryer, knelt down, and put his hand on one of the fins projecting from the drum on the hinge side of the door. He turned the drum until the fin was horizontal. He grabbed a pair of his boxer briefs from the rack, tossed them over the Birks box, and placed it on the fin. He made sure it was secure, then stood up and casually looked into the drum. A thief would have to get down on his hands and knees to see anything other than a pair of undies forgotten in the dryer. And he probably wouldn't even see that.

He dashed upstairs and threw on his blazer. Now it was the camera that felt clunky in his pocket. That was okay.

As he backed out of his driveway, the sun came out from behind a cloud and flooded the neighbourhood with what his mother called October magic. The autumn leaves — red, orange, green, gold, nutmeg brown — were suddenly glowing like lanterns, whether on the trees or scattered on the ground. Thousands, no millions, of points of light were shining like bulbs in a forest of chandeliers. It was as if Mother Nature, in a burst of brilliance, had turned every tree into a candelabra, every lawn into a river of light. Was she apologizing for the end of summer, for the coming of two months of misty grey, then two months of dirty white, then two more of barren brown? If she were, she could be forgiven, especially if Max and Colleen were enjoying the same treat in Forest Hill, and Mum and Dad as well on Jenkins Road. Less than two minutes later, the sun slipped behind another cloud and the lanterns dimmed. The leaves no longer glowed from the inside. What did Natasha call that? Something she'd learned in art history? Yes, a fleeting moment. Life was full of them.

He drove west on Scenic Drive parallel to the Escarpment and mused about this famous swath of geological drama. The continuous cliff-face sliced through the city on its eight-hundred-kilometre journey from Niagara Falls to Lake Huron. The people who had lived here for thousands of years had given the region its name, Neagara.

At two o'clock, he arrived at Duff's Corners, pleased to see that the Badger and his escorts were nowhere in sight. He ordered a large coffee, double cream, and was surprised how quickly the girl handed it to him. Then he remembered, this wasn't the Detour in Simcoe, where every cup was freshly brewed using an individual conical filter.

He found a seat with a good view of the front entrance and Wilson Street beyond it. A half-hour's drive to the left was Grand Basin Reserve. The centre of Hamilton was fifteen minutes to the right. The airport was twelve minutes behind him. Dennis should be here any minute.

His coffee was still hot when he saw a middle-age couple approaching one of the rooms in the seen-better-days Happy Hours

Motel on the opposite side of Wilson Street. Actually, only the man looked middle-aged; the woman looked younger by a decade or two. She was wearing a skimpy polka-dot dress and high heels. He sported a long coat open over a business suit. They had no luggage. He struggled with the key for quite a while before he finally got the door to open. Perhaps the delay had something to do with her lips locking on his neck, her left hand clamped on his back, and her right hand massaging his crotch.

At two-thirty, the last mouthful of Zol's coffee was cold. At two-forty he'd finished flipping through the issue of the *Auto Trader* he found on a counter. At two-forty-five, he wondered whether he should turn on his phone. He'd turned it off when he'd left the house, not wanting any interruptions during this meeting on which so many lives were hanging. He decided to leave it off. He hadn't given Dennis the number, so he wouldn't be calling it anyway.

The couple from the Happy Hours slipped out of their room at two-fifty. They weren't kissing or embracing; in fact they weren't even touching. The man looked anxious and walked left, his coat buttoned to the neck. The woman walked right, her dress still skimpy, but her heels exchanged for flats.

At three o'clock, Zol reckoned he'd waited long enough. He'd nursed a large coffee for the first half hour and a large decaf for the second. He'd started out anxious, but now he was frustrated, angry, and past the point of no return with the Badger. His bladder was demanding attention. Two more minutes and he'd go for a leak and call it a day.

A Native guy, husky, about forty, wearing a black nylon jacket came out of nowhere and made a beeline for Zol's table.

"You're Dr. Szabo, eh?"

"That's right. Are you with Mr. —"

He dropped a letter-size envelope on the table. "Then this is for you." He turned and strode out. Zol watched him climb into a black Silverado and drive off. No coffee, no explanation, no nothing.

Zol picked up the envelope. His name was hand-printed in blue ink. The top left corner said Office of the Chief, Grand Basin. Inside was a standard sheet of white paper. It took only a few seconds to read what was scrawled across it: *Dr. Szabo, Dennis Badger says forget the meeting. No point to it. He doesn't trade. A waste of time for both of yous. Sorry, Rob Falcon, Grand Basin Chief.*

Shit. He'd played it all wrong. He'd pushed Dennis too hard by expecting him to drop everything and fly halfway across the country on short notice. He'd made the Badger lose face to a White Man, making it impossible for him to cooperate. In retaliation, the Badger was holed up in his den, digging in his heels.

Zol read the chief's message again, folded it, and returned it to the envelope. He thought about it again. Maybe no one had ever pushed the Badger hard enough. The bastard was killing people. Directly and indirectly. And expecting to get away with it. What about Colleen's contacts at the DNA lab in Toronto? They'd been processing the Badger's discarded coffee cup for four days now and not a word. That sounded anything but hopeful; Colleen had expected a turnaround time of under seventy-two hours. The Badger was likely to be as slick at evading forensic science as eluding government authority.

Zol flipped open his 7-Eleven phone and turned it on. No notice of missed incoming calls, but there was an unread text message from Hamish sent over an hour ago: IMPORTANT DEVELOPMENTS. CALL MY CELL ASAP.

Hamish was going to have to wait. Zol pressed delete and the phone came alive in his hand, buzzing and chirping. Shit. What was happening? Had Hamish set some sort of cyber loop thing that told him Zol was ignoring his message?

No, it was an incoming call. A Toronto number he knew far too well.

An icy fist gripped his heart.

CHAPTER 43

"Dr. Szabo?" said the female voice from the Ministry of Health.

"Yes."

"Please hold for Dr. York." She parked him on hold without waiting for an answer. If the Muzak was supposed to Zen you out while you were waiting on the line, it wasn't working. His palms were so slippery he had to keep passing the phone from one hand to the other and wiping the sweat on his pants.

"Szabo?" Elliott said after an eternal three or four minutes.

"Yes, sir?"

"What are you up to?"

"Well, I've been waiting for —"

"I know who you're waiting for, and it's not going to happen."

"Sir?"

"I told you to watch your step down there in Indian country, and now I get a phone call from the vice commissioner of the provincial police. Says you've been threatening a prominent First Nations businessman. Even tried to blackmail him. Tell me this isn't true."

A vice commissioner of the OPP? How had such a heavy hitter got involved so quickly? The Badger's connections must run right to the top. What were those connections based on? Hush money? Political contributions? Family ties?

"Well, I've been negotiating with Mr. Badger to solicit his cooperation in our investigation of his tainted tobacco." The camera in his pocket now felt bulky and incriminating.

"Negotiating? The OPP are calling it bribery or extortion. Those are criminal offences, for God's sake."

Surely Dennis hadn't mentioned the pipes to the police. His complaint couldn't have been that specific without incriminating himself. He'd told them enough of his version of the story to get Zol off his back. "We've traced our cluster of fatal liver failures to a research project that went sour in Norfolk County."

"Research?" York made it sound like a curse. "Come on, man, a guy like Dennis Badger doesn't do research."

"But Caledonia University does, and a toxin-producing virus escaped the confines of a lab and infected most of the tobacco crop in Norfolk County. That's Dennis Badger's prime source for his cut-price cigarettes."

"You may have been reading too much science fiction, Szabo, but I've been reading your reports on those liver cases. There's a flaw in your logic. Your so-called toxin is affecting kids at only one high school and the firefighters at just one station. People smoke Dennis Badger's cigarettes all over the country. If his tobacco was causing your liver failures, we'd be seeing cases like them coast to coast."

"Yes, well . . . we're working on that puzzling aspect."

"You're working on it, are you. Isn't that dandy? At this point in your investigation you can't tell me how Dennis Badger's cigarettes have anything to do with the crux of your liver outbreak. Yet today you threatened to shut down his international tobacco sales? Goddammit, who the hell do you think you are?"

What was he supposed to say?

York hadn't finished. "You overstepped your jurisdiction, Szabo. Big time. Your territory is Norfolk County. Any public-health ramifications beyond your borders you leave to me. And if anyone is going to shut down Mr. Badger's international tobacco sales, it's the pertinent federal agency. Certainly not an upstart rural MOH who's too big for his britches."

This was so unfair. The Badger's tobacco was poisoning livers, there was no doubt about that. They just hadn't figured out the exact mechanism. In the meantime, of course it was appropriate to issue a public-health warning and suspend the Badger's operation until the mess got sorted out. That was how public health worked. When a restaurant was in violation of an important health and safety code, the health unit shut the place down by posting a red sign on the front door of the premises. When nursing homes indulged in faulty practices, the Ministry suspended their licences until they cleaned up their act. When paramedics refused their annual flu shots, Emergency Medical Services suspended them without pay.

The difference was, Dennis Badger was a multimillionaire with a direct line to the OPP.

"I'm taking a supervisory role in this case, Szabo. I want all your notes and data sent to me by tomorrow morning. And you'll call me every afternoon with an update."

"Is that necessary, sir? Isn't that too much of an imposition on your time?"

"You've left me no choice. And let me make this clear: if Dennis Badger needs to be approached by anyone working on behalf of the Ministry of Health, I'll arrange for one of my staff to interview him. From now on, you're under strict orders not to contact Dennis Badger or his associates in any way, shape, or form."

Zol said nothing. He was too busy thinking.

"You still there, Szabo?"

"I'm here."

"Did I make myself clear?

"Very, sir."

"Good," York said and hung up.

Zol closed the phone and gazed through the window at the Happy Hours Motel. The woman in the skimpy polka-dot dress was outside room number eight again. She'd put on her heels, and this time her client was a much younger man. He had the rakish ball cap, high-top sneakers, and baggy jeans of a rapper. She had that doorway routine of hers down pat: same lips on the neck, same left hand pressed against the back, same right-handed action on the crotch.

Zol was so drained he could hardly move. He felt like slouching on this chair for the rest of the afternoon and watching that hooker come and go, but his bladder was begging for relief, and he had a call to make. It didn't matter that he hadn't entered the number into the new phone's address book. He knew it by heart.

CHAPTER 44

At five thirty, Zol strode into Four Corners Fine Foods through the automatic doors off Concession Street. He loved this place, five minutes' drive from his house. It was a haven, and perhaps another addiction, for a professional chef turned doctor. There were so many aromas coming off the breads and cheeses, the tropical fruits, the European chocolates that they cancelled each other and let him browse in peace. No crossed-wire musical snippets assaulted him here. Sometimes, he and Max came with a list. Other times, like now, he let his imagination take him down the aisles and into the grocery cart.

It was amazing how good you felt when you'd wrestled a problem to the ground — in this case to the tobacco fields of Norfolk County — and decided on a plan. His visit with Art Greenwood had soothed him immediately. Art had listened without interrupting and validated Zol's concerns with his eyes and with that gentle way he clasped his hands and cocked his head. Then it had been Art's turn to speak, and Zol's world seemed to stop as Art put it back on course. The wily old fellow was a master at stripping away bullshit, zoning into the heart of a matter, and suggesting a course of action that fit the situation perfectly. No wonder he'd been such a whiz in the telecom industry, perfecting Canada's version of Touch-Tone service.

Zol was reaching for a warm, sourdough baguette when the flip phone buzzed in his pocket. It wouldn't be Colleen again. She'd called ten minutes ago to say that she, Max, and Allie were at Toronto Pearson Terminal Three waiting for Francine's flight from Hong Kong. Max was beside himself with excitement. At first Zol had bristled at the thought of them wandering around the city, but Colleen was a pro and assured him they weren't being followed. And by now, the Badger would have received word from his OPP contact that the pain-in-the-ass Simcoe MOH had been officially muzzled and was no longer a threat.

Zol dropped the baguette into his cart beside the masala hummus and Kalamata olives, and put the phone to his ear.

"Where the heck have you been?" Hamish said.

"Here and there. Sorry. Forgot about your message."

"No point in having a phone if you never turn it on."

"Long story. Spent an hour with Art Greenwood at his retirement residence. They don't like cellphones ringing there. They find them intrusive and interfere with their hearing aids. Old people didn't grow up with them the way we did."

"You could've left it on vibrate."

"To tell you the truth, I needed some space. It's been a tough afternoon. We went for a walk — well I walked, he drove his electric scooter thing. I needed some advice. He helped me put everything into perspective. We decided I needed to talk to the priest."

"Seriously? A priest?"

"Yep."

"But you never go to church."

"Sure, but don't forget I was raised a Catholic. Once they baptize you, they stick to you for life. My mother's in deep with the Catholic Women's League."

"When are you going to talk to the priest?"

"Have already. And now I feel a hell of a lot better. No matter what happens, I'll be able to live with myself." That's what counted in the end — making things safe for the next generation.

"Colleen told me she and Max moved their stuff to the Beach."

He knew that already from Colleen. Allie suggested they all stay at her house in Toronto. It made sense — Zol's place was a no-go zone and the Beach was a family friendly neighbourhood. Most of the city was accessible by way of the Queen Street streetcar. Max loved the Red Rocket.

"That okay with you?" Hamish continued. "Your son, your ex, and your girlfriend in one big happy sleepover?"

"I'm cool with it. Good to have them safely out of the way for a few days. The Badger and I aren't done yet."

"That's what I need to talk to you about. I've got great news. Now you can bypass Dennis Badger and stop the epidemic immediately. That's why I texted you to call me ASAP."

Zol wheeled the cart to the quiet corner where Four Corners kept the tasteless stuff for diabetics, imported from Germany: sugar-free chocolates, boring jams, and canned fruits packed in some sort of brine. He'd never seen anyone browsing here.

"What are you saying?" Zol said.

"We found the cofactor. You know, the agent that makes the kids at Erie Collegiate and the first responders at Norfolk Emergency Services uniquely susceptible to acute liver failure."

"You're kidding. What is it? Where'd you find it?"

"In the lunchroom at the Simcoe fire station."

"Just sitting there?"

"No, we had to ferret it out. Natasha and I."

"And?"

"It's something called Snooze-Free gum." Hamish's voice was getting higher and higher, his tone more and more camp, as he expounded on the details of the dodgy import from China.

"And exactly what is amentoflavone?" Zol asked.

"In high doses, it's a powerful modifier of cytochrome P-450 enzymes, which means it alters the way the liver metabolizes certain drugs, chemicals, and toxins."

"Let me guess, it sends Tammy Holt's 5-FNN down some sort of nasty biochemical pathway that turns it into a toxin."

"Oh." Hamish said, sounding surprised that a mere public-health doc knew the first thing about biochemistry. "I've done a little digging, some talking to a couple of biochem colleagues. And well, you're exactly right."

"Fancy that, eh?"

"Without the gum, 5-FNN is a nice little appetite suppressant with billion-dollar market potential. But if it's in your system and you chew that gum . . ."

Your liver fell apart from centrilobular necrosis, as if you'd inhaled a bottle of carbon tetrachloride, old-fashioned dry cleaning solution.

"Good work, Hamish. I presume Natasha's making sure no one in Canada chews any more of that stuff."

"No worries. She's on it. Called the CFIA's hotline immediately."

She'd probably had to leave a message on their machine. The Canadian Food Inspection Agency's hotline wasn't all that hot after three o'clock Eastern.

"Now," Hamish said, sounding calmer, "I guess you don't have to worry about Dennis Badger and his contaminated tobacco."

"How so?"

"If people don't chew that gum, they can smoke all the rez tobacco they can get their hands on and not get sick . . . oh . . . sorry." He cleared his throat. "Well, you know what I mean." Was Hamish suddenly getting sensitive, thinking about Zol's mum slowly dying of lung cancer acquired from forty years of smoking?

"It's okay, Hamish. I know what you mean. But," Zol reminded him, "there must be dozens of other chemicals, herbal and other-wise, that can send 5-FNN down that poisonous pathway."

"Like what?"

"Ginkgo biloba is in all sorts of so-called natural remedies, many of which are improperly labelled and could contain high levels of amentoflavone without anyone knowing it."

"Shouldn't you leave that to Health Canada and the CFIA?"

"And watch more livers shrivel and die after smokers consume other enzyme modifiers? I'm thinking St. John's wort, milk thistle, or even plain old grapefruit juice."

"I suppose, when you put it that way, but —"

"Of course I'm putting it that way. Can you imagine if we lobbied for a worldwide embargo on grapefruit juice so Dennis Badger could keep selling his contaminated tobacco to unsuspecting smokers all over the planet?" He had a strong image of the Badger sitting in his Learjet, the fringe of his deerskin jacket fluttering every time he lifted a flute of Moët & Chandon champers to his lips.

"You're exaggerating. There's no evidence that grapefruit is a problem here."

"But it could be. It interferes with the metabolism of quite a few drugs."

"But how are you going to get around the Badger without putting us all in danger?"

"You'll just have to watch."

CHAPTER 45

Zol drew the minivan into the garage and popped the back open. It was going to be fun putting a meal together with the two bags full of treats from Four Corners. They had the best hummus, which he'd have on the sourdough baguette while he prepared the pork tenderloin for roasting: garlic, onion, Herbes de Provence, and his secret ingredient, Tap 357 rye whisky flavoured with real maple syrup. Delicious.

He hit the garage-door button and braced for the screeching of the closing door. He walked into the mudroom and cursed himself for forgetting to set the alarm on his way out this afternoon. How dumb to be that distracted over a meeting that never happened. He threw on the lights and went to drop the groceries on the kitchen counter, but . . . what the hell? The place looked like San Francisco after the earthquake. Every drawer was hanging open, the contents dumped on the floor. Every cupboard had been ransacked. Even the fridge and dishwasher had been gone through. He grabbed a baseball bat from the garage and ran from room to room, throwing on the lights as he went. It was the same everywhere. Their entire life thrown to the floor. The computer room was particularly bad. Every one of Max's DVDs had been cleared from the shelf and tossed onto the carpet. The computer monitor had been upended, but not smashed.

When he thought about it, this wasn't vandalism. Nothing had been trashed. And neither was it wanton theft. None of the valuable electronics had been stolen. Even his collection of watches — some elegant, some fun, but none over the top in price — was still in the dresser in the bedroom. The boxes had been opened and tossed every which way, but the timepieces were still there.

Whoever had done this had been looking for something specific. Had they known what they were looking for or making an educated guess? Shit. He ran down to the basement, sweat pouring down the back of his neck. Had they found her? Oh, please, no. Please, let her be safe in the dryer.

When he got to the laundry room, he saw the clothes from the drying rack scattered on the floor along with a box of laundry detergent, a bottle of bleach, and another of fabric softener. The place had be turned over meticulously. The detergent box was upright, not a single granule spilled from it. Cursing at his stupidity, he forced himself to look in the dryer.

The door was closed. Had he left it that way? He couldn't remember. He pulled it open, knelt down, put his hand in. Nothing. Shit. He felt further up, brushed against the metal fin, found the smooth cotton of his boxer briefs, then yes, the box underneath. When he lifted it out, the weight of it told him the little bird was still there. Unless . . . would they be cruel enough to replace her with a rock?

He held his breath and removed the lid. She winked at him as if to say *It's about time you showed up*. Thank God.

He removed her from the box and slipped her into his jacket pocket, then went upstairs to call the cops. Colleen would be pleased. Finally, he was calling the police.

CHAPTER 46

"Hi, Dad," Max said the next morning, through the 7-Eleven phone.

Zol was standing in his Simcoe office, gathering the notes he needed to fax to Elliott York in Toronto. He didn't trust the landlines here, though the security company promised the bugs had been dealt with. He was going to use the fax machine at the mailbox store on Norfolk Avenue, just to be sure.

"Is it true, Dad? Colleen says the bad guys aren't following us anymore?"

How could he phrase it so it approached the truth yet sounded reassuring? "They're not actually bad, Max. They don't happen to agree with some of the things I have to do at work."

"I thought they had guns."

"I haven't seen any weapons." Which was true, remarkably enough, considering what had been happening these past few days. "They promised me they'd leave you alone as long as you stayed in Toronto for a little while longer. Are you having fun there?"

"I guess. Allie is a good sewer. She makes her own clothes and sells them at a store. She's making me a Halloween costume."

"Fantastic, bud. What are you going to be?"

"A zombie pirate."

"You mean with an eye patch and a wooden leg?"

"No, a real zombie. Wicked hair, grey skin that will make me look like a corpse, striped legs, and blood oozing from everywhere."

A corpse? Great. "Allie sounds pretty talented."

"She's really nice," Max said. "But Dad . . ." He'd lowered his voice. "Soksang is kinda different."

Sok-sang? Who was she? Did Allie have a maid? Or maybe it was a he? It would be no surprise if a friend of Francine's had a gardener on a day pass from a halfway house.

"Who?" Zol asked, trying not to sound anxious.

"You know. Francine, remember? She changed her name when she became a nun. And that's what I'm supposed to call her, Soksang."

"Sorry. I remember now." Soksang, Cambodian for peace. Zol cleared his throat. "Do you mean different in a nice way? She's not being mean, is she?"

"No. But she doesn't watch movies and she can't buy me anything. She's not supposed to touch money. Not even a credit card."

"So is Colleen paying for what she needs?"

"Soksang never goes shopping. She showed us her robe. She doesn't have any other clothes. It has to be orange, no other colour. And it has three different parts. She says it's so comfortable she doesn't need anything else. Not even jeans. Her suitcase is very small. She let me carry it for her. It wasn't heavy."

"That was good of you. I'm sure she was thrilled to see you at the airport."

"You know, Dad, it never gets cold in Cambodia. Kids there have never seen snow."

"I guess they wouldn't, would they?"

"Soksang doesn't eat dessert and she doesn't know anything about computers. Or how to use a cellphone. And she doesn't know who Hermione is in *Harry Potter*."

"But you're having a good time?"

"Sort of. Soksang sits by herself and prays a lot. She says I watch too much TV." It was sounding like Max had discovered for himself that Francine made a better pen pal than a mother figure. Music to Zol's ears. "Dad, when can Colleen and I come home? I miss Travis and my other friends."

Zol pictured the chaos in the house. No kid should have to see his room pulled apart by professional thugs. Max would have bad dreams for a month.

"It won't be long," Zol told him, not sure how normal their life was ever going to be again.

"I won't have to go trick-or-treating here on Halloween, will I? I don't know any of the kids."

"I hope not, Max. I hope everything will be settled before then."

"Promise? You mean I can go to school on Monday? Wear my costume, go to the Halloween assembly, and everything? Promise, Dad?"

Zol crossed his fingers and thought about the plans that were taking shape. Everything was hanging on Sunday morning. If things ran off the rails, Monday would have to take care of itself.

"I'm doing my best, Max. All I can do is my best."

CHAPTER 47

At five on Sunday morning, Matt Holt turned right off Bay and right again onto Murray, using his GPS for guidance. He'd only been down here once before, when a grateful client had taken him out in his sailboat. Sailing on Lake Ontario was okay, but he would have preferred something faster, with a nice throaty engine you could tinker with.

Dylan with the Irish accent had said to look for a two-storey detached brick with a large front porch, and he'd leave the lights on.

"You can't miss it," he'd added. "In my corner of North Hamilton, a detached house is as rare as an honest Yugoslav general. Look for the Sicilian Fratellanza Racalmutese, a social club that's basically a floodlit sign sitting atop a few blocks of Lego. Nice people and good neighbours, if you like garlic. We're half a block further on."

Matt parked at the curb in front of the house and knocked on the door. The living room curtains parted briefly before the door opened, and a presence filled the doorway. It introduced itself as Dylan and said what a pleasure it was to meet face to face after spending much of yesterday talking to each other on the phone.

He looked about thirty-five, bushy beard, black shirt and jeans over an athletic build. It was amazing how hairy some White people could be, but what was most impressive was the guy's height, about six-six. His eyes were grey, like a wolf's, and he flashed one of those big smiles White people use when they're anxious. Though on this guy, the smile seemed sincere. Perhaps that was because he was some sort of priest. At least, that's what Dr. Szabo had called him when he'd set them up. Or maybe that was his code name, Dylan the Priest. A real priest wouldn't have a Fisher-Price trike in his front hall beside a pair of women's boots.

"Good morning to you, my good man," said Dylan the Priest. "Come in. I've everything ready. Twenty boxes of fun." His eyes strayed to the massive scar running from Matt's left eye, through his cheek, down his neck to his collar bone.

"I see you like my scar," Matt said.

The smile vanished from the big guy's face. "Sorry, I shouldn't have —"

"It's a beauty, eh?" Matt said, touching it. "But it's fake. A friend did it for me last night. He works in the movies."

Dylan the Priest relaxed and let out a chuckle. "You certainly played me for a fool. It's going to make quite the fine impression on the guards."

That was the idea. They'd remember the scar and nothing else. His movie friend had lent him a Detroit Tigers baseball cap with a realistic fringe of blond hair sticking out from under it. The black work shirt and matching pants he'd bought at the Brantford Mall, where they'd embroidered *Upper Canada Security* above the shirt pocket. The woman had done it while he waited, without batting an eyelash. It was amazing what people let you get away with. Especially around Halloween.

The cardboard boxes stacked in Dylan's living room were each the size and weight of a two-four of Molson's. They'd been dabbed with green, grey, and brown paint. The camouflage looked pretty cool. It didn't take long to load them into the van Matt had prepared for the job. As per usual on a Saturday, he'd sent his staff home at noon, and then he'd spent the afternoon alone in his shop spray-painting the made-up name on the van's side panels: UPPER CANADA SECURITY. He'd added a fake but operational phone number to make everything legit. He was pleased with the paint job, although it didn't have to be perfect. This little charade didn't have to last long. The plan was to get the set-ups done before sun-up.

They stopped at an all-night Tim's on Barton Street for a couple of large double-doubles, but the caffeine didn't touch his partner. Instead of riding shotgun, Dylan the Priest snored all the way to Grand Basin.

Five hundred metres from their first destination, Matt stopped on the gravel shoulder of the rural side road running through the bush. He shook Dylan the Priest by the arm. "Wake up, Goldilocks, it's showtime."

"What? Oh, are we here? On the rez already?"

"You got it. Indian territory." Matt winked and pointed ahead through the windshield. "The first Rollies factory is just ahead. Target number one. You ready?"

"Most certainly," he said, sounding more confident than the look on his face. If he'd grown that bushy beard to hide behind, it wasn't working. "But would you be so kind as to run through the steps again."

"Good idea, partner." It was kind of fun having a White guy playing Tonto to his Lone Ranger. Although the real Lone Ranger was Dr. Szabo.

They ran through the details of the plan they'd worked out yesterday over the phone. Dr. Szabo had bought them pay-as-you-go cells from 7-Eleven to minimize the chance that Dennis and his boys could listen in. The Badger was a superior mastermind who controlled an impressive empire, but he wasn't a magician. The phones were secure. Weren't they?

Matt put on the Tigers' ball cap and a pair of safety goggles with yellow lenses, and drove the final half kilometre. Until now, this had felt like an adventure. It had been fun dreaming up the disguise and painting the van. But when the headlights caught the first glimpse of barbed wire through the trees, the double-double began to churn in his stomach.

He ignored the ruckus in his guts and stopped the van at the unmarked gate. Of course it was unmarked. Regular folk weren't supposed to know that this was one of the two major Rollies factories on Grand Basin Reserve. Factory seemed too fancy a word for the single, plain building enclosed in a ten-foot perimeter of barbed wire. One storey high, the placed looked like a long, narrow warehouse with an A-line roof, aluminum siding, and security cameras at the gate and above the front door. Colleen had said there were four more cameras mounted on the eaves — one on each corner. She'd also said there was only one guard on duty after midnight and on Sundays, and the shift changed at eight-thirty in the morning. The machines that made the cigarettes ran Monday through Saturday. The large gravel parking lot was bordered on three sides by dense bush. And all that barbed wire, of course. In the far corner were two cube vans — white, no special markings. A two-litre Acura CSX was parked close to the front door. It looked well taken care of, though you never knew the state of the shocks, the brakes, and the exhaust until you put a vehicle on the hoist and made a thorough inspection.

Matt put his window down and pressed the button on the intercom.

"Can't you see the sign?" said a voice through the speaker. "No trespassing?"

"Upper Canada Security, sir."

"We're closed."

"We're answering an alarm situation."

"I didn't hear no alarm."

"It's a silent one. Signalling a problem with your security cameras."

"Nobody called me."

"It's company policy to respond in person, sir. To be sure you're not experiencing a personal emergency situation and nobody's tampering with your equipment."

"I'm fine."

"I have orders to see that the guard on duty is not in danger and to check the security cameras immediately."

"I can't let you in here."

Shit. This was more difficult than he'd expected. "I do not need to enter the premises, sir, only the grounds of the compound. The situation in question is an exterior problem. If necessary, I can adjust the cameras with my handheld device. You can observe everything I do on your interior monitors." Sometimes it helped to use big words. What you said sounded good, so people felt your authority without admitting to themselves they weren't entirely certain what you'd said.

"You'd have to sign in."

"Certainly, sir. I wouldn't have it any other way. I'm sure you take security as seriously as we do."

The gate opened, and by the time they'd drawn next to the Acura the guard was standing outside holding a clipboard.

"Just two o' yous?" the guard said through the window of the van. His eyes widened at the sight of Matt's scar and stared at it longer than was polite. Good, he wouldn't forget it.

If the scar wasn't fake, and this was a normal encounter, the guy would have pissed him off. He was young, Asian, Canadian accent, and about twenty-two, though with Asians you could hardly tell whether they were twenty or forty. He had the bloodshot eyes of someone who'd been up all night and was desperate to get home to bed. Still, there was a tough-guy edge to his attitude, probably supported by the handgun clipped to his belt.

Matt reached for the clipboard, signed it, passed it to Dylan the Priest in the passenger seat, and handed it back to the guard along with one of the Upper Canada Security business cards he'd printed yesterday. The phone number on the card matched the one he'd painted on the van.

"Can you do me a favour?" Matt asked.

"Depends," said the guard.

Matt shrugged to give the impression it wasn't a big deal whether the guy did him the favour or not. "Dead simple. You're going to see the outside camera images go white for half a minute, maybe longer, one at a time. I need you to record the camera numbers and the times when the images go on and off. To the nearest five seconds will be fine. Can you manage that?"

The guy lifted the cuff of his nylon jacket to expose the Breitling on his wrist. If the gang was paying him marginally above minimum wage, it was a knock-off. If it was real, he was no rent-a-cop flunky; he was number-one son taking care of Daddy's million-dollar operation. And that made him all the more dangerous.

They waited until Mr. I've-got-a-Breitling returned to the building. Matt could hear him bolt the door. Was he phoning Upper Canada Security to verify the legitimacy of the call? If he did, he'd get another pay-as-you-go cellphone and Dr. Szabo's girlfriend working a shift at the "Upper Canada Security" call centre.

Matt backed the van away from the Acura and parked at the extreme right of the building's face, where they wouldn't be seen by the front-door camera, only the camera at that right corner. Matt got out first, then the priest. While the priest opened the rear doors of the van and got ready to remove three of his boxes, Matt stood in front of the roof-mounted camera, aimed his phone at it, and pretended to punch in a few numbers. He gave a confident salute for the guard's benefit, punched at the phone again, then shone his heavy-duty halogen flashlight straight at the camera lens.

The light was the priest's signal to walk into the shadows parallel to the long, right side of the building hefting three boxes at once. They were heavy, but not too much for him, and they had to make this quick. The guard wouldn't stay patient or duped for long. The priest had taken only four strides away from the van when the entire side of the building erupted in a blaze of light. Shit, motion detectors. They hadn't worked those into the plan. The priest froze, his eyes betraying his panic.

"No worries," Matt told him, then realized there could be microphones as well as the more obvious lights and cameras. "Halfway along will be fine. I'm nearly done here."

The priest nodded, then set two boxes on the gravel next to the building, just shy of the halfway point between the front and rear cameras. He adjusted the position of the two boxes. Apparently their orientation was critical to their ultimate function. He brought the third box back. This he set around the corner from the face of the building, where it wouldn't be visible by anyone entering or leaving the factory. He placed the box close enough to the building that it couldn't be seen on the guard's monitor when Matt turned off the blinding halogen flashlight.

The priest stood back and checked the box's position. He made a minor adjustment, then gave two thumbs up.

Matt killed the light and waved encouragingly at the camera. He joined the priest in the van and drove to the other side of the building. He blinded that front-corner camera, and the two of them went through the routine again.

When they had all six boxes in place, he knocked on the front door.

"It's all fixed," he told the guard. "A minor software issue. Good to go."

"Don't you want this?" the guard said, looking hurt that Matt was about to leave without asking for the record he'd taken such pains to complete.

"Of course." He made a show of carefully studying what the guard had written. "I'll take these stats back to the office and include them in my report. Thanks a lot. Do we need to sign out?"

"Oh yeah," the guard said. "I'll get the sheet."

Matt turned the van around while the guard fetched his clipboard. God, he could hardly wait to get the hell out of here.

The guard returned with the clipboard, and Matt and the priest signed the sheet. As Matt was handing it back, the guard narrowed his eyes, stared at Matt's face, and reached for his holster.

Matt's heart rate thundered into overdrive as its turbocharger kicked in. Had the guard recognized him from his shop? All he could do now was ignore the galloping in his chest and keep his face neutral. It was amazing how well that tactic worked on White guys. Drove them crazy and gave you the upper hand. Did it work on Asians?

"You're lucky," the guard continued, his right hand stroking the butt of his handgun. "Your dispatcher knows you pretty damned good." He was scrutinizing the left side of Matt's face and drawing a finger down his own cheek. "If she hadn't described you so accurate like, you would've been stayin' here till change o' shift."

Apparently pleased to have had the last word, the guard took the clipboard and strolled back inside. Seconds later, the gate opened.

Matt smiled and waved at the camera.

Shit. Was he going to be able do this twice more before sunrise?

And then he thought about Tammy and Donna. And Mum and Dad. Dennis Badger had taken a huge toll on his family. There was no doubt in Matt's mind that the Badger was responsible for Tammy's murder. And Donna was in a coma thanks to the contaminated cigarettes the bastard had no intention of pulling from the market. Getting the best of him wasn't going to dry Mum's and Dad's tears, but it might make them feel better. Being made to quiver like a helpless victim, again and again, gnawed your bones and sucked out the marrow.

CHAPTER 48

"We should be okay right here," Natasha told him.

The clock on the dashboard said 7:27. They were right on time. She put the car in park and set the emergency brake. There were no other cars in the lot.

"Hell's bells, woman," said Hamish from the passenger seat. "We can't stay here. It's far too close. They'll see us."

She pointed to the smoke shop and convenience store beside them, Evergreen Variety. "Sign says they open at ten on Sundays. No one will bother us."

"You said we would be parking at a discreet distance. These guys have got AK-47s. I've seen them. We have to get out of here."

"This isn't a Rollies Factory, Hamish. Dennis Badger makes a show of running this as a legitimate operation. It's even government licensed. His guys don't go around waving automatic rifles."

Hamish looked like a scared rabbit scanning the forest for foxes. He pointed to the bush encroaching on two sides. "But it's dark and we're in the middle of nowhere. If somebody doesn't like the look of us —"

"It's not actually dark, just dim. Look at the sky. The sun will be up in twenty minutes. We can see perfectly well. And we're right beside a convenience store, for heaven's sake. People come and go from here all the time."

She had to admit, it was a bit creepy out here, no one else around, three kilometres north of Grand Basin's village centre. If Colleen hadn't told her exactly where to come, she'd have never twigged that what she was looking at across the road was a cigarette factory. It looked like a secret government installation stashed in the middle of a forest, not Dennis Badger's Hat-Trick operation. His security was impressive. Ten metres of open gravel ringed the space around the five low-rise, windowless buildings. Then came the perimeter fence, three metres of barbed wire topped by razor wire. The gate looked particularly secure, and wide enough to admit transport trucks. Six tractor trailers were parked inside waiting to be loaded with Kings, Menthols, Filter-tips, and Plains. The entire length of what was obviously the main building was ablaze with security floodlights. Nobody could ever get near the place without permission.

A flicker of movement caught her eye. There they were. Two of them. Inside the compound. Dressed in black, throwing something — tools? — into the back of a van. She watched as they jumped into the front seats and drove toward the gate. She held her breath while the driver turned and waved at the man standing guard by the building's front door. One — two — three — four — the gate opened. They drove through. She couldn't let herself breathe until she'd seen the writing on the side panel.

The van headed north, and she caught it: UPPER CANADA SECURITY. She let her air out and sucked it back in again, then turned to Hamish and allowed herself to smile. Matt and the priest had done it. They'd completed set-up number three of three.

"Now what?" Hamish said.

"We wait. Until seven-forty-five. Ten minutes before sunrise. Matt's in contact with the trucks. If they're in place by then, the priest will do the honours with his remote control."

"I haven't the faintest idea how Zol roped three sets of firefighters into cooperating with arson, of all things."

"It's not arson. It's fireworks. The burning schoolhouse. Nothing is going to get burnt. It's just going to look that way."

"It's still flames and smoke."

"That's the idea."

"I don't like it."

Then why had he insisted she pick him up at his condo and bring him with her? It took her twenty minutes out of her way, which at five o'clock in the morning was no small inconvenience.

"Dr. Zol brainstormed the ethics with me on Friday," she told him, "and I think they're sound."

It wouldn't be anyone's fault if a demonstration of fireworks was misinterpreted as a real fire. And it was perfectly natural for a member of the Grand Basin volunteer brigade — Matt Holt, for instance — to find the brigade overwhelmed by three major fires and solicit the assistance of firefighting colleagues in Brant, Oxford, and Norfolk Counties. In fact, the fires would look so serious that every measure would have to be taken to put them out before the flames spread to the adjacent woodlands. It was obvious that any uncontrolled forest fires on Grand Basin Reserve would put many homes and lives at risk. As they liked to say in health units around the world: it was better to be safe than sorry.

"But the inciting incident is a hoax," Hamish insisted.

"That part we keep to ourselves. Dennis Badger has been given plenty of time to cooperate. And now it's time to fight fire with —"

A high-pitched alarm pierced the quiet of the morning. It was coming from across the road.

"Here we go," Hamish said. "Look, the rear corner of the building. It's on fire."

"Ahead of schedule. Everything must be in place."

"No, Natasha, it's real. And so is the fire alarm. The place really is on fire."

The guard ran out through the front door, looked at the smoke billowing from his right, ran back inside, then moments later returned with a small fire extinguisher. By then, the entire side of the building parallel to the road appeared to be on fire, and the flames were clearly too much for one man to handle. He dropped the extinguisher, pulled a phone from his pocket, and punched at it. 911?

Thirty seconds later, she could feel the rumble. It was coming from the north and accompanied by the wail of sirens and that weird, annoying buzzer-honker sound that fire trucks make.

"Ah," she said. "And here come the right men for the job."

Four fire trucks — BRANTFORD FIRE in huge letters along the sides — careened up the road and came to a roaring stop at the gate. They must have GPS.

By now, the entire front of the building was engulfed in smoke, and flames were starting to lick at the far side. The guard, clearly panicked, ran to the gate and shook it. He was shouting and miming to the driver of the first truck in the line. What was he saying? He kept looking back at all that smoke in front of the building and shaking his head.

"Oh my God," Natasha said. "The trucks won't be able to get in. The guard can't open the gate."

"Why not?"

"Because the switch is inside. The electric switch. The stupid switch. Nobody thought about it. If they don't get in there soon, the fireworks will be used up." And the so-called fire would go out.

It was going to look so pathetic. And Dennis Badger would be laughing all the way to the Supreme Court, his operation intact. She could see it now, she and Dr. Zol banished to North Overshoe.

"What do you mean fireworks?" Hamish said. "This is a real fire. Look at the roof."

Flames were shooting through the roof. Was the place actually on fire? And if so, was that a good thing or a disaster?

One of the firefighters jumped from the second truck in line and fiddled with a metal box attached to the side. One of his mates ran to join him and they pulled a heavy-duty tool and some sort of pump or power supply from the box, then ran with the gear to the gate.

"Hey, cool," Hamish said. "That must be the Jaws of Life. They'll cut that sucker open pretty quick."

And they did. Within a minute, they had the gate open. The trucks roared through it.

In no time, four men were up their ladders, hacking at the roof with mean-looking axes.

And then they started the water treatment. First, they blew the front door off its hinges. Then they blasted the corners off the eaves and exposed the attic. Then they aimed Niagara Falls through the holes they'd hacked in the roof. Once the smoke had cleared from the front door, they aimed the water cannon straight inside and gave the place a thorough soaking. When one pumper-tanker had delivered its load, the next one took its place. Four tankers held an awful lot of water.

After half an hour, maybe it was less, they halted their assault. Two men jostled the guard to keep him from foolishly entering the dangerous building while six of the them rushed inside carrying axes and other fierce-looking tools. Goodness knows what damage they were going to inflict on the machinery, the bales of tobacco, the rolls of cigarette paper, and the crates of filter tips in the interest of quenching every last ember. They would have to assure themselves there was nothing left that could spread to the adjacent bushland. Preventing a forest fire was their prime concern; no family should lose their home.

Her phone rang in her purse. Hamish made a face and handed her the bag.

"Matt here. How's it going?"

"Hamish thinks it was a real fire, but I'm not sure."

"Dylan the Priest will be pleased his simulation was that convincing. There a lot of damage?"

"Oh yeah. What a shame, eh?"

"Any trouble?"

"Just with the gate." She told him about the Jaws of Life.

"Same here. But these guys from Woodstock know what they're

doing. A bit rough with the water, though. The roof's gone, and so are two of the walls."

"Our place is pretty sturdy. Still standing."

"But give it to me straight," said Matt, his voice up an octave. "Is it out of commission?"

"For a very long time." She glanced at Hamish. His eyes were glued to the mess across the street. She thought of his carwash addiction. He hated mud, but loved the sight of water streaming out in jets. "Any trouble with guns?" she asked Matt.

"Nah," he said. "The guard looked so scared he forgot he was packing."

"And the other Rollies factory?"

"About to call them now. But I don't think anything could stop those Simcoe lads from doing a thoroughly professional job when called upon."

She pictured Norfolk County Fire and Rescue on the scene. Even an AK-47 would be no match for a crew of revengeful Norfolk firefighters with a water cannon.

CHAPTER 49

Zol had sat long enough biting his nails in the Tim's on Argyle Street. He couldn't wait here in Caledonia any longer nursing double-double decafs. By now, the fires would have been out for almost an hour. He was aching to see the damage for himself, but he had to have a legitimate reason for showing up at the Badger's ruined Hat-Trick factory. Without a good excuse for his presence there, it would be obvious he'd been in on the plan. As it was, Dennis may have already guessed that Zollie Szabo, that nerdy kid from Simcoe Composite, had masterminded it. The Badger and the other tobacco pirates would be beside themselves with anger, knowing they'd been victimized twice — first by arson and second by overzealous firefighting. They'd need to be handled with extreme caution.

He called Norfolk's fire chief, Grant Dyment, on his cell.

"How are things, Chief?"

"My team put out the fire, but in the process demolished that Rollies factory with three tanks of water. We have one tank to spare, which we're driving over to Mr. Badger's main operation in case there are some smouldering embers that might need further attention. I hear there won't be any Hat-Tricks coming out of that place for a long time. Maybe never."

"Is there a lot of run-off?"

"You mean, have our professional efforts created a big watery mess that is escaping the confines of the properties involved?"

"And do you suppose that watery mess might be full of contaminants?"

"I don't know, Doc. It's just tobacco. Some of us have been filling our lungs with those same contaminants for years."

"But theoretically speaking, could there be a fair bit of — let's say nasty waste water making its way into local streams and rivers? I'm thinking of our beautiful Grand barely a few kilometres north."

The chief paused for a moment, then admitted, "Now that you mention it, Dr. Szabo, it could be bad for the fish. And for the people who eat them. And disastrous for the local drinking water." He'd adopted the puffed-up tone of a politician making a stump speech. "Think of the wells on the reserve and the treatment plants all the way downstream to Lake Erie."

"Sounds like a host of public-health issues to me, Chief Dyment."

"Consider yourself officially involved," said the chief, stifling a chuckle. "I smell a drinking-water emergency that needs your immediate attention before it gets out of control."

"Thanks for the heads up. As it happens, I've been doing business this morning in Caledonia, which puts me in the vicinity. I can be there in a few minutes, make my assessment, and notify the appropriate government partner agencies immediately."

The Spills Action Centre at the Ontario Ministry of the Environment would be delighted to get a Sunday-morning call from a concerned MOH from Norfolk County. They had a twenty-four-hour Spills R Us hotline.

Next, he called Natasha.

"Dr. Zol! You missed all the excitement."

"I gather. Where are you? Tell me you haven't entered Dennis Badger's compound."

"Of course not. We're following your orders and staying out of trouble. Hamish and I are still in my car, across the street from the action. It's like being at a drive-in movie."

He was almost scared to ask: "And Al Mesic?"

"At home in bed."

"Hamish didn't tell him where —"

"He told Al he had to go to the hospital. A patient was crashing in the ICU."

"Good thinking. We can't let Al . . . well, you know. Look, you two sit tight. I'm coming in."

About twenty minutes later, he slid into the back seat of Natasha's little Honda. Sweat matted the curls at Natasha's neck; Hamish's cheeks were ashen.

"Have you seen Matt and Father Stoyan?" he asked them.

"Not since seven-thirty," Natasha said. "We saw them leaving after setting up."

"If Matt doesn't stay away from this mess, he won't be able to show his face on the rez for a long time, maybe never." It was essential that no one tied Matt to today's events. Not even with the cleanup.

Hamish rubbed his eyes. "Another priest? Who's Father Stoyan? We only know about Dylan."

"Same guy," Zol said. "Stoyan guides the flock, Dylan sets the fireworks."

Hamish thought about that for a moment, then said, "Well, I suppose one way or another he has his eyes on the heavens."

"How many fire trucks responded to the alarm here?" Zol asked.

"Four," Natasha said. "All from Brantford. Three of them did what they had to do and returned to base." She gestured across the road. "The fourth is still here. The other one you see is from Norfolk. It came later and hasn't had to do anything. Maybe it's for backup. I recognized Chief Dyment from our meeting on Thursday."

"He still here?" Zol asked.

"There he his," Natasha said, "by the side of the building, holding a garbage bag."

Hamish made a face. "What are they doing? They can't hope to clean up all that mud by shovelling it into garbage bags."

"I think they're collecting evidence for the fire marshall," Natasha told Hamish, then turned and winked at Zol. "You know, to determine whether arson was involved."

Zol winked back at her. "I'm sure they'd like us to hold it for safekeeping." He opened his door. "I guess I'd better go and perform my assessment. And face Dennis Badger when he gets here."

Natasha looked disappointed. Hamish looked relieved. There was too much mud over there for his liking.

Zol walked across the road, then picked his way around the worst of the puddles. The stench of mud mixed with smoke got stronger with every step, and before he knew it Mumford & Sons were treating him to an energetic chorus of "Little Lion Man." It was a terrific tune from one of his favourite folk-rock bands, but their lyrics predicted pure doom. God, he hoped they were wrong about how his inevitable face-off with the Badger was going to turn out.

He had almost made it to the front door of what used to be the main part of the factory when an authoritative voice boomed from behind him. "That's far enough, sir. The building's unstable. Could collapse at any time."

Zol turned and introduced himself to the stocky, ruddy-faced man behind him. He was an impressive figure, dressed in full fire-fighting gear — hip waders, heavy pants secured with suspenders, bulky yellow coat stained with mud and soot, and the classic fire-fighter's helmet.

"Glad to have you aboard, Doc," said the firefighter, removing his glove. "I'm Grant Dyment. We spoke on the phone."

They shook hands and took the measure of each other. It seemed they both admired what they saw. Zol pointed to the half-dozen garbage bags lying next to one of the fire trucks. "I see your men have done most of the environmental sampling already, Chief. Terrific. Makes our job a lot easier."

"Be my guest. I'm turning them over to you. The fire marshall's staff will want to gather their own samples. They're fussy about that." He touched his nose and threw Zol a knowing look. "But I'm sure they won't find anything out of the ordinary here." He shrugged. "An industrial fire like this? Probably an electrical short in a neglected piece of machinery."

There was a splash as an SUV hit the puddles by the gate. It was a Porsche Cayenne, the colour of cinnamon. An interesting mix of culinary metaphors. Zol could see the Badger riding shotgun. He was wearing his deerskin jacket.

Dennis couldn't have spent last night on the rez. If he had, he'd have stormed onto this scene long before this. His fortified mansion was only two side roads over. No, he'd come from somewhere a good deal farther away. Perhaps the brand new Four Seasons in Toronto.

As the Porsche inched through the open gate and into the flooded compound, Zol could see four men inside: Dennis, the driver, a henchman behind him, and Chief Bob Falcon.

The Badger had his door open before the driver pulled to a stop. For a big man, he moved quickly, though the mud was doing its best to destroy his Gucci loafers. He threw up his arms. "Holy shit," he shouted to no one in particular. He turned to Chief Falcon, who was struggling to keep up with him as they marched toward Zol and the fire chief.

"Look what they've done," Dennis shouted to the Native chief. "They've fucking killed my operation. Some bastard is going to pay for this."

Any semblance of traditional Native diffidence, learned or hard-wired, had vanished from the Badger's face. He was charging like a bull bison stung by a thousand wasps and out for blood — crimson cheeks, bulging blue eyes, and foam on the mouth.

"Who's in charge here?" he demanded. "And it better not be you, Szabo."

Zol felt the weight of the Badger's fist pressed against his chest, but he stood his ground.

The fire chief took a step forward. "That would be me, chief of Norfolk Fire and Emergency. Grant Dyment."

"I don't give a shit what your name is, but I do want my factory fixed. At your expense."

Zol exchanged looks with the fire chief.

"That's not the way it works, sir," said the chief. "We put the fires out. Any restitution is up to you and your insurance company."

"This is goddamn arson. Has to be. Three Native cigarette factories on fire at the same time? You don't have to be a friggin' genius to see arson when it's staring you in the face."

"You own all three factories, do you, sir?"

For a second or two, the Badger lost his momentum. His eyes flashed up and to his right before he answered. "No. Just this one."

"I've made a preliminary inspection of the other two sites," Grant Dyment told him. "No owner or manager has shown any interest in the damaged properties. No one has come to have a look. No one's come to claim anything that might be salvageable. That got me thinking — maybe the owner lives out of town. Or is ashamed to show his face on account of some funny business going on inside."

"Don't know what the hell you're talking about."

The fire chief took his time eyeing his boots and scraping them against the gravel. "Let me think . . . the processing of cannabis maybe?"

"Don't be absurd. We just process tobacco, and have been for two thousand years."

The Badger loved pulling that race card. Trouble was, his God-given, unrestricted right to sell tobacco was looking pretty soggy at the moment. He frowned and looked away. Clearly, he was as surprised as anyone that the Asians hadn't shown up to inspect the ruins of their investment.

Dennis straightened his shoulders and set himself back on the offensive. He glared at Zol. "What are you doing here anyways, Szabo? Joined the fire department, or just come to gloat?"

"I called Dr. Szabo in," said the fire chief. "To assess the situation from a public-health standpoint. All this water, full of factory pollutants, could poison the wells on your reserve."

"And whose fault is that?" The Badger turned to the Native chief, standing granite-faced beside him. It was impossible to tell what Bob Falcon was thinking. He hadn't moved a muscle during the Badger's entire tirade. "Come on, Bob," the Badger said, taking a step toward the factory. "Better see what's left of the operation that funded all those good things I brought to your reserve."

Grant Dyment held the Badger by the arm. "You can't go in there, sir. It's not safe." The fire chief's tone was fatherly and respectful.

"Take your hand off me," the Badger said, trying in vain to evade the fire chief's grasp.

Dyment stood firm. His arm didn't budge. He must have been in this situation many times before and prevented countless people from dashing into burning buildings to retrieve their belongings.

The Badger's eyes filled with hate. "I said, take your hand off me. This is sovereign First Nations territory." He looked at the Native chief, "Tell them, Bob. Tell them to get the hell out of here, to get off our land. They have no business here."

Five of them — Zol, the fire chief, the Badger's two silent body-guards, and the Badger himself — fixed their gaze on Chief Falcon, waiting for the man who said little to give the final word.

Falcon's face remained impassive, his thoughts hidden. If he was facing inner conflict and turmoil, he wasn't showing it. But he couldn't be missing the fact that the bodyguards had their hands hovering beside their holsters.

Finally, Chief Falcon looked at the Badger and said, "These men came to help us, Dennis. Of course they got business being here." He gestured toward the soggy factory. "And if that place is gonna fall down, I'm not gonna be inside it when it does."

Dyment released the Badger's arm, and Zol felt the tension drop a notch or two. Seconds later, everyone turned toward the thud-thud of two doors slamming. A couple dressed in business attire began walking toward them from a blue-grey Chevy Malibu. The pair looked like a middle-aged woman and her twenty-something son in need of directions to the local Baptist church.

From five paces away, the woman called out, "Dennis Joseph Badger?"

"Who's asking?" Dennis said.

"Sergeant Bergman," said the woman once the pair had reached the group. She gestured to the young man beside her. "And this is Constable Holloway. We're with the Ontario Provincial Police."

"Good," Dennis said. He pointed at Zol. "Arrest this man for arson. Look what he did to my factory. And put three hundred of my people out of work."

"Mr. Badger," said the woman, "I don't do windows and I don't do arson." She paused, flashed her badge, and let everyone feel the weight of her words. "But I do investigate homicides. In fact, I've been looking for you for more than a year."

She pulled a pair of handcuffs out of nowhere, and while the athletic-looking constable stood with his handgun poised for immediate action, she yanked the Badger's arms behind his back and slapped on the cuffs.

"Dennis Joseph Badger," she said in a clear, loud voice, "I'm arresting you for the murder of Dr. Tammy Holt. You do not need to say anything, but anything you do say may be used as evidence."

She dipped into her jacket pocket and held out a clear plastic bag that had OPP: CRIME EVIDENCE written across a seal at the top. Badger glanced at it and looked quickly away. Inside was what appeared to be a beaded star on a disk attached to a strip of leather. Was it a necklace? Whatever it was, it had the well-worn look of a keepsake or a Native artifact — and the detective looked triumphant to have it in her possession.

"You have the right to retain and instruct a lawyer right away," the detective said, returning the bag to her pocket. "Do you understand?"

Dennis looked too stunned to answer. He flashed Chief Falcon a look of utter confusion that morphed into revulsion as he stumbled toward the unmarked police car at the hands of the officers.

No one in the group said a word. The bodyguards gawked at the departing unmarked police car like bewildered sheep who'd lost their shepherd. Now that he looked at them, Zol saw that they were identical twins. One had a big ugly sore on his lip.

Zol's phone beeped in his pocket. An incoming text. He flipped it open and read the message from Colleen: NICE WORK WITH HIS TIM'S CUP. POLICE SAMPLE ALSO PERFECT MATCH. JUDGE GRANTED SEARCH WARRANT FOR BADGER'S HOUSE. BERGMAN MUST'VE FOUND EVERYTHING SHE NEEDED. XO

He looked up from the screen. A silver Mercedes had joined the huddle of cars parked across the street. Colleen gave a wave from behind the wheel. Al Mesic, smiling beside her, raised his notepad and his camera, then gave an appreciative thumbs up. Clearly, he was delighted with this scoop. His story of the Badger's arrest, complete with photos, would be huge for him. But hell, he better never discover that the firefighters' destruction of the factories was premeditated.

The Native chief was the first to stir. He turned to Zol. His dark, deep-set eyes were glistening, on the verge of tears. He cocked his head toward Dennis's suv, not so gorgeous now with mud smearing its alloy rims and cinnamon side panels. "Doc?"

"You want to talk?"

Falcon nodded and without a further word led Zol to the suv. He swung open a rear door and motioned Zol in, then climbed in beside him from the opposite side.

Seated in the back seat, staring at his hands, Robert Falcon looked like a man filled to bursting with a lifetime of bottled up opinions and no idea how to let them out. After a long silence, he said, "Donna Holt," and let her name hang in the space between them. And then he began. "She died 'bout an hour ago, eh?"

Zol didn't know what to say. *I'm sorry* wouldn't begin to cover it. For a long moment, he said nothing and hoped reciprocating the chief's initial silence conveyed the depth of his own regret. Finally, he ventured, "Donna's death is going to be very hard on Matt. Both his sisters were so —"

"Her mother called me. From Toronto. She's my sister, eh?"

"Sorry?"

"Tammy and Donna, they were my nieces. My sister's kids."

"Oh Chief, I'm so sorry. I had no idea."

"Looks like Dennis killed them both." Falcon turned and stared through the window at the charred remains of the cigarette factory. After a while, he dropped his gaze to his hands and studied them intently, as if contemplating his own culpability.

The elected chief of Grand Basin Reserve raised his head and, for the first time, looked into Zol's eyes. "Us guys were blind, eh? On the rez, Dennis's greed was like an infection. You know, contagious, eh? Like the White Man's smallpox that killed so many of us in the old days."

Talking like this was tearing the chief apart. But it was clear that an inner strength was compelling him to continue. He smudged the tears on his cheeks with the back of his hand. "It took me far too long to see that. I shoulda listened to my sister and her husband. We knew that Dennis brought bad people to the reserve — gangsters, gamblers, loan sharks, and, yes, even hit men. And my sister knew her daughter's death had everything to do with Dennis Badger's trade in pirate smoke. But all those dollars Dennis was throwin' around, they blinded me."

The chief put his hand in his pocket and pulled out what looked like a wad of newspaper. "I can't keep this any longer, Dr. Szabo. Dennis was showin' it off in Toronto last night. Told me to put it back somewheres safe in my office. I figure you know what to do with it. Give it to the right people. I heard you're the one that found it in the first place."

Zol didn't need to unwrap the paper to know what the chief had passed him. But when he saw those garnet eyes, his own stung. He caressed the smooth stone and remembered the autumn day when he'd got all excited after finding buried treasure with his dad's metal detector.

He passed the pipe back to the chief and said, "Hold him for a sec, will you."

Zol reached into his own pocket and pulled out the black-eyed mate. She hadn't left his side since Thursday night.

He'd expected the chief to be stunned at the sight of the pair of legendary birds sitting beak to beak. But the chief simply nodded, as if all along he'd known Zol was the custodian of the second loon.

"Do you have any pipe tobacco with you?" Zol asked. "Mine's at home, but I think we could both do with a smoke."

The chief swept the leather-and-maple interior of the Porsche with his discerning gaze. "Dennis doesn't let no one smoke in here."

"That's okay," Zol said. "He won't ever know."